SIDNEY SHELDON'S
ANGEL *of the* DARK

BOOKS BY SIDNEY SHELDON

Angel of the Dark

After the Darkness

Mistress of the Game

Are You Afraid of the Dark?

The Sky Is Falling

Tell Me Your Dreams

The Best Laid Plans

Morning, Noon & Night

Nothing Lasts Forever

The Stars Shine Down

The Doomsday Conspiracy

Memories of Midnight

The Sands of Time

Windmills of the Gods

If Tomorrow Comes

Master of the Game

Rage of Angels

Bloodline

A Stranger in the Mirror

The Other Side of Midnight

The Naked Face

SIDNEY SHELDON'S

ANGEL of the DARK

Tilly Bagshawe

DOUBLEDAY LARGE PRINT HOME LIBRARY EDITION

wm

WILLIAM MORROW
An Imprint of HarperCollins*Publishers*

ISBN 978-1-61793-711-8

This Large Print Book carries the
Seal of Approval of N.A.V.H.

For my sister, Alice

His wings are gray and trailing,
Azrael, Angel of Death,
And yet the souls that Azrael brings
Across the dark and cold,
Look up beneath those folded wings,
And find them lined with gold.

—ROBERT GILBERT WELSH, "AZRAEL" (1917)

PART I

CHAPTER ONE

LOS ANGELES
1996

He got the call at around nine P.M.

"Unit 8A73. Come in, please."

"Yeah, this is 8A73."

The patrolman yawned into the radio. It had been a long, boring night making the rounds in West Hollywood and he was ready for his bed. "What's up?"

"We got a 911. Female. Hysterical."

"Probably my wife," he joked. "I forgot our anniversary yesterday. She wants my balls in a jar."

"Your wife Spanish?"

"Nope."

"Then it ain't her."

He yawned again.

"Address?"

"Four-twenty Loma Vista."

"Nice neighborhood. What happened, the maid forgot to put enough caviar on her toast?"

The operator chuckled.

"Probably a DV."

Domestic violence.

"Probably?"

"The lady was screaming so much it was tough to make out what she was saying. We're sending backup, but you're closest. How soon can you guys be there?"

The patrolman hesitated. Mickey, his partner, had ducked out of their shift early to hook up with yet another skank on Hollywood Boulevard. Mickey got through hookers the way that other men got through socks. He knew he shouldn't cover for him, but Mickey was so goddamn charming, saying no to the guy was like trying to swim against a riptide. *What to do?* If he admitted he was alone, they'd both get canned. But the alternative—showing up solo at a DV—wasn't an appealing prospect either.

Violent husbands were not usually the LAPD's biggest fans.

Fuck it.

"We'll be there in five."

Mickey's skank had better be worth it.

Four-twenty Loma Vista turned out to be a vast, sprawling, Spanish Mission–style 1920s estate, perched high in the Hollywood Hills. A discreet, ivy-clad gate set into a fifteen-foot wall gave little clue of the opulence that hid behind it: a dramatic, sweeping driveway and gardens so enormous and perfectly manicured they looked more like a country club than the grounds of a private residence.

The patrolman barely registered the fancy real estate. He was looking at a crime scene.

Open gate.

Front door ajar.

No signs of forced entry.

The place was eerily quiet. He drew his weapon.

"Police!"

No answer. As the echo of his own voice faded, from somewhere above him he heard a low moaning sound, like a not quite boiling teakettle. Nervously, he mounted the stairs.

Goddamn you, Mickey.

"Police!" he shouted again, more loudly this time. The moaning was coming from one of the bedrooms. He burst in, gun drawn. *What the fuck?* He heard a woman screaming, then the sickening crunch of his own skull as it slammed against the floor. The wooden boards were as slick as an oil spill.

But they weren't slick with oil.

They were slick with blood.

Detective Danny McGuire from homicide division tried to hide his frustration. The maid was making no sense.

"¡Pudo haber sido el diablo! ¡El diablo!"

It's not her fault, Detective Danny McGuire reminded himself. The poor woman had been alone in the house when she found them. No wonder she was still hysterical.

"¡Esa pobre mujer! ¿Quién podía hacer una cosa terrible como esa?"

After six years in homicide, it took a lot to turn Detective Danny McGuire's stomach. But this had done it. Surveying the carnage in front of him, Danny was aware of the In-N-Out burger he'd eaten earlier fighting its way up into his esophagus in a desperate bid for freedom. No wonder the officer who'd arrived at the scene had lost it. In front of him was the work of a maniac.

If it weren't for the crimson sea of blood seeping into the floorboards, it might have looked like a burglary. The bedroom had been ransacked, drawers opened, jewelry boxes emptied, clothes and photographs strewn everywhere. But the real horror lay at the foot of the bed. Two bodies, a man and a woman. The first victim, an elderly male in his pajamas, had had his throat slashed in such a repeated, frenzied manner that his head was almost completely severed from his neck. He'd been bound, trussed almost, like an animal in an abattoir, with what looked like climbing ropes. Whoever killed him had tied his mutilated corpse to the naked body of the second victim, a woman. A very young, very beautiful woman, judging from the taut perfection of her figure, although her face had been so badly beaten it was hard to tell for sure. One glance at her bloodied thighs and pubic area, however, made one thing abundantly clear: she had been violently raped.

Covering his mouth, Detective Danny McGuire moved closer to the bodies. The smell of fresh blood was overpowering. But that wasn't what made him recoil.

"Get a knife," he said to the maid.

She looked at him blankly.

"*Cuchillo*," he repeated. "Now! And someone call an ambulance. She's still breathing."

The knife was produced. Gingerly Danny McGuire began cutting through the ropes binding the man and woman together. His touch seemed to rouse the woman. She began crying softly, slipping in and out of consciousness. Danny bent low so his mouth was close to her ear. Even in her battered state, he couldn't help but notice how beautiful she was, dark-haired and full-breasted with the soft, milky skin of a child. "I'm a police officer," he whispered. "You're safe now. We're gonna get you to a doctor." As the ropes loosened, the old man's head lolled grotesquely against Danny's shoulder, like some hideous Halloween mask. He gagged.

One of his men tapped him on the shoulder. "Definite burglary, sir. The safe's been emptied. Jewelry's gone, and some paintings."

Danny nodded. "Victims' names?"

"The house belongs to Andrew Jakes."

Jakes. The name was familiar.

"He's an art dealer."

"And the girl?"

"Angela Jakes."

"His daughter?"

The cop laughed.

"Granddaughter?"

"No, sir. She's his wife."

Stupid, thought Danny. *Of course she's his wife. This is Hollywood, after all. Old Man Jakes must have been worth a fortune.*

At last the ropes gave way. *Till death us do part,* thought Danny as Angela Jakes literally tumbled free from her husband's corpse into his arms. Slipping off his overcoat, Danny draped it over her shoulders, covering her nakedness. She was conscious again and shivering.

"It's all right," he told her. "You're safe now. Angela, isn't it?"

The girl nodded mutely.

"Can you tell me what happened, sweetheart?"

She looked up at him and for the first time Danny saw the full extent of her injuries. Two black eyes, one so swollen that it had closed completely, and lacerations all over her upper body. Scratch marks. Danny thought, *She must have fought like hell.*

"He hurt me."

Her voice was barely a whisper. The effort of speaking seemed to exhaust her.

"Take your time."

She paused. Danny waited.

"He said he would let Andrew go if . . . if I . . ." Catching sight of her husband's bloodied corpse, she broke into uncontrollable sobs.

"Someone cover him up, for Christ's sake," Danny snapped. How was he supposed to get any sense out of the girl with that horror show lying right next to her?

"We can't, sir. Not yet. Forensics isn't finished with the body."

Danny flashed his sergeant a withering look. "I said cover him."

The sergeant blanched. "Sir."

A blanket was draped over Andrew Jakes's body, but it was too late. His wife was already in deep shock, rocking back and forth, eyes glazed, muttering to herself. Danny wasn't sure what she was saying. It sounded like: "I have no life."

"Is the ambulance here yet?"

"Yes, sir. Just arrived."

"Good."

Detective Danny McGuire moved away out of the victim's earshot, beckoning his men around him in a tight huddle. "She needs a doctor and a psych evaluation. Officer Menendez, you go with her. Make sure the medical examiner sees her first and we get a full rape kit, swabs, blood tests, the lot."

"Of course, sir."

Tomorrow, Detective Danny McGuire would question Angela Jakes properly. She was in no fit state tonight.

"You'd better take the maid with you while you're at it," he added. "I can't hear myself think with her wailing in my ear."

A skinny, blond young man with horn-rimmed glasses walked into the room.

"Sorry I'm late, sir."

Detective David Henning might be a card-carrying nerd, but he had one of the best, most logical, deductive brains on the force. Detective Danny McGuire was delighted to see him.

"Ah, Henning. Good. Call the insurers, get me an inventory of everything that was taken. Then check out the pawnshops and Web sites, see what shows up."

Henning nodded.

"And someone get on to the security provider. A house like this must be alarmed up the wazoo, but it looks like our killer just strolled on in here tonight."

Officer Menendez said, "The maid mentioned that she heard a loud bang of some sort around eight P.M."

"A gunshot?"

"No. I asked her that, but she said it was more like a piece of furniture falling over. She was on her way upstairs to check it out, but Mrs. Jakes stopped her, said she'd go up herself."

"Then what?"

"Then nothing. The maid went upstairs at eight forty-five P.M. to bring the old man his cocoa as usual. That's when she found them and called 911."

His cocoa? Danny McGuire tried to visualize the Jakeses' married life. He pictured a rich, lecherous old man easing his arthritic limbs into bed each night beside his lithe, sexy young bride—then waiting for his maid to bring him a nice cup of cocoa! How could Angela Jakes have borne being pawed by such a decrepit creature? Danny imagined the old man's bony, liver-spotted fingers stroking Angela's breasts, her thighs. It was irrational, but the thought made him angry.

Did it make somebody else angry too? Danny wondered. *Angry enough to kill?*

Early the next morning, Detective Danny McGuire drove to Cedars-Sinai Medical Center. He felt excited. This was his first big murder case. The victim, Andrew Jakes, was a scion of Beverly Hills high society. A case like this could propel Danny's career into the fast lane if he played his cards right. But it wasn't just his career prospects that Danny was excited about. It was the prospect of seeing Angela Jakes again.

There was something uniquely compelling about the young Mrs. Jakes, something beyond her beauty and that violated, made-for-sex body that had haunted Danny's dreams last night. All the circumstantial evidence suggested that the girl was a shameless gold digger. But Danny found himself hoping that she wasn't. That there was some other explanation for her marriage to a man old enough to be her grandfather. Danny McGuire loathed gold diggers. He did not want to have to loathe Angela Jakes.

"How's the patient?"

The duty nurse outside Angela Jakes's private room eyed Danny suspiciously. "Who's asking?"

Danny flashed her his badge and most winning Irish smile

"Oh! Good morning, Detective." The nurse returned his smile, surreptitiously checking his left hand for a wedding band. For a cop he was unusually attractive: strong jaw, lapis-blue eyes and a mop of thick black Celtic curls that her own boyfriend would have killed for. "The patient's tired."

"How tired? Can I question her?"

You can question me, thought the nurse, admiring Danny's boxer's physique beneath his plain white Brooks Brothers shirt. "You can see her as long as you take it easy. She's had some morphine for the pain in her face. Her left cheekbone was fractured and one of her eyes is quite badly damaged. But she's lucid."

"Thank you," said Danny. "I'll be as quick as I can."

For a hospital room, it was luxurious. Tasteful oil paintings hung on the walls. A Wesley-Barrell upholstered chair stood in the corner for visitors, and a delicate potted orchid quivered by the window. Angela Jakes was propped up against two down pillows. The bruises around her eyes had faded from last night's uniform plum to a dark rainbow of colors. Fresh stitches across her forehead gave her the disconcerting look of a dressmaker's dummy, but still she remained quite astonishingly beautiful, alluring in a way that Danny could not remember ever encountering before.

"Hello, Mrs. Jakes." He held up his badge again. "Detective McGuire. I'm not sure if you remember. We met last night."

Angela Jakes smiled weakly. "Of course I remember you, Detective. You gave me your coat. Lyle, this is the policeman I was telling you about."

Danny spun around. Standing stock-still against the wall behind him was probably the most handsome man

Danny had ever seen this side of a movie screen. Tall and olive-skinned, with the perfect, aquiline features of a hunter, jet-black hair and blue eyes, flat and almond-shaped like a Siamese cat's, he scowled at Danny disapprovingly. He was wearing an expensively tailored suit, and when he moved it was like watching oil spread across a lake, smooth and fluid, almost viscous.

Danny placed him instantly. *Lawyer.* His upper lip curled. With a few honorable exceptions, Detective Danny McGuire was not a fan of lawyers.

"Who are you and what are you doing here? Mrs. Jakes is not supposed to have any visitors."

"Lyle Renalto." The man's voice was practically a purr. Walking over to Angela Jakes's bedside, he placed a proprietary hand over hers. "I'm a family friend."

Danny looked at the two preposterously attractive young people holding hands and drew the inevitable conclusion. *Yeah, right. And I'm the Queen of Sheba. Family friend, my ass.*

"Lyle was Andrew's attorney," said

Angela. Her voice was low and husky,
nothing like the frightened whisper of
last night. "Conchita called him last
night to let him know what happened and he came straight here." She
squeezed Lyle Renalto's hand gratefully,
her eyes welling with tears. "He's been
amazing."

I'll bet he has. "If you're up to it, Mrs.
Jakes, I'd like to ask you a few questions."

Lyle Renalto said curtly, "Not now.
Mrs. Jakes is too tired. If you submit
your questions to me, I'll see that she
answers them once she's rested."

Danny instantly bridled. "I don't believe I was talking to you, Mr. Renalto."

"Be that as it may, Mrs. Jakes has
just been through an indescribably har-
rowing ordeal."

"I know. I'm trying to catch the guy
who did it."

"Quite apart from witnessing her husband's murder, she was violently raped."

Danny was losing patience. "I'm
aware of what happened, Mr. Renalto. I
was there."

"I didn't witness Andrew's murder."

Both men turned to look at Angela, but her attention was focused wholly on Danny. Feeling a ridiculous sense of triumph, he moved toward her bedside, edging Renalto aside.

"Would you like to tell me what you *did* witness?"

"Angel, you don't have to say anything," the attorney butted in.

Danny raised an eyebrow at the endearment.

"Angel was my husband's pet name for me," Mrs. Jakes explained. "All his friends used to call me that. Not that I am an angel, by any means." She smiled weakly. "I'm sure I could be quite a trial to poor Andrew at times."

"I highly doubt that," said Danny. "You were telling me about last night. About what happened."

"Yes. Andrew was upstairs in bed. I was downstairs reading."

"What time was this?"

She considered. "About eight, I suppose. I heard a noise from upstairs."

"What sort of noise?"

"A bump. I thought Andrew might have fallen out of bed. He'd been having these spells recently. Anyway, Conchita came running in, she'd heard the noise too, but I said I'd go up. Andrew was a proud man, Detective. If he were . . ." She searched around for the appropriate word. "If he were incapacitated in any way, he wouldn't have wanted Conchita to find him. He'd have wanted me."

"So you went up alone?"

She inhaled deeply and closed her eyes, bracing against the memory.

Lyle Renalto stepped forward. "Angel, please. There's no need to upset yourself."

"It's all right, Lyle, really. The detective needs to know." She turned back to Danny. "I went up alone. As I was walking into the bedroom someone hit me from behind. That's the last thing I remember, the pain in my head. When I woke up, he was . . . he was raping me."

"Can you describe the man?" asked Danny. He knew from experience that the best way to calm emotional witnesses was to stick to the hard facts. Once you started with all the "I know this must be distressing for you" bullshit, the floodgates opened and you'd lost them.

Angela Jakes shook her head. "I wish I could. But he wore a mask, a balaclava."

"What about his build?"

"Most of the time he was behind me. I don't know. Stocky, I guess. Not tall, but he was certainly strong. I fought, and he hit me. He said if I didn't let him keep doing it, he would hurt Andrew. So I stopped fighting." Tears streamed down her swollen cheeks.

"Where was your husband at this time? Did he try to help you? To raise the alarm?"

"He . . ." A look of confusion came over her face. She glanced at Lyle Renalto, but he looked away. "I don't know where Andrew was. I didn't see him. On the bed, maybe? I don't know."

"It's all right," said Danny, sensing her anxiety levels rising. "Go on. You stopped fighting."

"Yes. He asked me for the combination of our safe and I gave it to him. Then he raped me again. When he'd finished, he knocked me out a second time. When

I came to . . . the first thing I remember is you, Detective."

She looked Danny in the eye and he felt his stomach lurch, promptly forgetting his next question. Lyle Renalto smoothly took advantage of the silence.

"Conchita, the Jakeses' housekeeper, told me that all Angela's jewelry was taken and a number of valuable miniatures. Is that correct?"

Before Danny could respond that he wasn't in the habit of leaking sensitive information about a murder inquiry to "family friends," Angela blurted out angrily, "I don't care about the damn jewelry! Andrew's dead! I loved my husband, Detective."

"I'm sure you did, Mrs. Jakes."

"Please find the animal who did this."

Danny cast his mind back to last night's crime scene: the blood-soaked floor, the old man's all-but-severed head, the disgusting, obscene scratches on Angela Jakes's thighs, buttocks and breasts.

Animal was the right word.

* * *

There was no sign of the pretty nurse outside Angela Jakes's room. As Danny stood waiting for the elevator, Lyle Renalto oiled up to him. "You don't have a very high opinion of attorneys, do you, Detective?"

The lawyer's tone had switched from hostile to ingratiating. Danny preferred hostile. Nevertheless, it was an unusually perceptive comment.

"What makes you think that, Mr. Renalto?"

Lyle smiled. "Your face. Unless, of course, it's just me, personally, whom you dislike."

Danny said nothing. Lyle went on.

"You're not alone, you know. My father hated lawyers with a passion. He was crushingly disappointed when I graduated law school. I come from a seafaring family, you see. As far as Pa was concerned, it was the United States Naval Academy or nothing."

Danny thought, *Why's he telling me this?*

The elevator arrived. Danny stepped inside and pressed *G* but Lyle stuck an arm out to hold the doors. His film-star features hardened and his cat's eyes flashed in warning. "Angela Jakes is a close friend of mine. I won't have you hounding her."

Danny lost his temper. "This is a murder inquiry, Mr. Renalto, not a game of twenty questions. Mrs. Jakes is my key witness. In fact right now, she and her maid are my only witnesses."

"Angela didn't see the man. She told you that already."

Danny frowned. "I thought Mr. Jakes was a close friend of yours too. I'd have thought you'd want us to find his killer?"

"Of course I do," snapped Lyle.

"Or perhaps you weren't *quite* as close to Andrew Jakes as you were to his wife. Is that it?"

This seemed to amuse Lyle Renalto. "For a detective, I must say you're a pretty poor judge of people. You think Angel and I are lovers?"

"Are you?"

The attorney smirked. "No."

Danny desperately wanted to believe him.

"This is a triple felony, Mr. Renalto," he said, removing the attorney's arm from the elevator door. "Rape, robbery and murder. I strongly suggest you do not attempt to obstruct my investigation by coming between me and the witness."

"Is that a threat, Detective?"

"Call it what you like," said Danny.

Renalto opened his mouth to respond but the elevator doors closed, denying him the last word. Judging from his twitching jaw and the look of frustration etched on his handsome face, this wasn't something that happened very often.

"Good-bye, Mr. Renalto."

Five minutes later, back on Wilshire Boulevard, Danny's cell phone rang.

"Henning. What have you got for me?"

"Not much, sir, I'm afraid. Nothing in the pawnshops, nothing online."

Danny frowned. "It's still early days."

"Yes, sir. I also checked out Jakes's will."

Danny brightened. "And?"

"The wife gets everything. No other family. No charitable causes."

"How much is everything?"

"After taxes, around four hundred million dollars."

Danny whistled. *Four hundred million dollars.* That was quite a motive for murder. Not that Angela Jakes was a suspect. The poor woman could hardly have raped and beaten herself. Even so, Danny thought back to the words Angela had murmured repeatedly to herself last night: *I have no life.*

With four hundred million in the bank, she certainly had a life now. Any life she wanted.

"Anything else?" he asked his sergeant.

"Just one thing. The jewelry. A little over a million bucks' worth was taken from the safe and Mrs. Jakes's jewelry box."

Danny waited for the punch line. "And . . . ?"

"None of it was insured. Seven figures' worth of diamonds, and you don't add it to your homeowner's policy? Seems strange, don't you think?"

It did seem strange. But Danny's mind wasn't focused on Andrew Jakes's insurance oversights. "Listen," he said, "I want you to run a check for me on a guy named Lyle Renalto. *R-E-N-A-L-T-O.* Says he was Old Man Jakes's lawyer."

"Sure," said Detective Henning. "What am I looking for, exactly?"

Detective Danny McGuire said honestly, "That's the problem. I have no idea."

CHAPTER TWO

MARRAKECH, MOROCCO
1892

The little girl gazed out of the carriage window at streets teeming with filth and life and noise and stench and poverty and laughter, and felt sure of one thing: she would die in this place.

She had been sent here to die.

She had grown up in luxury, in privilege and above all in peace, in a sprawling palace in the desert. The only daughter of a nobleman and his most favored wife, she had been named Miriam, after the mother of the great prophet, and Bahia, which meant "most fair," and from her earliest infancy had known nothing but praise and love. She slept in a room with gold leaf on the walls, in a bed of intricately carved ivory. She wore silks woven in Ouarzazate and dyed in Essaouira with ocher and indigo and madder, shipped in at great expense from the Near East. She had servants to dress her, to bathe her, to feed her, and more servants to educate her in the Koran and in music and poetry, the ancient poetry of her desert ancestors. She was beautiful inside and out, as sweet-faced and sweet-tempered a child as any noble father could wish for, a jewel prized above all the rubies and amethysts and emeralds that adorned the necks and wrists of all four of her father's wives.

The palace, with its cool, shady courtyards, its fountains and birdsong, its plates of sugared almonds and silver pots of sugary mint tea, was Miriam's whole world. It was a place of pleasure and peace, where she played with her siblings, sheltered from the punishing desert sun and all the other dangers of life beyond its thick stone walls. Had it not been for one terrible, unexpected event, Miriam would no doubt have lived out the rest of her days in this blissfully gilded prison. As it was, at the age of ten, her idyllic childhood ground to an abrupt and final halt. Miriam's mother, Leila Bahia, left her father for another man, riding off into the desert one night never to return.

Miriam's father, Abdullah, was a good and honorable man, but Leila's betrayal broke him. As Abdullah withdrew increasingly from life and the day-to-day business of running his household, the other wives stepped in. Always jealous of the younger, more beautiful Leila and the favoritism Abdullah showed to their child, the wives began a campaign to get rid of Miriam. Led by Rima, Abdullah's ambitious first wife, they prevailed on their husband to send the child away.

She will grow into a serpent, like her mother, and bring ruin on us all.

She looks just like her.

I've already seen her making eyes at the servant boys, and even at Kasim, her own brother!

In the end, too weak to resist, and too heartbroken to look his favorite daughter in the face—it was true, Miriam did look exactly like Leila, right down to the soft curve of her eyelashes—Abdullah acquiesced to Rima's demands. Miriam would be sent to live with one of his brothers, Sulaiman, a wealthy cloth merchant in Marrakech.

The child wept as the carriage clattered through the palace gates and she left the only home she had ever known for the first, and last, time. Ahead, the desert sands stretched out before her, apparently endless, a bleak but beautiful canvas of oranges and yellows, modulating from deep rust to the palest buttermilk. It was a three-day ride to the city, and until the walls of the ancient battlements loomed into view, they passed nothing but a few nomads' huts and the occasional merchant caravan weaving its weary way across the emptiness. Miriam had started to wonder if perhaps there *was* no city. If it was all a wicked plan by her stepmothers to throw her out into the wilderness, like they did to criminals in the poems Mama used to read her. But then, suddenly, she was here, inside this anthill of humanity, this wild mishmash of beauty and ugliness, of minarets and slums, of luxury and destitution, of lords and lepers.

This is it, thought the terrified child, deafened by the noise of the clamoring hands banging on the carriage as they passed, trying to sell her dates or cumin or ugly little wooden dolls. *The apocalypse. The mob. They're going to kill me.*

But Miriam wasn't killed. Instead, not twenty minutes later, she found herself sitting in one of the many ornate waiting parlors in her uncle's *riad* close to the souk, sipping the same sweet mint tea that she was used to at home and having her hands and feet bathed in rosewater.

Presently a small, round man with the deepest, loudest voice Miriam had ever heard waddled into the room. Smiling, he swooped her up into his arms and began covering her with kisses. "Welcome, welcome, dearest child!" he boomed. "Abdullah's daughter, well,

well, well. Welcome, desert rose. Welcome, and may you prosper and flourish evermore in my humble home."

In reality, Uncle Sulaiman's *riad* was anything but humble. Smaller in scale than her father's palace, it was nevertheless an Aladdin's cave of sumptuous wealth, beauty, and refinement, all paid for with the proceeds of the younger brother's thriving textile business. And Miriam *did* flourish there. Unmarried and childless, her uncle Sulaiman came to love her as his own daughter. For the rest of his life Sulaiman remained grateful to his brother, Abdullah, for bestowing on him so great and priceless a gift. If it were possible, he loved Miriam more than her natural parents had done, but Sulaiman's love took a different form. Where Abdullah and Leila had protected their daughter from the dangers of the outside world, Sulaiman encouraged Miriam to savor and explore its delights. Of course, she never left the *riad* unaccompanied. Guards went with her everywhere. But under their watchful eyes she was free to roam through the vibrant buzzing alleyways of the souk.

Here were sights and sounds and smells that she had read about in storybooks brought phantasmagorically to life. Marrakech was a delicious assault on every sense, a living, breathing, pulsing city that filled Miriam's tranquil soul with excitement and curiosity and hunger. As she grew into her teens, more beautiful with each passing day, her love affair with the city intensified to the point where even a proposed vacation to the coast caused her to feel irritated and impatient.

"But *why* do we have to go, Uncle?"

Sulaiman laughed his booming, indulgent laugh. "You make it sound like a punishment, dearest. Essaouira is quite beautiful, and besides, no one wants to stay in Marrakech in high summer."

"I do."

"Nonsense. The heat's unbearable."

"I can bear it. Don't make me leave, Uncle, I beg you. I'll devote twice as much time to my studies if you let me stay."

Sulaiman laughed even louder. "Twice nothing is nothing, dearest!" But, as al-

ways when Miriam really wanted something, he gave in. He would go to the
coast for two weeks alone. Miriam could
stay home with her guards and her gov-
erness.

Later, Jibril would remember it as the
moment his life began.
   And the moment it ended.
   The sixteen-year-old son of Sulaiman's chief factor, Jibril was a happy,
outgoing child, seemingly without a
problem in the world. Pleasant-looking,
with curly brown hair and a ready smile,
he was also bright academically, with a
particular aptitude for mathematics. His
father harbored secret hopes of Jibril
one day founding a business empire of
his own. And why not? Morocco was
becoming more cosmopolitan, its in-
habitants more socially mobile than they
had ever been. Not like it had been in
his day. The boy could have the world
at his feet if he wished it, as bright and
glittering a future as he chose.
   Unbeknownst to his father, Jibril had
secret hopes of his own.

None of them revolved around business.

They revolved around the incandescent, radiant, utterly lovely form of Sulaiman's niece, Mistress Miriam.

Jibril first met Miriam the day she arrived at the *riad* as a frightened ten-year-old. Then thirteen and a kind boy, sensitive to others' pain, Jibril had taken Miriam under his wing. The two of them quickly became friends and playmates, spending endless happy hours roaming the souk and squares of the city together while Jibril's father and Miriam's uncle worked long hours in the company offices.

Jibril couldn't say exactly when it was that his feelings toward Miriam had changed. Possibly the early arrival of her breasts, shortly after her twelfth birthday, had something to do with it. Or possibly there was some other, nobler reason. In any event, at some point during his fifteenth year, Jibril fell deeply, hopelessly, obsessively in love with his childhood playmate. Which would have been as wonderful a thing as could have happened, had it not been for one small, but undeniable, problem: Miriam was not in love with Jibril.

Tentative allusions to his feelings were met with peals of laughter on Miriam's part. "Don't be ridiculous!" she would tease him, pulling him by the hand in a way that made Jibril want to melt with longing. "You're my brother. Besides, I'm never getting married." Memories of her mother's flight and her father's despair still haunted her. Uncle Sulaiman's happy independence seemed a far safer, more sensible option.

Jibril wept with frustration and despair. Why had he ever behaved like a brother toward her? Why had he not seen before what a goddess she was? How would he ever be able to undo the damage?

Then one day, it happened. It was during the weeks that Miriam's uncle Sulaiman was away on vacation in Essaouira. Jibril returned to the *riad* after his morning's studies to find smoke pouring out of the windows. You could feel the heat from a hundred yards away.

"What's going on?"

Jibril's father, his face and hands

blackened with soot, coughed out an answer. "It started in the kitchens. I've never seen flames spread so fast. It's a miracle we got everybody out of there."

Huddled around them was a throng of frightened household staff, some burned and weeping, others coughing violently. They'd been joined by numerous neighbors and passersby. Soon the crowd was so big that it was difficult for the men with water buckets to fight their way through.

Jibril's heart tightened in panic. "Where's Miriam?"

"Don't worry," said his father. "She left early this morning to go to the baths. There's nobody in the house." But just as he spoke, a figure appeared at an upper window, arms flailing wildly. It was hard to make out who it was through the thick, acrid clouds of smoke. But Jibril knew instantly.

Before his father or anyone could stop him, he darted into the building. The heat hit him like a punch. Black smoke filled his lungs. It was like inhaling razor blades. Jibril fell to his knees, blinded, utterly disoriented. *I have to get up. I have to find her. Help me, Al-lah.*

And God did help him. In later years, Jibril described the feeling as some unseen person taking him by the hand and physically pulling him toward the stone stairwell. He had no idea how, in that hell, he fought his way to Miriam, how he lifted her in his arms like a rag doll and carried her downstairs through the flames and into the street. It was a miracle. There was no other word for it. *Allah saved us because He wills us to be together. It is our destiny.*

When Miriam opened her eyes, and looked into the eyes of her rescuer, Jibril's prayers were answered.

She loved him. He was a brother no more.

When Sulaiman returned home to his gutted *riad,* his only thought was for his beloved Miriam and how close he had come to losing her. He summoned Jibril to his study.

"My boy, I owe you my life. Tell me how I can repay you. What gift can I give in gratitude for your heroism? Money? Jewels? A house of your own? Name it. Name it and it is yours."

"I want no money from you, sir," said Jibril humbly. "I ask only for your blessing. I intend to marry your niece."

He smiled, and Sulaiman could see the love light up his eyes. *Poor boy.*

"I'm sorry, Jibril. Truly, I am. But that is not possible."

Jibril's smile crumpled. "Why not?"

"Miriam is of noble birth," Sulaiman explained kindly. "When her father entrusted her to my care, it was on the understanding that she would one day make an alliance befitting her class and status in life. I have already chosen the gentleman. He's older than Miriam, but he is well respected, kind—"

"NO!" Jibril couldn't contain himself. "You can't! Miriam loves me. She . . . she won't do it."

Sulaiman's expression hardened. "Miriam will do as I ask her."

Jibril looked so forlorn that the old man relented. "Look. I said I am sorry, and I meant it. These are the ways of the world, Jibril. We are all prisoners, in

our different ways. But you must forget
about my niece. Ask me for something
else. Anything."

Jibril did not ask. How could he?
There was nothing else he wanted. He
tried to tell himself that he still had time
to persuade Sulaiman. The older man
might change his mind. Miriam might
indeed refuse to wed the man to whom
she had been unknowingly betrothed,
though he knew in his heart that this
was a vain hope. Miriam loved Sulaiman like a father, and would never bring
dishonor on herself or her family by disobeying him, especially not in so grave
a matter as marriage.

Not even Jibril's own father could
help him.

"You must forget the girl, son. Trust
me, there will be scores of others. You
have a bright future ahead of you,
backed by Sulaiman's money, if only
you'd take it. You'll be able to afford a
house full of wives!"

Jibril thought darkly, *Nobody under-
stands.* And though Miriam tried to
comfort him, assuring him that she
would always love him no matter whom

she married, it was cold comfort for the boy, who burned for her body with all the fiery intensity of a volcano.

At last the day came when all Jibril's hopes died. Miriam was married to a sheikh, Mahmoud Basta, a paunchy, bald man old enough to be her father. If she was distraught, she hid it well, maintaining a serene grace throughout the ceremony, and afterward, when she bid good-bye to her second, much beloved home.

The newlyweds lived close to the city, in the Basta family palace at the foot of the Atlas Mountains, and Miriam was able to visit her uncle Sulaiman's house often. On these visits, she would sometimes see the hollow-eyed Jibril staring at her from across a room, pain etched on his face like a mask. At these times she felt pity and great sorrow. But the emotions were for Jibril, not for herself. Mahmoud was a kind husband, loving, indulgent and decent. When Miriam gave him a son at the end of their first year of marriage, he wept for joy. Over the next five years, she gave him three more boys and a girl, Leila. Over time,

Miriam's children came to fill the void that had been left by her doomed love for Jibril. Watching them play while their doting father looked on, she sometimes felt guilty that she was so happy, while Jibril, she knew, remained broken and lost. She had heard through friends that he drank heavily, and spent his days in the hookah bars and whorehouses of the souk, squandering all the money her uncle had given him.

The last time Miriam saw Jibril was at her husband's funeral. Mahmoud, who had never reined in his fondness for baklava and sweet Moroccan wine, died of a heart attack at the age of sixty-two. Miriam was forty, with a fan of fine lines around her eyes and a comfortable layer of fat around her hips, but she was still a beautiful woman. Jibril, on the other hand, had aged terribly. Shrunken and stooped, with the broken veins and yellow eyes of a heavy drinker, he looked twenty years older than he was, and was as sad and embittered as Mahmoud had been happy and generous-spirited.

He staggered over to Miriam, who

was standing with her eldest son, Rafik. She realized immediately that he was drunk.

"So," Jibril slurred, "the old bash-tard's gone at lasht, is he? When can I come to you, Miriam? Tell me. When?"

Miriam blushed scarlet. She had never felt such shame. *How could he do this? To me, and to himself? Today of all days.*

Rafik stepped forward. "My mother is grieving. We all are. You need to leave."

Jibril snarled. "Get out of my way!"

"You're drunk. Nobody wants you here."

"Your mother wants me. Your mother loves me. She's always loved me. Tell him, Miriam."

Miriam turned to him and said sadly, "Today I have buried two of my loves. My husband. And the boy you once were. Good-bye, Jibril."

That night, Jibril hanged himself from a tree in the Menara Gardens. He left a one-word note: خان.

Betrayed.

* * *

The young girl put the book down, tears welling in her eyes. She had read the story hundreds of times before, but she never grew tired of it and it never failed to move her. Sure, she lived in 1983, not 1892; and she was reading the book in a grim, freezing-cold children's home in New York City, not some Moroccan palace. But Miriam and Jibril's tragic love still spoke to her across the ages.

The girl knew what it felt like to be powerless. To be abandoned by one's mother. To be treated like an object by men, a prize to be won. To be shoved through life like a lamb to the slaughter, with no say whatsoever in her own destiny.

"Are you okay, Sofia?"

The boy put a protective, brotherly arm around her. He was the only one she'd told about the book, the only one who understood her. The other kids in the home didn't understand. They mocked her and her old, dog-eared love story. But he didn't.

"They're jealous," he told her. "Because you have a family history and they don't. You have royal blood in your veins, Sofia. That's what makes you different. Special. They hate you for that."

It was true. Sofia identified with Miriam's story on another level, too. A blood level. Miriam was Sofia's great-grandmother. Somewhere inside of her, Miriam's genes lived on. The book Sofia held in her hands, her most prized possession, was not some fairy tale. It was true. It was her history.

"I'm fine," she told the boy, hugging him back as she pulled the thin rayon blanket up over both of them. Even here, pressed against the radiator in the recreation room, it was bitterly cold.

I am not nobody, she told herself, breathing in the warmth of her friend's body. *I am from a noble family with a romantic, tragic history. I am Sofia Basta.*

One day, far away from here, I will fulfill my destiny.

CHAPTER THREE

The Parker Center in downtown L.A. had been the headquarters of the United States' third-largest law enforcement agency since the mid-1950s. Made famous by the 1960s television show *Dragnet,* the drab, nondescript concrete-and-glass building on 150 North Los Angeles Street housed, by 1996, some of the most expensive, state-of-the-art technology found in any police station in the nation, everything from retina recognition scanners to thermal imaging cameras. The Detective Bureau was particularly well equipped, with incident rooms lined with banks of computers and storerooms stocked with a veritable buffet of surveillance gadgetry.

Unfortunately Detective Danny Mc-Guire was too junior in rank for his investigation to be considered worthy of one of these rooms. Instead the six-man team that made up the Jakes homicide investigation had been stuffed like bad-tempered sardines into a windowless hole in the basement, with nothing but a whiteboard and a couple of leaky pens to fire their deductive instincts.

Standing in front of a chipped whiteboard, pen in hand, Danny scrawled a few key words: *Jewels. Miniatures. Insurance. Alarm. Background/Enemies.*

"What have you got for me?"

Detective Henning spoke first. "I talked to five jewelers, including the two in Koreatown you suggested, sir. All said the same thing. The Jakes pieces would've been broken up and the stones either reset into rings or sold loose. Chances of us recovering an intact necklace or pair of earrings are nil. Unless the job was done by some random junkie who doesn't know any better."

"Which it wasn't."

"Which it wasn't," Henning agreed.

One of the few certainties they had established was that whoever broke into the Jakes mansion was a pro, familiar with the estate's complex alarm system and able to disable it single-handedly. He'd also managed to subdue two victims, raping one and killing the other, with minimal disturbance and in a frighteningly short space of time. Angela Jakes was convinced she had never met her assailant before. He was masked, but she hadn't recognized his voice or the way he moved. Nonetheless, Detective Danny McGuire was certain that the man they were looking for had inside knowledge of the family. This was no opportunistic burglary.

"The art angle's a little more promising," said Detective Henning.

Danny raised a hopeful eyebrow. "Oh?"

"Jakes was a dealer, as we know, so naturally enough the house was stuffed with valuable paintings, most of them contemporary."

"Wow," another officer chipped in sarcastically. "I don't know how you keep coming up with these insights, Henning. You're like gold dust, man."

Everyone laughed. Henning's status as McGuire's teacher's pet was a running joke.

Henning ignored the interruption. "If the killer really knew his art, he'd have gone for the two Basquiats hanging in the study, or the Koons in one of the guest bedrooms."

Someone said, "Maybe they were too heavy? The guy was on his own."

"We're quite sure about that, are we?" asked Danny.

"Yes, sir," said Detective Henning. "Forensics confirmed there were only one set of prints found in the house besides those of the family and staff. But in any case the paintings weren't heavy. All three were small enough for one man to carry and they had a combined value of over thirty million dollars. But our guy chose the miniatures, just about the only antiques in Jakes's collection."

"Were they valuable?" asked Danny.

"It's all relative. They were worth a couple hundred thousand each, so maybe a million bucks in total. They're family portraits from the nineteenth century, mostly European. The market for them is pretty small, which makes them our best bet by far on the tracing-stolen-goods route. I got the name of a local expert. He lives in Venice Beach. I'm meeting him this afternoon."

"Good," said Danny. "Anyone else?"

The rest of the team reported their "progress," such as it was. The climbing ropes used to bind the couple were a generic brand that could have been purchased at any camping or sporting-goods store. The knot the killer used to bind the couple together was complicated—a double half hitch—another sign, if they needed it, that they were looking for a professional criminal. But other than that there was precious little physical evidence of any worth. The blood and semen tests didn't match any in the nationwide database.

"What about Jakes's background? Anything circumstantial that might help us?"

The short answer to that was no. Andrew Jakes's business dealings had been clean as a whistle. He was a prominent philanthropist, not to mention a significant donor to the LAPD's Policemen's Benevolent Association.

Danny thought, *I knew I'd heard the name somewhere. Strange a charitable guy like that left nothing to good causes in his will.*

The old man had no known enemies, and no family, close or otherwise, other than an ex-wife he'd divorced more than twenty-five years earlier who was now happily remarried and living in Fresno.

The door opened suddenly. Officer John Bolt, a shy redhead and one of the most junior members of Danny's team, burst into the room clutching a piece of paper. Everybody looked up.

"Mrs. Jakes's lawyer just released a statement."

The mention of Lyle Renalto made Danny's shoulders tense. Detective Henning's background search on Renalto had come up with nothing out of the ordinary, but Danny's suspicions lingered.

"Don't keep us in suspense, Bolt. What does she say?"

"She's giving away all the money she inherits from her husband's estate to children's charities."

Danny said, "Not all of it, surely?"

Bolt handed Danny the paper. "Every penny, sir. Over four hundred million dollars."

Reading the statement, Danny felt a strange sense of elation.

I knew she wasn't a gold digger. I just sensed it. I gotta learn to trust my instincts more.

An hour later, Danny pulled up outside the gates of a large, neo-Tudor mansion in Beverly Hills. Twenty-twenty Canon Drive was the address Angela Jakes gave when she was released from the hospital. It belonged to a friend.

"I can't go back to Loma Vista, Detective," she'd explained to Danny. "It's too painful. I'll stay with a friend until the estate is sold."

A uniformed maid showed Danny through to a warm, sunny sitting room filled with overstuffed couches and big vases of heavily scented freesias and lilies. It was a feminine room, and Angela Jakes looked quite at home in it, walking over to greet Danny in bare feet and jeans. It was now two weeks since the attack and the bruises to her face had mellowed to a soft apricot yellow. For the first time Danny could see the color of her eyes: a rich, liquid brown, like melted chocolate. No woman had a right to be that beautiful.

"Detective." She shook his hand, smiling. Danny felt his mouth go dry. "Is there any news? Have you found him yet?"

"Not yet."

A flicker of disappointment crossed her face and Danny felt disproportionately upset. Angela Jakes was the last woman on earth he wanted to disappoint.

"We're still in the early stages of our investigation, Mrs. Jakes," he assured her. "We'll find him."

Angela sat down on one of the couches and gestured for Danny to do the same. "Please, call me Angela. Can I get you anything? Some tea perhaps."

"I'm fine, thank you." Danny loosened

his tie. *Is it me, or is it hot in here?* "I wanted to ask you a couple more questions if I may. About your marriage."

Angela looked perplexed. "My marriage?"

"The better the picture we can build up of your life together, the easier it'll be for us to figure out who might have done this. And why."

She considered this, nodding thoughtfully. "All right. Well, what would you like to know?"

"Let's begin at the beginning. How did the two of you meet?"

"At an art class at UCLA."

Her eyes lit up at the memory and Danny thought, *My God, she really did love him.*

"It wasn't a regular degree course or anything. Just a night class I was taking. I used to enjoy art when I was in high school. Not that I was ever very good at it." It astonished Danny how such a gorgeous woman could have so little self-confidence, but Angela Jakes always seemed to be putting herself down.

"Where did you go to high school?" he asked idly.

"Beverly Hills High. Why?"

"No reason. Just curious. It's a bad habit we detectives have."

"Of course." She smiled again. Danny's stomach flipped like a pancake. "Anyway, Andrew came to UCLA to give a talk about the art business. How to get a gallery to look at your work, that sort of thing. What attracts collectors. He was so smart and funny. We just clicked right away."

Danny tried to picture Old Man Jakes and an even younger version of Angela "just clicking." It wasn't easy.

"Did your husband have any enemies that you were aware of?"

"None." Her tone was firm, almost defiant.

"You're sure?"

"Quite sure. Andrew was a sweetheart. Everybody loved him."

Not everybody. Danny tried another tack. "On the night of the murder, I don't know if you remember this, but you kept saying something."

"Did I?"

"Yes. You repeated the same words over and over."

She looked at him blankly.

"'*I have no life.*' That was the phrase you used. Can you think why you might have said that?"

She hesitated. "Not really. Only that when I met Andrew, he gave me a life. He rescued me. So perhaps I said 'I have no life' because I knew it was the end."

"The end?"

"The end of the peace and happiness I had known with Andrew. But I don't remember saying those words, Detective. I don't remember anything except Andrew and the blood. And you."

"You say your husband rescued you? From what?" asked Danny.

Angela stared awkwardly into her lap. "An unhappy situation."

Danny knew he ought to press her, but he couldn't bear to upset her again. Clearly she didn't want to talk about it. *She'll tell me when she's ready.*

"I see. And what about you, Mrs. Jakes?"

"Me?"

"Was there anyone who might conceivably have held a grudge against you, personally?"

Angela Jakes thought about this for a moment. "You know, I never thought so. Although, as you can imagine, Detective, with an age difference like the one between me and Andrew—over fifty years—people are quick to judge. I know there were many in Andrew's social circle who distrusted me. They assumed I was after his money. I imagine you thought the same thing."

"Of course not," lied Danny, avoiding her eyes.

"I tried to persuade Andrew to leave me out of his will, to prove to people our marriage was never about money. But he wouldn't hear of it. He said the naysayers were bullies and one should never give in to bullies."

"Is that why you gave all his money to charity? To prove people wrong?"

She shrugged. "Maybe that was part of it, subconsciously."

"Did your husband know that you were planning to give everything away when he died?"

"No." She shook her head. "It might have hurt his feelings. Andrew wanted me to have the money, and I wanted him to be happy. But the truth is, I have no use for that sort of wealth."

Without meaning to, Danny raised an eyebrow.

Angela Jakes laughed, a warm, mellifluous laugh, like honey oozing off a spoon. "You look dubious, Detective. But really, what on earth would I do with four hundred million dollars? I like to paint, I like walking in the canyons. Those things don't cost millions. Far better for it to go to people who need it, who can really make use of it. In some small way, it makes me feel as if what happened wasn't entirely in vain."

She looked down at her hands again and Danny could see she was fighting back tears. Instinctively, he reached out and put a hand over hers. He was embarrassed to admit it, but the intimacy felt wonderful. Electric.

"What the hell's going on?"

Danny jumped. Lyle Renalto's voice had shattered the mood like a stone crashing through a windshield.

"What are you doing here?" the lawyer demanded.

As he stood in the doorway, Renalto's handsome features were twisted into an angry mask and his shoulders thrust aggressively forward. He was wearing an identical suit to the one he'd worn at the hospital, with a pale blue silk tie that matched his eyes. Danny didn't think he'd ever been less pleased to see a person in his entire life.

"A police interview is going on," he replied coldly. "And as usual, Mr. Renalto, you're interrupting. May I ask what *you're* doing here?"

"That's easy," Lyle replied, "I live here. Didn't Angel tell you?"

Danny turned to Angela. "*He's* the friend you're staying with? You never mentioned it."

She shrugged. "You never asked. Lyle was kind enough to offer me a place to stay while I recuperate. As I told you, he's been a tremendous support through all of this."

Lyle Renalto said curtly, "If you're done harassing Mrs. Jakes, Detective, I'll be happy to show you out."

"Detective McGuire is not harassing me," said Angela. "He's been perfectly polite."

"Hmm." Renalto sounded unconvinced.

Ignoring him, Danny said, "I have one more question for you, Mrs. Jakes, if you don't mind. You mentioned that you first met Mr. Jakes at an art class."

"That's right."

"May I ask what your name was at that time?"

Angela glanced nervously toward Lyle Renalto. "My name? I don't understand."

"Your maiden name," Danny explained. "Before you and Mr. Jakes were married."

"Oh!" She looked palpably relieved. "I wondered what on earth you meant for a moment." She fixed Danny with the chocolate eyes for a third and final time. "Ryman. My maiden name was Ryman."

The room was small and drab and claustrophobic, and the smell of day-old Chinese takeout was overpowering. Detective Henning thought: *Stolen art isn't the booming business the media makes it out to be.*

Roeg Lindemeyer, an art fence turned occasional police informer, lived in a dilapidated single-story house in one of the more run-down Venice walk-streets, narrow, pedestrian-only alleyways that ran between Ocean Avenue and the beach. A few blocks farther north, 1920s "cottages" like Roeg's had been renovated by hip, young West L.A. types and were changing hands for seven hundred grand or more. But not here. This was Venice Beach as it used to be: dirt-poor. Roeg Lindemeyer's "showroom" was as seedy and impoverished as any junkie's squat.

"So? Have you seen any of them?"

Henning watched impatiently as Lindemeyer leafed through the insurance photographs of the Jakes miniatures. The fence was a wizened hobbit of a man in his midfifties, his fingers black with tobacco stains. He left thumbprints on each of the images.

"What's it worth to ya?"

With distaste, the young detective

pulled two twenty-dollar bills out of his wallet.

Lindemeyer grunted. "Hundred."

"Sixty, and I won't report you for extortion."

"Deal."

Greedily, the older man stuffed the cash into his pocket and handed back the now smeared photographs.

"So?" Detective Henning repeated. "Have you seen those miniatures on the black market or haven't you?"

"Nope."

"That's it? 'Nope'? That's all you got for me?"

Lindemeyer shrugged. "You asked me a question. I answered it."

Henning made a lunge for his money. Lindemeyer cringed.

"Okay, okay. Look, Detective, if they was for sale, I woulda seen 'em. I'm the only guy on the West Coast who can move that niche, Victorian shit. You know it and so does everybody else. So either your boy's skipped town or he ain't selling. That's real information, man. Maybe he wanted 'em for personal use."

A psychopathic, homicidal rapist with a love for obscure nineteenth-century portraiture? Detective Henning didn't think so. "Maybe he had a buyer lined up already," he mused aloud. "Then he wouldn't have needed your services."

"Mebbe."

"Do you know of any prominent collectors who might commission a job like this?"

"I might." Lindemeyer eyed the sergeant's wallet.

It was going to be a long and expensive afternoon.

"Could you do me a favor and check again?"

Detective Danny McGuire flashed the receptionist the same winning smile he'd used on the nurse at Cedars, but this time to no avail.

"I don' need to check agin. I checked awready."

Today's gatekeeper at the government records office on Veteran was black, weighed around two hundred pounds, and was plainly in no mood to take shit from some dumb-ass Irish cop who figured he was God's gift to women.

"We got no records for no Angela Ryman. Not Ryman *RY,* not Reiman *REI,* not any Angela Ryman. No births, no marriages, no deaths, no Social, no taxes. Not in California."

Danny's mind was flooded with doubts. One by one, he tried to rationalize them away.

Maybe she was born out of state.

Maybe she and Jakes got married in the Caribbean, or in Paris. Folks with that kind of money don't just run down to city hall like the rest of us. The marriage certificate could be anywhere.

It doesn't mean anything.

Even so, walking into the administration offices of Beverly Hills High School half an hour later, the sinking feeling in the pit of his stomach remained.

"I need the records of a former student." He tried to force some optimism into his voice. "She would have graduated eight or nine years ago."

The male clerk smiled helpfully. "Certainly, Detective. What was the young lady's name?"

"Angela Ryman."

The smile faded. "Well, I've been here ten years and that name doesn't ring a bell with me." He opened up a tall metal filing cabinet and pulled out a drawer marked *Ru–Si.* "I don't suppose you have a picture?"

Danny reached into his briefcase. He handed the man a shot of Angela that his officers had taken from the house. She was wearing her wedding dress and looked even more radiant than usual, her perfect features aglow with love and joy, her dark hair swept back from her milk-white face, her chocolate-brown eyes dancing.

The clerk said, "Oh my. Now, *that's* a face I wouldn't forget in a hurry. No, I'm sorry. That girl was never here."

"You're hurting me!"

Lyle Renalto was gripping Angela Jakes by the shoulders so tightly that his fingernails bit into the flesh.

"I'm sorry, Angel." He released his

grip. "But you have to get out of here. Now, today, before he comes back."

Angela started to cry. "But I . . . I haven't done anything wrong."

"Of course you haven't," said Lyle more gently. "I know that. You know that. But McGuire won't understand."

Angela hesitated. "Are you sure he won't? He seems like such a nice guy."

"I'm sure," said Lyle firmly. Pulling an overnight bag out of the closet, he handed it to her. "Get some clothes. We may not have much time."

Detective Danny McGuire woke at five in the morning. He'd gone to bed at two and barely slept. His mind was racing.

Angela Jakes had lied to him. About her name and about her education. What else had she lied to him about? And why?

Why would she fake a name and a past to the man who was trying to catch her rapist and her husband's killer? A man who was trying to help her? There could only be one reason. Angela Jakes must have something in her past that

she was ashamed of. Deeply ashamed
of. The obvious thought popped into
Danny's mind:

**Had she been a hooker back in the
day? Was that the "unhappy life" Andrew Jakes had rescued her from?**

It was a familiar enough story in L.A.:
young, beautiful, small-town girl comes
to Hollywood with dreams of making it
as an actress. Falls on hard times.
Hooks up with the wrong crowd . . .

Yet whenever Danny pictured that
angelic face, those eyes so full of trust
and goodness, he couldn't bring himself to believe that Andrew Jakes had
picked up his bride on Hollywood Boulevard. He hadn't believed Angela Jakes
was a gold digger either, even when all
the evidence pointed to it. *I was right
about that. I gotta trust my instincts
more.*

But what were his instincts telling him
now?

That was the problem. He had no
idea.

After leaving the high school yesterday, he'd driven around for an hour, trying to figure out his next move. The ob-

vious way to go would have been to drive back to Lyle Renalto's place and confront Angela on the spot. With any other witness, Danny wouldn't have thought twice. But he couldn't bring himself to grill the lovely Mrs. Jakes in front of her odious attorney, who would doubtless insist on remaining glued to her side. If she did have guilty secrets, and who of us didn't, she deserved a chance to confess them in private. Danny would understand. After everything she'd just been through, he owed her that much sensitivity at least.

So instead Danny had driven back to the station house to brainstorm with the rest of the team. Only it was actually more of a shit storm. Every lead his men had been chasing seemed to have turned into a dead end. Henning's Venice art expert had come up with a big fat doughnut on the miniatures. The insurance scam angle looked less and less promising, as the only people who could possibly benefit from a staged robbery would be the Jakeses themselves, one of whom was dead, while the other had given away all her money.

Two of Danny's officers had been checking out the lucky charities on the receiving end of Angela Jakes's generosity. Both seemed totally kosher, with sparklingly transparent accounts. A sophisticated computer program had gone through every violent rape in the L.A. area in the past five years, looking for any connection with art or jewelry thefts, or any connection at all that might link one of those suspects to the Jakes crime scene. *Nothing.* It was the same story with forensics. *Prints: nothing. Semen analysis: nothing.*

Danny pulled on a pair of sweatpants and stumbled into the kitchen to fix himself a strong cup of coffee. It was still dark outside. The tree-lined, suburban street in West Hollywood where Danny had lived for the past six years was empty and as silent as the grave. *Was Angela still asleep?* Danny pictured her, dark hair spilling over a soft white pillow, her glorious body warm and naked beneath Lyle Renalto's sheets. *Was she in the guest bedroom?* Christ, he hoped so.

He remembered Lyle's contemptuous

comment at the hospital: *"For a detective, you're a pretty poor judge of people. Angela and I aren't lovers."*

Detective Danny McGuire hoped with all his heart that Renalto's words were true.

He looked at his watch: 5:20.

If I drive over there now, they'll still be asleep. I can see for myself which beds were slept in.

He jumped into the shower.

It was six A.M. on the dot. The same uniformed maid who had been on duty yesterday answered the door. Danny thought, *Poor woman. How early does she have to be at work?*

The maid looked at Danny and thought, *Poor man. How early does he have to be at work?*

"I'm looking for Mrs. Jakes."

"Mrs. Jakes not here."

"Okay, look, I know Mr. Renalto's your boss. And I know he's not exactly thrilled about my questioning Mrs. Jakes, especially at this time in the morning. But this is a murder investigation. So I need you to please wake Mrs. Jakes, and Mr. Renalto if you have to."

"No, you don't understand. She not here. She leave last night. You're welcome to come in and search the house if you no believe me."

Unfortunately Danny did believe her. His heart began to race unpleasantly.

"Left? Where did she go?"

"I don't know. She have a suitcase. Mr. Renalto drive her to the airport."

Danny's career flashed before his eyes. *I should have come straight back here yesterday. I would have caught them. Now my key witness has flown the coop to God only knows where.*

"What about Renalto? Did he leave with her?"

The maid looked surprised by the question. "Of course not. Mr. Renalto, he is here. He is asleeping upstairs."

Danny pushed past her, bounding up the ornately carved staircase two steps at a time. Double doors at the end of the corridor clearly led to the master bedroom. He kicked them open. The sleeping figure under the covers didn't stir.

"Okay, asshole. Where is she?" Danny marched toward the bed. "And you'd better have a good fucking answer or I am going to book you for obstruction of a murder investigation and personally see to it that you never practice law in this town again."

Grabbing the heavy silk counterpane, Danny yanked it off the bed.

And really, really wished he hadn't.

CHAPTER FOUR

TWO YEARS EARLIER . . .

Sofia Basta hung up the phone and hugged herself with happiness.

Her husband was coming home. He'd be here in an hour.

Husband. How she loved saying the word, turning it over in her mind and on her tongue like a piece of succulent candy. They were married now. Actually married. Frankie, her only friend through the long, dark, desperate years in New York. Frankie, the most beautiful, brilliant, perfect man on earth. Frankie, who could have had anyone, had chosen her, Sofia, to be his bride. Most mornings she still woke up and felt nervously for her wedding band, unable quite to believe her good fortune. But then she reminded herself.

I am Sofia Basta, great-granddaughter of Miriam, a Moroccan princess. I'm special. Why shouldn't he have chosen me?

Their apartment was modest, a two-bedroom condo in the Beverly Hills postal district, but Sofia had made it warm and welcoming, delighting in creating the perfect nest for Frankie to come home to. Brightly colored cushions and throws adorned the couch in the living room, which was flooded all day long with blazing California sunshine. How Sofia loved that sunshine, after eighteen grim, overcast years in New York! The grimy city, the loneliness of the children's home. Sofia's life had been a nightmare back then. But it all seemed like a dream now, a story that had happened to someone else.

And what a story it was.

Sofia's mother, Christina, had been a drug addict and sometime hooker, as ill equipped to take care of her children as she was to take care of herself. But it had not always been like that. Christina Basta grew up in great wealth, first in Morocco and later in Paris, where her parents sent her to an exclusive girls' boarding school. Tall and slender as a gazelle with creamy skin and mellow, searching brown eyes, the spitting image of her grandmother Miriam, Christina quickly caught the eye of the Parisian modeling scouts who hung around the Rue Du Faubourg looking for fresh talent. By sixteen years of age Christina was working almost full-time. By eighteen she was living in New York, sharing a model apartment with three other girls from her agency and indulging in all the myriad pleasures the city had to offer.

Christina Basta's burnout was rapid and catastrophic. First came cocaine. Later it was heroin. At twenty, after one missed job too many, Christina was dropped by her agency. By now estranged from her family, and too proud to ask for help, she turned instead to "boyfriends" to fund her ever-growing habit—in reality dealers and pimps, who dragged her deeper and deeper into hell.

Sofia and her twin sister, Ella, were the result of Christina's third pregnancy. Christina had tried to abort them, as she had the other babies, but the procedure was botched and both babies survived. Born in the Berwind Maternity Clinic in Harlem, and abandoned there by their mother that same night, the Basta twins spent a few short weeks together before Ella, the prettier baby of the two, was adopted by a local doctor and his wife. From then on, Sofia began her life as she was destined to continue it: alone.

But not completely.

When Sofia was six years old and living at the St. Mary's Home for Girls in Brooklyn, the staff at the home received word, via a top-flight Madison Avenue law firm no less, that Sofia's mother had died. Christina had left a "small bequest" to her daughters. As the doctor and his family had moved away, taking Ella with them, it was decided that the bequest should go to Sofia.

"It's not very substantial," the lawyer explained, to the great disappointment of

the head of St. Mary's. "It may have sen-
timental value, though, perhaps when the
child is older. There's a book, an old
book. And a letter."

The book was the one that recounted
the love story of Miriam and Jibril, which
a few years later Sofia and Frankie
would spend so many happy hours por-
ing over together. The letter was from
Sofia's mother, explaining that the book
was not some legend, but the true story
of one of Sofia's ancestors, a relic of a
past that Sofia had never known, and
detailing the circumstances of her birth.

Frankie had seen the letter. Sofia had
shown it to him in her teens. He was
the only one she trusted and he understood that the book and the letter
changed everything for the orphaned
Sofia. Overnight, she had gone from
being nobody, the unwanted spawn of
a hooker and her pimp, to being somebody, somebody special, a royal Moroccan princess tragically separated
from her beautiful twin. Of course, the
other kids in the home made fun of her,
told her that her book was a load of
horseshit, that there was no twin, no

exotic royal past. But Frankie helped Sofia see past their envy and their mockery. He was her rock, her salvation, her only friend, and the book was her most treasured possession.

To this day, Sofia wasn't sure what had drawn Frankie to her. Perhaps it was that he was an orphan too, a genuine orphan, like her. Most of the kids in the home had families, just not ones that could take care of them. Frankie and Sofia had no one. But in other ways they were wildly different. Where Sofia had always been lonely and friendless, envied by the girls in the home for her beauty and harassed by the boys for the same reason, Frankie was adored by everyone, staff and kids alike. Handsome—*my God, he was so handsome!*—smart, funny, charismatic, he could make you feel special merely by casting his ice-blue eyes in your direction.

Frankie cast his eyes in Sofia's direction a lot. But not in the same, frightening, predatory way that the other boys did. Frankie's attentions were nobler, gentler somehow, and infinitely more precious than the others' testosterone-fueled advances. Sofia was flattered but frustrated. She longed for him to touch her, but he never made a move.

She had begun to despair that he ever would. And then one day a miracle happened. They were reading the book together in the rec room, as they so often did. Frankie loved the book almost as much as Sofia. He thought Miriam's story was wonderfully romantic and questioned Sofia endlessly about her family history and her long-lost twin, Ella. But on this day, he asked a different question. The most wonderful, unexpected, unhoped-for question. And of course Sofia had said yes, and Frankie had promised her that as soon as they were married, he would be with her, physically, as a man and wife should be.

From that point on, in her own mind at least, Sofia Basta's life had been transformed into one long fairy tale. She and Frankie married on her eighteenth birthday and moved out of the orphanage to a minuscule studio apartment in Harlem, where, as promised, Frankie had made love to her for the first time.

It was the happiest four minutes of Sofia's life.

For the next two years Sofia worked as a waitress while Frankie went to school. He was so smart he could have been anything he wanted to be, a doctor, a lawyer, a businessman. He was offered the job in L.A. before he'd even graduated, that's how smart he was. They moved to California, packing one single suitcase of possessions and waving good-bye to New York as happily as two people ever had.

Los Angeles was everything Sofia had dreamed it would be and more. In fact her life now was *so* perfect, she felt guilty when she complained about anything—like Frankie having to travel for work or stay late at the office. Or like the fact that, so far, they'd been unable to conceive a child. Although this probably had something to do with how rarely her husband wanted to make love to her.

"I want it to be special," Frankie explained. "It won't be if we let it become routine."

Sofia tried to convince Frankie that it

would be special for her no matter how many times they did it, but he wouldn't be moved. Sofia told herself she shouldn't let it bother her too much. He showed her his love in so many other ways—taking intimate photographs, burning up with jealousy when other men paid her attention, complimenting her constantly on her clothes, her perfume, her hair. The sexual side would come, in time.

She'd finished baking a batch of cookies and was in the middle of changing the sheets on their bed when she heard Frankie's key in the door. Squealing with delight, she flew into his arms.

"Baby." He kissed the top of her head. "Did you miss me?"

"Of course I did. Every second! Why didn't you tell me earlier that your flight was today? I'd have come to LAX to meet you."

"I know you would've. I wanted to surprise you."

Frankie looked at his adoring young wife and congratulated himself, once again. Sofia's beauty never failed to surprise him. After only a few days away from her, she seemed to have grown more lovely, more perfect. She was an angel. The thought of another man touching her put murderous thoughts into Frankie's head. Yet he knew with absolute certainty that he could never be the lover she wanted. It was a problem.

That night in bed, feeling her frustration as she lay next to him, Frankie asked, "Do you ever think about sleeping with other men?"

Sofia was horrified. "No! Of course not. I'd rather die. How can you ask me that?"

"You'd really rather *die*?" He looked at her with an intensity she'd never seen before. Sofia thought before answering, then said yes, because it was the truth. She wouldn't have been able to live with herself if she betrayed Frankie. He was her life now, the breath in her body.

"Good," said Frankie. "In that case there's a man I want you to meet. An important man." Slowly, he reached down between her legs. Sofia moaned helplessly. It had been so long since he'd touched her. *Please . . . please don't stop*. But Frankie did stop, pulling his hand away and placing a finger over Sofia's lips. She could have wept.

"I want you to be nice to this man. Do everything that I tell you to do. Even if it's hard."

"Of course, darling." She reached for him. "You know I'll do anything for you. But what did you have in mind?"

"Don't worry about it now. I'll set it up. You just do as I ask."

Frankie rolled on top of her. To Sofia's astonishment, he was hard. Sliding inside her, he gave five or six short thrusts and climaxed almost instantly.

For a while neither of them spoke. Then Sofia asked quietly, "What's his name?"

"Hmm?"

"This man you want me to meet. What's his name?"

In the darkness, Frankie smiled.

"Jakes. His name is Andrew Jakes."

CHAPTER FIVE

LYON, FRANCE
2006

Matt Daley looked at his watch. He had spent the last half hour sitting on an uncomfortable couch in a drab waiting room, deep within Interpol's headquarters in Lyon. The building, looming over the river on the Quai Charles de Gaulle, was a shrine to ugly functionality, a place built by bureaucrats, for bureaucrats. *A data analyst's wet dream,* thought Matt, noting the total absence of artwork or even an occasional colored rug or vase of flowers anywhere in the maze of corridors he'd seen so far. *No wonder the staff look so depressed.*

In fairness, he was basing this assessment on a sample of two people. The dour young Frenchman who had issued him his visitor's pass and led him to the office of the man he'd flown halfway across the world to see, and that man's secretary, a woman whose battle-ax features exuded about as much warmth as a Siberian nuclear winter.

"D'you think he'll be much longer?" Matt asked.

The secretary shrugged contemptuously and returned to her computer screen.

Matt thought of his father. Harry Daley had never been to France, but had always admired Frenchwomen from afar for their poise and charm and sexiness. *Boy, would Rosa Klebb over there have shattered his illusions!*

Thinking about his dad made Matt smile.

If it hadn't been for Harry Daley, he wouldn't be sitting here.

* * *

Harry Daley had been a wonderful father, and an even better husband. Harry and Marie, Matt's mom, were married for forty years and had been everything to each other. At Harry Daley's funeral last year, scores of friends had lingered at the graveside, sharing their memories of the man Matt and his sister, Claire, had loved for as long as either of them could remember.

During the ceremony, Matt got terrible giggles when the Croatian priest's "May he rest in peace" came out quite clearly as "May he rest in piss." Given that Harry had died of cancer of the bladder, this struck both Matt and his sister as hilarious.

Raquel, Matt's glamorous South American wife, didn't see the funny side.

"My God," she hissed in Matt's ear, "what is *wrong* with you? Have you no respect? It's your father's *funeral*."

"Oh, c'mon, honey. 'May he rest in piss'? It's funny. Dad would have seen the humor. Imagine what Jerry Seinfeld would've done with a line like that."

Raquel said cuttingly, "You are hardly Jerry Seinfeld, honey."

It hurt because it was true. Matt Daley was a comedy writer, but in recent years not a very successful one. Handsome in a boyish, disheveled sort of way, with a thick thatch of blond hair and apple-green eyes, his most distinctive feature was his contagious smile, a facial event that seemed to fold his entire physiognomy into one giant laugh line. In the early days of their relationship, Raquel had been attracted to Matt's sense of humor and was flattered when amusing incidents from their life together made their way onto the hit TV show Matt worked on briefly back then. But after eight years the novelty had worn off, along with the hope that Matt's residuals were ever going to earn them the glitzy Hollywood lifestyle Raquel yearned for. Matt now worked for a cable network that paid their bills but left them with little for the finer things in life.

"What's she bitching about this time?" Matt's sister, Claire, was not a fan of her sister-in-law.

"She doesn't like funerals," said Matt loyally.

"Probably scared somebody's going

to shine perpetual light upon *her* and we'll all get to see the scars from her latest eye lift."

Matt grinned. He loved Claire. He loved his wife too, but even he was beginning to come to the painful realization that the feeling was probably no longer mutual.

On the drive back to L.A. after the funeral, Matt tried to build bridges with Raquel.

"I'm about to start working on a new idea," he told her. "Something different. A documentary."

The faintest flicker of interest played in her eyes. "A documentary? Who for?"

"Well, no one yet," Matt admitted. "I'm writing it on spec."

The flicker died. *Just what we need,* thought Raquel. *Another unsold spec script.*

"It's about my father," Matt pressed on. "My biological father."

Raquel yawned. To be honest, she'd forgotten that Harry Daley wasn't Matt's real dad. Harry had married Matt's mom when Matt was a toddler and Claire a baby in arms.

"I found out recently that he was murdered more than a decade ago."

If this piece of news was intended to shock Raquel, or even pique her interest, it failed. "People get murdered every day in this city, Matthew. Why would anyone want to sit through an hour of television about your unknown father's demise?"

"Ah, but that's the thing," said Matt, warming to his theme. "He wasn't unknown. He was an art dealer in Beverly Hills. Famous, at least in L.A. And seriously rich."

Now he had Raquel's attention. "You never mentioned this to me before. How rich?"

"Filthy rich," said Matt. "We're talking hundreds of millions of dollars."

"*Hundreds of millions?* My God, Matt," Raquel gasped, swerving dangerously across lanes of traffic. "What happened to all the money?"

"It went to his widow," said Matt, matter-of-factly.

"What, all of it? What about you and Claire?"

"Me and Claire? Oh, come on, honey.

We hadn't had any contact with him for over thirty years."

"So?" Raquel's pupils dilated excitedly. "You're his children, his blood relatives. Maybe you could contest the will?"

Matt laughed. "On what grounds? It was his money to leave as he chose. But anyway, you're missing the point. The story gets juicier."

Raquel struggled to imagine anything juicier than a payout of hundreds of millions, but she forced herself to listen.

"The widow, who was only in her early twenties at the time, and who was violently raped by whoever killed my old man, gave *all* the cash away to children's charities. Every last penny. It was the biggest single charitable gift in L.A. history. But barely anybody knows about it because instead of sticking around to bask in the glory, this chick hops on a plane just weeks after the murder and disappears. Literally vanishes off the face of the earth and is never heard of again. It's wild, isn't it? Don't you think it's a great story?"

Raquel didn't give a damn about

Matt's stupid story. What sort of man didn't lift a finger to stake his claim to a multimillion-dollar fortune? She'd married a cretin.

"How come you never brought this up before?"

The anger in her voice was unmistakable. Matt's spirits sank. *Why do I always seem to make her angry?*

"To be honest, I sort of forgot about it. I heard about it a few months ago, but I thought it might upset Dad if I showed too much of an interest, so I let it go. But now that Harry's gone, I figure it couldn't hurt to explore it. Networks are really into 'personal history' right now. And murder and money always sell."

The rest of the car ride passed in silence. By the time the Daleys reached home, two obsessions had been born.

Raquel's was with a four-hundred-million-dollar fortune.

And Matt Daley's was with the unsolved murder of his biological father: Andrew Jakes.

* * *

Over the next few months, while his wife spent fruitless hours consulting lawyer after lawyer, hunting for the loophole that would restore "their" fortune, as she now thought of the Jakes estate, what started as a research project for a documentary became the all-consuming focus of Matt Daley's life. By day he would trawl the L.A. libraries and galleries, greedily digging up every scrap of information about Andrew Jakes he could find: his businesses, his modern art collection, his real estate portfolio, his friends, enemies, acquaintances, lovers, interests, pets, health problems and religious beliefs. At night, holed up in his study like a hermit, Matt did more research online. Soon he was barely sleeping. Like a cuckoo chick demanding attention, the file marked *Andrew Jakes* grew bigger and fatter each day, while what little was left of Matt and Raquel Daley's marriage slowly starved to death.

After a while even Claire Michaels became concerned that her brother was overdoing it. "What are you hoping to achieve with all this?" she finally asked one day.

Standing in the kitchen of her bustling house in Westwood, with a baby on one hip and a pot of tomato sauce in her hand, surrounded by the noise and mess of a cheerful family life, Claire made Matt feel happy and sad at the same time. Happy for her, sad for himself. *Would things have been different if Raquel and I had had children?*

"I told you," he said. "It's for a documentary."

Claire looked skeptical. "How's the script coming along?"

Matt grimaced. "I'm not at the scriptwriting stage yet."

"Well, what stage are you at?"

"Research."

"Who have you pitched the idea to?"

Matt laughed. "What are you, my agent?"

He tried to make a joke of it, but inside he knew his sister was right. All his friends had said the same thing. The mystery surrounding his biological father's murder was becoming an addiction, a dangerous, time-consuming habit that was distracting him from his marriage, his work, his "real" life. Yet how was Matt supposed to let it go when the LAPD investigation had left so many holes, so many glaring, unanswered questions?

According to the official file, Andrew Jakes had been killed by an unknown intruder, a professional thief who'd turned violent. No one was ever arrested for the crime. No specific suspects were even named. Meanwhile, his widow, Angela, seemed to have disappeared off the face of the earth, as had the jewelry and miniature portraits taken from the couple's house that night. Her attorney, Lyle Renalto, had driven her to the airport but claimed to have no idea where she was headed and had apparently not heard from her since. Police had questioned him repeatedly, but he never changed his story. There was some talk of Mrs. Jakes's being sighted in Greece, but nothing had ever been proven. Danny McGuire, the detective in charge of the case, quit the force not long afterward and left L.A., taking whatever insights he may have had with him. Meanwhile, the semen from Angela Jakes's postrape forensic examination had never been matched to any other crime, before or since. Neither were the few smudged fingerprints found at the crime scene at 420 Loma Vista.

Matt said to Claire, "It's like one day this couple was living their lives in their beautiful mansion, planning for the future. And the next day, *poof,* it's all gone. The house, the money, the paintings. The couple themselves. And after the murder, his widow just hops on a plane one morning and is never heard of again."

"Yes, Matt, I know the story," said Claire patiently.

"But doesn't it scare you? The idea that all this"—Matt waved around the kitchen at his nephews, their schoolbooks, all the detritus of Claire's full, busy life—"could be gone tomorrow? Gone." He clapped his hands for emphasis. "Like it never was."

Claire was quiet for a long time. Finally she said, "I'm worried about you, Matt. I think you need to talk to someone."

Matt agreed. He needed to talk to someone all right.

The problem was that the someone he needed to talk to lived in Lyon, France.

CHAPTER SIX

He glanced at the flashing blue lights in his rearview mirror and checked his speed. Sixty-five. A mere five over the limit, on a virtually empty stretch of road on the outskirts of the city.

Petty. It was little stunts like this that gave the Lyonnais police a bad name. Rolling down the window to give the overzealous gendarme a piece of his mind, his frown changed to a smile.

The officer in question was a woman. An extremely attractive woman. She had red hair—he had a thing for redheads—blue eyes and full breasts that not even her unflattering police uniform could fully conceal.

"What's your hurry, sir?"

Oh, and the voice! Low and husky, the way that only Frenchwomen could do it. Perfect. The voice clinched it.

He smiled flirtatiously. "Actually, Officer, I have a date."

"A date? You don't say." The gorgeous russet eyebrows went up. "Well, is she going to spoil if you don't get there right this second?"

"She's already spoiled."

Leaning out through the driver's-side window, he kissed her passionately on the lips.

"What time will you be home for dinner tonight, honey?" his wife asked him, when they finally came up for air.

Danny McGuire grinned. "As soon as I can, baby. As soon as I can."

Fifteen minutes later, striding into Interpol HQ late for his meeting, Danny hoped he wouldn't have to stay too late. Céline looked so sexy in her tight blue Officier de la Paix uniform, it was painful having to drive away from her. She'd been in uniform the day they met and it was still the way Danny liked her best.

Back in L.A. he'd never have dated someone else on the force. But here in France, everything was different. He'd moved here a decade ago, chasing a shadow. The shadow of Angela Jakes. He never found her. Instead Danny found Céline, love, French culture and cuisine, a rewarding career and a whole new life. Lyon was Danny McGuire's home now and he loved it, more than he would once have believed possible.

It had all been so different when he first arrived.

Danny McGuire hated France. He hated it because he associated it with failure. His failure. The 1997 Jakes murder had been a remarkable case in many ways, not the least of which was that it was the first and only complete failure of Danny McGuire's career. He'd never found the man who murdered Andrew Jakes in such a frenzied, sadistic fashion and who raped his stunning wife.

Danny would never forget the morning he'd arrived at Lyle Renalto's Beverly Hills mansion, pulling back the bedclothes to find the lawyer naked and in a state of obvious sexual arousal, laughing at him. Angela Jakes was gone, Renalto delighted in informing him. Overwhelmed by the pressure of Danny's "aggressive" questioning, according to Lyle, she had decided to begin a new life overseas. Hiding behind attorney-client privilege, Renalto stubbornly and steadfastly refused to divulge any further information to the police.

It was around this time that Danny McGuire had his first contacts with Interpol. Logging in to the I-24/7, Interpol's global database designed to assist member countries' local forces in tracking suspects across borders, he eventually traced Angela Jakes to Greece and began liaising daily with the authorities in Athens, trying to track her down, but to no avail. Meanwhile, back in L.A., his other leads dried up one by one, like tributaries of a drought-stricken river. Andrew Jakes's killer had vanished, just like his wife and the stolen art and jewelry. Indeed, all that was left of the Jakeses' life together was Andrew's fortune, which found its way safely (and tax-free) into the coffers of two different children's charities, both of which were naturally delighted to receive it.

Danny's LAPD superiors were deeply embarrassed. They ruthlessly killed any press interest in the Jakes case, ostensibly so as not to encourage "copycat killings" but actually to cover their own hides. The case was closed. Motive: theft. Assailant: unknown. Danny was moved off of homicide onto the fraud squad, a clear demotion, and told to forget about Angela Jakes if he wanted to keep his job.

But he couldn't forget. *How could anyone forget that haunting face?* And he didn't want to keep his job. Quitting the force, he spent the next two years and virtually all his savings traveling around Europe frantically searching for Angela. Working as a private individual, he found he got precious little cooperation from local police forces, and had to rely on unscrupulous private detectives to help him keep the trail alive. Finally, broke and depressed, he wound up in France, where an old contact in Lyon told him Interpol was hiring and suggested he apply for a job there.

Slowly Danny rebuilt his shattered career. He joined as a junior member of a crime IRT (Interpol Response Team) and rapidly earned a reputation for himself as a brilliant original thinker and strategist. IRTs could be deployed anywhere in the world within twelve to twenty-four hours of an incident in order to assist a member country's forces. Adaptability, quick thinking and an ability to work as a team under strained circumstances were all key to the unit's success. Danny McGuire excelled at every level. He won plaudits for his bravery and skill in a Corsican gangland murder case. Not many foreign cops could have persuaded people in that tight-knit community to talk, but Danny won over hearts and minds, successfully convicting five of the gang leaders. After that there was the ax murder of an Arab sheikh in North Africa—that one wasn't so tough to crack; the guy helpfully left his prints all over the vic-

tim's apartment—and the disappearance of a beauty queen in rural Venezu-
ela. The girl in question was the mistress
of a wealthy Russian oil magnate, and it
proved a great case for Danny, who got
a nice clean conviction. (Not so great
for the beauty queen. Her body parts
were eventually found in trash bags in a
Maracay motel.)

Danny enjoyed the work and the novelty of living in France, and began to
feel his confidence slowly coming back.
Meeting and marrying Céline had been
the icing on the cake. But through all
his later triumphs, as he rose meteori-
cally through Interpol's ranks, he never
forgot Angela Jakes. *Who was she before she married her husband? Why did
she run?* He knew it couldn't have been
his questioning that scared her off, as
Lyle Renalto claimed. There must have
been another reason. Most importantly
of all, *Who had raped her and killed her
husband in such a hideous, bloody
manner?* The official line, that a robbery
had gotten spectacularly out of hand,
was clearly nonsense. Art thieves didn't

slash an old man's throat so forcefully they all but severed his head.

In the end it was Céline who had finally persuaded Danny to drop it. Sensing that there was more to her new husband's feelings for Angela Jakes than professional interest, she told him straight out that she felt threatened.

"She's gone," she told him tearfully, "but I'm here. Aren't I enough for you?"

"Of course you are, darling," Danny assured her. "You're everything to me."

But for years afterward, in his dreams, Angela Jakes still bewitched him with her milky-white skin and reproachful chocolate eyes:

"Find the animal who did this."

Danny promised he would, but he had failed. The animal was still out there.

Gradually, however, Danny *did* move on. His marriage to Céline was supremely happy. Two months ago, when Danny got promoted to head up the entire IRT division, running twenty-eight global response teams for both crime and disaster assistance, it felt as if everything had come full circle since the nightmare of 420 Loma Vista and Andrew Jakes's murder. Professionally as well as personally, Danny McGuire was finally at peace.

Then he got the first e-mail.

Matt Daley's first message had been titled simply *Andrew Jakes*. Just seeing those two words on a screen made Danny McGuire's blood run cold. Daley gave little away about his own background, saying merely that he was an "interested party" and that he had "new information" on the case that he wanted to discuss with Danny in person. Dismissing him as a crackpot, Danny didn't reply. But the e-mails kept coming, then the phone calls to Danny's office, at all times of the day and night. Finally, Danny responded, informing Mr. Daley that if he had any new information he should make it available to the LAPD homicide division. But Daley wouldn't be fobbed off. Insisting that he *had* to talk to him personally, Matt Daley announced that he was flying to Lyon next week and that he "wouldn't leave" until Danny had agreed to see him.

Now, true to his word, he was here. Mathilde, Danny's excellent secretary, had called an hour ago. A "blond American gentleman" was sitting outside Danny's office, claiming he had an appointment and that it was urgent. What did Danny want her to do?

I want you to send him away. I want you to tell him to stop reminding me about Angela Jakes and to get the hell out of my life.

"Tell him I'm on my way in. But I don't have long. He'll have to make it quick."

"Mr. Daley." There was no warmth in Danny McGuire's tone. "You'd better come in."

McGuire's office was large and comfortable. Matt knew that the former detective had done well for himself since he left the LAPD, but he was surprised to find just how well. Photographs of a stunning, redheaded young woman were everywhere.

Matt picked one of them up idly. "Your wife?"

McGuire nodded curtly.

"She's very beautiful."

"I know. And she's at home right now,

waiting for me." Danny glared at him. "What can I do for you, Mr. Daley?"

Matt's heart rate quickened. *So much for small talk.* He took a deep breath and said, "You can reopen the investigation into Andrew Jakes's murder."

Danny frowned. "And why would I want to do that?"

"Because there's new evidence."

"Like I told you in my e-mail, Mr. Daley, if you have relevant evidence you should report it to the L.A. police. This case is no longer my business, or within my jurisdiction."

"You're Interpol," said Matt reasonably. "The whole world's within your jurisdiction, isn't it?"

"It's not as simple as that," Danny McGuire muttered.

"Well, I think it is." Matt Daley leaned forward, fixing Danny with a gimlet stare. He was as stubborn in person as he had been on the telephone. "The LAPD doesn't give a shit. They closed the case and gave up. That's why you quit."

Danny said nothing. He couldn't argue with that.

Matt Daley's next words turned his blood to ice.

"What if I told you there'd been another murder?"

Danny McGuire forced himself to sound calm. "There are a lot of murders, Mr. Daley. All over the world, every hour of every day. We humans are a violent bunch."

"Not like this." Reaching into his briefcase, Matt Daley pulled out a thick paper file and slammed it down on Danny's desk. "Same exact MO. Old man violently slaughtered, young wife raped, leaves all the money to charity, then disappears."

Danny McGuire's mouth went dry. His hands shook as he touched the file. *Could it be true? After all this time, had the animal struck again?*

"Where?" The word was barely a whisper.

"London. Five years ago. The victim's name was Piers Henley."

CHAPTER SEVEN

LONDON
2001

Chester Square is situated in the heart of Belgravia, behind Eaton Square and just off fashionable Elizabeth Street. Its classic, white-stucco-fronted houses are arranged around a charming, private garden. In the corner of the square, St. Mark's Church nestles serenely beneath a large horse chestnut tree, its ancient brass bells pealing on the hour, conveniently saving the square's residents the trouble of glancing at their Patek Philippe watches. From the street, the homes on Chester Square look large and comfortable.

They aren't.

They are enormous and utterly palatial.

It's an oft-repeated cliché in Belgravia that no Englishman could afford to
live in Chester Square. Like most cli-
chés, it is true. Roman Abramovich, the
Russian oligarch owner of Chelsea football club, owned a house there, before
he ran off with his young mistress and
left the property to his wife. Over the
years, Mrs. Abramovich's neighbors included two Hollywood film stars, a
French soccer hero, the Swiss founder
of Europe's largest hedge fund, a Greek
prince and an Indian software tycoon.
The rest of the houses on the square
were owned, without exception, by
American investment bankers.

Until the day that one of those American investment bankers, distraught
over the collapse of his investments,
put a rare Bersa Thunder pistol in his
mouth and pulled the trigger. His heirs
sold the house to a British baronet. And
so it was that Sir Piers Henley became
the first Englishman to own a house in

Chester Square for over twenty-five years.

He was also the first person to be murdered there.

Detective Inspector Willard Drew of Scotland Yard handed the woman a cup of sweet tea and tried not to stare at her full, sensual lips as she sipped the steaming cup. Beneath her half-open bathrobe, blood splatters were still clearly visible on her pale, lightly freckled thighs. The rape had been particularly violent. But not as violent as the murder.

While Inspector Drew interviewed the woman downstairs, up in the bedroom his men were scraping her husband's brain tissue out of the Persian carpet. The master-bedroom walls looked like a freshly painted Jackson Pollock. An explosion of blood, of rage, of animal madness had taken place in that room, the likes of which Detective Inspector Drew had never seen before. There was only one word for it: *carnage.*

Inspector Drew said, "We can do this

later, ma'am, if it's too much for you right now. Perhaps when you've recovered from the shock?"

"I will never recover, Inspector. We'd better do it now."

She looked directly at him when she spoke, which Inspector Drew found disconcerting. Beautiful was the wrong word for this petite redhead. She was sexy. Painfully sexy. She was creamy skin and velvet softness and quivering, vulnerable femininity, every inch a lady. The only incongruous note about her was her voice. Beneath her four-hundred-dollar Frette bathrobe, this woman was cockney to the bone.

Inspector Drew said, "If you're sure you're up to it, we could start by verifying some basic details."

"I'm up to it."

"The deceased's full name?"

Lady Tracey Henley took a deep breath. "Piers . . . William . . . Arthur . . . Gunning Henley."

Piers William Arthur Gunning Henley, the only son of the late Sir Reginald Henley, baronet, was born into modest, landed wealth.

By his thirtieth birthday, he was one of the richest men in England.

Never particularly successful at school—his housemaster at Eton had accurately described him as "a charming time-waster"—Piers had an instinctive gift for business. In particular, he possessed that rare alchemy that enabled him to sense *exactly* when a struggling company was at its nadir, if it would bounce back, when, and how far. He bought his first failing business, a small provincial brokerage in Norfolk, at the age of twenty-two. Everybody, including his father, thought he was crazy. When Piers sold the business six years later, they had offices in London, Manchester, Edinburgh and Paris and had reported pretax profits for that year of twenty-eight million pounds.

It was a small success for Piers Henley, but an important one. It taught him to trust his instincts. It also increased his appetite for risk. Calculated risk. Over the next thirty-five years, Piers bought and sold more than fifteen businesses and held on to two: his hedge fund, Henley Investments, and Jassops, a chain of high-end jewelers whose brand Piers had totally revitalized till they were outperforming the likes of Asprey and Graff. He also acquired (and later divested himself of) a wife, Caroline, and two children; a daughter, Anna, with his wife, and a son, Sebastian, with his mistress. Both children and their respective mothers were provided with comfortable homes and generous allowances. But Piers had neither the time nor the inclination to pursue a family life. Nor was he remotely interested in conventional notions of romance.

At least not until his sixtieth birthday, when a chance encounter with a young woman named Tracey Stone changed his life forever.

For his birthday party, Sir Piers (he'd inherited the baronetcy a month before on his father's death) hired a private room at the Groucho Club in Soho. A mecca for London's successful media and literary types, the Groucho was exclusive, but nevertheless managed to maintain a sort of threadbare, scruffy Englishness that Piers had always rather relished. It reminded him of his childhood, of the down-at-heel grandeur of Kingham Hall, the Henley family estate, where Constables and Turners hung on the walls but the heating was never switched on and all the carpets were riddled with moth holes.

Sir Piers Henley approved of the venue, but was depressed by the guest list. His secretary, Janey, had drawn it up as usual. Looking around at the same old faces, captains of industry and finance, accompanied either by their frozen-faced first wives or beautiful but grasping second wives, Piers thought bleakly, *When did everybody get so old? So dull?* When exactly had he exchanged his real friendships for this? Contacts and business acquaintances.

It was while he was pondering this important question that the waitress poured scalding lobster bisque directly onto his crotch. To the end of his life, Sir Piers Henley would have livid burn marks on the inside of his thighs. Every time he looked at them, he thanked his lucky stars.

The Groucho party had been Tracey

Stone's first day as a waitress, and her last. As Sir Piers Henley screamed and leaped to his feet, Tracey dropped to her knees, unbuckled his belt and pulled off his trousers faster than a whore on commission. Then, without so much as "May I, my lord?" she whipped off his Y-fronts and emptied a jug of ice water over the baronet's exposed genitalia. The cool water felt marvelous. The fact that he was standing in the middle of the Groucho Club in front of half of London society stark bollock naked felt . . . even more marvelous. Despite the searing pain in his legs and balls, Sir Piers Henley realized he felt more alive in those few moments than he had in the last fifteen years put together. Here he was, praying for a return of youth, of life, of excitement . . . and *poof,* a beautiful girl had dropped into his lap. Or rather, a beautiful girl had dropped lava-hot soup into his lap, but why split hairs? He couldn't have been more delighted.

Tracey Stone was in her late twenties, with short, spiky red hair, dark brown eyes and a skinny, boyish figure that looked quite preposterously sexy

in her black-and-white maid's get-up.
She's like a human matchstick, thought
Piers, *sent to light me up.*

And light him up Tracey did.

When Tracey agreed to go on a date
with Piers, her friends thought she was
crazy.

"He's about a hundred and nine,
Trace."

"And posh."

"With a cock like a burned cocktail
sausage thanks to you."

"It's disgusting."

Piers's friends were equally scandal-
ized.

"She's younger than your daughter,
old boy."

"She's a *waitress,* Piers. And not even
a good one."

"She'll rob you blind."

Neither of them listened. Tracey and
Piers knew their friends were wrong.
Tracey wasn't interested in Piers's
money. And Piers couldn't have cared
less if Tracey's parents were as cockney as Bow Bells. She had switched on
a part of him that he had believed long
dead. As the burns on his groin slowly

began to heal, all he could think about was going to bed with her.

On their first date, Piers took Tracey to dinner at the Ivy. They roared with laughter through three delicious courses, but afterward Tracey hopped into a black cab before Piers could so much as give her a peck on the cheek.

On the second date, they went to the theater. It was a mistake. Tracey was bored. Piers was bored. Another cab was hailed and Piers thought, *I've lost her.*

The next morning at seven A.M., the doorbell rang at Piers's flat on Cadogan Gardens. It was Tracey. She was carrying a suitcase.

"I need to ask you summink," she said bluntly. "Are you gay?"

Piers rubbed his eyes blearily. "Am I . . . ? *What?* No. I'm not gay. Why on earth would you think I was gay?"

"You like the theater."

Piers laughed loudly. "That's it? That's your evidence?"

"That and the fact you never try to shag me."

Piers looked at her incredulously.

"*Never try . . . ?* Good God, woman. You never let me within a mile of you. And by the way, for what it's worth I *don't* like the theater."

"Why'd you go there, then?"

"I was trying to impress you."

"It didn't work."

"Yes, I noticed. Tracey, my darling, I would like nothing more than to try to 'shag' you, as you so poetically put it. But you've never given me the chance."

Pushing past him into the hall, Tracey dropped her suitcase and closed the door behind her. "I'm giving you the chance now."

The lovemaking was like nothing Piers had ever experienced. Tracey was silken hair and soft flesh and pillowy breasts and wet, warm, delicious depths that craved him like no woman had ever craved him before. When it was over, he proposed to her immediately. Tracey laughed.

"Don't be such a tosser. I ain't the marrying kind."

"Nor am I," said Piers truthfully.

"Then why'd you ask me? You must stop asking me to do things that you don't even enjoy yourself. It's a bad habit."

"I asked because I want you. And I always get what I want."

"Ha! Is that a fact? Well not this time, your lordship," said Tracey defiantly. "I ain't interested."

Piers couldn't have loved her more if she'd been dipped in platinum.

They married six weeks later.

The first eighteen months of the Henleys' marriage were blissfully happy. Piers went about his business as usual, and Tracey never complained about his long hours, or his habit of taking telephone calls in the middle of dinner, the way that other women he'd dated had. Piers had no idea how his wife occupied her time during the days. At first he'd assumed she went shopping, but as the monthly AmEx statements rolled in he saw that Tracey had spent almost nothing, despite having an unlimited platinum card and a generous cash allowance. Once he'd asked her, "What do you do when I'm at the office?"

"I make porn films, Piers," she replied, deadpan. "That's Monday, Wednesday and Friday. Tuesday's armed robbery. Thursday's me day off."

Piers grinned and thought, *I'm the luckiest man on earth.* He carried her up to bed.

Tracey was the perfect sexual partner, always eager, always inventive, never demanding on the nights when he was too tired or stressed with work to screw her. The only cloud on the marital horizon was the fact that, according to Tracey, she could not have children.

"Nothing doing in that department, I'm afraid. Me equipment's broken," she told him matter-of-factly.

"Well, what part of your equipment?"

"I dunno. All of it, I 'spect. Why? Aren't you a bit old to be thinking about changing nappies, luv?"

Piers laughed. "*I* won't be changing them! Besides, *you're* not old. Don't you want a child of your own?"

Tracey didn't. But no amount of her repeating this message would make her husband believe her. Over the next year,

Piers dragged his young wife to every fertility specialist on Harley Street, subjecting her to round after round of IVF, all to no avail. Determined to "think positive," he bought a large family house in Belgravia and hired an interior decorator from Paris to design children's rooms, one for a boy, one for a girl and one in neutral yellow.

"What's that for? In case I give birth to a rabbit or summink?" Tracey teased him.

She remembered what he'd said to her the night he proposed. *"I always get everything I want."* Unfortunately, it seemed that in Mother Nature, Sir Piers Henley had met his match.

"Your children." Detective Inspector Willard Drew tore his eyes away from Tracey's breasts, enticingly encased in a peach lace La Perla bra. For such a slender woman, Lady Henley was remarkably well endowed and she did seem to be having enormous trouble keeping her bathrobe belted. "They're away for the night?"

Her beautiful face clouded over. "We don't 'ave kids. It was me. I couldn't."

Inspector Drew blushed. "Oh. I'm sorry. I saw the bedrooms upstairs and I assumed . . ."

Tracey shrugged. "That's all right. Why wouldn't you assume? Was there any other questions?"

"Just one."

She'd already been incredibly helpful, giving detailed descriptions of the stolen items of jewelry—Lady Henley knew a *lot* about jewelry, settings, carats, clarity, you name it—as well as of her attacker. He was masked at the time of the attack, so she never saw his face, but she described him as being of strong build, stocky, with a scar on the back of his left hand, a deep voice, and a "strange" accent she couldn't quite place. Considering the ordeal she'd just been through, it was a lot to remember. She was certain she'd never met him before.

"This might be difficult," Inspector Drew said gently, "but did your husband have any enemies? Anyone who might have borne a grudge toward him?"

Tracey laughed, a full, raucous, barmaid's laugh, and Inspector Drew thought what fun she must have been to be married to. A few hours ago Sir Piers Henley must have considered himself one of the happiest men alive.

"Only a few thousand. My 'usband had more enemies than Hitler, Inspector."

Inspector Drew frowned. "How so?"

"Piers was a rich man. Self-made. In the 'edge fund business, wasn't he? Nobody likes a hedgie. Not the blokes who do up their kitchens, not their partners, not their competitors, not even their investors half the bloody time, no matter 'ow much money you make them. It's a dog-eat-dog world, Inspector, and my Piers was a fuck-off Doberman with a mean set of teeth." Tracey Henley said this with pride. "People hated him. And that's just 'is fund. If you want to get into the personal stuff, there's the bloke he gazumped to buy this place, the car dealer he never paid for the Aston 'cause he didn't like the way he looked at me, everyone he blackballed at White's—that's a long list, I can tell you. Then there's 'is ex-wife, 'is ex-mistress. His current mistress, for all I know."

Inspector Drew found the idea that any man married to Tracey Henley would seek sexual pleasure elsewhere extremely hard to believe. According to her statement, she was thirty-two but she looked a decade younger.

"Piers had an army of enemies," Tracey continued. "But he only had one real friend."

"Oh? And who was that?"

"Me."

For the first time that night, Tracey Henley gave way to tears.

CHAPTER EIGHT

Danny McGuire looked up from the file in front of him as if he'd just seen a ghost. He'd been reading, in total silence, for the last twenty minutes.

"How did you hear about this case?"

Matt Daley shrugged. "I read about it online. I got interested in the Jakes case and I . . . well, I came across it. The Henley killing was a big deal in England. There was a lot of press at the time."

"What exactly *is* your interest in the Jakes case, Mr. Daley?" Danny asked. "You never said in your e-mails."

"I'm a writer. I'm fascinated by unanswered questions."

Danny's eyes narrowed suspiciously. "You're a journalist?"

"No, no, no, a screenwriter. TV. Comedy, mostly."

Danny looked suitably surprised. He nodded toward the file. "Not much to laugh about in here."

"No," Matt agreed. "But I also have a personal connection. Andrew Jakes was my father."

Danny did a double take. *Had Andrew Jakes had children?* It took him a few moments to dredge up the memory. That's right. There'd been a first wife, decades before he met Angela. One of the junior members of his team had gone to check out the lead but obviously thought it was nothing significant. Was there a kid? *I guess there must have been.*

"I never knew him," Matt explained. "Jakes and my mother divorced when I was two. My stepfather adopted and raised me and my sister, Claire. But biologically, I'm a Jakes. Do you see any family resemblance?"

An image of Andrew Jakes's almost severed, graying head lolling from his torso flashed across Danny's mind. He shivered.

"Not really, no."

"When I learned my father had been murdered, I got curious. And once I started reading up on the case, I was hooked." He grinned. "You know how addictive it can be, an unsolved mystery."

"I do," Danny admitted. *And how painful. This guy seems nice, but he's so eager, like a Labrador with a stick. He wouldn't look so happy if he'd seen the bloody carnage in that bedroom. The bodies trussed together. Jakes's head hanging from his neck like a yo-yo on a string.*

"When I read about the Henley case, I tried to get in touch with you, but that's when I learned you'd left L.A. I tried Scotland Yard directly, but they weren't too helpful. Didn't want to talk to some crackpot American writer any more than the LAPD did." Matt Daley smiled again, and Danny thought what a warm, open face he had. "You cops sure know how to close ranks when the shit hits the fan."

That's true, thought Danny, remembering his own years in the wilderness, begging for help finding Angela Jakes, before he joined Interpol. It felt like a lifetime ago now.

"Anyway, it took me awhile after that to track you down. I couldn't believe it when I discovered you were at Interpol. That you were actually in a position to help me."

Danny McGuire frowned. "Let's not get ahead of ourselves. I agree that the two cases have similarities. But for my division to get involved, for Interpol to authorize an IRT, we have to be approached by a member country's police force directly.

Matt leaned forward excitedly. "We're not talking about 'similarities.' These crimes are carbon copies. Both the murder victims were elderly, wealthy men, married to much younger wives. Both wives were raped and beaten. Both wives conveniently disappeared shortly after the attacks. Both estates wound up going to charity. No convictions. No leads."

Danny McGuire felt his heart rate began to quicken.

"Even so," he said lamely, clutching at straws. "It could be a coincidence."

"Like hell it could. The guy even used the same knot on the rope he used to tie the victims together."

A double half hitch. Danny McGuire put his head in his hands. This couldn't be happening. Not after ten years.

"Look, I know you have procedures you have to follow," said Matt Daley. "Protocol and all that. But he's still out there, this maniac. Matter of fact," he announced, playing his trump card, "he's in France."

"What do you mean?" Danny asked sharply. "How could you possibly know something like that?"

Matt Daley leaned back in his chair. "Two words for you," he said confidently. "Didier Anjou."

CHAPTER NINE

SAINT-TROPEZ, FRANCE
2005

Lucien Desforges sauntered down the Rue Mirage with a spring in his step. Life, Lucien decided, was good. It was a gorgeous late spring day in Saint-Tropez with omens of summer everywhere. On each side of the road running from La Route des Plages down to the famous Club 55, bright pink blossoms were already bursting forth from the laurel bushes, pouring like floral fountains over the whitewashed walls of the houses. Lucien had often been struck by those whitewashed walls. It seemed incongruous to have such humble exteriors surrounding such lavish mansions, each one stuffed full of every luxury money could buy.

Lucien was on his way to one of those very mansions, one that many Tropeziens considered the grandest of them all: Villa Paradis.

Terrible name, thought Lucien. *Talk about vulgar. But then what was one to expect from a former pop star and matinee idol, a street kid from Marseille who made fantastically, miraculously good? Certainly not good taste.*

Villa Paradis was owned by one of Lucien's clients. One of his best, most important, most consistently lucrative clients. True, he wasn't always the easiest of clients. His continued association with the organized criminals he grew up with, two-bit Marseillais mafiosi with a taste for extortion, fraud and worse, had caused Lucien innumerable headaches over the years, as had his utter inability to keep it in his pants (or, if out of his pants, safely shrink-wrapped in Durex). But at the end of the day, Lucien Desforges was a divorce lawyer. And if there was one thing Villa Paradis's owner knew how to do, expensively, publicly and repeatedly, it was get divorced.

Over his morning coffee in Le Gorille earlier, Lucien had laughed out loud when he realized that he had, in actual fact, forgotten how many divorces he had handled for this particular client. Was it four, or five? Would this one make five? Lucien had made so much money in fees from this man, he'd lost count. *Que Dieu bénisse l'amour!*

Keying the familiar code into the intercom on the gate, Lucien wondered how long he could draw out this latest marital parting of the ways. His client had only been married to this particular wife for a matter of months, so the case wouldn't be as lucrative as some of those from the past. *If only the old goat had fathered a child with her. Then we'd really be in business.* But as the gates swung open and the crystal-blue Mediterranean twinkled before him like an azure dream, Lucien reminded himself never to look a gift horse in the mouth.

The point was that Didier Anjou was getting divorced.

Again!

It was going to be a beautiful day.

The marriage had begun so well. Which was strange, given that all of Didier Anjou's other marriages had begun so very, very badly.

First there was Lucille. *Ah, la belle Lucille!* How he'd wanted her! How he'd pined! Didier was twenty at the time, and starring in his very first movie, *Entre les draps* (Between the Sheets), which was exactly where Didier longed to be with Lucille Camus. Lucille was forty-four, married, and played Didier's mother in the movie. The director had begged her to take the role. He'd always had a soft spot for Lucille.

It was probably why he'd married her.

In 1951, Jean Camus was the most powerful man in French cinema. He was a Parisian Walt Disney, an old-world Louis B. Mayer, a man who could make or break a young actor's career with a nod of his shiny bald head or a twitch of his salt-and-pepper mustache. Jean Camus had personally cast Didier Anjou as the male lead in *Entre les draps,* plucking the handsome boy with the black hair and blacker eyes from utter obscurity and propelling him into a fantasy world of fame and fortune, of limousines and luxury . . . and Lucille.

Looking back, decades later, Didier consoled himself with the fact that he'd never really had a choice. Lucille Camus was a goddess, her body a temple begging, no, *demanding* to be worshipped. Those swollen, matronly breasts, those obscenely full lips, always parted, always tempting, inviting . . . Didier Anjou could no more *not* seduce Lucille Camus than he could breathe through his elbows or swim through solid stone. *Elle était une force de la nature!*

Of course, had he stopped at seduction, things might have worked out better than they had. Unfortunately, three weeks into their affair, Didier got Lucille pregnant.

"I don't see the problem." A baffled Didier defended himself, dodging another hurled item of china that Lucille had propelled furiously onto a collision course with his skull. "*Chérie,* please. Just say it is Jean's. Who's to know?"

"Everyone will know, you cretin, you *imbecile!*" Didier ducked as another plate narrowly missed his windpipe. "Jean's infertile!"

"Oh."

"Yes. Oh."

"Well then, you'll just have to get rid of it."

Lucille was horrified.

"An abortion? What do you think I am, a monster?"

"But, *chérie,* be practical."

"*Jamais! Non,* Didier. There is only one solution. You must marry me."

The Camus divorce was the talk of Cannes that year. A heavily pregnant Lucille Camus married her boy-toy lover, and for a few wonderful months, Didier was genuinely famous. But then the baby died, Jean Camus took the grief-wrecked Lucille back, and the ranks of the film community closed around them. For the next eight years, until Jean died, Didier Anjou couldn't get so much as a laundry-detergent commercial in France. He was washed up at twenty-three.

It wasn't until he hit thirty that things finally started to look up. Didier married his second wife, Hélène Marceau, a beautiful, innocent heiress from Toulouse. Hélène was a virgin, unwilling to sleep with Didier until they were married. This suited Didier perfectly. He fucked around throughout their courtship, all the while looking forward to the day when he would take possession of Hélène's tight *chatte* and fat bank balance. Who could ask for more?

The wedding was a coup, the happiest day of Didier's life. Until night fell and, alone at last in the marital bed, Didier discovered why his new bride had been so coy about sleeping with him. It appeared that poor Hélène had grotesquely deformed genitals, a secret she'd kept since birth. The whole innocent, scared-of-sex shtick had been a front, a ploy. The bitch had trapped him!

The union was miserable from the start, yet Didier stayed with Hélène for five years. Naturally he cheated on her constantly, siphoning off every last franc of her fortune into privately produced movies, all of them star vehicles for himself. Hélène knew what her husband was up to, but loved him helplessly anyway. Didier had this effect on women. Each day Hélène prayed fervently that Didier would see the light and come to return her love, despite her unfortunate physical affliction. But it never happened. At thirty-five, famous for the second time in his life and rich for the first, Didier Anjou finally divorced Hélène Marceau. He was back on the market.

Next came Pascale, another heiress who made Didier even richer and bore him two sons but took a regrettably inflexible view about his extramarital dalliances.

One of these dalliances, Camille, became the fourth Madame Anjou the year Didier turned fifty. Thirty years his junior and stunningly beautiful, the top fashion model of her day, Camille reminded Didier of himself at her age. Physically perfect, selfish, ambitious, insatiable. It was a match made in heaven. But after three years of marriage, Camille slept

with Didier's teenage son, Luc. With
Lucien Desforges's help, Didier cut both
of them off without a penny and vowed
never to marry again.

He retired to Saint-Tropez, where he
became legendary for his vanity, in particular for the vast collection of toupees
that he housed in a special dressing
room at Villa Paradis, much to the
amusement of the Russian hookers who
regularly warmed his bed there. No one,
least of all his lawyer, ever expected Didier Anjou to take another wife.

But four months ago, out of the blue,
the old roué had done just that, secretly
marrying a Russian woman whom none
of his friends had ever heard of, never
mind met. Her name was Irina Minchenko,
and the general assumption was that
she was one of the hookers and had
somehow managed to bewitch Didier
into wedlock.

The general assumption was wrong.
In her midthirties, aristocratic and educated, Irina was wealthy in her own
right. Even if she'd been poor, she was
far too beautiful and smart to be a

hooker. From the day they met, at a house party in Ramatouelle, Didier was besotted.

He took his new bride to Tahiti for their honeymoon, to a secluded beach-side cottage. For the first time in his life, Didier Anjou did not want the media to follow him. He told Lucien, by now a friend, "Irina is too exquisite to be shared with the world. Whenever I see some-one so much as look at her, man or woman, I want to kill them. It's crazy what she does to me!"

Whatever Irina did to him, it's over now, Lucien thought wryly, strolling around onto the villa's private rear ter-race. Just two weeks back from the honeymoon and Didier Anjou had called him, literally howling with rage and fury.

"I want a divorce!" he'd screamed into the phone. "I want to fuck that bitch over, do you hear me? I won't give her a goddamn penny!"

That was last night. Hopefully Didier would be in a calmer mood this morn-ing. It was too early for screaming.

Unfortunately, when Lucien Des-forges stepped through the French windows into the living room, the screams were deafening. But they weren't Didier's.

They were his own.

CHAPTER TEN

Danny McGuire stared at Matt Daley for a long time. Or rather, he stared into space for a long time. Matt's crooked, genial, hopeful face just happened to be in the way.

Of course, Danny knew about Didier Anjou's murder. Like everybody else in France, he'd heard about it on the TV and read about it in the papers. Everyone from *Le Monde* to *Le Figaro* had published accounts of Anjou's colorful romantic past and speculated as to which wronged husband or unpaid creditor might have ordered a hit on the elderly roué. But little had been written about the matinee idol's latest wife, other than that she was Russian and was believed to have returned to her home country after the killing. Certainly Danny had heard nothing about a rape. He said as much to Matt Daley.

"No official complaint was ever made," Matt agreed. "But the blogs are alive with rumors that Mrs. Anjou was sexually assaulted by the killer, and that the guy who discovered the crime scene found the two of them tied up together. Problem is that, once again, the widow's not around to ask. She's gone."

"Yes, but only back home to Russia. She hasn't vanished like the others."

Matt shrugged. "So the papers say. But who knows what the truth is. The police down there are so corrupt they make Chicago City Hall look like the Peace Corps."

Danny laughed. But it was a hollow laugh, one filled with foreboding. If Andrew Jakes's killer really was still out there, repeating his awful crimes, then two more innocent men's deaths were on Danny McGuire's conscience. And what about the widows, the beautiful young women who had so conveniently disappeared just weeks after the killings? If they were dead too, he had even more blood on his hands. This man, this animal, would be getting more emboldened with every successful hit. Danny couldn't just sit by and do nothing, let him strike again. On the other hand, what he'd told Matt Daley was true. It wasn't just his reluctance to reopen old wounds and upset Céline that was holding him back. Without a local police force requesting Interpol's help, officially Danny's hands were tied.

He told Matt Daley, "We can't be sure it's the same man. I don't know about Sir Piers Henley, but Didier Anjou had a long line of people who wanted him dead."

"I agree we can't be sure," said Matt excitedly. "That's why we need to reopen the case. Or start a new case, looking at all three murders together. There's so much we don't know. All I can tell you is I feel in my bones that this is one guy, one crazed fucking lunatic, and that we're getting closer to him."

Danny McGuire thought, *He's using* we *already. He's assuming I'm in.*

"I'll make some calls to Scotland Yard and the local French police. See what I can dig up. But I can't promise anything."

If Matt was disappointed, he hid it well. "I understand. I know it probably sounds weird, seeing as my father abandoned my sister and me and all. But I'd like to see justice done for him. I figured, if you had this information, maybe you could help."

"What will you do now?" asked Danny. "Are you heading back to the States?"

Matt looked at him incredulously. "Back to the States? Hell no. Why would I do that? Like I told you, I think the killer's here, in France. I'm on a flight to Nice at six o'clock tonight. I should be in Saint-Tropez by ten."

"Be careful," Danny warned. "If the Mafia was involved in Didier Anjou's death, you could be putting yourself in danger."

"You don't really believe it was a Mafia hit? Come on. That's just lazy detective work, the path of least resistance."

"I don't know," said Danny. "I don't know anything concrete at this point and neither do you, Mr. Daley. Blog gossip does not a homicide case make. Plus, even if you're right, and the three killings are all connected . . ."

" . . . which they are. You *know* they are."

" . . . local French police don't take kindly to outsiders trampling all over their turf and meddling in their investigations. Especially Americans."

Matt threw his arms out wide in a gesture of innocence. "Don't worry about me." He grinned. "I'll charm them into submission."

Later that afternoon, in the departures lounge at the Lyon airport, Matt Daley tried out his charm on his wife.

"I'll be here another week, honey, ten days at most. I'll bring you back some goodies from Chanel, how about that?"'

"I don't want *goodies*!" Raquel snarled. "I want our share of that money! Don't you realize that every day you're gone, those fucking charities are spending *our* cash? I can't fight this alone, Matt, and I can't fight it with no money. There's a lawyers' meeting on Tuesday in Beverly Hills. I expect you there."

"But, honey, this Anjou murder—"

"Is not gonna pay our bills," snapped Raquel. "I mean it, Matt. Either get home by Tuesday or don't bother getting home at all."

Across town, at home with Céline, Danny McGuire lay sprawled out on the bed in postcoital bliss.

"How did it go today?" his wife asked him. "Your meeting, with that American. Your stalker! What did he want in the end?"

"Hmm? Oh, nothing." Reaching out, Danny caressed her breast. "He's some TV guy, making a documentary about the LAPD. It wasn't important."

It was the first time Danny could ever remember lying to her. The guilt of it lay heavy in his stomach, like lead.

That night, while Céline McGuire slept, Danny lay awake, thinking of Angela Jakes's perfect face.

CHAPTER ELEVEN

Matt Daley stared out of the window of Hélène Marceau's medieval château feeling like he'd strayed into the pages of a fairy tale. It wasn't just the house. It was the entire town of Eze, a ludicrously picturesque hilltop village less than twenty miles outside Monte Carlo. Walt Disney couldn't have drawn the place better, with its turrets and steeples, its winding cobblestone streets, its gas lamps and flower boxes and quaint, higgledy-piggledy artisans' cottages. Matt thought: *It's perfect. A ready-made movie set for* Beauty and the Beast.

Twenty years ago, Hélène Marceau would have made a wonderful Belle. Even now, in her fifties, Didier Anjou's ex-wife number two was an attractive woman. With her slender figure, fine bone structure and sparkling emerald eyes, Hélène could still turn heads. Of course, everybody in Eze knew the rumors: that Hélène was *déformée, down there*. But it didn't seem to have prevented her from landing two more husbands after Didier, both of them wealthy. The furniture in this room alone must be worth six figures.

"I'm sorry I can't be of more help, Mr. Daley." Hélène's English was perfect. "But Didier and I hadn't had any contact for many years. I read of his death in the newspaper, like everybody else."

Matt sighed. Much to Raquel's fury, he had been in the South of France for nine days now and badly needed a lead. Any lead. He took a sip of his *thé au citron*. "Did you part on bad terms?"

"Didier left me, Mr. Daley. Just as soon as he'd spent every centime I had to my name."

"I see. So you did part on bad terms."

Hélène smiled. "We divorced, Mr. Daley. It's fair to say that, at the time, Didier was not at the top of my Christmas-card list. But I'm not a great bearer of grudges. Time passed. I remarried. I was sorry when I heard what had happened to Didier. Nobody deserves to end their life that way."

One glance at Hélène Marceau's face told Matt that she was sincere. This woman did not wish Didier Anjou dead, and clearly had nothing to do with his murder. It was the same story with his other exes. Matt had tracked each of them down. Lucille Camus was now a frail octogenarian, barely able to remember her own name, still less plot a murder of a man she hadn't seen in decades. Pascale Anjou had remarried a Greek property tycoon and was far too rich to care. Camille, the fourth Madame Anjou, still lived happily with Luc, Didier's estranged son, on a farm in the Pyrenees. She sounded genuinely upset when Matt contacted her to ask about Didier's murder.

Not that Matt had ever had much faith

in the "hell hath no fury . . ." theory, which seemed as flimsy to him as the Mafia link that the police were so keen to pursue. He was sure that the same man who killed his father and Sir Piers Henley had done away with Didier Anjou. But Danny McGuire was right. They needed more than conjecture to build a criminal case, or even to make a half-decent documentary. Matt had to explore every angle.

Of course, the one ex he really *did* want to talk to still eluded him. The police claimed that Irina Anjou had returned home to Russia, as she was entitled to do after giving her witness statement. But no one seemed to know where, exactly, she had gone, who her family was or, indeed, anything about her at all. All Matt's inquiries about Irina had been met by bored Gallic shrugs from the Saint-Tropez police, and few locals seemed ever to have met her. Only one man was willing to talk to Matt about Irina Anjou. Taking his leave of Hélène, Matt Daley set off to meet him.

* * *

Set in the very heart of Saint-Tropez's bustling harbor, Café Le Gorille was *the* place to see and be seen. Sipping your morning coffee as the superyachts sailed in, ogling the glamorous occupants as they emerged on deck in their Cavalli silk shirts and Eres bikinis, you could almost imagine you were one of their number. Privileged. Golden. Untouchable. And all for the price of a café au lait and an hour sitting on the rather uncomfortable wicker chairs that made the backs of one's thighs look like you'd sat on a waffle iron.

Lucien Desforges recognized Matt Daley instantly. Not because they had met before, but because Matt had that earnest, trusting, idiotic look common to untraveled Americans. *How odd,* Lucien thought, *that a nation of people so generally loathed abroad should have such unparalleled faith in their own likability.*

"Mr. Daley."

"Monsieur Desforges. Thanks for seeing me."

Lucien Desforges had thought twice about agreeing to today's meeting. He'd had nothing to do with the police since they effectively ignored what he'd told them about Irina Anjou having been violated. "One crime at a time," the moronic detective in charge had told Lucien, making no effort to record the details of his statement. If the lady declined to report it—and apparently she had—the rape did not officially exist. Less hassle, less paperwork, and everyone was happy.

Everyone except Lucien Desforges, who still had nightmares about the things he'd seen at Villa Paradis that awful morning. The blood everywhere, on the walls, the carpet, the couches. The horrific wounds to Didier's neck and face. Irina, naked and bruised, trussed together with her husband's tattered corpse. Truth be told, he no longer wanted to talk about it, not with this persistent young American, not with anyone. But in the end curiosity got the better of him. Matt Daley claimed that his father had been killed in the same sadistic fashion as poor Didier. There had been a rape in that case too, and Daley seemed convinced that there was a link between the two killings. So convinced that he had given up his job and traveled halfway across the world to pursue it.

"I don't know how much help I can be," Lucien confessed.

Matt said, "Well, you can't be any less help than the cops, that's for sure. Those guys take 'not interested' to a whole new level."

Lucien Desforges's face hardened. "They failed in this case. The killer is gone and they know nothing. We French do not like to be reminded of failure. Especially by Americans. How can I help you?"

Matt pulled out a pen and notepad. Like most writers, he carried a pen and pad everywhere, in case he saw or heard something funny he could use as material. Investigating a murder wasn't exactly like writing a sitcom, but it still required a scrupulous attention to detail.

"I want to know about Irina."

"What do you want to know? I told the police that she was raped. The poor thing had bruises all over her thighs and breasts and choke marks round her neck. She was hysterical when I found her. But nobody gives a shit."

"I do," said Matt. "I need to know more about who she was. Who she is. They were planning to get divorced, right?"

Desforges nodded.

"How bad were things between the two of them?"

"Bad enough, I guess."

"What I mean is, none of Didier's other exes wanted him dead. But did Irina?"

Lucien Desforges took a sip of his coffee. "I am a divorce lawyer, Mr. Daley. In my experience most women want their husband dead at one time or another. However, I can tell you one thing with certainty. There is no way that Irina Anjou had anything to do with Didier's murder. The rape . . . what she suffered . . ." He shook his head, as if trying to dislodge the memory. "This man, this animal, he is not normal. His is *fou,* crazy. *Détraqué.*"

Matt noticed the blood rushing to the lawyer's face and waited for him to regain his composure.

"Didier wanted to get out of the marriage. That's why I was going to the villa that day, to discuss a divorce. He was furious with Irina about something, but I never found out what it was."

"Do you know anything about her background?"

Lucien Desforges shook his head. "Not really. She was Russian, new to the area. I never met her until that day. The marriage surprised everyone. But I understand she was wealthy in her own right. She had no need of Didier's money. Which is not to say that others didn't. Didier Anjou kept some pretty shady company right to the end of his life. He was 'friendly' with a number of senior Mafia figures in Marseille."

"So I hear."

"Those guys don't play around. If Didier had fallen foul of them in some way, they're more than capable of killing him and of raping his wife. They're animals."

A pretty dark-haired waitress came

over to take Matt's order, smiling co-
quettishly at his broken French.

"She likes you," said Lucien as the
girl walked away, deliberately swaying
her hips.

"Really?" Matt turned and stared after her, twisting his wedding band mis-
erably.

"Why don't you ask her out?"

"I can't. I'm married."

This seemed to amuse the Frenchman enormously. "So?" He guffawed.
"I'm hyperglycemic, but I still like ice
cream."

It was a good line. In another life,
Matt would have written it down. As it
was, he wrenched the conversation
back to the subject at hand.

"What do you think happened to
Irina? The widows in the other two cases
I'm investigating disappeared shortly
after the attacks and were never heard
from again."

Lucien shrugged. "I'm not surprised.
I imagine they wanted to leave it all behind them, all the gruesome memories,
and start again. You can't blame Irina
Anjou for getting out of France."

Matt frowned. "Well, you *could* blame her. You could say that she took the money and ran."

Lucien Desforges looked genuinely surprised. "Oh no. That's the one thing no one can accuse her of. Didier wasn't as well off as people assumed he was, you know. After four divorces, few men are. But before Irina left, she emptied her and Didier's joint bank account and gave away everything they had to charity."

Matt watched the goose bumps pop up on his forearms and felt the hairs on the back of his neck start to rise.

"Are you sure about that?"

"Quite sure," said Lucien. "Face au Monde, I believe the charity was called. Some surgical thing in Paris having to do with cleft palates. They help children."

CHAPTER TWELVE

Danny McGuire sped up the treadmill, hoping the pain in his legs might distract him. It didn't.

There was a fully equipped gym at Interpol headquarters, but Danny preferred to frequent Sport Vitesse on the Rue de La Paix. Partly because he needed to get away from other Interpol officers every now and then. As much as he enjoyed his job running the IRT division, the organization itself was bureaucratic and inward-looking, a veritable shrine to red tape. But mostly because the treadmills at the club all faced giant windows overlooking the rush-hour traffic, which reminded him of L.A. Danny loved living in France, the slower pace of life, the history, the architecture, the food. But there were occasional moments when he missed the States, *Monday Night Football* and buffalo wings. Meeting Matt Daley had brought his homesickness back with a vengeance.

Danny McGuire liked Matt Daley. He liked his honesty, his sense of humor, his tenaciousness. But he wished with all his heart Matt Daley had never tracked him down.

Since the second Matt had walked out of his office, Danny had thought of nothing but the Jakes case and these other, apparently linked homicides. After Matt called him in high excitement from Saint-Tropez to announce that Irina Anjou had also left all her husband's money to a children's charity, he finally broached the subject with his superiors.

"The May-December marriages, the rapes, the frenzied nature of the killings, the binding of the victims together. These alone suggest a pattern. But the fact that all three widows evaporated after the fact, and all handed over their inheritance to kids' charities, including Irina Anjou . . . it's got to be worth checking out, hasn't it, sir?"

Deputy Director Henri Frémeaux blinked inscrutably, his fat face giving nothing away. In his midsixties, totally bald and with the sort of distended belly that might have looked jolly on a less humorless man, Henri Frémeaux was everything Danny McGuire disliked about Interpol: officious, unyielding, deliberately narrow-minded. He was also brilliantly intelligent, a dogged problem solver with a first-class logical mind. But that wasn't why Henri Frémeaux had risen to the top at Interpol. That he'd achieved by slavish adherence to the rules.

"Which member country has requested our assistance?" he asked Danny bluntly. "I don't recall seeing anything like this come across my desk."

"No, sir. It hasn't yet. I received the information from a private source."

Deputy Director Frémeaux's eyebrows slowly lifted. "A private source?"

"Yes, sir."

"Assistant Director McGuire. As I hardly need to remind you, Interpol is not like other law enforcement agencies. Our purpose is to function as an administrative liaison between the law enforcement agencies of our member countries, providing communications and database assistance."

Danny sighed. "Yes, sir. I've read the manual. But if this killer is out there, preparing to strike again, then don't we have a duty to act?"

"No. Our duty is clear: to provide communications and database assistance to our member countries, *when requested*. Has such a request been made with regard to these crimes?"

Danny might as well have been talking to a brick wall.

It was the same story with Scotland Yard. Chief Inspector Willard Drew had been a lowly detective inspector when he ran the Henley murder investigation. He received Danny's phone call with a frostiness bordering on arctic.

Yes, Tracey Henley had left the country. No, the authorities were not aware of her current whereabouts, but neither did they suspect any foul play. No, no one had ever been charged with Sir Piers Henley's murder, despite exhaustive interviews of over eighty possible suspects. No, Chief Inspector Drew had not the slightest interest in reopening the file "because some minor French film star got bumped off by a local mafiosi."

Danny understood Willard Drew's defensiveness. He'd felt the same way himself, after Andrew Jakes's killer got away. The failure stung, like salt in an open wound. But he was also frustrated by it.

The French police were even worse, taking days to return Danny's call, then laughing off his suggestion of links with the L.A. and London murders as "fanciful" and Matt Daley's evidence as "circumstantial at best." No one wanted to reopen this case, to prize the lid off such a horrible, violent, blood-slick can of worms. Around the globe, the sound of collective hand washing was deafening.

Sweat poured down Danny's back, pooling at the base of his spine as his feet pounded the moving rubber track beneath him. As he ran, his own doubts came creeping back. Yes, the French police were lazy and the British defensive. But were they also right? Lots about the three murders didn't add up. Interpol's I-24/7 database was the largest and most sophisticated of its kind in the world, maintaining collections of fingerprints and mug shots, lists of wanted persons, DNA samples and travel documents. Their lost and stolen travel-document database alone contained more than twelve million records. But after an exhaustive search, Danny had found no other crimes that even vaguely matched the Jakes, Henley and Anjou cases. If it really *was* one killer, why had he waited so long between attacks? And why had he chosen victims so geographically spread out? What did he do between murders? How was he supporting himself? Almost all serial killers that Danny knew of worked within a territory, a familiar "killing patch," and stuck to it. Professional assassins moved around, but they focused on their targets; they didn't hang around and rape innocent bystanders.

And there were other discrepancies in Matt's "carbon-copy" killings. Didier Anjou and Andrew Jakes had both been knifed to death. Sir Piers had had his brains blown out. Jewelry was stolen from the Henley and Jakes homes, but not from Didier Anjou's, despite the fact that he had an extensive collection in plain view on his bedroom dresser. And what of the Jakes art thefts? The rare Victorian miniatures? Where did they fit into a possible motive?

Exhausted, Danny slowed the treadmill to a fast walk, letting his heart rate drop. Matt Daley was on his way back to Los Angeles. At some point next week Danny would have to call him, to update him off the record on "progress." What a joke. He had nothing, nothing except a single number: *three.*

Three victims. Andrew Jakes, Sir Piers Henley, Didier Anjou.

Three countries.

Three missing wives. Angela Jakes, Tracey Henley, Irina Anjou.
Three.
Hardly the breakthrough of the century.

Instinctively, Danny felt that the key to unraveling the mystery lay in the rape of the young wives. Somewhere behind these crimes was a woman hater. A violent, sexually motivated beast.

He thought about his own wife, Céline, and felt a wave of revulsion and disgust wash over him, tinged with fear. If anything should happen to her, anything, he didn't know what he would do. He wondered for the umpteenth time about the beautiful Angela Jakes and the other women, Tracey and Irina. Were they alive, living new, unobtrusive lives somewhere, as the police in L.A., London and Saint-Tropez all so badly wanted to believe? Or were they dead too, their three corpses rotting in unmarked graves, silent victims of this most ruthless and cunning of killers?

* * *

Matt Daley pulled into his driveway feeling as nervous as a teenager on his first date. He'd been gone for almost three weeks, the longest he'd been physically apart from Raquel since they married. Despite her anger—since he refused to fly home for her lawyers' meeting a week ago, she hadn't contacted him once and had refused to return his calls or e-mails—Matt was surprised to find that he'd missed her. The break had given him a renewed determination to put things right with his marriage.

I've been neglecting her, he told himself. *No wonder she spends so much time chasing an imaginary pot of gold in her lawyer's office. Why wouldn't she, with me cooped up in my office all day, or flitting around the world trying to solve these murders?*

The thought crossed his mind that if he actually cracked this case, with Danny McGuire's help, if he found the killer and brought him to justice, he might make Raquel proud of him again. Then he could write a screenplay about it, sell it to a major studio, and make more money than even Raquel could dream of. It was a nice fantasy, but in the meantime he had to spend more time with her. And he would. Now that he was back, he'd make everything right between them again.

Inside, the house was in darkness. Matt pushed aside his disappointment. *It's still early,* he told himself. *She'll be home soon.* At least this way he'd have time to shower and change after his long-haul flight. Air France's economy seats had clearly been designed by a double-jointed munchkin and Matt's lower back was killing him.

Upstairs, the bedroom was pristine, a testament to his long weeks away. Matt threw his suitcase down on the pale pink counterpane and began to un-dress. Only then did he see the enve-lope propped up against his bedside lamp. His name was on the front, in Raquel's distinctive large-looped hand-writing.

Matt's stomach lurched.

Stop thinking the worst. It might be a welcome-home card.

But even as he tore open the letter, he knew that it wasn't.

* * *

It was the banging that roused him. It was deafening. Lying on the floor, a small pool of saliva staining the peach shag carpet in front of his face, his first thought was, *Someone's trying to demolish my house. With me inside it.*

His second thought was, *Good luck to them.*

Raquel was divorcing him. He'd driven her away and she was never coming back. At that moment few things seemed preferable to being crushed instantly to death by a giant pile of rubble, the debris of what had once been a happy home.

BANG, BANG, BANG!

Not a wrecking ball. A fist. On a door. An angry fist.

"Open up, Matt. I know you're in there."

The voice was familiar, but Matt couldn't place it. Then again, after two bottles of wine washed down with the dregs of a bottle of vodka left over from last New Year's Eve, Matt had trouble placing his own legs. Tentatively he lifted his head off the floor, pushing back with his arms so that he was on his knees. The bedroom swam around him in peach swirls. He retched.

BANG, BANG, BANG!

"I'm coming! Jesus." Matt staggered downstairs, clutching the banister like a paraplegic in a bounce house. Every step was torture, but he had to stop the noise. He opened the front door. "Oh. It's you."

Claire Michaels wrinkled her nose as a waft of alcohol fumes hit her in the face. Her brother looked as if he'd aged ten years.

"Raquel's left me."

"I know," said Claire matter-of-factly. "She stopped by my place to leave a stack of unpaid bills for you, 'in case you should ever deign to come home,' as she put it."

"What am I gonna do?" sobbed Matt hopelessly. "I love her, Claire. I can't live without her."

"Oh, baloney," said his sister, pushing past him into the hall. "Go upstairs and take a shower and I'll make you some breakfast. You can tell me about

France. Oh, and Matt . . . ? Drink a bucket of mouthwash while you're up there, would you? Your mouth smells like something that died two weeks ago."

Claire's breakfast was delicious. Freshly made pancakes with blueberries, walnuts and maple syrup, smoked salmon frittata and a huge pot of strong Colombian coffee. Afterward, Matt actually felt semihuman again.

"She's already filed for divorce, which has to be some kind of world speed record," he told Claire gloomily. "She wants half of everything."

"Except the bills."

"Except the bills. Which I totally can't pay. When they slice my credit cards in half, I'll make sure to send her her share." He smiled weakly. "What the hell am I going to do?"

Claire began clearing away the plates. "You could always try working. You know, getting a job? It's this thing where you go into an office and do stuff for other people, and they pay you for it. It's really catching on."

"Ha ha," said Matt. "I have a job. I'm a filmmaker."

"Oh!" Claire's eyebrows shot up sarcastically. "I see, Ingmar Bergman. And how's the great opus going? Was France everything you dreamed it would be?"

"It was great." Matt's eyes lit up for the first time that morning. He told his sister about his meeting with Danny McGuire and the unexpected developments in the Didier Anjou case, with Irina leaving her husband's estate to charity, just as the other two widows had done. "I know it's the same killer, the man who killed our dad. And I'm pretty sure McGuire knows it too, though he's cagey about promising too much."

Claire frowned. "Andrew Jakes was not 'our dad.' Dad was our dad. Jakes was just some fucking sperm donor."

Matt was taken aback by her anger. "Okay. Maybe he was. But he didn't deserve to have his head hacked off by some psycho, and for the guy to get away with it."

"Maybe he did deserve it?" said

Claire, loading Matt's dishwasher with a series of loud clangs. "Maybe he was a lousy SOB. Maybe they all were." She turned to face her brother. "You've already lost your marriage, Matt. Mom's upset with you, *I'm* upset with you. You're flat broke. Isn't it time you gave up this wild-goose chase and got your life back together? If three police forces and Interpol have all failed to solve these murders, what makes you think you can do it?"

"I'm smarter than them?" Matt grinned, earning himself a look of withering disdain from Claire. He knew she was right. He had to find paid work, and soon, if he was going to survive this divorce and keep a roof over his head. He could still work on the documentary, still keep in touch with Danny McGuire. But he couldn't let the unsolved murders consume him the way they had been.

The phone rang. They both stared at it, thinking the same thing. *Raquel.*

"Keep your cool," cautioned Claire. "Don't yell at her. And don't cry."

Matt picked up the handset, shaking. "Hello?"

Danny McGuire's voice sounded distant and tinny, but the excitement and adrenaline were both clear as a bell. "There's been another murder. Last night, in Hong Kong."

"Is it our guy?"

"Same MO," said Danny. "Rape, bodies bound together, rich elderly victim. Miles Baring."

Matt was silent for a moment. It took a few seconds for the full import of what McGuire was telling him to sink in. The killer was not only still out there. He was becoming bolder and more active. It had barely been a year since his last hit, and yet here he was, striking again on the opposite side of the world. Almost as if he knew that someone was watching him, knew that someone had finally found the scattered puzzle pieces and cared enough to try to arrange them into a coherent picture. *After ten long years, he's playing to an audience,* Matt found himself thinking. *He's playing to me.*

"Where's the widow?"

The elation in Danny McGuire's voice was unmistakable. "That's the best part. The Hong Kong police have her in protective custody. I called the guy in charge and told him what happened with the other wives. Lisa Baring's not going anywhere."

Matt hung up in a daze.

"Who was that?" asked Claire. "Not Raquel, I take it?"

"Hmm? No," said Matt. "I need to go pack."

"Pack?" Claire looked at him despairingly. "Matthew! Have you listened to a word of what I just said?"

Matt walked over to his sister and kissed her on the cheek. "I have. And I agree with it all. You're absolutely right, and I promise to look for a job the moment I get back from Asia. In the meantime, how are you fixed for time? I don't suppose you could give me a lift to the airport, could you?"

PART II

CHAPTER THIRTEEN

Hong Kong was like nothing Matt Daley had ever seen before.

He considered himself a man of the world. Not in the James Bond sense, obviously. No one could call Matt Daley sophisticated; still less, suave. Most days he considered it an achievement if he remembered to go out wearing matching socks. But neither was he some Midwestern farm boy who'd never been exposed to other cultures. Matt might have grown up in a small town, but he'd lived in New York and traveled extensively in Europe and South America when he was in his early twenties. Even so, Hong Kong filled Matt Daley with genuine awe.

Central, the island's main commercial district, was packed with towers so impossibly tall they made Manhattan look like Lilliput. Lan Kwai Fong, the nightlife quarter and red-light district, glittered and screamed and stank, its narrow streets packed with some of the weirdest specimens humankind had to offer: juggling midgets, armless dancers, blind transvestite hookers and the ubiquitous, wide-eyed U.S. servicemen on shore leave, drinking it all in. It reminded Matt a little of Venice Beach, multiplied to the power of a thousand. Come to think of it, the whole of Hong Kong was like that. *Intensified.* The grass out in the New Territories was so green it glowed like a cartoon. In New York and London, shopping streets were crowded. Here they were overrun, infested, alive with humanity like a rotting corpse riddled with maggots. Matt's overriding impression was of a place where everything happened in excess. Noises were louder, scents were stronger, lights were brighter and days were longer, apparently endless. Forget New York. Hong Kong was the real "city that never sleeps." After a week Matt still couldn't decide whether he loved it or hated it.

Not that it really mattered. He wasn't here on vacation. He was here on a mission.

It had seemed such a simple proposition on the phone to Danny McGuire. Danny's division at Interpol was now "actively assisting" the Hong Kong Chinese police. In practice, this meant little more than that the two organizations were exchanging information. There was no talk of a response team on the ground or anything like that. But McGuire at least now had the legitimate Interpol-endorsed go-ahead to devote time to the case, including delving deeper into the prior murders "where relevant." Matt's job was to fly out to Hong Kong, meet with Lisa Baring, the widow of the latest victim, and find out whatever he could. He would then feed that information back to Danny—strictly off-the-record, of course.

"If my bosses found out I was using

civilian contacts in the field, or meddling in a member country's domestic investigation, I'd be canned faster than a dolphin in a tuna net."

Ignoring Claire's handwringing injunctions to be careful, Matt had hopped on the Qantas flight to Hong Kong with high hopes. So far those hopes had shown no sign of realization. Making contact with Lisa Baring was proving to be mission impossible. Miles Baring, her husband, had been Hong Kong's Donald Trump, and his murder and the sexual attack on his stunning young wife were front-page news on the island. Media interest in the case was heightened by an almost total lack of available information. The Hong Kong police ran a tight ship and were not prone to giving press conferences merely to satisfy the curiosity of a salacious public. Miles and Lisa Baring had always fiercely guarded their privacy, and Mrs. Baring clearly saw no need to break this habit simply because her husband had been slaughtered in cold blood. Ensconced in the Queen Elizabeth Hospital on Gascoigne Road, she had made no public statement and apparently had no intention of doing so. Thanks in part to Interpol's warnings, the hospital building was surrounded by armed police. Other patients' visitors were strictly monitored, and not even deliverymen or medical staff came and went without a daily grilling. As for Mrs. Baring herself, the only people allowed access to her were her doctors and Chief Superintendent Liu, the Chinese detective in charge of the local investigation.

Unable to use Danny McGuire's name, or claim any connection with Interpol, Matt had fallen back on tried and tested telephone ruses.

He was a reporter with *60 Minutes,* putting together a piece on the wonderful efficiency of Liu and his team.

He was an attaché from the U.S. embassy, paying a courtesy visit to a fellow citizen in distress. (Lisa Baring was American by birth, a New Yorker, if the papers were to be believed.)

He was a lawyer bearing vital documents that only Mrs. Baring was permitted to sign off on.

The answer was always the same: "No visitors."

Initially Matt stayed at a little guest-house on the Peak. But the proprietress asked him to leave after a sinister-looking unmarked car with smoked windows took to parking outside the building day and night, leaving only when Matt did. Matt told Danny McGuire about the car.

"Do you think the Chinese might be watching me?"

Danny sounded worried. "I don't know. It's possible, although I can't think why. Be careful, Matt. Remember, the killer may still be local. While Lisa Baring's in Hong Kong, there's a good chance he's sticking around, biding his time till he can spirit her away like he did the others."

"You think he tricked the other widows into leaving?"

"I think it's possible, yes. Maybe he had an accomplice, someone who lured the women away from the safety of their own homes and police protection so he could finish them off too."

Matt wasn't convinced. "If he wanted

the wives dead, why not just kill them at the scene? Why go to all the trouble of two separate murders?"

"I don't know," said Danny. "Maybe as far as he's concerned, it's no trouble. Maybe he enjoys it."

Matt shivered.

"All we know for sure about this guy is that he's dangerous as hell and he doesn't mess around. If he suspects you're on to him, you could be in real danger."

Matt moved to the Marriott, a large, faceless hotel downtown, and the dark car disappeared. Occasionally he still had the eerie sensation that he was being followed, on the DLR, Hong Kong's subway, or on his way to the Starbucks next to the hospital, where Lisa Baring remained under armed guard. But he never saw anyone, or had anything concrete to report back to Danny.

With his funds running low and still no nearer to talking to the elusive Mrs. Baring, Matt was seriously contemplating flying back home empty-handed when an e-mail arrived from Danny McGuire's personal Gmail address.

"Delete this as soon as you've read it," Danny wrote. "Liu sent it through today. I thought it might give you some leads."

The next word of the e-mail sent Matt's heart rate racing.

Deposition

Lisa S. Baring
16/09/2006, Queen Elizabeth Hospital, Hong Kong

I confirm that my name is Lisa Baring, and that I am the wife of Miles Baring, deceased. I confirm that I was with the deceased on the night of his death, 04/09/2006, at 117 Prospect Road, Hong Kong. I confirm that the account given below is a true and complete record of events, to the best of my knowledge and memory.

Miles and I were at home as usual. Anita, our cook, had made a dinner of chicken and rice and we shared a bottle of red wine. I would not say that either of us was intoxicated. After dinner, we retired upstairs to our bedroom, where we watched television—CNN global business news—and made love. We turned out the lights at around 10:30 P.M. and both went to sleep.

I woke to find a masked man holding a knife to my throat. I saw Miles move toward the panic button beside our bed, but the man shouted at him to stop or he would cut my throat. Miles did as he asked. The man tied me up first with rope and placed me on the floor. He said if either of us made a sound, he would kill us. Miles asked him what he wanted, but he did not reply. Instead he moved toward Miles. Miles tried to fight him off, and that was when the man stabbed him.

I know I screamed. I was not aware of Miles screaming, only of his being stabbed again and again. There was a lot of blood. I felt certain that one of the servants would have heard something by this point, but no one came. I must have passed out.

When I came to, the man was raping me. He cut me with the knife on my back, buttocks and legs. Miles was lying on the floor bleeding. I do not know whether he was dead or not. I think he was. After approximately five minutes the man stopped raping me. I don't think he ejaculated. He produced a gun, which I had not seen before. I remember thinking it was strange that he had chosen to use a knife to subdue us when he had a gun all along. I assumed he was going to kill me, but instead he turned and fired a single shot into Miles's head at close range. It was very quiet. Then he dragged Miles's body over to me and tied the two of us together with the same rope he had used on me before. He covered my mouth with duct tape. And he left.

I did not see him steal or attempt to steal anything from the room. He did not ask either me or Miles at any time about the safe. I have no idea what happened after he left the room, how he escaped from the property. I lay on the floor for a further five hours until one of the maids, Joyce, discovered us early the next morning and called the police.

I confirm that at no time did I recognize the man who attacked us, either from his voice or any other physical characteristic. I confirm that our infrared security system had been disabled, but I have no knowledge as to when or how this happened.

Signed:
Lisa S. Baring

Matt read the statement again and again, his mind crowded with questions. So much of what Lisa Baring said didn't make sense. Why had the servants not heard anything, or seen the man once he entered the house? There must have been scores of them there that night. How was a sophisticated security system disabled without anybody realizing? Why would Miles Baring, an intelligent man in his late seventies, decide to physically challenge an armed assailant rather than press a panic button? He must have had opportunities to reach for the button while his wife was being tied up. Why, as Lisa Baring herself pointed out, did the attacker use a knife when he had a gun with a silencer?

Matt Daley didn't sleep that night. Instead he lay staring at the ceiling of his hotel room, his mind refusing to shut down. He realized he was starting to think of this killer as a shadow, unreal, like a character in some kind of potboiler mystery. But of course, he wasn't a shadow. He was human, flesh and blood, and he was out there tonight, sleeping and eating and thinking and living his life, despite the series of horrific crimes he had committed. Lisa Baring knew that man, not by name, but in a far more intimate, more real way. Lisa Baring had touched him, just like Angela Jakes, Tracey Henley and Irina Anjou had all touched him before her. She had heard his voice, smelled his breath and his sweat, felt the weight of him on top of her, inside her. To Matt he might seem like an enigma, a ghost. But to Lisa Baring he was very, very real.

I have to do it. Somehow I have to meet Lisa Baring.

I have to get to her before he does.

Inspector Liu closed his eyes and counted to ten. He had never much liked Western women. They were too opinionated, too stubborn, too arrogant. He couldn't imagine why Miles Baring hadn't chosen a more docile, pliable, Chinese woman as a wife. It would certainly have made his—Liu's—job a lot easier.

"I've told you why, Mrs. Baring," he repeated patiently. "Your life may be in danger."

Lisa Baring continued packing her things into a Louis Vuitton overnight case, ignoring him. Her doctors had discharged her from hospital that morning and she was up and dressed for the first time in weeks, wearing clothes her Hong Kong housekeeper, Joyce, had brought from home: Hudson jeans that accentuated her long legs, a white mus-

lin blouse from Chloé and her favorite
Lanvin ballet pumps. Her dark hair was
tied back in a loose ponytail, and simple Tiffany diamond studs gleamed at
her ears and neck, illuminating a face
so naturally lovely that no makeup could
have improved it. Inspector Liu knew
her to be in her midthirties, but as he
watched her now, it was hard to believe.
Her skin glowed like a teenager's. Unfortunately, she was as headstrong as a
teenager too.

"I appreciate your concern, Mr. Liu,"
she said breezily, "but I have no intention of living the rest of my life like a
prisoner, looking over my shoulder. I
don't want police protection."

"You need it, Mrs. Baring."

"Be that as it may, I refuse it. I de-
cline it. I'm grateful for the offer, but my
answer is no."

Famed though he was for his equa-
nimity, Inspector Liu felt a rare flash of
real anger. "This isn't simply about your
own safety, Mrs. Baring. As you know,
we understand from Interpol that whoever raped you and killed your husband
has raped and killed before. He will al-

most certainly try to do so again. We have a duty to prevent that from happening, to protect possible future victims. Surely you can see that."

Lisa's perfect face looked pained. "Of course I can see that. No one is more eager to bring this bastard to justice than I am, Inspector, or to stop him from striking again. As I told you before, if he tries to make any sort of contact with me, or anything remotely suspicious happens, I will let you know immediately. But in the meantime, I must be allowed to live my life as I see fit. Miles and I have a holiday villa in Bali. It's secluded and safe. I'll be staying there until the media frenzy here dies down."

Inspector Liu drew himself up to his full five feet four inches and said authoritatively, "I'm sorry, Mrs. Baring, but I'm afraid that's absolutely out of the question."

Fifteen minutes later, in a blacked-out limousine on her way to Chek Lap Kok Airport, Lisa Baring spared a thought for the hapless Chinese policeman. He seemed like a sweet man, and he obviously meant well. But Lisa had seen enough cops in the past three weeks to last her a lifetime. Hong Kong was full of memories of Miles and what had happened, not to mention the media attempting to beat down her door. She had to get away.

At the North Satellite Concourse, the Barings' G6 was waiting. Seeing it brought a tear to Lisa's eye. Miles had loved that plane. It was his pride and joy.

"Welcome back, madam."

Kirk, the pilot, welcomed Lisa aboard.

"I'm so sorry about what happened. If there's anything I can do, anything at all . . ."

Lisa put a hand on his arm. "Thank you, Kirk. But all I want is to get out of here."

"We're next up," he assured her. "Make yourself comfortable."

Make myself comfortable, thought Lisa as the jet's engines roared to life. Wasn't it wrong to be comfortable with Miles lying dead on a slab somewhere, his cold corpse mutilated by knives and bullets? Fresh tears welled in her eyes. *I can't let myself think about Miles. I've got to block it out. Nothing's going to bring him back.*

It was easier said than done. As the plane lifted up through the clouds, reminders of her husband were everywhere. There was Miles's office tower, nestled next to the giant Bank of China building like a baby hiding beneath its mother's wing. *If only it could have protected him! If only anything could have.* She closed the window blind, but Miles was everywhere inside the plane too. The soft tan leather seats that he'd lovingly picked out himself when they upgraded the plane. His own seat, beside Lisa's, still bearing the faint imprint of his body. Even his kindly eyes staring down at her from the portrait on the wall. *Poor, poor Miles. What crime did he ever commit, beyond being rich and happy? Who in the world had he hurt? Who did either of us ever hurt?* Miles had tried to make Lisa happy too. But not even the brilliant Miles Baring could achieve the impossible.

It wasn't until they began their descent that it occurred to her. *We came to Bali on our honeymoon.* Suddenly, being here felt wrong. Disrespectful. But it was too late now. She'd told Inspector Liu that she would be in Bali. Until the case was closed, and the press lost interest in Miles's murder, this must be her chosen prison.

That was all her life was in the end, she thought sadly: a series of prisons. Some of them had been luxurious, like this one. Others, long ago, had been cold and lonely and dark. But for as long as she could remember, she had never been free.

She knew now that she never would be.

As she closed her eyes, a memory came back to her. Or perhaps it wasn't a memory? Perhaps it was a dream.

Italy.
Happiness.
A warm beach.
She let herself drift away.

Positano was beautiful. So beautiful she had almost forgiven him for France.

The hotel was old and distinguished.

Its clientele was exclusive, rich but not flashy, European aristocracy mostly.

"You're a sucker for a title, aren't you, darling?" he teased her.

She liked it when he teased her. It reminded her of the old days.

"What you wouldn't do for a coronet on that pretty little head of yours, eh? It'd suit you too. You were born for it, I'd say."

They were at the poolside bar, sipping martinis and watching the sun go down. She thought, *I wish we could do this more often. Just relax.* The barman smiled flirtatiously as he refilled her glass. He was handsome, olive-skinned and dark-haired, with mischievous almond eyes. For a moment she panicked, afraid that her husband had seen the smile, that he would be angry. It was strange how he could make her feel so safe, yet at the same time she remained afraid of him. But he hadn't noticed anything. In fact he seemed more interested in the old man playing chess with his daughter at the far end of the bar than he was in her.

They finished their drinks and walked

back to their room as the sun oozed into the horizon. Once they were inside, her husband locked the door and undressed, as unselfconscious as a savage in his nakedness. And why wouldn't he be, with that body? Michelangelo couldn't have sculpted a better one.

"I saw that barman looking at you."

He walked toward her and she felt the hairs on her forearms stand on end.

"I . . . I don't know what you mean," she stammered. "No one was looking."

He pushed her down onto the bed. "Don't lie to me. You liked it when he looked at you, didn't you? You wanted him."

"That's not true!"

Hands tightened around her neck. "It *is* true. Did you want that old man too, at the end of the bar? Hmm?" With his knee he forced her legs apart. "Let's face it, he's more your type. Old and rich."

"Stop it!" she pleaded. "You're the one I want. The only one."

But the last thing she wanted him to do was stop. He was aroused for the first time in months. She reached for him, clawing at his bare back, squirming out of her bikini bottoms, desperate to pull him inside her. *Please let him make love to me now. It's been so long.* But after a lingering kiss, he did what he always did. Wrapped his arms around her like a cocoon and waited until she fell into a fitful, frustrated sleep.

It was a long wait. Finally the regular rise and fall of her chest let him know it was safe to move. He slipped out of bed and down the hotel corridor. Outside it was pitch-dark, but he knew where he was going. Behind the main building, past the tennis courts to the low-built employees' residence.

Two knocks. The door opened.

"I'd almost given up on you."

"Sorry. I couldn't get away."

He kissed the almond-eyed barman passionately on the mouth. "Let's go to bed."

The Barings' villa, Mirage, on the north side of the island, was idyllic and as secluded as anyone could have wished. The perfect marriage of luxury and simplicity, with its Infinity pool, whitewashed walls and colonial dark wood floors, Villa Mirage was surrounded by thick jungle on one side and shimmering ocean on the other. Even so, Lisa had taken extra precautions, installing round-the-clock details of security men to circle the perimeter and two armed bodyguards inside the property, in addition to the housekeeper, handyman and butler who lived at the villa year-round. Not for a moment did she believe Inspector Liu's warnings about her attacker returning to kidnap or harm her. That was preposterous. But the media attention was another matter. In the absence of any information, or a viable suspect on whom to focus their anger, the Chinese press had chosen to vilify Miles Baring's much-younger American wife. Overnight, it seemed, Lisa had gone from innocent victim to calculating gold digger in the minds of most ordinary Hong Kong citizens. She knew from bitter experience that the paparazzi would stop at nothing to steal a picture of her, which the newspapers would no doubt twist to make it look as if she were living it up in Bali. As if she weren't grieving Miles. Lisa wasn't about to let that happen.

It was late when she arrived at the villa and she was tired.

"I think I'll go straight to bed if you don't mind, Mrs. Harcourt."

"Of course, ma'am. I'll have Ling bring you up some warm milk."

Karen Harcourt, Villa Mirage's housekeeper, was short and round and motherly. She wore her gray hair in tight curls and had always reminded Lisa of the sweet old grandmother from the Tweety Pie cartoons.

If only I'd had a mother like that, my life might have been so different. If only I'd had a mother at all.

"Thank you."

Upstairs, Lisa's bedroom had been prepared for her arrival. The mahogany four-poster bed had been turned down and draped with fine-mesh mosquito nets. Diptyque candles cast a warm glow over the room and filled it with the soothing scent of gardenia. The doors to the balcony were open, allowing Lisa to hear the soft lapping of the waves against the shore below. The only jarring note was the silver-framed pictures of her and Miles that were still propped up on her teak dressing table. *Mrs. Harcourt probably thought I'd want to see them. To hold on to the memories.* Lisa slipped them into a drawer and sighed.

Turning around, she froze. There was a man by the door, lurking in the shadows. Lisa couldn't see his face, but she didn't need to. He was a man. A stranger. In her bedroom. She screamed at the top of her lungs.

"Help! Guards! Help me!"

The man stepped into the light. "Please, stop screaming. I'm not here to hurt you."

Lisa's voice got louder. "INTRUDER! HEEEEELLP!"

He walked toward her. "Really, I didn't mean to scare you. I only want to talk. I—"

He slumped, lifeless, to the floor. Behind him, Lisa's housekeeper, Mrs. Harcourt, stood shaking like a leaf. Lisa stared at the heavy, blood-smeared frying pan in her hand and promptly fainted.

CHAPTER FOURTEEN

The man on the floor was quite still. Blood poured from a wound in the back of his head where the housekeeper had hit him. Belatedly the two security guards burst into the room, just as Lisa began to come around.

One said, "I'll call the police."

"No." Lisa was surprised by how firm her own voice sounded. "No police. Is he dead?"

One of the guards knelt low over the body. "No, ma'am. He's breathing."

The man on her bedroom floor was pale and blond. He was not the man who'd killed Miles. His voice alone could have told her that. But who was he, and what was he doing here?

"How badly is he injured? Does he need a doctor?"

The guard felt the man's wrist. "He's got a strong pulse. But he ought to see someone, just in case. Concussions can be tricky things."

Lisa nodded. "I'll call Frank."

Dr. Francis McGee was on old friend of Miles's with a villa just across the bay. Frank was retired, but his mind was still sharp. More importantly, he could be relied on to maintain absolute discretion.

Mrs. Harcourt bustled forward. "We need to stop the bleeding right away. I can bandage him, but I'll need help getting him upright."

When Frank McGee arrived forty minutes later, the man was propped up on pillows in one of Mirage's guest suites. The wound on his head had been cleaned and tightly bandaged. As he drifted in and out of consciousness, two guards stood at the door, intently watching his every move.

"He wasn't armed," Lisa told the doctor. "But I didn't know that at the time. He just appeared in my bedroom and I screamed. Mrs. Harcourt only meant to disable him."

"You don't have to explain yourself to me, my dear. Housebreakers deserve everything they get in my book. Mrs. Harcourt did the right thing." Dr. McGee unwound the bandages and looked at the wound. Then he pulled open the man's eyelids and shone various lights in his eyes. The doctor's hands were liver-spotted and crisscrossed with thick, gnarled veins, but Lisa noticed how still and sure they were when he worked. "He'll live. I'll put in some stitches eventually, but for now he needs rest. Someone must keep an eye on him throughout the night, though. If he starts vomiting or bleeding out of the nose, call me immediately. You're quite sure you don't want to call the police?"

"Quite sure. He owes me some answers before I hand him over to anyone else."

Only after Frank McGee left did Lisa realize how truly exhausted she was.

Was it really only that morning that she'd left the hospital in Hong Kong, walking out on the enraged Inspector Liu? It felt like weeks ago. She longed to go to bed, but she was determined to be at her would-be attacker's bedside when he woke up. Curling up on an armchair in the corner of the room, under the watchful eye of the security guards, she pulled a cashmere blanket over herself and fell instantly to sleep.

"Jesus. My head."

The blond man was awake. Groggily, Lisa checked her watch. It was five A.M. *Morning.*

"What did you hit me with? An anvil?"

He was American. For some reason Lisa hadn't registered that last night.

"A frying pan. And *I* didn't hit you. It was my housekeeper."

The man reached up and touched his bandages. "Your housekeeper's got quite a swing on her. I feel like I've done ten rounds with Andre Ward."

"I've no idea who that is," said Lisa

briskly. "But what you actually did was one round with a seventy-two-year-old grandmother."

The man smiled sheepishly. "That's kind of embarrassing."

"I'd say embarrassment is the least of your worries." A cold edge had crept into Lisa's voice. "Who are you? And what the hell were you doing breaking into my home?"

The man extended a hand. "Matt Daley. Pleased to meet you."

"I'm not going to *shake your hand*! You were trying to rob me"—Lisa shivered—"or worse. Give me one good reason why I shouldn't have you arrested and thrown into jail this instant."

Matt couldn't help but admire the way her full breasts rose indignantly out of her low-cut Chloé blouse and her cheeks flushed when she was agitated. *She's beautiful. Just like the others.*

"Because you're in grave danger," he said solemnly. "And not from me. Mrs. Baring, I know you have no reason to trust me. But the man who killed your husband, the man who hurt you, has killed before. And the wives of his victims have a disconcerting tendency to go missing—"

"Yes, I know, I know." Lisa waved her hand dismissively. "Inspector Liu told me. He wants to keep me under lock and key until they catch this guy. But as the police in . . . four countries is it now? . . . seem to have singularly failed to catch this man for the past decade, the idea of hanging around was not exactly appealing."

Matt smiled. He wasn't sure what he'd expected of Lisa Baring. If he was honest, he thought she'd be some sort of meek and mindless trophy wife, the kind that rich old men usually went for. But she was nothing like that at all. She was feisty and fiery and sharp-tongued. If there was a soft center underneath, she did a good job of hiding it. He liked her.

Lisa looked at him suspiciously. "You still haven't answered my first question. Who are you? And what interest do you have in me and my safety? Are you a reporter?"

"No, absolutely not. I'm a victim, of

sorts. Like you. The man who killed your husband also killed my father."

The blood drained from Lisa Baring's face. *Was it possible?*

"Who was your father?"

"A man named Andrew Jakes." Matt closed his eyes. A wave of nausea and dizziness washed over him. He slumped back onto the pillows. "I don't feel so good."

Lisa summoned one of the maids for a glass of water. She handed it to Matt. "Drink this."

Matt sipped the water slowly and began to revive. Lisa, on the other hand, still seemed to be reeling with shock.

Eventually she asked him, "How did you know I'd be here? In Bali."

"I didn't," Matt said. "I thought you were still in the hospital in Hong Kong. But no one would let me near you there, and I knew you and your husband had a place in Bali, so I came out looking for clues."

"What sort of clues?"

"Anything that might link you or Miles to the other victims. I hoped you might come here, eventually. To get away from the media circus. But I wasn't expecting you to be in the villa last night. That's the truth."

There was no earthly reason for Lisa to believe him. Yet she found that she did. There was an honesty in his face, an openness that invited trust. It was an emotion Lisa Baring had almost forgotten she was capable of.

"And did you find any?"

Matt looked puzzled.

"Clues?"

"Well, no." He rubbed his head ruefully. "Some old lady whacked me over the head with a frying pan before I got the chance."

"Do the police know you're here? Interpol?"

Matt was taken aback. He hadn't expected her to ask him such a direct, specific question. He didn't want to lie to her, it felt wrong, but Danny McGuire had made him swear up and down not to mention their connection, and a promise was a promise.

"No."

"All right, Mr. Daley." Lisa Baring stood up. "Try and get some rest. We've both had a long night. I'll have Mrs. Harcourt bring you some food later. If you're up to it, perhaps we can discuss this further at dinner this evening."

Matt's eyes widened. "You're letting me stay here?"

"For now."

Lisa turned to the guards at the door. "If he needs to use the bathroom, or anything else, one of you is to go with him. Don't let him out of your sight."

Matt held tightly to the banister as he came downstairs. His head felt a lot better, but he was still unsteady on his feet. The villa radiated peace and tranquillity, like the Aman hotel in Morocco he and Raquel had stayed in on their honeymoon. Since arriving in Asia, Matt realized guiltily, he'd barely thought about Raquel or the divorce at all. Perhaps it was a defense mechanism. Denial. Why worry about things you can't change? That sort of thing. He knew he'd have to go home and face the music eventually. But here in this magical, idyllic, otherworldly spot, his domestic problems barely seemed real.

"Feeling better?"

Matt swallowed hard. Lisa had changed into a simple white cotton sundress. She wore plain, twisted-rope sandals, and her hair was piled up into a messy crown of dark curls on top of her head. The effect was at once innocent and knowing, pure and alluring. Raquel was a great-looking woman, but hers was a brash sexuality, a take-no-prisoners, in-your-face, va-va-voom appeal that required short skirts and a lot of makeup to achieve its full effect. Lisa Baring was the opposite. It was an overused phrase, but Lisa fit it perfectly: she was a natural beauty.

"Much better, thank you," said Matt.

Lisa took a seat at one end of a simple oak dining table, laden with a buffet of fresh local produce: squid sautéed in garlic; fresh, sliced papaya; warm, baked *roti gambang,* a delicious, seeded Indonesian bread. She gestured for Matt to sit. "Are you hungry?"

"I am now," said Matt. "This looks incredible."

"Help yourself."

She was being friendly, welcoming even, but there was still a wariness there. Probably inevitable, under the circumstances, but Matt did his best to dispel it. "I don't blame you for doubting my motives," he said, heaping his plate with bread and delicious-smelling seafood. "I'd be cautious too in your position. But I promise you, I only want what you want."

"And what's that?"

"To know the truth, presumably. And to catch this bastard, whoever he is."

Lisa poured two glasses from a carafe of red wine on the table and handed one to Matt.

"I'm not sure I believe in 'the truth.' As if there's only one. Everybody's truth is different, isn't it?"

The wine was excellent, full-bodied and fruity. Matt swirled it around in his mouth thoughtfully, enjoying the array of different tastes on his palate before answering.

"I disagree. I think the truth is the truth. People lie to themselves, that's all. They see what they want to see."

"And what do *you* see?" Lisa asked archly.

I see an intelligent, gorgeous, desirable woman I'd like to take to bed this instant. It was clear she was avoiding the subject of her husband's murder. Maybe it was still too early for her to talk about it. Too painful. "I see someone who acts tough but feels terrified inside."

This seemed to amuse her. "That's quite some X-ray vision you have, Mr. Daley. But I'm afraid it's off the mark. I'm neither tough nor afraid. I'm just putting one foot in front of the other, trying to get from one day to the next."

"And what *is* next for you, after all this?" Matt asked. "You can't hole up in Bali forever."

Lisa looked wistful. "No. I suppose not. But I don't like thinking about the future, Mr. Daley."

"Please, call me Matt."

"Things happen, Matt, things that you can't control. Bad things. None of us controls our own destiny. I've learned the hard way that that's just an illusion. Why make beautiful plans only to see them collapse into pain and death and dust?"

Watching her sad brown eyes, Matt felt an overwhelming urge to protect her, to comfort her, to make everything all right. Danny McGuire had admitted to feeling something similar for Angela Jakes after his father's murder, but it had distracted him from pinning Angela down, from unraveling the truth before she took off for Europe and slipped forever from his grasp. Matt Daley wasn't about to make the same mistake with Lisa Baring.

"How much did Inspector Liu tell you about the other murders?"

Lisa frowned. "Must we talk about that?"

"It's why I'm here, isn't it? Why you let me stay. Deep down you want to know the truth."

Lisa didn't respond to this. It was unnerving being psychoanalyzed by this attractive blond stranger, especially when he was right. Instead she answered Matt's first question. "Liu didn't tell me much. Just that similar crimes had been committed before, that Interpol thought it possible we were dealing with a serial killer, and that my own life might be in danger. He didn't get into specifics."

"Fine. I will." Over the course of the next hour, Matt told her all he knew about his father's murder and the killings of Sir Piers Henley and Didier Anjou. He and Lisa finished the first carafe of wine and she called for a second. Lisa listened calmly throughout his narrative, showing little or no emotion.

When Matt finally finished, she said: "I'm not sure it's the same man."

"What do you mean? Of course it's the same man."

"It may have been the same man for the earlier attacks. But I'm not sure the person you're describing is the man who killed Miles."

"What makes you say that?"

Lisa tore off a chunk of bread and dipped it pensively in her wine. "Little things. Like the giving-the-money-to-charity part. Miles didn't leave a penny to charity, and I haven't even begun to think about what I'm going to do with my inheritance. But more importantly, the whole thing smacks a little too much of some kind of Robin Hood complex, don't you think? Taking from the rich to give to the poor?"

Bizarrely, this idea had not occurred to Matt. It seemed so obvious when Lisa said it now. "Possibly, yes."

"Well, I know nothing about the man who raped me. But I can tell you this: he was no Robin Hood."

At the mention of the word *rape,* a heavy silence settled over the table, an almost visible cloud of shame. Matt found himself wishing that he knew this woman better, well enough to take her in his arms and comfort her, to assure her that none of this was her fault. As it was, he changed the subject.

"Tell me about Miles. About your marriage."

Lisa smiled, but it was a sad smile. "You mean tell you whether I married a man thirty years older than myself for love or for his money? What do you think?"

Matt blushed. That *was* what he meant, but he didn't realize he'd been so obvious.

"I'm sorry. I didn't mean to offend you."

"It's all right," said Lisa. "We may as well be honest with each other. I didn't love Miles. That much is true. But I liked him. He was a kind man and he treated me well. I've reached a point in my life where I value kindness. I was lucky that he chose me."

She speaks about it so passively, thought Matt. *"He chose me." As if it were an arranged marriage, and she had no say in the matter.*

"How did the two of you meet?"

"At a conference in Shanghai about a year ago."

"A year?" Matt looked surprised. "You hadn't been together very long, then?"

Lisa played with her napkin under the table. "No. We were married for nine months. It all happened very quickly. Our romance. Miles was a brilliant man and very considerate toward me."

"But not toward everyone?"

"He was in his later years. I think, when he was younger, he was probably a bit more ruthless, a bit more ambitious. He had a first wife, before I was born, and children. I don't think he treated them very well. But by the time we met, he had mellowed considerably."

Matt thought about Andrew Jakes. What a crappy husband he'd been to his mom, how he'd abandoned him and Claire without a shred of remorse, but how in later years he'd transformed into a doting partner to Angela.

"People change, I guess."

"Yes, they do. But the past can't be changed, and justice can never be outrun. We must all make atonement for the wrongs we do. We must all pay the price."

It was such a strange thing to say, Matt wasn't sure how to react. Was she saying that Miles Baring somehow *deserved* what had happened to him? Surely not. Her grief for her ex-husband seemed genuine, and she spoke of him with obvious affection and respect. But then what "price," what "atonement," was she talking about? Perhaps they'd both had too much wine.

Either way, Matt was grateful when the maid returned to clear away the plates, bringing decaf coffee and a slab of bright green *pandan,* a sweet Balinese rice cake to break the awkward silence. Sipping their coffee, they talked about other things, each of them evidently enjoying the other's company. Lisa asked Matt a lot of questions about his childhood. She seemed fascinated by Andrew Jakes's abandonment of his mother, and openly disbelieving that he, his mom and Claire could have gone on to have such happy lives afterward. Yet when Matt quizzed her about her own childhood, she was reluctant to talk. She grew up in New York but wasn't particularly happy there. She had a sister but they'd lost touch a long time ago. That was the most he was able to get out of her.

Noticing Matt rubbing the back of his head, she said, "I'm sorry about that clobbering you took. I'd really like you to stay here while you recover."

"What about the guards?" asked Matt, half jokingly. "Will they be watching me pee the whole time, or do you trust me to go by myself now?"

Lisa grinned. "I trust you. You'd be here as my guest."

"Are you sure you don't want your privacy?" Matt asked, more seriously now. "I'd be happy to find a guesthouse or a local hotel. I wouldn't want to intrude. I mean, obviously technically I *am* an intruder . . ."

Lisa laughed. "I'm quite sure. I'm not planning on leaving here anytime soon. And I could use the company. And who knows? Perhaps, together, we'll unravel this mystery, find the missing link that connects these terrible murders . . . if there is one."

"Well, if you're really sure," said Matt, "I'd be delighted. Thank you."

"Good." Lisa Baring smiled. "Miles always used to say that two heads were better than one."

That night as he lay in bed, Matt stared at the ceiling fan spinning around and thought how his life seemed to be spinning equally fast. *How on earth did I wind up here, in a luxury villa in Bali of all places, the guest of quite possibly the most interesting, attractive woman I've ever met? And how ironic that a sadistic killer, the man who murdered my father and raped that woman, should have played Cupid.*

He ought to call Danny McGuire in Lyon and inform him of developments. And he would. But not quite yet. Matt Daley wanted to keep Lisa Baring to himself for a little while longer. To figure out what made those intelligent eyes so sad in the peace and tranquillity of this magical island.

Think of it as a vacation, he told himself as he drifted off to sleep between soft Egyptian-cotton sheets. *A long-overdue vacation.* Raquel, the divorce, Danny McGuire, and everything about life on the outside felt wonderfully far away.

For the first time in months, Matt Daley fell asleep happy and excited at the prospect of what tomorrow might bring.

CHAPTER FIFTEEN

Mrs. Joyce Chan. Interview commencing, nine A.M."

The plump Chinese woman blinked at Inspector Liu nervously. She was afraid of policemen generally, but of this one in particular. He carried himself with importance and kept frowning, tapping his left foot against the leg of his chair in an irritated manner. Joyce knew she hadn't done anything wrong, but that didn't necessarily matter when it came to the Hong Kong police. If they wanted a scapegoat and chose her, there was nothing she could do about it.

Inspector Liu *was* in a bad mood. But it had nothing to do with Joyce Chan. In fact, he was very much hoping that the housemaid from the Barings' mansion might finally provide him with the breakthrough he so desperately needed in this case. With Lisa Baring being so stubbornly uncooperative, Inspector Liu had made precious little headway in catching Miles Baring's killer, a failure that was starting to embarrass not just Liu himself, but his superiors. Indeed, it would not be stretching the point to say that Inspector Liu had come to hate Miles Baring's widow, with her arrogant, Western beauty and her refusal to submit to his authority. Any sane woman would have been grateful for police protection, under the circumstances. And any genuinely grieving woman would have *wanted* to stay and help the police catch the man responsible for her husband's death, not to mention her own violation. The fact that Lisa Baring hadn't done these things, but had fled to a compound in Bali, outside of Inspector Liu's jurisdiction, further hardened the detective's heart against her. Lisa Baring was listed as the sole beneficiary in her husband's will. That gave her motive. By her own admission, she was present when the murder took place. That gave her opportunity. Of course, she hadn't raped herself. But did she know more about her "attacker" than she was letting on? And if so, was she afraid of him, or protecting him?

Inspector Liu would have dearly loved to force Lisa Baring to return to Hong Kong and answer these questions herself. But short of arresting her, for which he had no grounds, his hands were tied.

That was where Joyce Chan came in.

"How long have you worked at 117 Prospect Road, Mrs. Chan?"

Sweat trickled down the maid's fat cheeks. "Long time. Mr. Baring buy house, 1989. I working there two year later. Long time."

"And what were your duties?"

Mrs. Chan looked at Inspector Liu blankly.

"Your job. What was your job?"

"Oh. I in charge all the maids on bedroom floors. Level two and three. They change sheet, keep it clean. I organize."

"I see. So you were a supervisor. You did not clean yourself."

She nodded eagerly, pleased to have provided a correct answer. "Supervisor. Yes. Only sometime I clean for Mrs. Baring. Special thing."

Inspector Liu's ears pricked up, like a deer scenting danger on the wind.

"What sort of 'special thing'?"

Mrs. Chan's hands shook. She mumbled, "Private thing."

Belatedly, Liu realized that the poor woman was terrified. He tried to reassure her. "You're not in any trouble, Mrs. Chan. This is all very helpful information, I assure you. It may help us to catch the man who killed Mr. Baring. Do you understand?"

She nodded dumbly.

"What private cleaning did you do for Mrs. Baring?"

The maid squirmed. "Mrs. Baring have a friend. Sometime visit in the day."

"A friend? You mean a man?"

Joyce Chan nodded. "After, she like me make everything clean. Only me."

Inspector Liu could barely contain his excitement. This was more than the kind of conjecture the tabloids were running wild with. This was hard fact. The lovely Lisa Baring was having an affair!

"And did you ever meet this man? Mrs. Baring's 'friend'?"

Mrs. Chan shook her head no.

"But you saw him, presumably. Can you describe him to me?"

"Never see him."

Inspector Liu frowned. "You must have seen him. You said he visited during the day. Who let him into the house? Did he drive there? What kind of car did he have?"

But the maid only repeated more firmly, "Never see him. Never. Only missus tell me afterward, come and cleaning everything."

Inspector Liu grilled Mrs. Chan for a further thirty minutes, but the well of revelations appeared to have run dry. Yes, Mrs. Baring had a lover, but she had not asked for any "special" cleaning on the day of the murder, or in the week leading up to it. She *had* dismissed the domestic staff early that day and asked not to be disturbed, but apparently this was not uncommon. According to Joyce Chan, Mr. and Mrs. Baring often requested to be left alone together.

After Joyce Chan left the interview room, Inspector Liu sat thinking for a long time.

It was time for another chat with the helpful American from Interpol.

Many people described Bali as a paradise. But for Matt Daley it was more than that. Bali was a place of magic, of healing, of transformation. It brought him back to life.

When Lisa Baring first asked him to stay, Matt assumed he'd be at Villa Mirage for a few days until his head fully healed. He'd find out everything he could about the night of the murder, and about Miles and Lisa themselves: Was there something about them that had led them to be targeted? Some link with the other victims that he hadn't seen before, that might help them trace the killer? Then he'd report back to Danny McGuire at Interpol and head to

Los Angeles to deal with his mounting problems back home.

But as he and Lisa spent more and more time together, something strange started to happen. Matt found himself caring less and less about the case, and more and more about Lisa. Though he didn't dare ask her, he was pretty sure she felt the same way. Here in the idyllic surroundings of the villa, days turned into weeks, weeks into months, and the pair of them barely left the property at all. Domestics were dispatched to the local farms and villages for food. Books and other luxuries were ordered online. It was the longest period Matt had spent confined to one property in his entire life, but he didn't feel trapped. Quite the opposite in fact. It was liberating.

Danny McGuire had been attempting to contact him frantically, bombarding him with e-mails and calls, but Matt couldn't bring himself to read or respond to the messages. He'd even stopped responding to calls from his sister, Claire, or the other occasional calls he received from home. Once he opened the door to reality, to life outside the bubble, the idyll would be shattered. And Matt wasn't ready for that. Not yet.

Villa Mirage was a world unto itself, an infinitely dazzling miniature ecosystem. Matt and Lisa would work in the morning, Matt (officially at least) on his documentary and Lisa on the mountains of paperwork already being generated by Miles's estate. Bali might have granted her a respite from the police and the media, but there were still trustees and tax attorneys and mortgage companies to be dealt with, not to mention the shareholders of Miles's various companies. Luckily, Lisa had excellent secretarial skills. One of the few nuggets of information Matt had managed to glean about her pre-Miles life was that she'd once worked as a paralegal in a lawyers' office in L.A.

But both Matt and Lisa soon began living for the afternoons, when they would take off and explore Mirage's limitless delights together. Sometimes Lisa hired local guides to lead them into the thick jungle that bordered the villa's grounds, a world bursting with exotic and sometimes dangerous life. As the guides pointed out potential dangers— a coral snake here, a green pit viper, or a two-striped telamonia spider there— and educated them about the breath-taking flora, Matt and Lisa listened entranced, like children released into a strange, tropical Narnia. Other times they went fishing in the lagoon, or swimming in one of the deep, volcanic rock pools hidden at the foot of the cliffs. Matt loved to watch Lisa swimming. She was a slight woman, but her slender body was strong and athletic and she fairly glided through the water with all the deft grace of a young otter. There was something else there too, when she swam. Joy. Delight. A lack of inhibition that he rarely saw in her at other times. One afternoon he asked her about it.

"I've always loved the water." Standing on a rock, rubbing her damp hair with a towel, Lisa looked luminous. Her dewy skin glowed like a teenager's and her eyes sparkled with light and life. "There's a freedom to it. The silence.

The weightlessness. No one can touch you there. No one can hurt you. It's what I imagine death to be like."

"Death? That's a morbid thought, isn't it?"

"Is it?" She laughed, wrapping the towel around her hips Turkish style. "Not to me. I've always seen death as an escape. It doesn't frighten me."

Matt had heard people say this before, and had always taken it with a grain of salt. How could anyone not be scared of dying? Surely it was humanity's most basic instinct to want to survive. Clinging to life was like breathing, a fundamental fact of human nature, a flaw or a strength depending on how you looked at it, that all of us shared. But when Lisa expressed the thought, somehow it was different. He could see in her face that she meant it. There was a strange, fatalistic aura of peace right where the fear should be. He envied her.

"Lucky you," he said, stuffing his own clothes into a rucksack to take back to the villa. "That must help a lot, I imagine. Coming to terms with Miles's death."

Since their first days together, when he'd bombarded her with questions about her marriage and her past and gotten precisely nowhere, Matt had stopped asking Lisa about the murder and her husband. By unspoken mutual consent, Miles Baring's name was no longer mentioned between them. Hearing it now, Lisa looked stricken.

"Not really," she said bleakly. "Come on, let's get inside. I'm cold."

Matt could have bitten his tongue off. He hated when this pall of sadness came over Lisa, and hated even more when he was the one who cast it. Back in the villa, they dried and dressed and took some hot, sweet tea out onto the veranda. Lisa had changed into cutoff jeans and a plain white T-shirt. Barefoot, with her still-damp hair slick against her face and her knees drawn up to her chest, she looked more like a teenager than a grown woman, never mind a woman who had lived through such tribulations. Matt realized with a jolt that at some point during his long, happy days at Mirage, he had begun to view his life in a new way, as *before* Lisa Baring and *after* Lisa Baring. It had happened almost without him realizing it, but he was in love with her.

Before Lisa, Matt had been lost. It wasn't just Raquel's decision to leave him, although that blow had certainly hit him hard. It was many things, things he hadn't had time to process until now, here in the deep peace of the Balinese jungle. His failed career. His adopted dad's death. Not being able to have children with Raquel. Never knowing Andrew Jakes, the man who had given him life but then abandoned him, apparently without a moment's regret or remorse. Researching Jakes's murder and becoming so obsessed with this documentary, Matt now realized, had been his way of detaching from the pain. But Lisa Baring had shown him a better way.

After Lisa, it was as if a weight he hadn't even known he'd been carrying had been lifted off his shoulders. Matt felt hopeful, happy, alive. Whatever the future held, whatever the outcome of his work with Danny McGuire to track down this elusive killer, being with Lisa made Matt realize that there *was* a future for him, a future as bursting with possibility as the jungle all around them was throbbing with life. Increasingly, Matt found himself hoping that his future included the presence of Lisa.

There were problems, however. Nothing physical had yet happened between them. Sometimes Matt thought he could sense her staring at him as he sat at his computer or reading a book on the sofa. But whenever he looked up, her attention was elsewhere. Even so, an unspoken hum of mutual attraction seemed to linger in the air between them.

Last week, out fishing on Mirage's private lake, Lisa had lost her footing on the bank and Matt instinctively slipped an arm around her waist. Lisa froze. But after a moment's hesitation she did not object, gradually allowing herself to relax against Matt's body. It felt wonderful. Matt longed to go further, but he knew better than to rush her.

I have to be patient. Let her come to me. She's just lost her husband. She's just been raped.

That was the other problem. Lisa

never spoke about the night of Miles's murder or her rape. As if by refusing to talk about it, she could make it go away. And much to his shame, Matt saw himself colluding in that silence. He wanted to forget the past as well. But this killer was *not* just a part of the past. He was out there, somewhere, watching and waiting, planning his next kill.

Matt had come to Bali looking for clues, clues that might help him unearth a serial killer, but he'd allowed his love for Lisa and his happiness in her company to distract him. Watching Lisa sip her tea now, he forced himself to remember:

The man I'm looking for raped and terrorized Lisa. If his past crimes are anything to go by, his next step will be to kidnap her. To have her "disappear" like Angela Jakes, Tracey Henley and Irina Anjou.

Lisa was in danger. And Matt still had no idea how, or where or when that danger might strike. The thought crossed his mind that his own prospects looked none too rosy either. This man, whoever he was, had a pretty gruesome track record of dispatching the men involved with his female victims. But it was Lisa's safety that tortured him inside.

I can't lose her. I can't lose another person I love. If I do, I'll lose my mind.

Inspector Liu turned on his tape recorder as Jim Harman began to speak.

An Englishman who had grown up in Hong Kong, the son of well-to-do expat parents, Jim ran his own security and electronics business on the island. He had personally overseen the installation of the alarm system at the Baring estate on Prospect Road.

"I'll tell you this, mate," he told Inspector Liu firmly. "There was nothing wrong with that alarm system."

Tall and skinny, with a face like a weasel and small, widely spaced eyes, Jim Harman was prepared to defend his reputation vociferously.

"I installed it myself, with more failsafes than the fucking White House, pardon my French."

Liu asked calmly, "Then how do you

explain the fact that Mr. Baring's killer was able to get around it?"

"He didn't 'get around it,'" Jim Harman said matter-of-factly. "Someone let him in."

"And why would they do that?"

Harman shrugged. "I'm a systems guy, not a detective, Inspector. You tell me. But the only explanation is that someone deliberately disabled the system and let the guy in."

"And who knew how to do that?"

For the first time, the weasel-faced Englishman looked perplexed. "That's the thing. No one. Mr. Baring and myself were the only ones who knew how to work that security system. It makes no sense."

The interview over, Inspector Liu hopped on the DLR to Wan Chai, in the northern part of the island, in search of some lunch. The underground trains were clean and ran on time, a rarity in Hong Kong. Taking them calmed Liu and helped him to think.

"It makes no sense," Harman had said. But it did make sense. Indeed, the possibilities were clear and satisfyingly

finite: either Miles Baring had given his wife instructions on how to disable the security system, or Miles had disabled it himself, unwittingly opening the door to his killer.

Was it someone he knew?

Was it Lisa's lover?

Was Lisa's lover a friend of her husband's?

Stranger things had happened.

Inspector Liu emerged from the subway blinking into the Wan Chai sunshine like a reluctant mole. His phone rang the very same instant.

"Liu speaking."

"Sir." It was one of his surveillance team, a small, elite group who'd been dispatched to Bali to keep an eye on the beautiful, headstrong Mrs. Baring. "We got some better shots of the villa today from the long-range cameras."

"She still hasn't left the property, then?"

"No, sir."

Villa Mirage, the Barings' Balinese retreat, was so secluded as to be almost completely inaccessible and extraordinarily difficult to photograph. Liu had tried to have the place bugged, but Mrs. Baring's private security detail was excellent. None of his men had been able to get near her. He'd hoped he might have more success if, by a piece of luck, she should venture out of the place by car, but so far she had lived as a virtual recluse. It was as if her every action, or inaction, had been specifically designed to frustrate him.

"We do have some good news, though, sir. It appears there's a man staying at the house with Mrs. Baring."

Liu almost choked. "A man?"

"Yes, sir. A Westerner. They had breakfast together on the terrace this morning. They looked . . ."—the detective searched for the appropriate word— "intimate."

Had Inspector Liu been a different kind of man, he would have punched the air with excitement. *Lisa Baring's lover! She's smuggled him in!* It was hard to believe that anyone could be so reckless. Surely she must know that the police would still be watching her? Inspector Liu had never been in love and he hoped he never would be. What fools passion made of people.

All they needed now was some physical evidence. If this man's fingerprints or any trace of his DNA were found at the Baring house, they'd have enough evidence to arrest the two of them. Danny McGuire from Interpol had warned him that the killer was likely to stay close to Mrs. Baring. That as long as Liu held Lisa Baring, he held the bait.

The problem was that Inspector Liu no longer "held" Lisa Baring.

He had to get inside that villa.

CHAPTER SIXTEEN

Alone at the corner table of a quiet café, Danny McGuire picked flakes from the top of his *pain au chocolat* and waited for his team to arrive. After Inspector Liu formally requested Interpol assistance, Danny's boss, Deputy Director Henri Frémeaux, had reluctantly authorized a small task force to devote "no more than eight hours per week" collating evidence for the case now codenamed Azrael.

"It's from a poem," Danny had explained to Frémeaux, back at headquarters. "Azrael's the Angel of Death."

Frémeaux stared at him blankly. He wasn't interested in poetry. He was interested in statistics, facts and results. Danny had better justify this use of manpower, and quickly, if he wanted his agency support to continue.

By "small task force," it turned out Henri Frémeaux meant two additional men. Danny chose Richard Sturi, a German statistician with about as much personality as the croissant Danny was currently eating, but with an uncanny gift for seeing meaningful, real-life patterns in unintelligible strings of numbers, and Claude Demartin, a forensic specialist. For the nitty-gritty detective work he would have to rely on himself and Matt Daley, his "mole on the ground" in Hong Kong.

So far, Daley had been his biggest disappointment. He'd seemed so gung ho in the beginning. Indeed, if it hadn't been for Matt Daley, the Azrael investigation would never have gotten off the ground. But after a fruitless first week in Hong Kong, Matt had sent Danny precisely one brief e-mail about "casting his net further afield" and proceeded to disappear on some jaunt around Southeast Asia. After weeks of unreturned e-mails and phone calls—other than a single voice mail left in the middle of the night assuring Danny that Matt was "okay" and "working on it"—Danny had officially given up. Inspector Liu threw him occasional tidbits of information, but like most local police chiefs, the man in Hong Kong was more interested in receiving data from Interpol than sharing his own. As Henri Frémeaux reminded Danny repeatedly, "This is a Chinese case, McGuire. Our job is merely to support and facilitate."

It was then that Richard Sturi showed up, wearing his usual suit and tie and clutching his laptop like a security blanket. Sturi's eyes blinked uncomfortably in his round, owl-like face as he took in the "unusual" meeting place Assistant Director McGuire had chosen. External team meetings were unusual at Interpol, and frowned upon, but Danny was determined to get his little team bonding and throwing ideas around outside of the stifling atmosphere of HQ. When he arrived moments later, Claude Demartin was also formally dressed, but being French, unlike Sturi, he was never averse to meeting in a café. He ordered himself a *café crème* and a *croque-monsieur* before things got started.

"Okay, guys," Danny began. "Right now we have nothing tangible out of Hong Kong. What we do have is a huge paper file on the Jakes case, which I believe you've both seen, and you've been inputting into the I-24/7. Richard, is that right?"

The German statistician nodded nervously. He seemed to do everything nervously and wore the permanent expression of a man who was about to be hauled before the Gestapo and summarily shot.

"In terms of maximizing the use of our time, I suggest we focus on the Henley and Anjou cases, see if we can dig up anything that the local investigators missed."

"Are the local police being cooperative?" asked Claude Demartin, downing the last of his coffee.

"In a word, no. We've all got to tread carefully and try not to upset too many applecarts. There's a lot of professional pride on the line. Up to now this guy has gotten away with murder three times, and it looks as if he's going to make it a fourth in Hong Kong. Frémeaux's already looking for an excuse to shut us down, and if we piss off Scotland Yard or the LAPD or any of the other local forces, he'll have one. You understand what I'm saying?"

Two nods.

"Good. So what do we have so far? Our killer is male. He targets wealthy, older men with young wives. His motivation is at least partially sexual. And he is unusually savage in his murders. Anything you would like to add to this?"

Claude Demartin looked like he was going to say something, then thought better of it and clammed up.

"What?" Danny urged.

"I'm a forensics guy. I'm not an expert in any of this other stuff."

"I'm not looking for experts. I'm looking for ideas, theories. Just go with your instincts."

Richard Sturi visibly winced.

"Okay," Demartin began. "Well, then I'd say he's a sophisticated man."

"Because?"

"He's well traveled. Probably he speaks several languages. The crimes took place all over the globe."

Danny nodded encouragingly. "Good."

Demartin warmed to his theme. "Also he plans pretty meticulously. And he seems to have a knack for handling complicated security systems. Makes me suspect he's an electrical engineer or a computer whiz of some sort."

The security angle had always bothered Danny. Thinking of the Jakes case, he remembered that the alarm system at 420 Loma Vista had been highly sophisticated, state-of-the-art in its day. The Henleys had a straightforward but reliable Banham system in London, and Didier Anjou's Saint-Tropez home was surrounded by CCTV cameras, all of them suspiciously blank the night of his murder. According to Inspector Liu of the Hong Kong police, Miles Baring had installed a security system to rival the one at Fort Knox. And yet in all four cases, a single man had slipped in and

out of the victims' homes entirely unnoticed.

A killer with unusual expertise in matters of technology was one possibility.
But there was another, simpler one, one
that had haunted Danny since his days
on the Jakes case.

"Maybe someone in the household
knew the killer," he said out loud. "Someone let them in. A servant or something."

"Or the wives." Claude Demartin
baldly stated what Danny couldn't bring
himself to utter. "Here's a theory. This
killer, this sophisticated, intelligent guy,
targets the bored young wives of his
victims. He grooms them, winning their
trust, maybe seducing them sexually.
Then, once he has them under his spell,
he cons them, persuading them to give
all their husband's money away to charity."

"Then what?" Danny asked skepti-
cally. "He breaks into their homes?"

"Why not? By then he already has inside knowledge of the property, security codes, camera positions, et cetera.
He conceals his identity with a mask . . .
does something with his voice presum-

ably so the women don't recognize him. Murders the husbands. Rapes the wives. Then he returns later as the shoulder to cry on for the widows. Once the money's safely in the accounts of the charities, he persuades the widows to disappear with him. Safely removed from the crime scene, he kills them too, disposes of the bodies and moves on to the next hit."

All three men were silent. Demartin's theory was a serious stretch on many levels. Assuming that the killer attempted to disguise himself at the time of the break-in, was it actually possible that a woman would fail to recognize her own lover? It seemed pretty far-fetched. And wouldn't the cops have come across the killer in his shoulder-to-cry-on guise? Surely if some slick, presumably handsome, intelligent young man was hanging around the vic-tims . . .

Danny froze.

There *had* been such a man. With Angela Jakes. Hanging around her like a bad smell.

Lyle Renalto.

Demartin was talking again, enjoying his newfound role as Sherlock Holmes. Stuck in a forensics lab at Interpol, he rarely got a chance to let his imagination run wild.

"Or we could consider some alternatives. How about this? The killer does *not* conceal his identity. The wives know full well who he is and they let him into their homes deliberately. The wives aren't his victims. They're his accomplices."

Danny McGuire thought back to Angela Jakes's terrible injuries after her rape. She was so badly beaten that when he first saw her, tied to her husband's corpse, he'd thought she was dead. He shook his head. "No. No way. There was nothing faked about those rapes. Not the one I saw, anyway. Not in a million years was that sex consensual."

Claude Demartin raised an eyebrow. Americans could be dreadful prudes when it came to sex. "Are you sure? Some women like it rough."

"Not that rough," said Danny. *Not that*

woman. She was so sweet and gentle. An angel.

Demartin shrugged. "Don't forget there were hundreds of millions of dollars at stake in each of these killings. People will tolerate extreme suffering to obtain enormous amounts of money."

"But none of the widows kept the money. They gave it away."

"Except Lisa Baring."

"Except Lisa Baring. So far."

Silence fell again. Demartin's theory was plausible. One killer. *Possibly Lyle Renalto?* Grooming wives. Gaining access. Killing husbands. Diverting funds. Of course it still begged a number of questions. Not the least of which was "why?"

Danny said, "Motive's still a problem."

Richard Sturi laughed loudly. It was the first sound he'd made in a good fifteen minutes and both Danny and Claude Demartin turned to stare at him in surprise.

"*Motive's* a problem? Everything's a problem! You haven't a shred of hard factual evidence to support any of what you've just said."

The German's tone was contemptuous. His French colleague instantly bridled. "All right, then, Albert Einstein.
Let's hear what you've got to say about
the crimes."

Wordlessly, Richard Sturi removed
his sleek Sony laptop from its case and
placed it on the table. As he lovingly
stroked its cover, Danny had a sudden
image of Blofeld, from the *Austin Powers* movies, with his cat.

"This is just some initial analysis. Very
basic."

Danny McGuire and Claude Demartin
both gazed at the screen in awe. The
graphs lit up the screen one by one in
an array of eye-popping colors. Red for
the Jakes murder, blue for the Henley
case, green for Anjou, and livid purple
for the Barings. There were time lines,
showing the length of time between the
date of each marriage and the respective husband's murder, and from each
murder to the wife's disappearance. Bar
graphs, analyzing everything from the
age gap between each couple to
the geographical distance between the
crimes. Richard Sturi had done his

homework and then some. On the last screen, in yellow, was another, as-yet-untitled set of graphs.

Danny pointed at them. "What are those?"

"Projections. Not conjecture, you understand." Sturi looked at Demartin with an expression hovering between pity and contempt. "Mathematical probabilities, drawn from the limited *known* facts. I've been building up a profile of the killer based on past data. The yellow lines predict his statistically probable next move."

Danny swallowed hard. "You mean his next kill?"

"Precisely. It occurs to me that the most effective way for us to assist a member country in actually apprehending this individual would be to anticipate his next move and prepare for it. Of course, we can't say *who* specifically his next victim will be. But we can predict that individual's age, net worth, geographical location, most likely wedding date. There is a plethora of factors that can be statistically determined, telling us how the killer will behave in the future based on how he has behaved in the past."

Danny stared at the jagged yellow lines and for some reason thought of the Wizard of Oz. *Is that how we're going to find him? By following Sturi's yellow brick road? Perhaps we've had the answers all along, like Dorothy and her friends. We just didn't know where to look.*

Beneath the graphs were numbers, pages and pages of them. Statistical analysis of everything from the DNA evidence, to the dates of the bank transfers, to comparative data about each of the children's charities, to the four victims' dates of birth. A sea of numbers that all but made Danny's eyes cross.

Richard Sturi concluded, "In my opinion, it is a poor use of our limited time and resources to focus on *who* the killer might be and *why* he does what he does. We simply do not have enough factual evidence to answer those questions. This data tells us *how* he operates, *when* and *where* he kills. Look here." Sturi flashed between screens so fast that Danny saw nothing but a blurry rainbow. "The rate at which he commits his crimes appears to be increasing rapidly."

"No 'appears' about it," said Danny. "Nothing happened for four years after the Jakes case, but the Baring murder occurred a year after Didier Anjou's."

"Ah. But you are assuming that Sir Piers Henley was his first kill after Andrew Jakes."

Demartin's eyes widened. "You think there was another murder in between? One that we don't know about?"

"I don't think anything. Thinking's not my job. But statistically, such a case is likely, yes. Probably in South America, in 1998 or early 1999. I'm looking into it."

"Jeez." Danny whistled. "Okay. Go on."

"He kills every two to three years, moving east around the globe, changing his identity, and possibly his appearance, between each strike. He is highly intelligent and a skilled manipulator. The age difference between his victims and their wives is dropping an average of five years with each murder."

"The victims are getting younger?"

"No. The wives are getting older. As, of course, is our killer."

Danny thought about this, grasping for something that had eluded him up to now. The age thing felt significant, but he didn't know why. After a long silence, he asked, "Do you think the wives are dead?"

Richard Sturi hesitated. "Probably. There is no plausible reason, at least none that I can think of, for him to keep them alive."

"Except for Lisa Baring," Demartin said again.

Except for Lisa Baring. How Danny wished Matt Daley had gotten further with Mrs. Baring. He'd picked a hell of a time to drop off the radar.

"Okay. Division of labor. As you know, we've only been allotted eight hours per week of official work time on Azrael. We all have other cases that need our attention, so I don't want to overload you. Richard, I want you to keep doing what you're doing. But nothing goes directly onto the I-24/7 database. Any stats and projections connected with this investigation come to me first. Understood?"

The German raised an eyebrow but nodded his consent. Delaying the inputting of data onto Interpol's systems was highly irregular. But not as irregular as disobeying a direct instruction from a superior officer.

"Claude, for now I need you to focus on forensics. See if there's anything in the semen, blood or fingerprint analyses that the local police missed."

"Yes, sir. If you don't mind my asking, what will you be working on?"

"I'm going to make a few inquiries in Los Angeles," said Danny. "There's a man there I'd like to talk to again. An attorney by the name of Lyle Renalto."

Inspector Liu could not reach Assistant Director Danny McGuire. According to McGuire's secretary, an obstructive French matron named Mathilde, McGuire was at a meeting and was not expected back in the office "for some time." So much for Interpol's promised 24/7 support.

Irritated, Liu left a message.

Mrs. Baring had a lover whom they now suspected of involvement in her husband's murder. As such, Mrs. Baring herself was now a suspect in the investigation. She remained in Bali, and photographic evidence suggested that this man was staying with her there. Could Assistant Director McGuire organize an Interpol response team to help Liu and his men gain access to the villa and, if necessary, arrest the suspects? The Indonesian authorities were being less than helpful.

Hanging up, Liu looked at his watch. Four P.M., Hong Kong time.

If he didn't hear from McGuire by morning, he'd take matters into his own hands.

Céline McGuire was not a happy woman.

She was not happy because the *boeuf bourguignon* she had so painstakingly cooked for her husband had been reduced to a viscous, charred mass at the bottom of a casserole dish.

She was not happy because she'd

done her hair and put on her prettiest dress, all for nothing.

She was not happy because all the excuses Danny was about to give her for his lateness would be lies, but she was too frightened to challenge him with the truth:

Angela Jakes was back in their lives.

Sometimes Céline likened Angela Jakes to a mistress. *Pretty pathetic to be jealous of a woman your husband has never made love to and never will, a woman who's almost certainly dead.* This time around, Céline saw Angela more as an addiction, like alcohol or crystal meth or a glistening white line of freshly cut cocaine. After five happy years, Danny had fallen off the wagon. The addict's lies had already started.

"Frémeaux called me into a meeting."

"Mathilde's off sick so I got stuck with a load of paperwork."

"The IRT division's up for a review next month. I'm gonna have to put in some extra hours."

Céline had checked out each story, but she already knew what she'd find. *If you want to lie through your teeth,*

Danny, you shouldn't have married a fellow detective. He hadn't even had the balls to tell her that a new investigation—Azrael—had been authorized, still less that he was heading the team. But if Danny's lies were laughably transparent, Céline's own tactics were just as risible. Fancy meals. Date nights. Sexy clothes. As if she stood a chance against his addiction. Against Angela.

"Sorry I'm late." Danny burst through the door, a stack of files under one arm and a bursting-at-the-seams briefcase under the other. "You didn't cook, did you?"

"What do you think?" snapped Céline, glancing over her shoulder at the smoky remains of the beef.

Danny looked stricken. "I'm sorry, honey. You should have told me."

"I should have told you? *I* should have told *you*?" She stormed past him, an angry flash of red silk, grabbing her coat from the peg by the door on her way out. "Fuck you, Danny. And fuck Azrael."

Before Danny could say another word, she was gone.

Azrael. So she knows already. Shit.

His instinct was to go after her, but he knew from experience that when Céline was *this* mad she needed space. Anything he said to her now would only fan the flames of her wrath. Wearily, he set down his work on the kitchen table. It had been a long, draining, fruitless afternoon. He'd spent most of it on the phone to L.A., tracking down every lead and calling in every favor he could think of in an effort to get hold of Lyle Renalto. But no one had seen or heard of the guy since 1997. He quit his law practice in that year apparently, barely twelve months after Andrew Jakes's murder and ten since Angela's disappearance. The same year Danny left town himself.

According to colleagues, Lyle was supposed to be taking up a new position back in New York—he was from the city originally—but Danny could find no trace of him in any of the public-records databases he checked there. Phone and utility bills, DMV, Social Security Administration, all had drawn a blank. Of course it was early days. But key players in the Jakes investigation had an uncanny tendency to evaporate into thin air just when Danny wanted to talk to them. Already the old feelings of frustration and helplessness and despair had started to return. Back in L.A. in the nineties, Danny had felt as if the truth he was seeking was a wet bar of soap: in his grasp one moment, but slipping through his fingers the next. Was that how it was going to be with Azrael?

He wondered for a moment who had spilled the beans about the investigation to Céline, then let it go. What did it matter, really? He should have told her himself. Now she would never understand, never forgive him. *Unless I solve the case quickly. Unless I succeed this time, catch this bastard and put an end to this nightmare once and for all.*

After a hastily made supper of a Brie-and-*jambon* baguette washed down with ice-cold Sam Adams—the French did a lot of things right but beer wasn't one of them—he began working through his mountain of notes. It was almost ten before he got as far as checking his voice mails. Three were internal memos

about budgeting, one was a lead on a
case his division was working on in Bo-
gotá and the fifth was from his mother
in L.A. asking if he'd remembered his
grandmother's ninetieth birthday (he
hadn't). But it was the sixth and final
message, from Inspector Liu, that made
the hairs on Danny's arms stand on
end.

Lisa Baring had a lover. All of a sudden Demartin's wild theory wasn't looking so way out there anymore. Was it
Lyle Renalto, all these years later, using
a different name and identity? He'd be
older, of course, in his late forties by
now, but he was probably still attractive
enough to lure a lonely, bored young
housewife into his net.

Liu said something about him staying
at the Barings' Bali villa. If it were true,
if there was even a chance of it being
true, they couldn't let him slip away
again.

He thought about calling Liu back,
but decided it could wait. What if Renalto, or whoever it was, was packing his
bags right now, and Lisa's. Spiriting her
away so he could kill her like he had the

others? Liu had asked for help with the local Balinese police, and that's what Danny was going to give him.

Danny dialed the number for the Interpol switchboard.

"I need clearance for an operation in Bali. Put me through to the chief of police in Jakarta."

Inspector Liu checked his BlackBerry. Still no word from Lyon.

Interpol could go fuck itself and so could the Indonesians.

This is my investigation. I'm done asking for permission.

The call to Indonesia did not go well.

They had not requested Interpol assistance and knew nothing about the Azrael murders.

The Hong Kong police had already made a nuisance of themselves, harassing private citizens on Indonesian territory. Having failed to observe the basic courtesies, Inspector Liu now had the audacity to demand their cooperation, asking them to issue an arrest warrant despite having provided no evidence of any criminal activity by anybody at Villa Mirage.

Inspector Liu (and Interpol) could stick their demands where the sun didn't shine.

Depressed, Danny returned to his mountainous to-do list, but his heart wasn't in it. Maybe he should call Céline? She still wasn't home, which was unlike her. After a fight, she typically stormed off for a few hours then came home a few glasses of wine later ready for a screaming match and some passionate make-up sex.

Pushing the paperwork to one side, a fax cover sheet slipped out of the file; Danny noticed that it was also from Liu's office in Hong Kong. How had he missed it earlier? Behind the cover sheet was a scanned photograph. It was black and white and grainy. Clearly it had been taken from some distance. It showed a man and a woman on a balcony, embracing. Danny looked at the man closely, scanning what little he could see of his features for any resemblance to Lyle Renalto. It was impossible. The picture quality was too poor. Although there *was* something familiar about the image. The shape of the head, the stance as the man extended his hand toward the woman—Mrs. Baring, presumably—the way that the facial features looked stretched out, almost as if he were cracking a huge smile . . .

Danny's stomach lurched.

Oh my God. No.

It can't be.

Shaking, he picked up the phone.

CHAPTER SEVENTEEN

Matt Daley was sitting by the pool, enjoying the sunset and sipping one of Mrs. Harcourt's perfectly mixed gin and tonics, when his cell phone rang. Danny McGuire's number flashed across the screen.

Damn, thought Matt. He felt guilty about McGuire. Guilty that he'd been avoiding the guy's calls, guilty that he hadn't told him about Lisa. He couldn't fully explain his silence, even to himself. It was just that what he had with Lisa felt so private and so precious, he was scared that once he cracked the door to the outside world, the floodgates would open and the dream would be shattered.

But he had to talk to McGuire at some point. For one thing, there was still a deranged killer out there, a maniac who had to be caught, for Lisa's sake as much as anyone's. Bracing himself for the inevitable abuse, he picked up.

"Danny, hi. I'm sorry I've been so tough to get hold of."

"Listen to me very carefully, Matt." Danny McGuire's voice sounded strained rather than angry. "You need to get out of there. Right now."

"Out of where?" Matt laughed. "You don't even know where I am."

"You're in Bali, staying at Lisa Baring's villa."

The laugh died on Matt's lips. *How the hell did Danny McGuire know that?* "I was going to tell you."

"Tell me what? That you were lovers?" For the first time a note of anger crept into McGuire's voice.

"Tell you I was here," said Matt stiffly. "That I'd met her. For what it's worth, we aren't lovers." *Yet.*

"It's not me you have to convince," said Danny. "It's Inspector Liu. Were you aware that the Chinese view Lisa Baring as a suspect in her husband's killing?"

Matt laughed out loud. "That's insane. Lisa had nothing to do with Miles's death, and that's a fact."

"Is it? Or do you just want it to be?"

It was a warm night, but Matt suddenly felt a distinct chill in the air.

Danny went on: "She had lovers, Matt. At least one that the police are aware of. Possibly more."

"Bullshit."

"Matt, listen to me. She brought men to the house for sex while Miles was at work."

"You're wrong." *You have to be wrong.*

"It gets worse. Liu thinks you're one of them. His men have been watching the pair of you at the villa. You've been under surveillance for weeks now. You were supposed to be lying low and instead you end up a goddamn suspect!"

"A suspect?" Matt spluttered. "That's ridiculous. I wasn't even in Hong Kong when Miles Baring was murdered."

"I know that," said Danny. "That's why I'm telling you all this now and not racing to have you arrested like Liu and his men. But you haven't exactly helped your own cause, my friend."

"I can't believe the Chinese have been spying on us," Matt said indignantly.

At this, Danny lost his temper. "It's a murder investigation! Hello? You're not out there on vacation. Or had you forgotten?"

Matt hadn't forgotten, but he certainly wanted to. He wanted to forget all of what he'd just heard, especially the lies that McGuire had told him about Lisa. He wanted to take Lisa far, far away, to protect her and love her and never have to think about death or pain or betrayal ever again. He tried to keep calm.

"You don't know Lisa, okay? I do. She would never have cheated on Miles. She just isn't that sort of person."

Danny McGuire's eye roll could practically be heard down the telephone line. "Come on, man . . ."

"And even if she did, so what?" Matt's voice grew increasingly desperate. "It doesn't make her a killer."

"No, it doesn't. But it might make her an accomplice."

"To what, her own rape?"

"Maybe it wasn't rape. Maybe it was consensual."

"Take that back," Matt said quietly.

"I'm sorry," said Danny, picking up the hurt and anger in Matt's voice. "I'm not saying this is what *I* think."

"I should hope not."

"I still have no idea what happened that night. But Liu has Lisa in his sights, and he has good reason for it. She *did* have a boyfriend—still does, for all we know. She was the only person who stood to gain financially from Miles's death. She instructed her staff not to come to the top floor the night of the attack. She was the only person, other than her husband, who knew how to disable the security alarm. And by the way, it *was* disabled earlier in the day, if you want to talk about facts. Whoever killed Miles Baring had inside help."

Matt didn't want to hear it. "If Liu had enough evidence to arrest Lisa, he'd have done it. But he hasn't. He's grasping at straws because he's got nothing.

Just like you had nothing in the investigation of my father's murder."

It was a low blow, but Danny had no choice but to suck it up. All he wanted was for Matt Daley to get out of Bali, before this whole thing blew up in both their faces. If anyone linked Matt Daley to Danny McGuire, Operation Azrael would be over and so would Danny's career.

"Do you remember what you said to me the day we met, in my office in Lyon?" Danny asked.

"'What kept you so long, you time-wasting bastard'?" quipped Matt.

"After that. You said: 'It's the wives. They're the key to all this.' Do you remember that?"

"Not Lisa."

"Why not Lisa?" Danny challenged him. "Because you're in love with her?"

Yes! "No. Of course not."

"How long have you known this woman, Matt? A month? Two? Has it occurred to you she might be using you?"

"Hmm, let me see," said Matt. "She's a drop-dead gorgeous millionairess;

and I'm an out-of-shape, bankrupt, soon-to-be-divorced ex–comedy writer. Yeah, I can see where you're coming from. She's definitely using me."

Danny smiled. Daley was infuriating, but his deadpan humor still hit home.

"I meant, using you for information. You know as much about these murders as the police, if not more. If Lisa's boyfriend was behind them . . ."

"He wasn't."

"How do you know?"

"Because she doesn't have a boyfriend! Haven't you been listening to a word I said?"

Danny's exasperation got the better of him. "Let me break it down for you. If you don't get out of that villa—assuming you aren't hacked to death in your bed by your girlfriend's lover in the meantime—Liu's men *will* arrest you and they *will* throw you into some stinking Chinese jail, and I will *not,* repeat *not,* come riding to your rescue."

"Fine," said Matt petulantly. He hung up the phone.

"Hey. Is everything all right? I heard you shouting."

Lisa walked out to the pool. She wore a long midnight-blue kimono robe belted at the waist and her long hair loose, brushed, clearly ready for bed. Matt lit up at the sight of her. *She's an angel. My angel. I mustn't worry her with this nonsense.*

"Everything's fine." Matt forced a smile. "Nothing to worry about. Just a misunderstanding with a friend."

"Someone from home?"

Home. Wasn't this home?

"Sort of."

Lisa flicked a switch and the stone fire pit burst into life. The flames cast a warm orange glow over her skin. "May I sit with you?"

Matt's smile broadened. "Of course." He patted the seat beside him. The urge to reach out and touch her was so strong it was unbearable. "Have you been working?"

"Trying to." A shy smile. "Being the executor of someone's will is harder work than it sounds. The numbers make my eyes swim. I can't seem to concentrate."

They sat in silence for a moment, watching the dancing flames.

"They had a fire pit like this in Positano," Lisa murmured vaguely. "Miles loved it so much he had the same one put in here."

Matt said nothing. He didn't want to talk about Miles or hear about his and Lisa's past vacations. Not now.

Then suddenly Lisa blurted out, "I keep thinking about what happened to me. The rape."

Matt held his breath. It was the first time she had spoken about the night of the attack in months, and the first time he'd ever heard her use the R-word.

"Do you want to talk about it? You don't have to if you don't want to."

Pulling her knees up to her chest, Lisa leaned in against him, slipping a silk-robed arm around his waist. She'd never come this physically close to him before, not of her own accord. Matt closed his eyes, lost in her warmth, her scent—jasmine and patchouli oil—the gossamer caress of her hair. Had he ever felt like this with Raquel? This desperate with longing, this intoxicated with desire? If he had, he couldn't remember. In fact, at this moment he could barely remember his wife at all.

When Lisa spoke, her voice was quiet but firm. "I want to talk about it. I need to. I need to talk about it with you."

Afterward, Matt Daley would struggle to remember every detail of that night. Lisa pouring her heart out about the rape. Nervously at first, her voice halting and awkward, but becoming surer as her fear turned to anger. She told him how the man had punched her and choked her, forcing her to perform hideous, perverted acts while Miles watched. How she had tried to detach, to separate her psyche from the vicious assaults on her body. How she knew all along that the man would hurt Miles, but yet how shocked, how terrified she was when she saw the gun.

Her words speeded up, a snowball of pain gathering speed and bulk as she hurtled through the whole, awful story. Then suddenly, *bang,* the snowball exploded, her anger spent, and the tears began to flow.

She sobbed in Matt's arms. "He shouldn't have done it. He knew I didn't want him to do it. I told him to stop, I begged him! But what could I do? What power did I have? What power have I ever had?"

She was rambling, her words a complex mixture of emotions, part sorrow, part anger and part guilt. It was the last part that tortured Matt the most, although he knew it was common for rape victims to feel guilty, as if they were somehow to blame for what had happened to them. The last thing Lisa needed was Inspector Liu or Danny McGuire trying to implicate her with their half-baked theories. He had to protect her from that.

She cried for what felt like hours. Matt cried too—for her, for himself, for the violent, twisted world that allowed this sort of horror to happen to an innocent, beautiful woman like Lisa. Somewhere during that long, tearful embrace, the last barriers between them fell, the last shards of restraint gave way.

Matt couldn't remember who had undressed whom or who had initiated the first kiss. All he remembered was giving himself to Lisa body and soul, surrendering in a way he had never surrendered to a woman before. And Lisa gave herself to him just as fully, her need and longing every bit as great as his own. Their lovemaking was beautiful. *She* was beautiful, silken and warm and all-consuming. They made love under the stars on the deck by the pool, then in the water. Then Matt dried her like a child and carried her to the bedroom and she begged him to do it again, and again and again. That was the most wonderful thing of all. Lisa's desire, her hunger, was a glorious surprise after so many long weeks of diffidence and uncertainty. It was as if Matt had unlocked a door and another woman entirely had taken control of Lisa's body: a sexual, wanton, completely uninhibited woman.

Matt moaned with pleasure as she took him in her mouth, then straddled him, bucking and gasping as she exploded into yet another orgasm. When she climaxed she dug her nails into his back, pulling him inside her as if she wanted to consume him, to possess him. Matt joyously submitted, losing himself in the moment. The funny, reserved, thoughtful woman he'd come to know these past few weeks was gone, replaced by this magnificent creature, this animal, ravenous, desperate and wild.

Matt lost count of the hours they spent exploring each other's bodies. All he knew was that they were still awake, wrapped in each other's arms, when the first rays of dawn crept through the shutters. And that sometime shortly afterward he sank into a deep, delicious, utterly sated sleep.

When he woke, bright sunlight stung his eyes like acid. Protectively pulling the bedclothes up around Lisa, Matt raised his forearm to shield himself from the glare. Mrs. Harcourt must have opened the blinds, her way of saying that she needed to make up the room.

"Karen, would you mind closing those please?" Matt rasped. "We, er . . . we had a late night."

A brusque male voice shouted something in Indonesian and it suddenly hit Matt: *That's not the housekeeper.* Before he could say or do anything, six armed police had surrounded the bed, guns drawn.

"Lisa Baring?"

Lisa stirred.

Then opened her eyes.

Then screamed.

"Lisa Baring. We have a warrant for your arrest."

"On what charge?" demanded Matt.

The Chinese officer looked at him and smiled. Then he smashed his gun into the side of Matt's face. The world faded to black.

CHAPTER EIGHTEEN

Lisa Baring looked intently at the man sitting opposite her. The last time she'd seen Inspector Liu was in her hospital room at the Queen Elizabeth Hospital. On that occasion she'd paid little attention to him, a grave mistake, as it turned out. She remembered Liu only as short, physically nondescript and deferential. Despite his frustration about her refusing police protection, he had treated her with the respect due to a patient, a rape victim, and the widow of an important and powerful man.

Today, he looked different. Transformed. As he sat behind a Formica-topped desk in this plain white interview suite in Hong Kong's Central District, his round face, glossy black hair and small, neatly manicured hands remained the same as she remembered, as did his cheap suit and thin polyester tie. But his manner had changed utterly. His formerly placid features seemed suddenly to have come alive, his mouth animated, his eyes glinting with something that Lisa couldn't quite place. *Excitement? Cruelty?* His body language was aggressive, legs apart, hands spread wide on the table, torso and head thrust forward. *He thinks he's in control, and he likes it.*

"I'll ask you again, Mrs. Baring. How long have you and the man you were arrested with this morning been lovers?"

"And I'll answer you again, Inspector. His name is Matthew Daley. And it's none of your goddamn business."

She knew she was provoking him, probably not the smartest thing to do under the circumstances, but she couldn't seem to help herself. He was so arrogant, so *rude.* And the things he was suggesting about Matt were just preposterous.

It was strange how confident she felt, under the circumstances. When she'd awoken this morning in her bedroom at Mirage to find six men training guns on her head, the flashbacks to Miles's murder were so strong she honestly thought she would pass out. If Matt hadn't been there to calm her down, she probably would have. *Darling Matt.* How could anyone think he was mixed up in any of this? She wondered where he was now, and prayed he wasn't being mistreated. She'd had no time to process what had happened between them last night, what with being frog-marched onto a plane, bundled into a squad car and dumped unceremoniously into this bleak interview room in a squat building in Central with the obnoxious Inspector Liu firing questions at her like poison darts.

Closing her eyes, Lisa could feel Matt Daley's hard, passionate body pressed against hers. The rush of desire was so strong, she blushed. But it was mingled with other emotions. Fear. Guilt. It was so hard to untangle anything of what she was feeling with the awful Liu breathing down her neck. Still, she was not as afraid as she thought she would be.

Because I'm not alone anymore. I have Matt now. Matt will save me.

The door opened.

"Lisa, darling. I got here as fast as I could."

Not Matt Daley, but a salvation of sorts. John Crowley, Lisa's attorney, was the managing partner at Crowley & Rowe, one of Hong Kong's leading law firms. In his midfifties, tall, dark and distinguished-looking, John Crowley positively radiated authority. He wore monogrammed cuff links and a bespoke suit that cost more than Inspector Liu earned in a year, and smelled of Floris aftershave and self-assurance. Lisa noticed the way Liu visibly shrank in his presence.

"John! How did you know where to find me? They wouldn't let me call."

"I know," said Crowley, taking a seat without being asked. "Just one of Inspector Liu's many breaches of proto-col. I was contacted by a friend of yours, a Mr. Daley."

Lisa's eyes widened. "They've re-leased Matt already?"

"Naturally. Once he produced his passport, it became clear he wasn't even in the country on the night of Miles's murder. Any suggestion of his involvement is pure fantasy. As is any suggestion of yours." John Crowley looked at his vintage Cartier watch impatiently. "Inspector Liu, on what grounds are you detaining my client?"

"We have the necessary authority." Liu handed over a stack of papers, ap-parently warrants, all in Chinese. John Crowley glanced at them as if he were contemplating using them to blow his nose, then tossed them imperiously aside.

"Has Mrs. Baring been charged?"

"Not yet. She's here to answer some questions. There are discrepancies, se-rious discrepancies, between Mrs. Bar-ing's account of what happened on the night in question and her staff's."

John Crowley turned to Lisa. "When were you arrested? What time?"

"This morning. Around ten o'clock, I think. I'm not sure, I was asleep when they broke in."

Crowley looked again at his watch. "That was nine hours ago. Which means that Inspector Liu has a maximum of three additional hours in which to finish his questions. If he doesn't charge you by then, you're free to go."

Inspector Liu glowered at the lawyer. He suspected that Danny McGuire from Interpol was involved in this somehow. That instead of returning his, Liu's, call, McGuire had taken matters into his own hands and contacted the U.S. embassy, preferring to deal with expats than with the local Chinese police. Interpol was supposed to be impartial, but McGuire, Crowley, Lisa Baring, and Matt Daley were all American. Americans had a way of sticking together.

"As you rightly say, Mr. Crowley, time is limited. So I'd appreciate it if you stopped wasting it. Mrs. Baring . . ." Liu turned on Lisa. "At the Queen Elizabeth Hospital you told me that your husband had no living relatives that you knew of that we needed to contact. In fact, as you well knew, Miles Baring had a daughter by his first marriage. Alice."

"That's true. But Miles had no contact with her, nor she with him. After his divorce his ex-wife moved back to Europe and he lost all contact with her and the child."

"A man of your husband's means could easily have taken steps to trace them, or could have instructed his estate to do so after his death. Indeed, Mr. Baring *had* made such arrangements, had he not, before he met you?"

"I . . . I've no idea," Lisa stammered.

"It was you who convinced him not only to marry you but to leave his entire fortune to you upon his death. Isn't that right, Mrs. Baring?"

Lisa opened her mouth to speak, but John Crowley stepped in. "She's already told you, she knew nothing of the provisions in Miles's will before he met her. It's not unusual for men to change their wills in favor of their wives after marriage."

"What *is* unusual, Mr. Crowley, is for

bereaved widows to lie repeatedly to the police who are attempting to apprehend their husband's killer," Liu shot back. "Mrs. Baring, you made a sworn statement that you did not know how to disable the security system at Prospect Road. Yet your maid, Joyce Chan, asserts that Mr. Baring explained it to you on numerous occasions."

"I . . . he might have tried. I'm not very good with technical things."

"Why did you instruct the servants not to enter the upper floors of the property the night your husband was killed."

"I don't remember."

"Was it so that you could admit your lover?"

"No!"

"Do you deny you had a lover?"

"Yes, I deny it. Of course I deny it."

John Crowley did his best to deflect and obstruct, but Liu kept hammering away, insisting that this lover existed, that Lisa had helped him into the house, and demanding over and over again to know his name. Were there so many that she couldn't remember? How many men had she slept with before Miles?

And during the marriage? How many men had she slept with since Miles's death, when she was supposedly grieving? Or was Matthew Daley the only one? How did she know Mr. Daley? She must have invited him to join her in Bali, which implies she knew him from before.

By the time the three hours were up and Inspector Liu released her, on condition that she not leave the island and "cooperate fully" with his investigation, Lisa was emotionally and physically exhausted. But she'd managed not to tell Liu anything about Matt's past. At the end of the day, Matt was a victim too. If he wanted to talk about his father's murder, or his interest in the other crimes, that was up to him.

John Crowley took Lisa's arm as they left the building. The poor thing was still shaking. "You did very well. Try not to worry about it too much. I highly doubt they're going to charge you with anything."

Lisa shook her head. "He looked at me with such hatred. Like I *wanted* this to happen. Like I *wanted* Miles to die. I didn't want any of this. It just happened. Maybe it had to happen, I don't know. But there was nothing I could do to stop it."

John Crowley looked at her strangely. It seemed a bizarre choice of words, to say the least. Why on earth would Miles's murder have "had to happen"? Then again, after the grilling Liu had just put Lisa through, perhaps it was a miracle she could string a sentence together at all.

"You must rest. Can I drive you home?"

Lisa looked at him blankly. *Home?* Where was that? Certainly not the house on Prospect Road. "You said Matt Daley was the one who called you about me. Do you know where he is staying?"

"I'm right here."

Matt's sweet, tired, good-natured face emerged from the sea of Asian faces still crowding the sidewalks even at this time of night. Lisa didn't think she'd ever been so happy to see another person in her life. She fell into his arms.

"Are you okay?" he whispered, hugging her tightly. "Did they hurt you?"

"No. I'm fine." She kissed him, making no attempt to hide her affection in front of John Crowley. The lawyer suppressed an irrational wave of jealousy. He didn't have many clients as attractive as Mrs. Baring, and he'd enjoyed playing her white knight this afternoon.

Matt said, "You must be Mr. Crowley. Thanks for showing up so quickly."

"Not at all. Thank you for contacting me." The two men shook hands. "Everything went well today. I think Liu's grasping at straws. But make sure you don't hand him any ammunition," he added to Lisa. "Stay in Hong Kong, lay low and keep in touch. If the police contact you again, let me know immediately."

"Of course."

Matt watched John Crowley jump into a cab. His eyes narrowed suspiciously. "He's damn good-looking for a lawyer."

Lisa laughed. Wrapping her arms around Matt's neck, she pressed her lips lightly to his. "Are you jealous?"

"Horribly."

They kissed again, and Lisa marveled at how happy she felt, how safe. She'd experienced more than her fair share of male jealousy in the past, and up till now that had only meant pain. But with Matt Daley it was different. Safe in Matt's arms, she could look back and see that most of her life had been spent under a dark cloud of fear, waiting for a man's jealousy to explode in rage and violence, waiting to be hurt. She'd accepted it because it was all she knew. And because of the secret, the secret that had destroyed not only her life but the lives of so many others. The secret to which only one man had the key, and that Matt must never, ever know.

Matt took her face in his hands. "You look so troubled. Is it Inspector Liu?"

"Yes," she lied. "He's out to get me."

"Well, he won't succeed," Matt assured her. "Not while I'm around. Listen, Lisa, I know it's not really the time. And I know last night was unexpected, for both of us. But I have to tell you. I've never felt like this before. I—"

Lisa put a finger to his lips. "Not here.

Liu and his men will probably coming scuttling out of that door any moment."

She was right. A busy street outside of a police station was no place to declare his undying love. Matt stretched out his arm. A cab stopped instantly.

"The Peninsula."

Lisa raised an eyebrow. The Peninsula was the grandest hotel in Hong Kong. They could afford it, now that the authorities had unfrozen Miles's accounts and allowed Lisa access to his money. But it was hardly lying low.

"I figured if we're going to be kept here under virtual house arrest, we might as well make our cage a gilded one," said Matt. "I want you to be happy."

Lisa knew all about gilded cages. "I'll be happy anywhere," she told him truthfully, "as long as I'm with you."

If only I could stay with him forever.

If only I could tell him the truth.

But she knew she never would.

* * *

Their suite was generous. There was a small, exquisitely furnished living room and two full-size marble baths adjoining a grand double bedroom with spectacular harbor views. After a hot shower and a room-service club sandwich, Lisa felt revived enough to talk to Matt about her interview with Inspector Liu.

"He had new information. He must have spoken to Joyce Chan. Frightened her into speaking out."

"Who's Joyce Chan?"

"Our housekeeper at Prospect Road. She's the only one who could have put the idea into Liu's head that I was having an affair."

So that's where the rumor started, thought Matt, remembering his heated conversation with Danny McGuire. *Malicious servant's gossip.*

"Spiteful bitch."

"Oh no!" Lisa looked horrified. "No, no, Mrs. Chan's lovely. She would never knowingly try to hurt me."

"Then why on earth would she say such a thing?"

"Because she was frightened," said Lisa. "And because it's true."

* * *

"I haven't been fully honest with you."

It was twenty minutes later and the two of them were in bed. Naked, wrapped in each other's arms . . . it felt like the right time to share confidences.

"I wanted to. But I didn't know where to start."

"That's okay." Matt stroked her hair soothingly. The truth was, he hadn't been fully honest with Lisa either. She still knew nothing about his connection with Interpol and Danny McGuire. All this time she'd been sharing her home, and now her bed, with a police mole. If that wasn't a betrayal, he didn't know what was.

Nervously, stumbling over her words, Lisa told Matt about the affair. There had only been one lover, not a string of them, as McGuire had implied. She'd denied the relationship to the police in order to protect the young man involved. She had never loved him, nor he her, but he'd helped alleviate the loneliness of her marriage to Miles.

"When Miles and I dated, we were intimate. It wasn't the most passionate relationship in the world—Miles was a lot older—but we did make love. But after we married, things changed. Miles was kind to me and affectionate. But he put me on a pedestal in his mind. As if I were this pure, untouchable thing. Relations between us were . . . rare."

For a second, Matt felt an affinity with Miles Baring. Lisa was incredibly desirable. Yet at the same time she was *so* perfect, *so* good, he understood the urge to cast her as a Madonna, something to be worshipped rather than defiled.

"It was a sex thing, then. Between you and this man?"

Lisa blushed and looked away. "Do you hate me?"

Matt pulled her close, breathing in the warm scent of her. "I could never hate you. You're everything to me."

Lisa looked pained. "Don't say that."

"Why not? It's true. You know it's true. I think I might hate *him,* but that's a different matter. And I certainly don't think you should be protecting him at your own expense."

"I have to protect him," said Lisa.

"Why?"

"Because. It's my duty. We promised not to reveal each other's identity."

"Yeah, but that was before Miles was murdered and you were raped. That kind of changes things, don't you think? Liu obviously suspects he was involved."

Lisa shook her head in silent misery. "Nothing changes a promise. Breaking a vow is wrong. It's wrong." She rolled away from him to the other side of the bed.

"How well do you know this guy?" asked Matt, his blood running cold. What if Inspector Liu and Danny were right? Not about Lisa being an accomplice to the murder of her husband—that was ridiculous—but about her lover being the killer? He clearly still had some sort of hold over her.

Lisa answered with her face to the wall. "How well does anybody know anyone?" *More riddles.* "How well do you and I know each other, if it comes to that?"

The echoes of Danny McGuire's words were uncomfortable. Had that conversation really only been last night? It felt like a lifetime ago.

"Tell me his name, Lisa."

"I can't. I'm sorry."

Matt said bitterly, "You don't trust me."

Lisa turned back around, propping herself up on her elbow, her magnificent breasts tumbling onto the Frette sheets between them. "I do trust you, Matt," she said indignantly. "You have no idea what a big deal that is for me. At least I'm being honest, which is more than I can say for you."

"What do you mean?"

"That phone call last night. You brushed it off when I asked you about it. But it wasn't just a 'misunderstanding with a friend,' was it? It was about me."

Matt sighed. "Okay. Yes, it was." After all this time it was a relief to admit it. He told her about Danny McGuire, how he'd worked on the original investigation into Andrew Jakes's homicide and since moved to Interpol, but how Matt had tracked him down and told him

about the other murders, of Didier Anjou and Piers Henley.

"The other widows all disappeared,
as you know, but you were still safe, at
the Queen Elizabeth Hospital. I flew out
here to find out what I could and report
back to McGuire."

The blood drained from Lisa's face.

"And did you? 'Report back,' I mean?
Oh my God. Is that why you slept with
me? To try to get more information out
of me, to get me to open up?"

"No!" Matt shook his head vehe-
mently. "That's why I came out here,
but once I met you, everything changed.
I haven't contacted McGuire once, I
swear. That was part of the reason he
was pissed at me last night on the
phone. I disappeared on him."

Lisa drew her knees up to her chest,
the sheet wrapped defensively around
her. She thought about what Matt had
said. Eventually she asked him, "What
was the other part? You said that was
'part of the reason' he was pissed. What
was the other part?"

Matt swallowed. In for a penny, in for
a pound. He might as well tell her now.

"He'd spoken to Liu. He told me you were cheating on Miles and that he thought you might have been an accessory to his murder."

Lisa gasped.

"I know, I know. I told him he was blowing smoke out of his ass, that you had nothing to do with it. But he wanted me to leave you, to get out of Mirage and come home. Liu had pictures of you and me together. He'd put two and two together and made about a thousand. I think Danny was worried that if I got arrested it would come out that he and I were working together. The folks at Interpol aren't too thrilled about having amateurs meddling in their cases. Danny might have gotten in trouble, or at the very least been pulled off the case."

"So you knew I was cheating on Miles," said Lisa. "You knew and it didn't bother you?"

"I didn't know. McGuire told me you were, but I didn't believe him. It didn't jibe with the Lisa I know."

The Lisa you know! It was so poignant, so pathetic in a way, Lisa didn't know whether to laugh or cry.

Matt said, "I love you so much. I don't care what happened before you and I met."

"You should, Matt. The past—"

"—is gone. You know, last night Danny McGuire asked me the same question you just did: How well do I really know you? How well do you really know me? And you know what the answer is?"

"What?"

"The answer is, we know what we need to know. We know we love each other. That's enough."

Lisa stroked his cheek tenderly. "You don't really believe that, do you?"

"Yes. I do."

"But what if someone's past is a nightmare. What if it's worse than you can possibly imagine? What if it's unforgivable?"

"Nothing's unforgivable." Matt reached for her. "I'm not in love with your past, Lisa. I'm in love with you."

Their lovemaking was more restrained than it had been the previous night.

Less explosive, but closer, more tender. If Matt had had any doubts about Lisa's feelings, they evaporated at the touch of her hand, the caress of her lips on his skin, his hair, the soft, lulling cadence of her voice. *I love you, Matt. I love you.*

Afterward Matt called room service and ordered two whiskeys. It was very late, past one, but both of their minds were racing.

Matt spoke first. "Let's run away together."

Lisa laughed. She adored Matt's sense of humor. She'd laughed more since meeting him than at any time she could remember, despite the desperate circumstances.

"I'm serious. Let's take off."

"We can't," said Lisa, putting a finger to Matt's lips.

"Sure we can. We can do whatever we want."

"Shhh." Lisa snuggled into him, her heavy eyes at last beginning to close.

"I'm serious," said Matt.

"So am I. Now go to sleep."

* * *

By the time Lisa opened her eyes, Matt was already at the desk, hammering away at his laptop. He'd had the fore- thought to have Mrs. Harcourt send over both his and Lisa's computers from Bali in the Barings' private plane, along with a small case of clothes and other essentials. They'd arrived at the Penin- sula overnight.

Lisa watched him work, naked except for a small white towel knotted at his waist. *He's so beautiful,* she thought with a pang. Not model handsome like some of the men she'd known over the years, but sexy in his own warm, loving, quirky way. She allowed herself a mo- ment's fantasy: she and Matt, married, happy, living far away from Hong Kong, far away from the rest of the world. Safe. Free. Together.

Catching her staring, Matt looked up and smiled. "Breakfast?"

Lisa grinned. "Sure. I'm starving."

They ordered fresh fruit salad and croissants with hot coffee and a side of crispy bacon for Matt. Lisa ate hers in bed, but Matt remained glued to the screen.

"What are you doing?" she asked him eventually, spooning the last of the honey onto her third croissant and biting into it greedily.

"I told you last night," said Matt. "Planning our escape."

"And I told *you* last night," said Lisa. "We can't just disappear together. Inspector Liu only released me from custody on condition that I stay in Hong Kong. Remember what John Crowley said last night? Don't give him any ammunition. It's vital that we play things by the book."

Matt closed his computer. "Screw John Crowley."

"Matt, come on. The jealous boyfriend shtick's cute and all, but this is serious."

"I know it is. Lisa, the Chinese police are trying to frame you for Miles's murder. They've already got Interpol buying into their theory, that you and your mystery boyfriend staged the whole thing. Just because Liu hasn't charged you yet doesn't mean he's not going to."

"But he's got no evidence."

"Sure he has evidence. It's circumstantial, and it's bullshit, but convictions have been built on less, believe me. If you continue to refuse to name this other guy—"

"We've been through that." Lisa sounded exasperated.

"I know. I'm not trying to change your mind. I'm simply stating the fact that they don't have him, but they *do* have you. And a bird in the hand is worth two in the bush. Liu knows that the American, British and French police were all left with a fistful of feathers. He won't let you go till he's made something stick."

Lisa hesitated. It wasn't that the idea of running away with Matt Daley wasn't appealing. It was wonderful, a fantasy, a dream. But it couldn't be done. *Could it?*

"Every day we stay here, we're like sitting ducks," said Matt. "Either for Liu or for the killer, whoever he is. Is that what you want?"

No. You're right. It's not what I want. But my life isn't about what I

want. It's about what I have to do. My duty. My destiny.

"If I run, I'll look guilty."

"You *look* guilty now, angel. I'm afraid that's part of the problem. The tabloids already hate you."

"Thanks a lot!" Lisa tried to make light of it, but the laugh caught in her throat. Matt walked over to the bed and kissed her.

"I'm just being realistic."

"I know you are." Lisa pushed aside her breakfast. She wasn't hungry anymore. "So what do we do? Theoretically, I mean, in this grand escape plan of yours. Where would we go?"

Grabbing his laptop from the desk, Matt brought it over to the bed. He clicked open a map of the world.

"You tell me."

He wanted to pick somewhere special, someplace that Lisa had happy memories of. But he realized when he woke up this morning that he still knew next to nothing about Lisa's life before she met Miles. She was American, raised in New York. Her parents were both dead and she had no family, save for one estranged sister. She was obviously well traveled. Her conversation was peppered with references to Europe and North Africa. And at some point she'd taken a job in Asia, where she'd met Miles. But that was it. If she had roots anywhere, Matt didn't know about them.

"Where do you think you'd be happy?"

Where would I be happy? I've been to so many wonderful places. Rome, Paris, London, New York. I've soaked up the sun on a Malibu beach and swum in the Mediterranean off the Italian Riviera. But have I ever truly been happy?

"Anywhere significant. Anywhere that means somewhere to you . . . outside of the States, obviously. I don't think it'd be the smartest move for either of us to go back there."

Lisa stared at the map, her mind a blank. Then suddenly the answer came to her, as blindingly obvious as the nose on her face. She stroked the screen lovingly with her finger.

"Morocco. I'd like to go to Morocco."

CHAPTER NINETEEN

"I'm not happy about this, McGuire. Not happy at all."

Henri Frémeaux didn't look happy. Then again, Henri Frémeaux never looked happy.

"I understand that, sir."

"We are here to assist and facilitate. *Assist* and *facilitate*. Which part of those two words do you not understand?"

"I do understand, sir."

"Oh, really? Then why do I find myself on the receiving end of an extremely tense telephone call with Hong Kong's chief of police, informing me that the

Azrael team has been obstructive, difficult and unavailable, and that . . ."—he consulted his notes—"Inspector Liu cannot even get his phone calls returned."

"With all due respect, sir, Liu asked me to 'assist' him by liaising with the Indonesian authorities. I was in the process of doing that when he decided to take matters into his own hands, arresting at least one innocent American citizen and possibly two. The legality of his actions was dubious at best."

"I'm not here to pass judgment on how the Hong Kong Chinese conduct their affairs!" Frémeaux shot back angrily. "My job is to see to it that we, Interpol, are doing *our* job. These protocols exist for a reason, you know."

Yeah, thought Danny, *to satisfy uptight pen pushers like you.*

Still, he could understand Henri Frémeaux's irritation. So far the Azrael task force had made little or no headway, other than Richard Sturi's brilliant statistical analysis; but without any forthcoming arrest on the horizon, that too was academic. Azrael had also taken up a phenomenal amount of time and resources, far more than the eight man-hours Frémeaux had grudgingly allotted. It was mostly Danny McGuire's time, although Danny had just sent Claude Demartin on a fact-finding mission to Aix-en-Provence to delve deeper into the scant DNA evidence surrounding Didier Anjou's murder. *Thank God Frémeaux doesn't know about that yet. Or about Matt Daley's involvement in the Hong Kong fiasco. Then we'd really be up shit creek.*

"I'll give you a month, McGuire," Henri Frémeaux grunted. "That's assuming I get no more calls from member countries complaining about your attitude."

"You won't, sir. I guarantee it."

"If I don't see tangible progress in that time—and by *tangible* I mean something that justifies the money we're spending chasing our tails—Azrael is finished."

Danny McGuire walked back to his own office despondent. Céline was barely talking to him. At work, his own IRT division, who had always been extremely loyal to him personally, was starting to get pissed at the amount of time he was devoting to Azrael, which most of them considered to be the wildest of wild-goose chases. When he started all this, he'd thought of Matt Daley as a partner, a fellow American who cared about catching the Jakes killer, as Danny still thought of him, as much as he did. But now even Matt had deserted him, apparently besotted by the beautiful Mrs. Baring, the latest of the widows. It was a long time since Danny McGuire had felt this alone. Not since the wilderness years, after Angela Jakes went missing.

Initially he'd been focusing his own energy on trying to track down Lyle Renalto, unable to shake the idea that Angela Jakes's lawyer was a key piece of the puzzle. It was Claude Demartin who'd put forward the "lover-killer" theory, although the seeds of Danny's distrust in Lyle Renalto had been sown more than a decade ago, when first they'd met at Angela's hospital bedside. But after weeks of intensive digging, trawling through databases in every country connected with Azrael, as well as all the major U.S. cities, he'd drawn a complete and total blank. The first official reference to Lyle Renalto was a tax return filed in Los Angeles just a year before Andrew Jakes was killed. Before that, there was nothing. And a year after the murder, *poof,* he was gone again, as if he'd never existed.

Angela Jakes's words on the night of the murder floated back across Danny's mind. *"I have no life."* Lyle Renalto had no life either. Officially, neither Angela nor Lyle had either a past or a future. Looking for some sort of pattern, Danny began digging into the backgrounds of the other victims' widows, Tracey Henley and Irina Anjou. In both cases it was the same thing. There were marriage certificates, but no birth certificates. No family had ever come forward to search for these missing women, or even officially to report them missing. They too apparently "had no life" before or after the terrible crimes that came to define them.

"Oh, there you are. I've been trying to get hold of you all morning." Mathilde, Danny's secretary, pounced on him the

moment he walked through the door.
She ran through the long litany of re-
quests and demands on Danny's time,
the myriad other IRT cases that he'd
been neglecting and the names of the
various colleagues who were baying for
his blood. When she was finally done,
Danny headed into his private office. As
an afterthought, Mathilde called out to
him, "Oh, and Claude Demartin called.
He says he has news and would you
call him back as soon as possible."

At the Peninsula, things began moving
at lightning speed. Every morning, almost every hour, Lisa Baring had the
same thought: *I've got to stop this. We
can't simply run away.* But Matt's en-
thusiasm, his self-belief, was so strong
and so intoxicating that she allowed
herself to be swept along with it, to believe the impossible: that maybe, with
him, she *could* escape. Outrun her destiny. Be happy.

Matt spent the bulk of each morning
making Skype calls from his computer.
Having decided air travel was too risky,

he'd planned a route using only boats and trains, booking under false names and transferring money anonymously via DigiCash from Lisa's Alpha Offshore account. Matt hoped that, in Asia at least, a hefty bribe would prove an acceptable alternative to picture ID. The plan was for Matt to leave first, in the small hours of the morning. Assuming they were being watched twenty-four hours a day by Inspector Liu's men, the idea was that Matt's departure would lure the surveillance crew away from the hotel. He would then have to lose them somewhere on the DLR and head for the harbor. This should provide enough distraction for Lisa to slip out at six A.M., dressed in the plain knee-length blue uniform worn by all the Peninsula maids, hopefully without being noticed.

Lisa asked Matt, "How on earth are we going to get hold of a uniform? Hit some poor girl over the head?"

"No. We'll ask her nicely. Failing that, we'll try a fifty-dollar bill and a signed photograph of Matt LeBlanc."

Lisa laughed out loud.

"You think I'm kidding? *Friends* is still

huge over here." Sure enough, he pulled a sheaf of publicity head shots out of a drawer. "You'd be amazed how far these go with our Chinese friends. Like cigarettes in jail."

Lisa shook her head. "So our grand escape plan begins with Joey Tribbiani?"

"Uh-huh. Have some faith, Lise. I know what I'm doing."

After Lisa's getaway, the next stage was a fishing boat to the mainland, where a "fixer"—Mr. Ong—had agreed to arrange their passage via the South China Sea and Sunda Strait to Cape Town. From there a long series of overnight train rides would ultimately bear them north. It would be a month at least before they arrived in Casablanca.

"Simple," said Matt, which made Lisa laugh again, because, of course, the plan was anything but simple. In truth, it was fraught with danger at every turn. But Matt's confidence was unshakable, and the fantasy too sweet and perfect to resist.

We'll live anonymously in some tranquil *riad,* watching the birds flit

around the fountain in the courtyard.
All will be peace and calm and beauty.
He'll never find me.
The madness will end.

At nine o'clock the night before they were due to leave, Matt left a sealed envelope with cash at the front desk. Running for his life or not, Matt Daley wasn't the sort of guy to disappear without paying his bill. Upstairs in their suite, he and Lisa drank a last nightcap of whiskey and settled down for a few short hours of sleep.

The alarm was set for two A.M.

For the plan to work, Matt had to be on his way before three A.M.

Claude Demartin had been on the autoroute for five straight hours before he took the exit marked *Aix-en-Provence*. Skirting the ancient city itself, he finally pulled in outside a nondescript light-industrial complex.

Wedged between the autoroute and the railway line, Laboratoire Chaumures was a forensic facility used by all the police forces of southern France. Two days earlier, Danny McGuire had received a call from one of their senior

research technicians, confirming that
the lab had indeed provided DNA sample analysis on the Anjou murder and
rape case last year.

"But there were no such results filed
in the police case notes," said Danny.

The technician sighed. "No. I'm afraid
that's typical. Unless there's a trial and
the prospect of fortune and glory, the
Tropezien police's attitude to evidence
preservation is laissez-faire, to say the
least."

Thirty-six hours later, Claude Demartin was meeting the technician face-to-
face. His name was Albert Dumas. In
his early fifties, tall, thin and angular,
with a white lab coat so crisp you could
get a paper cut from looking at it, and
a pair of round, wire-rimmed glasses
perched on the end of his volelike nose,
he was instantly recognizable to Demartin as a fellow forensics nerd. The two
men took to each other instantly.

"Come inside, Detective." Dumas
pumped Claude Demartin's hand en-
thusiastically. "I think you'll be excited
by what we found."

Inside, the lab was one giant, open-

plan space, with a series of glass-en-
closed cubicles arranged around the
perimeter. Some of these were offices,
simple, IKEA-furnished affairs. Others
were teaching rooms, set up with white-
boards, benches and laser pointers,
and with banks of microscopes neatly
arranged along the back walls. Others
still were labs. Albert Dumas led Claude
Demartin into one of the offices, where
a neat stack of printouts sat next to a
computer on the desk.

"So the local police kept no record of
this data?" asked Claude.

"So your boss told me. I can't say I
was surprised."

"But you keep your own independent
records?"

Dumas sounded offended. "Of
course. We have semen analysis, hair
analysis, blood work, fingerprints. It's
all here. I've run a comparison with the
data you sent us from the other cases."

"And . . . ?"

"The bad news is that the blood work
you've sent us is pretty much useless."

Claude frowned. *That's supposed to
get me excited?*

"The Henley samples had clearly been contaminated somehow in the Scotland Yard lab."

"How about the Jakes results?"

Albert Dumas flipped through his printouts. "No blood other than the victims' was found at the Los Angeles crime scene. Which was the same with the Anjou case, by the way."

"So we've got nothing?"

"Not quite. Hong Kong was a little more promising. There were three distinct samples taken from the Barings' home. But the blood that did not come from the victims themselves was standard type O, I'm afraid."

"Which narrows our suspect pool to about forty percent of the world population," Claude Demartin said bleakly. "Terrific. So what's the good news?"

"Ah, well." Dumas brightened. "At first I thought there wasn't any. Most of the fingerprints were compromised, so there were no clear matches there, and the semen results were conflicted."

"Conflicted how?"

"Both Mrs. Henley and Mrs. Jakes had had intercourse with their husbands on the nights in question, and there was no ejaculation during the Baring rape. That left us with only one decent semen sample: ours, from Irina Anjou. I sent the data to Assistant Director McGuire's office first thing this morning while you were driving down here, but unfortunately it didn't match with any of the sex offenders on Interpol's systems."

Demartin waited for the "but." *Please let there be a "but."*

"But," Albert Dumas said obligingly, "I had a thought a few hours ago about other physical evidence. There were numerous hair samples collected at the Hong Kong crime scene. Nowhere else. Just at the Baring house."

Claude Demartin vaguely remembered. "The Chinese ran tests on those at the time, though, and got nowhere. And those guys don't mess around. Their forensic facilities are some of the best in the world."

"True. But the Anjou evidence was never logged in any police database. They could only study what they had, and they never had access to our data."

Claude felt the familiar tingle of excitement he always got when a case was about to break. Human behavior was riddled with errors and inconsistencies. But forensic evidence, if properly handled, never lied.

Albert Dumas grinned. "I am now able to tell you, with a hundred percent certainty, that one of the hairs found in Mr. Baring's bedroom—item 0029076 in Inspector Liu's evidence log—is an exact DNA match to the semen retrieved from Mrs. Anjou." He handed Claude Demartin the relevant piece of paper.

"It was the same man," Claude whispered excitedly. "The same killer."

Albert Dumas frowned. "That's for you to decide, Detective. I couldn't possibly hazard a guess."

"But the results . . ."

"Tell us only that the man who inseminated Irina Anjou on May 16, 2005, was the same man whose hair was found in Miles Baring's bedroom. That much is a scientifically provable fact. Anything beyond that is mere conjecture."

Claude Demartin practically ran out to his car.

"Put me through to Danny McGuire. Tell him it's Claude Demartin. I have some news."

The moment Matt Daley's head hit the pillow he felt intensely drowsy. Projecting confidence was one thing. Feeling it was another. The stress of choreographing his and Lisa's escape plan must have taken more out of him than he'd thought.

Once we're away from here, in Morocco, I'll be able to protect her. We'll start again, just the two of us. New jobs, new lives, new identities.

He felt guilty about his sister, Claire, and his mother. It wasn't just Danny McGuire who Matt had disappeared on these past couple of months. It was his entire life back home. His past life, as he was now beginning to think of it. Before he met Lisa. Before he was reborn. His divorce attorney left daily messages, the tones of his e- and voice mails becoming increasingly desperate. If Matt didn't sign this or that paperwork, or show up to this or that hearing, Raquel would get everything.

Everything and nothing, thought Matt. *Let her have it. Lisa has enough money for both of us, and it's not as if we need much.*

He was already half asleep when his cell phone rang.

Danny McGuire.

Wearily, Matt hit ignore then switched the handset off.

The last thing he remembered was Lisa's lissome fingers softly stroking his hair.

"Hi, you've reached Matt Daley. Please leave a message."

Danny McGuire could have wept. He *hadn't* "reached" Matt Daley. No one, it seemed, could reach Matt Daley, not now. His obsession with Lisa Baring had made him unreachable.

"Matt, this is Danny. We have firm forensic evidence placing Lisa Baring's lover at the crime scene on the Anjou case. Are you hearing this? Whoever raped Irina Anjou conveniently left us a hair sample in your girlfriend's bedroom. So you were right. The killings are linked. And I was right. You're in serious danger right now. You need to get the hell away from that woman, and you need to call me back. Please, Matt. Call me."

Danny hung up.

With a heavy heart, he dialed Inspector Liu's number.

Matt Daley had horrible dreams. He woke gripped with panic. *Where am I?*

Everything seemed unfamiliar. The bed. The room. Even the smell in the air was foreign, thick and wet and heavy like a rain-soaked blanket. He sat up. Slowly, things came back to him, like distant objects emerging from a deep fog.

The Peninsula. The escape plan.

I have to get up.

He staggered to the window and opened the blinds. Daylight flooded the room. But it wasn't the pale lemon light of dawn. It was the brilliant blinding glare of midmorning. Something had gone terribly wrong. He'd slept through his alarm. But how?

His head throbbed painfully. *The whiskey . . .* Had he been drugged?

Spinning around, he stared at the empty bed.

Empty bed. It hit him like a punch in the stomach.

The bed was empty.

Lisa Baring was gone.

PART III

PART III

CHAPTER TWENTY

The hotel was glorious. It boasted a sumptuous lobby, hallways lined with red velvet carpets, a spectacular Roman-themed spa and a bedroom suite larger than most Manhattan apartments. Best of all were the views, across Sydney Harbor to the famous opera house, rising like some grand ship with sails billowing against the skyline.

Lisa had always wanted to come to Australia. But not like this.

"What's the matter?"

In linen Ralph Lauren pants and a blue silk shirt, he looked as handsome as ever. With more money to spend than he'd had before, he'd developed expensive tastes in clothes and watches that would have looked flashy on some men, but he wore them well. Then again, he wore everything well.

"Nothing. I'm tired." *Tired of looking over my shoulder. Tired of the nightmares, the loneliness, the deceit.*

Lisa was standing by the window. Walking up behind her, he started rubbing her shoulders.

"Did all that sex with Matt Daley take it out of you?"

"Stop it," she snapped. "He's a nice man, okay? Besides, you were the one who told me to get close to him."

It was true. He had told Lisa Baring to get close to the American, to find out what he knew. Inspector Liu was clearly stumbling around in the dark, like all the other detectives he'd dealt with. But Daley was different. He didn't think like a cop, he thought like a human being, like somebody's son. That alone made him dangerous.

"You fell in love with him, didn't you?"

"Don't be ridiculous," said Lisa. She

didn't want to talk about Matt. Not here. Not with him. She comforted herself that at least, with her out of the picture, Matt would be safe. He'd get over her eventually. Then he could go back to L.A. and his life and pick up where he'd left off. What she wouldn't give to be able to do the same!

She turned around to face him. "Look, I've done what you asked. With Miles. With Matt Daley. I have the money, I can wire it wherever you want. But what about your side of the bargain? When can I see my sister?"

"Soon."

" 'Soon'? Soon when? You promised!"

He grabbed her violently by the throat. Lisa whimpered in fear. How had she ever been attracted to him? Ever trusted him?

"When it's over, that's when. When all the guilty have been punished."

The guilty. Who are the guilty? Was Miles guilty, really? Did he deserve to die? And what about the others, the men you slaughtered all those years ago? What about their poor wives?

There was a time when she'd believed that Miles *was* guilty. When she'd seen the world the way *he* saw it. But meeting Matt Daley had changed all that. It was as if Matt had woken her from a trance, brought her back to reality. But by then it was too late.

He released his grip and Lisa slumped back against the wall, tears streaming down her cheeks. When he reached for her again, she cowered in fear, but this time his touch was gentle, brushing away the tears.

"Don't cry, my angel. Just one more, I promise, and it will all be over. How would you like to go to India?"

"No!" Lisa sobbed. "Please. I can't. I won't."

"Yes, you will . . ." He stroked her hair. "You need to rest first, that's all. Like you said, you're tired. But you know you'll help me in the end. We'll help each other. Remember: your sister's counting on you."

Danny McGuire turned right onto Cliff-wood, enjoying the sensation of the breeze on his face and the warm L.A. sunshine on his back as his open-topped rental car sped up the hill. It had been so long since he'd driven in Los Angeles, and his last memories of the place had been so grim, he'd entirely forgotten how much he had once loved it. Brentwood especially was glorious in the sunshine, with its clean, wide suburban streets lined with blossoming trees of every size and color, its pleasant Spanish-style homes and neatly kept yards, its white picket fences and yellow school buses and smiling, healthy-looking residents.

I must bring Céline here, he thought, *just as soon as she can stand the sight of me again.* Since Claude Demartin's breakthrough at the Chaumures Laboratory, relations had thawed not only with Inspector Liu in Hong Kong but with the French and British police forces too. Even the powers that be at the LAPD were suddenly willing to let bygones be bygones and get behind Operation Azrael. As a result, Henri Frémeaux had finally given Danny a half-decent budget, more manpower and free rein to devote the bulk of his time to the operation for the next six months. Danny was delighted, but Céline had burst into tears when he told her, especially when he announced that he was kicking things off with a monthlong trip to the States.

"So this is how it starts. A month here. Six weeks there. And what about us, Danny? What about our marriage?"

He'd done his best to explain to her. A crazed killer was on the loose. Lives were in danger. But her answer was always the same: "So let someone else save them. You can save other lives here, in Lyon, like you have been doing for the last five years. You can save *us.*" She hadn't even gone to the airport to see him off.

Making a left on Highwood, Danny pushed his marital troubles out of his mind. He was on his way to see Matt Daley at Matt's sister's house and glean what evidence he could about Lisa Baring firsthand. Lisa's disappearance was front-page news in Hong Kong and she was now openly spoken of in the Chinese media as a suspect in her husband's murder. Danny McGuire was reserving judgment.

All he knew right now was that Lisa Baring was a link—*the* link—to the Azrael killer. And that Matt Daley was a link to Lisa Baring.

"You must be McGuire. I guess you'd better come in."

Claire Michaels answered the door with a distrustful look on her face. She was blond, like her brother, and had the same open, animated features, even though at this moment they were set into a scowl.

"Thanks for letting me stop by."

She showed him into the living room. "Matt's upstairs getting dressed. He'll be down in a minute." She started to leave, then apparently thought better of it. "Look," she said to Danny, angry tears in her eyes, "this thing with the Baring woman has really taken it out of him, okay? He's not himself. Ever since he got involved with this stupid documentary, he's changed, but when he met Lisa Baring, it went to a whole new level. He's already lost his marriage, his home and now his heart. I honestly don't think he can take any more."

"I understand, Ms. Daley."

"Michaels. It's Mrs. Michaels," snapped Claire. "I'm married. And I don't think you *do* understand, Mr. McGuire. Matt needs to forget all about this stupid case. He needs to rebuild his life. Why can't you just leave him the hell alone?"

It was at that moment that Matt walked in. Danny hadn't seen him in person since their meeting in Lyon last year. It was all he could do not to gasp. Stick thin, his once-merry eyes sunken in an ashen face and his blond hair graying aggressively at the temples, Matt looked like he'd aged twenty years. No wonder his sister was worried.

"Hello, Danny." They shook hands. Despite his frail appearance, Matt looked delighted to see him.

"Hello, Matt."

Claire's two children ran into the room, jumping up and down at Matt's heels like puppies, trying to get their uncle's attention.

Matt turned to Danny. "Let's sit out in the gazebo. I've got most of my files out there anyway and it's quieter. We won't be disturbed."

* * *

For the next two hours, the two men compared notes. Danny filled Matt in on all the latest developments at Interpol. The DNA evidence, the holes in the backgrounds of all the Azrael wives, and, most recently, the anonymous depositing of large amounts of cash into the bank accounts of two Hong Kong–based children's charities. "We don't know for sure that it was Baring's money. We're having a lot of trouble tracing the funds' origins. But given the timing and the amounts involved, it's looking likely."

This last piece of news seemed to upset Matt immensely.

"Once the money's in, he'll have no reason to spare her. He'll kill her, just like he killed the others!" His eyes welled up with tears. "How could I have fallen asleep? Why didn't I hear something, feel something? He took her, Danny. He snatched her right from my bed. Oh Jesus."

Danny did his best to calm Matt down. "Let's not get ahead of ourselves. First, we don't know for sure that it was

Lisa's money that went to the charities. Second, we don't know for sure that the other widows are, in fact, dead. We don't have any bodies." Matt raised an eyebrow, but Danny pressed on. "Third, you're assuming Lisa was kidnapped. But it's far more reasonable to assume that she left of her own accord."

"No." Matt shook his head.

"But, Matt," Danny said reasonably, "your drink was drugged, right? That had to be her. She needed you unconscious so she could get away."

"No!" Matt slammed his frail fist down on the coffee table. With his rational brain he knew McGuire was right. But his heart wouldn't let him believe it, or at least wouldn't let him acknowledge the truth out loud. "She loved me. She wouldn't have gone willingly."

"I'm not saying willingly, necessarily. Maybe it was under duress. Maybe this guy has some sort of hold over her."

Matt was staring into the middle distance. "We were going to run away together. To Morocco."

Danny looked dumbfounded. "You were *what*?"

"Liu was trying to frame her," muttered Matt. "We had to get away. To disappear."

"And what about me?" said Danny. "Were you going to disappear on me too? I'm not trying to frame anybody, Matt. All I want is the truth. To find out who's been committing these savage murders, to *know* what happened to those women. What might be happening to Lisa Baring right now."

"Don't!" Matt clamped his hands over his ears and squeezed his eyes shut, rocking back and forth like an autistic child. "I can't bear it."

Maybe his sister's right, thought Danny, concerned. *Maybe he really has lost it.* Then he remembered how far gone he himself had been in the dark days after Angela Jakes's disappearance. For all Céline's fears, Danny McGuire had never loved Angela Jakes the way that Matt Daley clearly loved Lisa Baring. But dark thoughts of Angela being tortured, abused or killed had still brought Danny to the brink of a nervous breakdown. Was it any wonder that Matt was so screwed up?

"It's okay," he said quietly. "We'll find her. But we have to work together. And you have to promise me you won't do anything stupid."

"Stupid? Like what?"

"Like taking off again. Like going to look for her yourself. The one thing we do know is that this guy, this killer, is extremely dangerous. Leave any showdowns to the professionals, for Lisa's sake as much as your own."

Matt put his head in his hands. "I can't just do nothing. I can't sit by while she . . . she . . ." His voice trailed off into an anguished moan.

Danny said, "I'm not asking you to do nothing. I'm asking you to help me. Help me to help her."

"How?"

"By talking." Danny switched on his pocket tape recorder. "Tell me about Lisa Baring, Matt. Tell me everything you know."

Later that day, back in his hotel room in Santa Monica, Danny McGuire lay on the bed, eating a big bag of Lay's po-

tato chips and inputting everything Matt
Daley had told him into the Azrael files.

Later, he'd have Richard Sturi work
on the data to see where it fit into his
statistical patterns. Danny had enormous admiration for Sturi, for the way
the German could take raw information
and give it life and meaning, like a potter fashioning a sculpture out of a lump
of clay. But Danny McGuire also respected something that Richard Sturi
would have dismissed as superstitious
nonsense. He respected instinct. Intu-
ition. Especially his own.

What pieces of what Matt Daley had
told him today were important? Of all
the minute details, what leaped out at
him?

Without thinking, Danny started typ-
ing.

New York. Morocco. Sister.

He'd come to L.A. primarily to do
some more hands-on digging into the
whereabouts of Lyle Renalto. But today's meeting with Matt Daley had
changed his mind. Lisa Baring was the
key to all this. If he found out *who* Lisa
was, he stood a chance of figuring out

where she was. And if he found Lisa, Danny McGuire felt sure, he'd find the killer.

A few miles across town, Matt Daley was also in bed, staring at a computer screen.

But it wasn't his computer. It was Lisa's.

He'd thought briefly about handing it over to McGuire this morning. Maybe Danny's crack team of Interpol experts would uncover something that he himself had missed. But the truth was, as much as he liked the man, Matt no longer fully trusted Danny McGuire. He was a good guy and his heart was in the right place. But he wasn't convinced of Lisa's innocence. He hadn't said he suspected her in so many words. But Matt could just sense it, in his questions, his facial expressions, in all the things he didn't say.

Danny McGuire's job was to find the killer, to get a conviction. Matt Daley wanted that too, but it was no longer his primary focus. His primary focus was to save Lisa.

Since smuggling her laptop back from Asia, he'd already searched every crevice of every drive it contained, from old e-mails to photo files to Word documents, looking for something, anything, that might tell him who this man was. Lisa's lover. The one she was protecting. The one who had stolen her from him. But there was nothing. The only lead Matt had was a single vacation photograph, an amateurish shot showing Lisa hand in hand with a man. Lisa's face suggested that the photo was relatively recent, a year or two old perhaps but no more. She was just as Matt pictured her every night in his dreams. But the man's face was obscured by a dazzling light. Very bright sunshine, perhaps, or a reflected camera flash. Both of them were dressed in shorts and T-shirts, and standing in front of an aged stone harbor wall.

Bringing up the photo, Matt examined it again. The wall looked European. *Europe in the summertime.* A sign in the top left-hand corner caught his eye. He zoomed in, waited for the image to refocus, then zoomed in again. At last he saw it, a single word, hand-painted in cursive, italic script: *GELATO.*

Italy! They were in Italy. An Italian harbor. Somewhere on the coast.

With a jolt Matt's mind jumped back to Bali. On the veranda at Mirage with Lisa . . . staring into the fire . . . watching the flames dance the night they first made love . . . What was it that she had said?

"We had a fire pit like this in Positano. Miles loved it."

The man in the picture wasn't Miles Baring. But maybe it had been taken on the same trip to the Amalfi coast.

Was that where she met him? Was that where the nightmare all started, where she somehow fell into his trap?

Matt Daley had promised Danny McGuire he wouldn't do anything stupid. Breaking promises to Danny McGuire was starting to become a bad habit.

Closing the computer with trembling hands, he started to pack.

CHAPTER TWENTY-ONE

David Ishag gazed out the window of his twenty-third-floor office in Mumbai's central business district, grinning like an idiot.

David Ishag wasn't an idiot. Born to an Indian mother and an English father of Jewish descent, David Raj Osman Kapiri Ishag was one of the most well-respected entrepreneurs of his generation. He had engineering degrees from both Oxford and MIT, and was the founder and CEO of Ishag Electronics, India's fastest-growing exporter of component hardware. At forty-eight years old, though he looked much younger, with his mother's smooth coffee skin and his father's strong patrician features, David Ishag was handsome, brilliant and obscenely rich. Although he considered himself Indian—Ishag Electronics had offices all over the world, but the Mumbai tower overlooking Nariman Point would forever be its headquarters—in reality, David Ishag was a true global citizen. Raised in India, educated in England and America, steeped in not one or even two but *three* religions—his mother's Christianity, his father's Judaism, and the Hinduism of his native land—David could fit in almost anywhere. More even than his academic brilliance, it was his global worldview, and his ability to relate to people from all cultures and walks of life, that had made David Ishag the business phenomenon that he was.

This morning, however, his famed commercial acumen was in sleep mode.

This morning, all David Ishag could think about was a beautiful woman's face.

* * *

They had met two months earlier at a charity function. It was one of those tedious, overdone white-tie affairs at the Oberoi, where hedge fund and private equity types bid hundreds of thousands of dollars for lackluster raffle prizes ostensibly in order to "Raise Money for Street Kids" but more truly in order to show off in front of their girlfriends. Normally David avoided these things like the plague. He gave plenty of money to charity, anonymously and by bank transfer, like any normal, decent human being, and had zero interest in being pursued around a ballroom by dozens of frenzied, money-hungry socialites. The women at these events were worse even than the men, shameless gold diggers with faces shot up with Botox and craniums full of nothing at all. They could virtually smell your net worth from across a room, the way trained police dogs sniffed out hidden caches of drugs. They scared him.

Unfortunately, being a prominent member of Mumbai's business com-

munity meant that occasionally David
Ishag had to put in an appearance at
such charitable functions. On this particular evening, for the first time ever, he
was glad he had.

He saw her at a corner table, looking
as bored as he was. Not the arrogant,
affected boredom of the models who
eyed David when he walked in, so intoxicated by their own beauty that they
considered everybody else beneath
them, but the genuine, profound boredom of an intelligent person who finds
herself stuck making small talk with a
table full of braying donkeys.

She was simply dressed in a decid-
edly noncouture black column, but her
beauty needed no adornment. With her
high cheekbones, pale skin and intelligent dark brown eyes, framed by a
sharply cut Cleopatra bob of black hair,
she had a presence, almost an aura
that drew David to her. Catching him
staring, she looked up and smiled.

Her name was Sarah Jane Hughes.
She was a schoolteacher, working for a
charity that helped educate slum children across the subcontinent. She was

Irish, only a few years younger than David and hilariously funny. Her imitations of the investment banking bores at her table had David in stitches for days afterward, just as her haunting face had him skipping out of meetings early just to check if she'd called him back and agreed to go out on a date.

She hadn't.

David Ishag had dated other girls who played hard to get. The smart ones knew that Mumbai's most eligible, and also its most confirmed, bachelor was unlikely to be impressed by neediness. But Sarah Jane wasn't playing. She was genuinely busy, with the children at her school, her teaching, her life. She'd had no idea who David was when they met, and when she found out, she didn't care.

David Ishag already knew he was in love. For him, it was instantaneous. But once Sarah Jane agreed to go out with him, it had taken him a month to persuade her that she felt the same way. Just when he'd started to believe it was never going to happen for him, that the tabloids were right when they said he simply wasn't the marrying type, David had found the woman of his dreams. He was sublimely, ridiculously happy.

The buzzer rang. "Someone here to see you, Mr. Ishag. A young lady."

David's heart soared. *Sarah Jane!* They weren't supposed to see each other till dinner tonight. After she'd accepted his marriage proposal last week—David had wanted to fly her to the perfect romantic location, Mauritius or at the very least Goa, to pop the question, but Sarah Jane point-blank refused to take time off work, so in the end he was forced to produce the ring over dinner at Schwan's—they had a lot to discuss. But David knew that if he had to wait another six hours to see her, he wouldn't get a stroke of work done today. He was delighted she'd bothered to come all this way, leaving her beloved classroom.

But when the office door opened, David's heart sank. *Not Sarah Jane. Elizabeth Cameron. My lawyer.* He'd totally forgotten about their meeting.

Elizabeth Cameron smiled. "Thank you for seeing me at such short notice."

David tried hard to maintain his professional demeanor, but the disappointment was etched on his face. "Not at all, Elizabeth. What can I do for you?"

Elizabeth Cameron was blond, attractive and ambitious. A promising young lawyer, she knew how important a big client like David Ishag was to her firm, not to mention to her own career. *Please, please don't let him shoot the messenger.*

"It's not good news, I'm afraid. Ms. Hughes has returned the documents to us. Unsigned."

"Oh."

If David Ishag looked surprised, it was because he was. The papers in question were a fairly standard prenuptial agreement. Sarah Jane was the one who'd wanted a quick wedding, somewhere private and low-key, with no elaborate preparations. "As soon as you sort out the legals, we'll do it" had been her exact words.

"Are you sure she understood what the papers were?"

Elizabeth Cameron shifted uncomfortably in her seat. "Quite sure. She read them thoroughly. I handed them over myself. Her response was . . . well, it was . . ." She trawled her memory banks for an appropriate word. *Forthright . . . pithy . . .*

"Spit it out, girl," said David with uncharacteristic anger. "What did she say? Exactly."

The lawyer swallowed hard. "Well now . . . exactly . . . she said she wouldn't marry you if you were the last man on earth. She said I could give you back your wretched contract, along with this." Reaching out her hand, she pressed an exquisite Bombay sapphire-and-diamond engagement ring into David's palm. "If I'm being completely honest, she did then suggest that you might like to, quote, stick, unquote, both the ring and the documents up your—"

"Yes, yes, I get the picture." David was already on his feet. "Where was she when you saw her? At the school?"

Elizabeth Cameron nodded glumly. "I'm not sure I'd go rushing straight over there, though. She was very, *very* angry. Speaking as a woman now, not as your attorney . . . you might want to give her a chance to cool down first."

"Sound advice, I'm sure," said David, pulling on his coat. "Unfortunately I'm completely incapable of taking it. You see, Ms. Cameron, the trouble is, I love this woman. And if she doesn't marry me, I'm going to have to jump out a window. You'll see yourself out?"

Sarah Jane's colleagues had never seen her so angry. In fact, they'd never seen her angry at all.

Sinéad, the teaching assistant, said, "It's probably just a misunderstanding."

Rachel, the headmistress, said, "Take the day if you need to, Sarah. Go and sort it out."

But Sarah Jane didn't want to "take the day." She wanted to take an ice pick to David Ishag's skull. Yes, theirs had been a whirlwind romance. And yes, in many ways they were still getting to know each other. But if David thought, *dreamed,* that she was going to begin their marriage by signing some horrible, legal insurance policy, clearly he didn't know her at all.

The school where Sarah Jane taught was a one-room building, really little more than a long shed, in the heart of the Dharavi slums. Over a million people lived in this fetid network of alleys and makeshift shelters, spread over half a square mile between Mahim in Mumbai's east and Sion in the west. Two-thirds of that number were children, less than five percent of whom received any formal education at all. The two hundred kids who crammed into Sarah Jane's school building every day were the chosen few, delighted to be there, eager to learn and, in many cases, remarkably bright. Despite the lack of facilities and the hundred-degree-plus heat in which they worked, Sarah Jane and her colleagues considered theirs to be a dream job.

Meeting David hadn't changed that. His daily life might have been about as far removed from hers as it could possibly be. But that was one of the things Sarah Jane loved about India. It was a place of extremes, a place where a love affair like theirs might actually work. Of course, it was probably easier for her to take the sanguine view, from the bottom looking up, than it was for David, with the world at his feet. He might be dark-skinned, and have Raj as a middle name, but when it came to living and working among the poor and dispossessed, Sarah Jane was already far more Indian than he was. David had visited Sarah's school only once. The fear on his face on that occasion as they walked through Dharavi had amused Sarah Jane hugely.

This was his second visit. Walking into the packed schoolroom, he looked even more terrified than he'd looked the first time, but for quite a different reason.

"Can we talk?"

Two hundred chattering kids fell silent in unison. Ms. Hughes's beau was from another planet, rich and handsome and wearing a suit that none of their parents could have afforded if they'd worked a lifetime.

"No."

"Please, Sarah. It's important. I don't know what Elizabeth said to you but—"

"Don't blame your lawyer!" Sarah Jane shot back. "You sent her."

"I did, yes. But if you'd just let me explain."

"I'm teaching."

"Fine." Scared of losing her as he was, David Ishag was no pushover. Pulling a hard wooden chair out from one of the desks at the back of the room, he sat down and folded his arms. "I'll wait."

It was a long wait. An hour. Two. Three. The heat was unbearable. David took off his jacket and tie and, eventually, his shoes. He longed to peel off his sweat-sodden business shirt as well, but felt a full impromptu striptease might not help his cause with Sarah Jane at this point. She was having enough trouble holding her class's attention as it was. If there was one thing young Indians loved, from the mansions to the slums, it was a good soap opera. This afternoon, the CEO of Ishag Electronics was providing it, waiting like a naughty schoolboy to explain himself to teacher.

Finally, class was dismissed. Sinéad and Rachel made themselves scarce. The lovebirds were alone.

"Why did you come here, David? What do you want?"

Anger still flashed in Sarah Jane's eyes. David chose his words carefully.

"You. I want you."

"On your terms." Sarah Jane gathered up her books and started stuffing them furiously into her briefcase.

David put a hand on her arm. "I'm not going to let you go over some stupid miscommunication. I want you, Sarah Jane. On any terms."

For a moment a look of real sadness crossed her face. "You don't even know me."

David recoiled, stung. "How can you say that?"

Because it's true. Because I barely know myself sometimes. It's like I'm playing a role, the leading role in my life, but somehow I only received a copy of half the script.

"If you really knew me, you'd know I don't give a fig about your stupid money."

"I *do* know that," David protested.

"Then why do you need a prenup? You might as well have written me a letter saying 'I don't trust you.'"

David tore at his hair in frustration. "I'm worth the better part of a billion dollars, Sarah Jane, okay? Whether you like it or not, that sort of money brings complications. Trustees, shareholders, tax implications. I can't simply run off and get married without considering my responsibilities."

"Well, you won't need to worry about them now, will you? Because we *won't* be getting married!"

Not since his college girlfriend, Anastasia, had David had to deal with such an unreasonably stubborn female. Ironically, Anastasia was the only other girl he'd ever been in love with. But when she got pregnant with his child, she had not only refused to marry him, but refused to have anything more to do with him at all, insisting he was "too immature" to be a father. After running back to her parents in Moscow to give birth to a baby girl, she severed all contact. By the time David recovered sufficiently to fly out to Russia and insist on seeing his daughter, Anastasia had gone. No letter, no forwarding address, no nothing.

He was not about to let history repeat itself.

"For God's sake, Sarah Jane." Pulling her to him, he refused to let go. "I thought that was what you meant when you told me to 'sort out the legals.' It never crossed my mind it would upset you like this."

"You thought I meant a prenup?"

"The documents Elizabeth brought you today were nothing out of the ordinary. Not for a man in my position. But if I made a mistake, I'm sorry. I do trust you, totally. And I need you to be my wife."

He kissed her. Despite herself, Sarah Jane melted into him. He was such a good man. So decent. So attractive. So strong. He reminded her of someone, someone she needed to forget. It was all so confusing, so hard to tell right from wrong.

David whispered in her ear. "Please say you'll marry me."

"No prenup?" Sarah Jane whispered back.

"No prenup."

Matt Daley sat on the harbor wall in Positano, Italy, pulling hunks of bread from a freshly baked loaf and eating them slowly. The bread was delicious, flavored with rosemary and sea salt, soft and satisfying beneath the hard, seeded crust. Matt could have happily wolfed down the lot, but knew he had to make it last.

He'd been in Italy for ten days and his money was running out at an alarming rate. What Raquel had left him after the divorce barely amounted to a deposit on a Hershey bar. What little he had left didn't go far in a country that charged you two euros just to use a public bathroom and where gasoline seemed to cost roughly the same as liquid platinum. Restaurants were a total no-go. For the last two days Matt had survived on salami sandwiches and water from drinking fountains, but at this point meat of any kind was becoming a luxury—hence the bread-only lunch. He'd already traded in his modest room in a local guesthouse for a hostel, which was half the price but looked and felt like prison, complete with communal showers, bunk beds and a strict midnight curfew. And after all that, he was no nearer finding Lisa's mystery lover than he had been when he arrived.

On the plus side, the nightmares had at least stopped. If Matt had woken up screaming Lisa's name at two A.M., the way he had been doing at Claire's place, he'd have been kicked out of the hostel for sure. *It's because I'm doing something. I'm not sitting on my ass crying, I'm out there, trying to find this bastard, trying to save her.* Not that Matt didn't think about Lisa constantly. But he'd learned to compartmentalize the worst of his terrors. Every hour spent torturing himself about what might have happened to her, or what might be happening to her *right now,* was an hour wasted. *If I fall to pieces, she'll have no one.*

Armed with a printout of the picture from Lisa's computer, Matt had visited every hotel in town, from the scummy

Pensione Casa Guillermo to the palatial Hotel San Pietro.

"All reservations are confidential," said the snooty receptionist at the San Pietro. "We don't give out information on our guests, past or present."

"Never seen her," said the bored desk clerk at the Casa Guillermo.

"Don't think so. But fifty euros might jog my memory," said the fat manager of the Britannia Guesthouse, rubbing his hands together hopefully. Matt demurred. It was clear the greasy-vested idiot didn't recognize Lisa. Besides which, Matt could not imagine Lisa ever checking in to a dive like the Britannia, no matter how broke she was.

Carefully wrapping the last of the bread in a plastic bag and stuffing it into his backpack, Matt headed back into the old town. He had one last contact to see. If that came to nothing, he would leave Positano, perhaps go back to Hong Kong and see what he could dig up there.

The contact had come from a maid at the San Pietro. Witnessing Matt's curt dismissal by the reception staff, she'd taken pity on him and followed him out to his car.

"If it's gossip about the guests you're looking for, you ought to talk to Michele," she told him. "Michele saw everything. Heard all the secrets."

Michele, it transpired, had worked as a barman at Positano's grandest hotel until late last year when he'd been fired for petty theft. Unemployed since, he had a serious drinking problem and a major grudge against the San Pietro's management, neither of which made him a very reliable source of information. But beggars couldn't be choosers, and at this point Matt Daley was definitely a beggar, both figuratively and literally.

Michele lived in town in a run-down apartment above a fishmonger. Matt found the place easily. Even without the San Pietro maid's directions he could probably have smelled his way there. The stench of mackerel and sardines, mingled with sweat and human piss from the alleyway running alongside the building, was bad enough to make him gag.

"Come in. Valeria told me you were coming."

The man who opened the door was younger than Matt expected, and considerably more attractive. He'd been expecting a middle-aged, drunken slob, but other than a five o'clock shadow of stubble and faintly bloodshot eyes, Michele Danieli seemed to be in good shape.

"I hear you're looking for someone."

"Yes." Inside the apartment, evidence of a life in disarray became more apparent. Take-out boxes littered the floor, along with empty beer bottles and old newspapers. A half-empty bottle of Scotch was plainly visible next to the kitchen sink. *How did a fit, handsome kid like this get so down on his luck?* Matt found himself feeling sorry for Michele.

He handed him the printout of Lisa's photograph. The barman's reaction was instantaneous.

"Yes, I know them. They stayed for five days or so."

"When?" Matt asked breathlessly.

"Late summer, two years ago."

The summer before she married Miles Baring.

"You're sure?"

"Absolutely," said Michele. He pulled a cigarette out of a pack on the coffee table and lit it, blowing smoke in Matt's face. "I never forget a lover."

Matt inhaled sharply. He felt like he'd been hit over the head with a baseball bat.

"A lover? You slept together?"

Michele nodded. "Just once."

Clearly, there was much about Lisa's past that Matt didn't know. He'd accepted that fact long ago. But the idea that she would go on vacation to Italy with one man, then jump into bed with the first good-looking barman who asked her . . . that hurt. It wasn't the Lisa he remembered.

"The guy was a total asshole," Michele continued. "Violent, depraved. I was bruised so bad the next day, I couldn't go to work."

It took a few seconds for his words to sink in.

"You mean . . . the *man* was your lover?"

Michele laughed. "Of course! I don't do women, sweetheart. Can't you tell?" He winked at Matt flirtatiously, but a few seconds later his mood darkened. "I'm sure it was him who complained to the hotel about the missing cuff links. Like I'd want to touch his stinking jewelry after the way he treated me."

"Just to be clear. You're saying the man in the picture was gay?"

"Yes, dear."

"But he checked into the hotel with *this* woman? As a couple?"

"Uh-huh. Married. Don't look so shocked." Michele laughed. "It happens all the time."

Matt sank down onto the filthy, litter-strewn couch. After ten days of coming up empty, he was getting more from two minutes with Michele Danieli than he'd bargained for. If Danieli was telling the truth, and Lisa's mystery "lover" was actually gay, he couldn't be the Azrael killer. Whoever butchered those old men also raped their wives. He got off on sex with women.

"Do you remember their names, this couple?"

"He told me his name was Luca. His wife called him something else though. Franco, Francesco . . . something Italian. I never knew their last name, but the hotel should have records."

Not any that they'll show me, buddy. Interpol, though, could probably find out easily enough, if Matt decided to come clean and share this new information with Danny McGuire. Danny's team also had money to pursue new leads, something Matt Daley sorely lacked. But McGuire had admitted that he was cooperating with Inspector Liu, and Inspector Liu wanted to frame Lisa. For practical purposes, this made him dangerous. The enemy.

"What's your interest in this guy?" Michele piped up. "If you don't mind my asking."

"It's the woman I'm more concerned about," said Matt. "I have reason to believe . . . I'm afraid she might be in danger."

"If she's still with Luca, I'd say it's a certainty." Michele lit another cigarette. Matt noticed that his hand was trembling. "That guy was strange. Scary, actually. I got the feeling she was intimidated by him when I saw them at the bar, but it wasn't till after I slept with him myself that I realized why. I honestly thought he might kill me that night."

"Is there anything else you remember about them, anything at all that might help me find this man? Did he talk about his home, his friends, his job at all? Did she?"

Michele shook his head. "Sorry, man. Nothing springs to mind."

Matt got up to leave. When he reached the door, Michele called out, "Oh! There was one thing. It's probably not important, though."

"Try me."

"The woman, Luca's wife. She was lonely, I think. Anyway, she became friendly with another guest, especially during her last few days here. He was an old man, superwealthy, and he was here on his own. Anyway I remember at the pool, the old guy asked her where her family was from. And she said Morocco."

Matt froze. "Morocco?"

"Yeah. Which was weird, because

this girl was as American as apple pie. I mean, like, if she was North African, I'm from Nova Scotia."

"Would you recognize the old man if I showed you a picture?" Matt asked, his voice shaking.

"Don't need a picture," said Michele. "He was the biggest tipper I ever had, so I remember his name. It was Baring. Miles Baring."

CHAPTER TWENTY-TWO

Danny McGuire pulled his puffy jacket more tightly around him and braced himself against the cold as he walked through the busy streets of Queens. It was only late September, but New York was already in the grip of its first fall cold spell. Above Danny's head, russet leaves tipped with frost shook in the chill northeasterly wind. On the corner, three homeless men huddled around a burning oil drum, warming their gloved fingers over the flames. It felt as if it might snow. The FBI had been generous with their time, bending over backward to help Danny dig into Lisa Baring's early life. But it was like hunting the proverbial needle in a haystack. All they had to go on was what Danny gave them—Lisa's photograph, her blood type, her presumed age (based on the date of birth on her passport) and a range of dates during which she might have lived in the city as a child.

"You got anything on her family?"

Danny shook his head. "We think she had a sister, but no details on that. Parents believed dead. That's it."

The assistant director shrugged. "It's not much to go on."

"I know. I'm sorry."

"Give me a couple of days and I'll see what I can find."

While the FBI worked away, Danny spent the next forty-eight hours ricocheting around Manhattan like a deranged shuttlecock. He made a total of 116 phone calls to various high schools, for which his only reward was 116 "sorry, no such name in our records." He'd gone in person to the DMV, a Social Security Administration branch, the head offices of six retail banks and numerous administrative offices of eight major hospitals. He'd e-mailed Lisa's picture to the *Times,* the *Daily News* and the *Post,* on the off chance it might ring a bell with someone, and completed an exhaustive search for local news stories about orphaned sisters and/or any references to Morocco and children. Absolutely nothing.

Depressed and defeated, he'd returned to FBI headquarters only to find his helpful agent in a similarly glum mood.

"I'm sorry. But like I said, it's a big city and there's a *loooot* of Lisas in it. And that's assuming her real name is Lisa to begin with. You're talking about an anonymous kid who may have lived here twenty years ago."

Danny sighed. "Thanks for trying."

"The only other angle I can think of is the dead parents. If they died when she was young and there was no other family, she might have been placed in some kind of orphanage. The child welfare system doesn't usually separate siblings, if they can help it, so if she had a sister, they'd probably have gone somewhere together. You want the number for the offices of New York State Children and Family Services?"

That was yesterday evening. After a long night spent letting his fingers do the walking, today Danny was tramping the freezing streets of New York hitting the children's shelters in person. Lowering his head against the cold, he checked the GPS on his phone. *Almost there.* The Beeches was the last institution on his list. With so many homes closing down because of a lack of funds, and a shift in state policy in the nineties that favored fostering orphans out to families rather than keeping them in an institutional setting, there were in fact only twelve orphanages still running that had been operational back in the early eighties. Four of them only took in boys. Of the other eight, Danny had visited seven. Two kept no records at all. Of the five that did, none had taken in a pair of sisters during the dates in question. One had housed a Lisa, surname Bennington, but she was currently serving a thirty-year sentence for aggravated armed robbery in a

Louisiana penitentiary. Another dead end.

The Beeches in Queens was the largest remaining facility for homeless teens in the city. Most children's homes ceased to provide care after the age of thirteen, when kids were shoved out onto the streets or into halfway houses or foster homes. An ugly, redbrick Victorian building with small windows and a forbidding-looking black front door, the Beeches reminded Danny of something you'd find in a Dickens novel. Once he was inside, however, the decor was surprisingly cheery. Some budding artist had spray-painted a brightly colored, graffiti-style frieze on the reception walls. Through double glass doors at the end of the corridor Danny saw a group of young men gathered around a foosball table while another, largely female group was watching *American Idol* reruns on a communal TV, shouting loudly but good-naturedly at the screen.

I've seen worse places to grow up, thought Danny, thinking of the East L.A. streets he used to work back in his twenties or even the run-down neighborhoods of Lyon. *Maybe these kids were the lucky ones.*

"Mr. McGuire? I'm Carole Bingham, the director here. Would you like to take a seat in my office?"

In her early forties, with short blond hair, a handsome rather than conventionally pretty face and a trim figure elegantly covered by a wool Ann Taylor suit, Carole Bingham looked professional and organized. She was clearly more of an administrator than a housemother type, but perhaps that was what kids of this age needed.

Danny explained his quest. He was at pains to point out that the woman he was searching for was not necessarily suspected of murder, or indeed of any crime, but she was a link between four particularly gruesome homicides.

Carole Bingham pulled out a heavy metal drawer from a large, old-fashioned filing cabinet in the corner. "We're computerized from 1999 onward," she explained. "Back during the years you're talking about, whatever information we have is in here."

"You never had anyone input this stuff

into your electronic files?" asked Danny, gazing despondently at the mountain of disorganized, dog-eared documents.

Carole Bingham smiled sweetly. "Are you volunteering for the job? Look, you're right, of course. We should organize our old records. But the truth is we don't have either the budget or the time." She glanced at the clock on the wall. "I have a meeting with some bureaucrats from Albany in ten minutes in the main hall. Are you all right sifting through all this stuff on your own?"

"Of course," Danny said gratefully. "Hopefully I'll be out of your hair before too long."

It turned out to be a forlorn hope. It was astonishing just how much paper could be stuffed, squeezed, folded and crammed into a single metal drawer. Birth certificates, medical records, police and caseworker reports lay side by side with private letters, children's sketches and even old candy wrappers. Nothing was labeled, and though some official documents were dated, it didn't look like anyone had made even a perfunctory attempt to put things into any sort of order.

After two hopeless hours, a kid wandered in and handed Danny a much-needed cup of coffee. He was about sixteen, lanky and awkward and with punishing acne covering a good third of his face. But he looked Danny in the eye when he spoke—always a good sign—and you could see from his bone structure that he was going to grow up into a good-looking young man.

"Mrs. Bingham said to ask if you could use any help."

Danny looked up from the midst of the mountainous piles of paper. "Nah, that's okay. If I knew what I was looking for, maybe. But there's no point in two of us wasting our time."

"It's all stuff from the eighties, right?" said the boy.

Danny nodded.

"Have you seen the old yearbooks? If nothing else, they'll put a smile on your face. The clothes were, like, tragic." Grabbing a chair, the boy climbed up to the top shelf of a tall cabinet and pulled down a stack of black binders, dropping them on the floor beside Danny with a loud *thud*.

"These are kept separately?"

"Um, sure," said the boy, looking a little embarrassed. "Not officially. It's kind of sad, I guess, but sometimes we use them to play 'hot or not.' You know that Web site, where you put up your picture and kids can vote on how attractive you are? It's kind of like a lame version of that. Anyway, these are the eighties ones."

The boy left, and Danny started flicking through this new treasure trove. Not that he seriously expected to see a photo of a teenage Lisa Baring jump out at him. The odds of that had to be thousands to one. But at least these were pictures, with names, pictures of real kids.

Quite a number of years were missing. The books jumped from 1983 to 1987 and again from 1989 to 1992. It wasn't until he flipped open the ninth yearbook that he saw it.

The photo was dated, and the fashions as unflattering as the boy had warned him they would be. The face staring out at Danny was younger than he remembered, of course, and less polished. The teeth were not quite straight, and the hair was worn loose and long. But it was a face Danny McGuire would never forget. The long, aquiline nose. The regal curl of the lips. The arrogant sparkle in the azure-blue eyes. Beneath the photograph, some female hand from a later decade had scrawled the word *HOT* with several exclamation points.

He was hot, even then. And didn't he just know it.

The head shot was captioned *Frances Mancini—Most Likely to Make It to Hollywood!* But Danny McGuire knew him by another name.

Lyle Renalto.

Claire Michaels thought twice about making the call. She felt guilty, but she had to do something. She was desperately worried about her brother, and had no idea who else to turn to. She dialed the number.

"Hello?" Danny McGuire sounded extremely upbeat. For some reason, this threw Claire off her stride.

"Oh, hello," she stammered. "It's me. Claire Michaels. Matt Daley's . . . you know. We met."

"In L.A., of course. You're Matt's sister," Danny said kindly.

"Right. Have you heard any news from him?"

This brought Danny up short. Why would Claire be asking him such a question? Wasn't Matt staying at her house?

To be honest, the last thing Danny McGuire wanted to think about right then was Matt Daley. After stumbling across Lyle Renalto's picture—Frankie Mancini's picture—in the Beeches' yearbook earlier that day, he had hunted down Carole Bingham in high excitement. The director had introduced him to Marian Waites, one of the facility's catering staff and the only individual still on payroll who had been around in Mancini's day.

Danny hadn't expected much from Mrs. Waites, but it turned out the old lady had an encyclopedic memory, and was able to point out another face from the yearbook, a face that belonged to someone who had known Mancini well. "Thick as thieves, they were, those two." His name was Victor Dublenko. A quick call to the NYPD revealed that *they* knew Dublenko well, as a pimp and occasional dealer, still alive, currently out of jail and living in Queens, not six blocks from the Beeches, where Danny was standing at that very moment. Danny had been about to head off to Dublenko's apartment when Claire called.

Reluctantly, he turned his attention back to Matt Daley. "No. I haven't heard a word from him since I saw him at your place. He's not there with you?"

"If he were here with me, I wouldn't be calling, would I?" snapped Claire. "I'm sorry. I don't mean to take it out on you. But I'm worried about him. He left me a voice mail last night that literally made no sense."

"Did he say where he was?"

"Yeah. He's in Italy."

"Italy?"

"Uh-huh. The Amalfi coast. He said he had some lead about the man who may have abducted Lisa. To be frank with you, I'm surprised he had the money for a plane ticket. God knows how he's surviving out there."

Danny's heart sank. Matt had sworn to him that he'd let it go, that he wouldn't go chasing down this maniac on his own. Now that the powers that be at Interpol had officially sanctioned Operation Azrael, the last thing Danny needed was a mentally unstable Matt Daley crashing through his case like a bull elephant, interfering with potential witnesses and, for all he knew, withholding key evidence. He'd made no mention of an Italian "lead" when he and Danny met.

"Did he say anything else?"

"He said a lot of things, but like I said, he was rambling. He said Lisa's lover wasn't her lover. He was gay. He said that she knew him before she knew Miles, which for some reason he thought was important, but that he 'couldn't be Azrael,' that you and the other officers were on the wrong track. Who the hell is Azrael?"

"No one," said Danny. "It's a code name. Don't worry about it."

He too was worried about Matt, personally as well as professionally. "I appreciate your calling me," he told Claire. "I'm on my way to an important meeting right now, but afterward I'll try to contact your brother again. In the meantime, if you hear anything else, anything at all . . ."

"I'll let you know. He's not . . . he's not in any danger, is he?"

Danny could hear the anxiety in her voice.

"No," he lied. "I don't think so. I'll put a call in to the local police in Amalfi, just in case. Ask them to keep an eye out for him."

The conversation with Claire Michaels was bothering him. Had Matt Daley really gotten a useful lead on Lisa's lover? Without talking to him, it was impossible to figure out how much of what he'd told his sister was real, and how much a figment of his fevered, anxiety-racked imagination. By the time Danny reached Dublenko's apartment, his train of thought was hopelessly muddled.

Lyle Renalto. Frankie Mancini. What connection could the boy in the year-book photograph possibly have to Italy and Lisa Baring? Why was Danny even here?

Five minutes later Victor Dublenko appeared to be asking himself the same question, glaring at Danny from his grimy, vinyl La-Z-Boy recliner.

"I got nothing to say."

Dublenko's living room was disgusting, a fetid dump littered with stained cushions, needles, dead marijuana plants and half-eaten plates of food. Down the hallway, the two bedrooms were cleaner. Clients expected a certain standard of hygiene, and Victor Dublenko made sure he provided it. Bedrooms were for business. But for himself, Victor was quite happy to live in shit.

"I don't like cops."

Danny McGuire shrugged amiably. "I don't like pimps. But hey, what are you gonna do? We're each an occupational hazard of the other."

Victor Dublenko laughed, a phlegmy, guttural sound that quickly morphed

into a hacking cough. Pulling a hand-
kerchief out of his pocket, he spat
something vile into it and stuffed it back
into the pocket.

"So we don't like each other. But we
can still do business, right? You pay, I
talk."

Just then a very young, very skinny
girl in shorts and a vest wandered into
the room looking disoriented. Victor
Dublenko snarled at her and she scur-
ried out like a frightened beetle. *Poor
kid,* thought Danny. She couldn't have
been more than fifteen. Scum like
Dublenko made him want to puke. But
he reminded himself why he was here,
how many lives might depend on
Dublenko's information, and bit his
tongue. Pulling a wad of fifties out of
his jacket pocket, he licked his fingers
and made a show of counting them before carefully putting them back.

"I prefer 'you talk, I pay,' if it's all the
same to you, Mr. Dublenko."

Without taking his eyes off the pocket
with the money in it, the pimp said flatly,
"So whaddaya want to know?"

Danny handed over the yearbook picture. "Do you remember this guy?"

"Jesus!" Dublenko smiled, revealing a crooked collection of mostly gold teeth. "Frankie Mancini, man. Where the fuck you get this?" The coughing was back with a vengeance. Danny McGuire waited for Victor to clear his tobacco-ruined lungs, gasping for breath like a stranded fish.

"From the Beeches. I was there earlier. A Mrs. Waites mentioned that you and Frankie were both residents of the home between 1986 and 1988 and that you were close. Is that correct?"

Victor Dublenko's green eyes narrowed. "Mrs. Waites. That old bitch is still alive?"

"Is that correct, Mr. Dublenko?"

Victor nodded. "You know a lot about my past, Detective. I'm flattered."

Danny didn't bother to conceal his contempt. "Frankly, I'm not interested in your past. I'm interested in Frankie Mancini. When did you last see him?"

Dublenko shook his head. "A long time ago, man. Years, too many years. Maybe twenty?"

"Where?"

"Right here, in New York. He got transferred to another home the year after this picture was taken and we kept in touch for a while. But then he got a job out west somewhere and that was that."

Out west. Los Angeles . . . Where he became Lyle Renalto and met Angela Jakes . . . Where it all started.

"You never heard from him again?"

"We weren't exactly the pen-pal types," Dublenko sneered. "So what are you after him for? He done something wrong? Robbed a bank?"

"Would it surprise you if he had?"

Dublenko reflected for a moment. "Yeah, it would, actually. I always figured he'd do well for himself."

"Why'd you figure that?"

"Well, for one thing, he was smart. Foreign languages, math, there was nothing that kid couldn't do. And for another, just look at him. With a face like that, your life is easy."

The words could have been interpreted as bitter, but there was no resentment in Dublenko's tone. Quite the opposite in fact. He sounded admiring. Nostalgic. Affectionate, even.

"Easy in what way? You mean he was successful with girls?"

A grin spread across Dublenko's toadlike features. "Frankie wasn't interested in girls, Detective. That wasn't his team, if you know what I mean."

A shiver ran down Danny's spine. What had Claire Michaels said to him about Matt Daley's call from Italy? *"Lisa's lover wasn't her lover. He was gay. He couldn't be Azrael. You're on the wrong track."*

"Now, that's not to say women weren't interested in *him*. The bitches were all over him like flies. And like I say, Frankie was smart. He used that power to his advantage."

Danny thought of Lyle Renalto, the way that he'd wheedled his way into Angela Jakes's life, how he'd gotten her to trust him, perhaps even lured her to her death.

"Used it in what way?"

"Oh, you know. He'd get girls to do stuff for him, get him gifts, cover for him when he broke curfew. Little shit like that. But he never really *dug* women, if you know what I mean."

Danny was growing tired of Dublenko's less than subtle euphemisms. "I get it, Dublenko. Frankie was gay."

"Yeah, he was gay, all right, but it was more than that. I kinda got the feeling that women, like, repulsed him. Not just sexually, but as people. Apart from the princess, of course."

"The princess?"

Dublenko's expression soured. "Princess Sofia. That's what he called her. Fuck knows what her real name was. Frankie was totally obsessed by her."

"You resented their friendship?"

"Ah, whatever." Dublenko waved a hand dismissively. "It was bullshit, that's all. I remember Frankie telling me she was descended from the Moroccan royal family. Like, sure. That's how she wound up dumped on the streets in Brooklyn, right?"

Danny hesitated. Something Dublenko just said had reminded him of something, but he couldn't think what.

"I left the Beeches before Sofia arrived there, but I met her once, right before Frankie left town, and a precious little bitch she was too. I heard that before she met Frankie, the male staff at her previous home used to pass her around like one of those blowup dolls. Give it to her up her royal ass." Victor Dublenko laughed lecherously at the memory. "She was just another skank, used goods, but Frankie didn't want to hear it. 'My princess,' he called her. She put some kinda spell on him."

After satisfying himself that Dublenko had told him all he knew, Danny paid him and caught a cab back to his hotel. It was dark now and bitterly cold outside. Retreating to the warm cocoon of his room, he locked the door, threw his notes, tape recorder and briefcase on the bed and checked his messages. Nothing interesting. After a brief call to Céline—for the third night in a row Danny got to tell his wife's voice mail how much he loved and missed her— and another failed attempt to reach Matt Daley, he dialed Claire Michaels's number.

"This gay guy that Matt mentioned, Lisa's lover. Did he tell you his name?"

"I don't think so," said Claire. "Oh, wait. He might have said something in passing. Franco? Francesco? Is that possible?"

Hanging up, Danny stripped off his clothes and jumped into the shower. Something about pounding jets of hot water always helped him think. He felt as if today he'd been handed multiple pieces of the jigsaw puzzle. And if he could only somehow see how they fit together, he might have the answer to this riddle. The problem was that they weren't the pieces he'd been looking for.

He came to New York looking for information about Lisa Baring's past. Instead, he'd learned a lot about Lyle Renalto's. Only there *was* no Lyle Renalto, there was only this Frankie Mancini. Frankie Mancini . . . who was gay . . . so he couldn't be Azrael the rapist-killer, right? . . . but who *was* apparently linked with Lisa Baring. Though not as her lover. Just as Frankie had not been "Princess Sofia's" lover, whoever she may have been. Just as Lyle Renalto had not been Angela Jakes's lover.

Everything was linked, but each link came full circle back to itself rather than connecting with the others.

Lisa . . . Lyle . . . Frankie.

Lisa . . . Angela . . . Sofia.

What am I not seeing?

It wasn't just the people who came full circle but the places too. New York, L.A., Hong Kong, Italy, New York. *And Morocco. That's it. Dublenko said Frankie's Princess Sofia claimed to come from Morocco. That's where Matt Daley and Lisa were going to run off to, before Lisa disappeared.*

Was Morocco important, or just a coincidence? Danny's head ached.

Drying himself off, he sat down on the bed and looked again at Frankie Mancini's photograph in the Beeches yearbook. Lyle Renalto smiled mockingly back at him. Frankie was younger than Lyle, his face more fleshy and rounded. Yet despite the differences, they were clearly the same person.

On instinct, without really knowing why, Danny switched on his computer and pulled up the picture Inspector Liu had provided of Lisa Baring, the one

he'd given the NYPD and various agencies and organizations in the city with
so little success. He stared at Lisa's
face for a long time, almost as if he expected her to speak, to reveal her secrets. Finally, he zoomed in on her eyes,
the eyes that had bewitched Matt
Daley—and presumably Miles Baring
before him—reducing him to a shadow
of his former self. They reminded Danny
of other eyes he had seen. Eyes he had
seen somewhere else. Eyes he had
seen long ago.

All at once, there it was. Literally staring him in the face.

Heart pounding, Danny McGuire
picked up the telephone.

How could I have been so blind?

CHAPTER TWENTY-THREE

Inspector Liu looked at the hotel manager distastefully. The man was bald, apparently uneducated and morbidly obese, his whalelike blubber squeezed into a gray polyester suit two sizes too small for him and so shiny it was almost silver. Yet he seemed to be running one of the most expensive establishments in Sydney, a five-star hotel right on the harbor whose clients included rock stars and politicians. There was no justice in this world.

"You're quite sure it was her?"

"Look, mate," the manager wheezed,

handing back the photograph of Lisa Baring. "I might not be Stephen friggin' Hawkins, all right, but I know how to recognize a face. Especially a face that gorgeous. It's part of my job." He scratched his armpits unselfconsciously. "It was a couple of months ago now. Stacey upstairs'll have the exact dates for you. She checked in with a bloke, good-looking fella, but she paid the bill. I'm pretty sure they reserved under 'Smith.'"

"You don't verify your guests' passports?"

The manager snorted derisively. "We're not the bloody FBI, Mr. Liu."

"*Inspector* Liu," Liu said coldly.

"And no offense, but we're not the Chinese police state either," the fat Australian went on, ignoring him. "If I started sniffing around every Mr. and Mrs. Smith who checked in here, I'd soon go out of business, let me tell you."

"Who paid the bill?"

"She did, the sheila. In cash."

"But they left no forwarding address, no credit-card billing address, nothing?"

"Like I said, I don't think so, but check

with Stacey. She's the eyes and ears of this place if you know what I mean."

Stacey was a meek mouse of a woman in her sixties who corroborated everything her boss had already told the inspector. Mrs. Smith had paid in cash. No, she'd never mentioned anything about future plans, at least not at the front desk. Mr. Smith was "quiet" and "attractive." Stacey declined to hazard a guess as to his age.

"I'd like to see their room."

The suite was palatial, even by the hotel's grand standards. "Mrs. Smith" must have needed a wheelbarrow of cash to pay for a week's stay here. Then again, Lisa Baring could afford it, what with her old man's money burning a hole in her thieving, conniving pocket. He and his men scoured the rooms for fingerprints, hair, or other forensic evidence, but after two months and God knows how many subsequent occupants, not to mention twice-daily cleaning by the hotel staff, they weren't hopeful.

Every chambermaid was interviewed, along with the concierge, bar and restaurant staff and someone named Liana at the spa where Mrs. Smith had availed herself of the hotel's signature hot stone massage.

"She seemed a little emotional, to be honest," Liana remembered, batting her heavy false eyelashes in Inspector Liu's direction and almost asphyxiating him with a gust of CK One perfume. "She was tearful during her treatment, I remember that. But guests often are. So much gets released when you really hit those meridians, you know what I mean?"

"Did she say anything about what might have been upsetting her? Any information at all might help us."

Liana thought about it. "She didn't. But I'd say it was man trouble. I saw her with her hubby in the lobby a couple of times and he was always holding her hand or fussing over her, but she didn't seem into it. She kept shrugging him off."

By the end of the day, Inspector Liu was frustrated. He'd flown out to Sydney in person, because the Australia sighting was the first solid evidence he'd managed to get hold of, since Mrs. Baring's second attempt at absconding, that she was (a) alive, and (b) a free agent, not locked up in some sex offender's dungeon, as certain bleeding-heart factions seemed to believe. But the trip had been a bust. He'd discovered nothing that he couldn't have learned from a ten-minute phone call from Hong Kong.

Leaving three men behind to finish collecting the physical evidence, he took his leave. "One of our chauffeurs can take you to the airport," the fat manager offered magnanimously. "If you have to leave Sydney, you might as well do it in style."

Sitting in the back of the plushly upholstered, air-conditioned limo, Liu brooded on the fact that Lisa Baring and her lover seemed always to manage to remain one step ahead of him. You could bet your bottom Hong Kong dollar that *they* had left Sydney in style. Suddenly a thought occurred to him. He rapped on the window that separated passenger from driver, which promptly rolled down.

"There's a call button if you want it, mate. You see that console there on your left?"

But Inspector Liu wasn't interested in call buttons and consoles.

"How many chauffeurs does the hotel employ?"

"There's six of us."

"And do you keep records of your journeys? Which guests go where?"

"There's a logbook, yeah. It's in the office."

"Turn around."

"But . . . your plane. I thought you said the last flight to Hong Kong—"

"Turn around!"

Stacey in the office was dismayed to see the grumpy Chinese policeman back so soon.

"Inspector. I thought you said you were—"

"I need the drivers' logbook," said Liu. He gave her the dates. "I need to know who chauffeured the Smith party to the airport."

"Not all of our guests use the cars," the woman warned him. "Most check out under their own steam."

But Liu wasn't listening. There it was. *Smith, 10:20 A.M. Marco.*

"I need to speak to Marco. Right now."

"I'm afraid that won't be possible," Stacey said nervously. "Marco's off on compassionate leave. His mother passed away a week ago."

Inspector Liu could not have cared less about Marco's mother. "Give me his address."

Marco Brunelli was still in his underwear and a stained vest when the Chinese policemen knocked on his door. Actually they didn't so much knock as hammer.

"Can I help you gentlemen?" Marco swallowed nervously, thinking about the stash of weed lying there in plain sight on his bedside table, his failure to pay his last year's tax bill and an incident with a pole dancer at Blushes nightclub that had occurred the previous month. Not that the latter was his fault.

"You work at the Huxley Hotel, as a driver?"

"That's right. I'm on leave. It's my mum you see. She—"

"Saturday the sixteenth, in the morning, you drove a party named Smith to the airport. Do you remember?"

"Smith." Marco frowned. "Smith, Smith, Smith." The policeman handed him a photograph of a very attractive dark-haired woman. "Oh, *her.* Yeah, I remember her. And her husband. Yeah, that's right, I drove them to the airport. Why?"

"Did you know where they were flying to?"

"You know, that's a funny thing," said Marco, more relaxed now that he realized it was these clients the police were after, not him. "Normally clients are chatty in the back of the car, especially the Americans. They want to talk about what a great stay they've had, where they're going next, all that guff. But those two were silent as the grave. Didn't say a word."

Inspector Liu felt his hopes fading.

"But after I dropped them, on my way back into town, I noticed that the bloke had left his briefcase on the backseat. So of course I hightailed it back there and went racing into the terminal. The guy was so happy to see me he gave me a big hug and a two-hundred-dollar tip. They were just in time for boarding. So that's why I remember where they were going."

Marco smiled broadly. Inspector Liu could hardly bear the suspense.

"Mumbai, India," the driver announced proudly. "Was that all you wanted to know?"

Claude Demartin was having an unusually enjoyable afternoon at work. The Azrael team's office, deep in the bowels of Interpol headquarters, had begun its life as a windowless cubicle. But thanks to Danny McGuire, it had evolved into something of a happy bachelor's pad, complete with squishy couches, dartboard, and a minifridge stuffed full of the sort of cheap, high-calorie American food Claude was never allowed to eat at home.

Better yet, today Claude was manning the fort alone. Richard laugh-a-minute Sturi was off diddling with his statistical projections somewhere, the boss was still in the States, and the three other junior detectives were in London, attempting what Danny Mc-Guire had hopefully described as a "charm offensive" with Scotland Yard to get them to share more information from the Piers Henley case files.

So far, after a little light updating of the database and a token call to Didier Anjou's bank in Paris, tying up some loose ends, Claude had beaten himself three times at darts, enjoyed a satisfying session of World of Warcraft and eaten two family-size bags of Cheetos, which was probably officially a crime in certain parts of France. So when the phone rang, he answered in high spirits.

"Interpol, Azrael desk. How may I be of service?"

"Put me through to McGuire."

Claude Demartin recognized Inspector Liu's voice. Cheerless as ever, there was an impatience in his tone today—part excitement, part anger—that Claude hadn't heard before.

"It's urgent."

"Assistant Director McGuire isn't in

the office this week, I'm afraid. He's traveling. Can I help you? This is Officer Claude Demartin."

"No."

"Well, perhaps I can take a message. It's Inspector Liu, isn't it? From Hong Kong?"

Liu was silent. He didn't want to exchange pleasantries with this French monkey. He wanted to talk to the organ grinder. On the other hand, he did have vital information to impart.

"Did you make any progress in Australia?" Demartin pressed. "I assure you the moment we hear something from McGuire, I'll insist that he contact you. But is there anything the team should know? Any way we can help you?"

"Tell McGuire they're in India," Liu said tersely. "If he wants to know more, he can pick up the damn telephone."

The line went dead.

India. All Demartin could think of was how nicely the news fit with Richard Sturi's theories of where Azrael would strike next. The German was cocky enough already. He'd be insufferable after this. Before he could pick up the phone to call McGuire, it rang again.

"Azrael," Demartin said, more businesslike this time.

"Hi, Claude. It's me."

"Boss. Great timing. Listen, I just got a call from Liu."

"Never mind that," Danny McGuire said briskly. "I need you to e-mail me the clearest pictures we have of all the widows. Face shots only."

"Sure, I can do that. But about Liu. He wants you to call him urgently. He—"

"Now, Claude. I'll be waiting by my laptop." Danny McGuire hung up.

What was it with these big-shot detectives? Didn't anybody have the time to let you finish a sentence anymore?

On the bed in his New York hotel room, Danny gazed at his in-box.

One minute. Five minutes. Ten. What the fuck? How long did it take to download and send a few lousy JPEGs?

When at last he heard the longed-for *ping* of a new message in his coded Azrael folder, Danny's heart leaped, then sank when he saw that there were no attachments.

"Pictures to follow," Claude Demartin wrote. "And by the way, Inspector Liu's message was: 'They're in India.' You need to call him right away."

India! That was good news indeed. So was Demartin's use of the word *they*. It meant Lisa Baring was still alive and that she was still with . . . who? Frankie Mancini? Danny would call Liu in a moment and get the whole story. Just as soon as Claude sent him those damn images.

Finally, after what felt like millennia but was in fact about a minute and a half, a large file landed in Danny's in-box. The e-mail was entitled: *WIDOWS*.

Danny clicked it open with a trembling hand.

There they were, smiling at him across the years, their faces running along the screen from left to right in chronological order.

Angela Jakes . . . Lady Tracey Henley . . . Irina Anjou . . . Lisa Baring.

At first it wasn't obvious. There were the superficial differences: hair color and length, subtle changes in makeup and some of the images, particularly the ones of Irina, were blotchy and blurred. Age had wreaked its usual black magic, etching a spiderweb of fine lines over once-smooth skin. Weight had gone up and down, making some of the faces look gaunt while others looked blooming and chipmunk-cheeked. Then there were the more fundamental things. Angela Jakes's face was the loveliest of the four, youthful and innocent, untouched by the passage of time. Tracey Henley, the red-head, on the other hand, seemed harder and more artificial-looking. While she was still undeniably beautiful, Danny now saw that her nose was unusually narrow at the tip, almost as if she'd had some plastic surgery. Lisa Baring had the same small nose, although on her it appeared more natural. Her brow was higher, though, and smoother.

What really leaped off the screen, however, were the four women's eyes. Laugh lines and crow's-feet might come and go, cheekbones and mouths and noses might be surgically altered. But the eyes themselves remained the same.

Deep brown, like molten chocolate. Sad. Sultry. Mesmerizing.

The first time Danny McGuire saw them he'd been untying Angela Jakes from her husband's corpse. Slipping in and out of consciousness, Angela had opened those eyes and looked at him. Danny's life had changed forever.

Years later, those same eyes had lured Sir Piers Henley to his death.

They had hypnotized Didier Anjou.

Enchanted Miles Baring.

Made a besotted fool out of Matt Daley.

Mocked Inspector Liu.

Each of the women's faces was different. But the eyes gave them away.

Azrael isn't a "he." He's a "she."

They're all the same woman.

CHAPTER TWENTY-FOUR

The man quickened his pace. The alley
was dark and smelled of spices and
human shit. *Saffron, cumin and excre-
ment: the essence of India.* The man
laughed at his own joke, but it was a
nervous laugh, only a shade or two from
hysteria.

He was being followed again.

Weaving his way between the rickshaws and scurrying brown bodies, he
ducked behind a baker's stall. A narrow
passage opened through a brick arch-
way into a yard where kilns heated the
flat naan bread and *paratha*. Curious

half-naked children swarmed around him, intrigued by his foreign, white man's face. He brushed them away, his heart pounding. The only way out of the yard was the way he came in. If his pursuer had seen him slip behind the bread stall, he would catch him for sure. Catch him and kill him. The man expected no mercy.

At first he thought his pursuers must be police, but no longer. The shadows lurking behind him were far more sinister. Wherever he went in the city, he could feel their presence, cold and threatening like a malignant ghost. His nerves were in tatters. It was getting harder to make decisions.

This time, however, he seemed to have lost them. No one had followed him into the baker's yard. He must have given them the slip. Cautiously, he made his way back into the alley. A few blocks later he emerged onto a main road where the ubiquitous rickshaws made way for the more modern yellow cabs. *Almost like New York.*

He stuck out his arm.

  "Taj Mahal Palace, please. *Jaldi karna!*"

The man had sat at the bars of some of the most luxurious hotels in the world. The Chateau Marmont in Los Angeles, the San Pietro in Positano, the Peninsula in Hong Kong. But for sheer opulence, nothing could beat the Taj Mahal Palace hotel in Mumbai. A sumptuous mishmash of Moorish, Oriental and Florentine design, it was as majestic a home away from home as any maharajah could wish for. The main bar was accessed from the lobby, a vast space with marble floors and vaulted alabaster ceilings. An intricately carved arch supported by two onyx columns led into the darker, candlelit bar. The vibe there was more intimate, but just as luxurious, with wine-red velvet couches so soft you felt you were sitting on clouds and antique Persian rugs woven in every imaginable color. All around, richly dressed couples were laughing, their cut-crystal glasses glinting like diamonds as they sipped *caipir-*

inhas or Long Island iced teas. Royalty for a day.

He took his usual seat in the darkest, most recessed alcove and ordered a Diet Coke and some of the grilled cumin chicken they served as a bar snack. He wasn't hungry, but he had to eat. He had a long night of waiting and watching ahead of him.

Sarah Jane Hughes didn't notice the American man taking his seat in the corner. She was too agitated to think about anything other than David. It wasn't like him to be late.

Maybe he's had a change of heart after all the shit I've put him through?

She couldn't work out if the idea of him bailing on their prospective wedding made her frightened or relieved. The pressure was unbearable at times.

"I'm worth the better part of a billion dollars, Sarah Jane, okay? Whether you like it or not, that sort of money brings complications."

Complications. Talk about an understatement.

Pulling a small black mirror out of her purse, Sarah Jane touched up her makeup and arranged her hair the way she knew David liked it. Smoothing down her knee-length skirt, she unbuttoned the top of her blouse just enough to hint at the glorious figure beneath. Like most men, David Ishag liked the demure look. It made him feel secure. That the delights of Sarah Jane's body were for his eyes only. Which, of course, they were.

Till death do us part.

And there he was, walking toward her, lighting up the room the way that only he could, a human fireball of charisma. So handsome. So charming.

I can't go through with it.

She forced herself to take deep, calming breaths.

"Darling. Sorry I'm late."

"Very late." She kissed him on the lips, running her hands through his glossy dark hair only faintly tinged with gray at the temples. "I was starting to worry."

Envious female eyes bored into her. Sarah Jane blinded them with a dazzling flash of her sapphire-and-diamond engagement ring.

David Ishag kissed her back.

"Silly girl. You never need to worry. Not now, not ever again. Not with me to take care of you."

The man in the corner had the shakes. He couldn't bear to watch them, Sarah Jane and David. It was too painful. Yet he couldn't bring himself to look away.

A waitress approached him. "Are you all right, sir? Can I get you something?"

My sanity, please. If you're out of that, I'll have Prozac on the rocks with a twist of chlorpromazine.

"I'll take a bourbon. Straight up."

On the other side of the bar, a different man was watching.

This man noticed everything: the pallor of the foreigner's skin, the cruel tremor in his hand as he sipped his drink. He'd been following the white man for days now and had come to think of him almost as an old friend.

Poor devil. His heart cannot accept the truths that his eyes see. Is there any madness in this world greater than the madness of love?

The man's heart swelled with compassion, with pity for a fellow lost soul.

It really was too bad he was going to have to kill him.

CHAPTER TWENTY-FIVE

"We cannot wait until after the wedding. It's out of the question. We have to strike now."

Rajit Kapiri, a senior officer in India's elite IB (intelligence bureau) division, folded his arms across his chest, as if to indicate that the subject was closed. He was sitting in Interpol's Mumbai field office across the table from Danny Mc-Guire, whose body language was equally stubborn and uncompromising.

"We can't," Danny repeated. "We must catch Azrael red-handed. It's the only way to be sure of a conviction."

"But at what cost?" Kapiri spluttered. "Mr. Ishag's life? I'm sorry, McGuire. I'm not going to sit by while you play Russian roulette with the life of one of Mumbai's wealthiest and most prominent citizens."

Danny McGuire bit back his frustration. He couldn't afford to alienate the IB officer. If Kapiri complained to Danny's bosses at Interpol that the Azrael team was taking matters into its own hands and riding roughshod over local decision makers, Henri Frémeaux would disband the task force faster than you could say "spineless bureaucrat." But Danny needed Rajit Kapiri's cooperation for other reasons too. The IB had manpower, not to mention priceless local expertise when it came to intelligence gathering. It was they who'd provided the Azrael team with a shortlist of likely local targets—very wealthy, older, unmarried men based in Mumbai with no known family ties. Ironically David Ishag had only just made the cut, being so much younger than the other victims. But when it emerged that the electronics magnate had recently made sudden, unexpected wedding plans, and that his bride-to-be was a relative newcomer in town, McGuire's surveillance team moved in. It wasn't long before they'd tracked down Ishag's fiancée, a woman calling herself Sarah Jane Hughes. Despite the lighter hair extensions and dowdy clothes, and the new identity as an Irish schoolteacher, the surveillance pictures showed that Sarah Jane bore an uncanny resemblance to Lisa Baring.

"What if she kills him during the honeymoon?" Kapiri asked.

"None of the attacks have happened during the honeymoon. They've all taken place in the victims' own homes. She knows the territory there. Plus, let's not forget that she's not doing this alone. She needs her accomplice, and he doesn't go on the honeymoons."

Rajit Kapiri still looked uncomfortable. A wedding and a honeymoon meant allowing the suspect out of his sight and jurisdiction, out of his control. Four prior police forces had made that mistake.

Danny McGuire said, "I understand your anxiety. I share it, believe me. You think I'm not tempted to pick her up now?"

"Then why don't you?"

"I've told you why. Because this is our best chance, our only chance, to catch her red-handed, and to catch her accomplice too. If we move now, we'll have her, but he'll run."

The thing that bothered Danny most about the surveillance operation on Sarah Jane Hughes was that so far they had yet to make any sightings of a third man. If Frankie Mancini/Lyle Renalto was in Mumbai, he was lying very low.

"We'll track them on their honeymoon every step of the way. Remember we have a global network of agents. This is what we do."

"Humph." Rajit Kapiri did not sound reassured.

"As soon as they're back in India, we'll go to Mr. Ishag together and put him in the picture. Nothing will be done without his consent. If he declines to help us, you can arrest Sarah Jane then. Of course," Danny added slyly, "she won't actually have committed any crime on Indian soil at that point. Nothing you can prove anyway. You'd have to extradite her, probably to Hong Kong, so the Chinese authorities would get all the glory. But that would be your call."

Rajit Kapiri's eyes narrowed. He knew he was being manipulated and he didn't like it. On the other hand, if anything did go wrong during Mr. Ishag's honeymoon, he had a formal record of today's meeting and could lay the blame squarely at Interpol's door.

"Fine," he said. "But I want to be kept informed of their movements the entire time they're away."

"You will be. You have my word." Danny extended his hand across the table. Grudgingly the Indian shook it. "I do have one other request. Our boy may well come out of the woodwork while the couple themselves are gone. I don't have enough men to watch Ishag's house and office as well as Sarah Jane's school and apartment twenty-four/seven. Do you think you could help us out with that?"

The American had the cheek of the devil. But even Rajit Kapiri had to admire his chutzpah.

"I'll see what I can do, Assistant Director McGuire. You just focus on keeping David Ishag in one piece."

Less than five miles from the building where the Azrael team was meeting, a woman stared at her naked image in the mirror.

She ran her long fingers over each of her limbs, caressing the scars and bruises. They were the only parts of herself that felt familiar, that felt real. On her face she traced the faint signs of middle age that had begun to plague her in recent months: the fan of lines around the eyes and lips, the deepening of the purple shadows beneath her eyes, the more pronounced grooves running downward from the corners of her nose. She felt like crying. Not because she was getting older. But because the face was the face of a stranger.

She felt like crying, but she couldn't, she mustn't. She had to stay strong for her sister. Her sister needed her. The woman clung to that need desperately, like a newborn monkey clinging to its

mother. It was literally all she had to live
for.

"Why so sad?"

The man walked up behind her, kissing her neck and shoulders. The gesture should have been tender, but it was
not. It was possessive. Chilling. She
shivered.

"I'm fine. Just tired. "

"Try to sleep, angel."

She had changed so much since they
first met, but he had barely altered, inside or out. Behind her in the mirror he
was still dazzling, his beauty as con-
stant as the sun, as inescapable as
death. A few months ago she had
dreamed of escape. Now she knew how
foolish that had been. Now she hoped
only for her sister.

One day soon, he had promised, her
sister would be free.

CHAPTER TWENTY-SIX

"Good morning, Mr. Ishag. Welcome back!"

David Ishag smiled at his secretary. "Thank you, Sasha. It's good to be back."

Oddly, it *was* good to be back. As perfect as his life was right now, David Ishag was ready for a return to something like normality.

His honeymoon with Sarah Jane had been utterly magical. After an intimate, very private wedding service at the Catholic chaplaincy on Vidyanagara—only David's best man, Kavi, and Sarah Jane's colleague Rachel had attended—the happy couple flew to England to break the news to David's elderly mother before jetting off on a grand European tour.

"Do you think she'll ever get over it?"

Sarah Jane turned to David as they were touring St. Mark's cathedral in Venice.

"Who? Get over what? You must stop being so cryptic, my darling. I feel as if I've married a *Times* crossword setter."

"Your mother. Do you think she'll ever get over you marrying a Catholic? And one so far beneath you too?"

David stopped, cupping Sarah Jane's perfect angel's face in his hands. "Beneath me? You're so far above me I get vertigo just looking at you." He kissed her, then staggered backward, clutching at his head. "See? I'm dizzy already."

Sarah Jane giggled. "Idiot."

David Ishag had never been one to play the fool, or to go gaga over a woman. But he was a fool for his new wife and he wanted the world to know it. He took Sarah Jane to the finest hotels in the most romantic cities—the Georges V in Paris, the Hassler in Rome, the Dorchester in London, the Danieli in Venice. He made love to her in penthouse suites, on his newly refurbished Learjet and on the deck of his superyacht, *Clotilde,* as they cruised the Mediterranean together. But as joyous as the trip was, coming home to Mumbai was equally special, because it marked the start of their real life together.

David had expected them to start trying for a baby right away. Sarah Jane was over forty, so they didn't have time to waste, but surprisingly she was hesitant, insisting on going straight back to work at her school and taking things "day by day." While David adored her independent spirit, and the fact that clearly her head had not been turned by his immense wealth, part of him wished he could lock her up in his castle and keep her all for himself.

"You need to get back to your other love: work," Sarah Jane told him. As usual, she was right. Walking into Ishag Electronics offices this morning David had felt a renewed fervor and sense of purpose. He had the energy of a teenager again, which could only mean better times ahead for the business.

I should have gotten married years ago.

"So," he asked his secretary, "what's on the agenda?"

As ever, his schedule was packed. After an hour to respond to the most pressing of his thousands of new e-mails, David had a board meeting at nine, a business development presentation at ten fifteen, lunch with the CEO of Zenon Technology, one of Ishag Electronics' clients, at one, then an afternoon reviewing new product sales figures with his head of components, Johnathan Wray. A board meeting at the end of the day meant David would be lucky if he got home to Sarah Jane before eight o'clock that night.

Sitting down at his desk, he turned on his computer and immediately buzzed Sasha again.

"Book me a table for two at Jamavar for eight thirty tonight. Something secluded, by the fire, if they can do it."

"Yes, Mr. Ishag. By the way, there's a gentleman here to see you."

"There is? Who?"

"He won't give me his name and he's not on your schedule." There was no mistaking the disapproval in Sasha's voice. "I've asked him to leave, but he refuses. He says he must see you in person. Shall I call security?"

David hesitated. *A mystery!* He'd had a feeling today was going to be interesting. Since he married Sarah Jane—actually, since the day he met her—his life had become one long series of unexpected events. He hadn't realized quite how dull it had been before.

"No, that's all right. The e-mails can wait a few minutes. Send him in."

A few moments later, David Ishag's office door opened. He stood up, smiling broadly.

"Hello there. I'm David. And you are?"

The smile died on his lips when he saw the gun.

CHAPTER TWENTY-SEVEN

"Who are you? What do you want?"

Fear coursed through David Ishag's body. A year ago, the idea of death wouldn't have fazed him. If it was his time, it was his time. But now that he had Sarah Jane, everything was different. The thought of being torn away from her so soon after they'd found each other filled him with utter terror.

The pistol protruded from the man's inside jacket pocket. He reached for it. David closed his eyes, bracing himself for the shot. Instead, he heard a polite

American voice asking him, "Are you all right, Mr. Ishag? You don't look well."

David opened his eyes. The man was holding up an Interpol badge and an ID card. They must have been in the same pocket as the gun.

The relief was so overpowering David felt nauseous. He clutched at the desk. "Jesus Christ. You almost gave me a heart attack. Why didn't you say you were a cop?"

Danny McGuire looked perplexed. "I didn't have much of a chance."

David sank back into his chair. He reached for a glass of water with shaking hands. "I thought you were going to shoot me."

"Do visitors to your office often try to shoot you?"

"No. But they aren't usually armed either. Your inside jacket pocket?"

"Ohhhhh." Pulling his regulation Glock 22 automatic out of its holster, Danny McGuire laid it down on the desk. "Sorry about that. It's standard issue. Half the time I forget I'm carrying it. Danny McGuire, Interpol."

The two men shook hands.

Now that his heart rate had slowed to something approaching normal, David Ishag asked, "So how can I help you?"

Danny McGuire frowned. This was going to be difficult. But he'd learned long ago that when you had bad news to break, it was best not to beat around the bush.

"I'm afraid it concerns your wife."

Those six words ripped into David Ishag more powerfully than any bullet.

"Sarah Jane?" he said defensively. "What about her?"

Danny McGuire took a deep breath. "Not to put too fine a point on it, Mr. Ishag, but we think she's planning to kill you."

Even in Danny McGuire's no-nonsense, unflowery prose, it took over an hour to fill David in on the long and convoluted history of the Azrael killings. An hour during which David listened intently, searching for flaws in McGuire's thinking, for reasons *not* to believe that any of this crazy story had anything to do with Sarah Jane, his wife, and the one woman on earth with whom he believed he could be truly happy.

When McGuire finished, David was silent for a long time. He wasn't going to roll over and simply accept that his marriage, his entire relationship with Sarah, had been a sham, just because some unknown police officer told him it was. Eventually he said, "I'd like to see the photographs of the other women."

"Of course. You can come down to our headquarters and see them, or I can have them e-mailed to you here."

"Let's say you're right. Let's say Sarah Jane *has* lied about her name and background."

"That much is a provable fact."

"Okay, fine. But it doesn't make her a killer, does it?"

McGuire felt bad for the guy. He didn't want to believe that his wife was a murderer, any more than Matt Daley wanted to accept that Lisa Baring had conspired in Miles's death, or than he, Danny, wanted to blame Angela Jakes for *her* husband's death all those years ago. Even now, despite knowing what he did, Danny McGuire found that part the hardest to accept. That the Angela Jakes he remembered, that sweet, good-natured, innocent angel of a woman had never really existed. She was a character, an act, a shell. An identity assumed for a purpose—a deadly purpose—just like Tracey Henley was an act, and Irina Anjou and Lisa Baring and now Sarah Jane Ishag.

Angela Jakes's words on the night of the first murder came floating back to him.

"I have no life."

If only he'd realized then that she meant it literally. Angela had no life. She didn't exist, had never existed. And neither did Sarah Jane.

"It makes her an accessory to multiple homicides," Danny said bluntly. "It also makes her a liar."

David longed to jump in and defend Sarah's honor, but what could he say? At a minimum she had lied to him. He clung to the hope that the pictures McGuire sent him of the other Azrael widows would somehow exonerate her, but deep down he knew that they would not. Interpol wouldn't have sent a senior director to see him if all they had were wild accusations.

Even so, it all sounded so preposterous, so impossible to believe.

McGuire went on: "Clearly, she's not acting alone. As I said, there's been a sexual element to all the Azrael killings, with each of the 'wives' apparently raped and beaten at the scene. We have clear forensic evidence that a man was present at each homicide. We don't know whether the rapes were conceived as a cover, to throw us off the scent, or whether violent sex is a part of the motive. This woman, whoever she really is, may get off on the sadomasochistic element."

David groaned. *No, not my Sarah. She loves me.* The pain was so intense that he felt it physically, like someone injecting acid into his veins.

"Certainly money does not seem to be the primary motive. Despite the fact that all four prior victims have been wealthy, and their wills altered in their wives' favor, most of the money has wound up going to children's charities.

May I ask if you and Sarah Jane signed a prenuptial agreement of any kind?"

David stared out of the window bleakly. "No," he said wearily. "No prenup."

Sarah Jane's voice rang in his head: *"You might as well have written me a letter saying 'I don't trust you.'"*

"And your will?"

David put his head in his hands.

It had started out as a joke between them. One night in Paris, in bed in the palatial honeymoon suite at the Georges V, Sarah Jane had teased him for not wanting to make love.

"Is this what I've let myself in for, marrying such an old man? Long nights of celibacy?"

"It's the wine we had at dinner!" David protested. "And then that Château d'Yquem with dessert. It's done for me."

Sarah Jane shook her head in mock disappointment. "I knew I should have gone for a younger man. Next time around I'm going for a boy toy."

"Next time?"

"When I'm living the life of a merry widow."

David grinned and rolled on top of her. "I'll put a provision in my will. One sniff of a boy toy and you'll be penniless."

Sarah Jane laughed, that deep sexy laugh that fired up David's libido like a blowtorch. In the end, he made love to her that night with more passion than he'd ever felt before. The next morning, thinking back to their banter, he realized guiltily, *Shit. She isn't even* in *my will. I'd better change it before she has another cow about me not trusting her with money.*

He'd faxed the amendments to his attorney the next day.

Danny McGuire asked gently, "Is she sole beneficiary?"

David Ishag nodded. He looked so stricken that for one awful moment Danny McGuire feared he was going to break down in tears.

"I understand how hard this is for you, Mr. Ishag, believe me. I'm truly sorry." *Hard?* The understatement was so hilarious, David almost laughed.

"But we need your help if we're going to catch this woman and the man who's helping her. We got to you in time. But if Sarah Jane figures out we're on to her and takes off, her next victim may not be so lucky."

David Ishag closed his eyes. In a dull, lifeless monotone he asked, "What do you want me to do?"

Outside, in the punishing Mumbai heat, Danny pulled out his BlackBerry and sent a private, encrypted e-mail. It was addressed to Rajit Kapiri of the Indian IB and all six members of the Azrael team, and was cc'd to Henri Frémeaux back in Lyon.

The message read simply: "Ishag's in. Operation Azrael a go."

CHAPTER TWENTY-EIGHT

"Will you be late tonight, darling?"

Sarah Jane Ishag leaned over the breakfast table to kiss her husband. David had been unusually distracted lately. They hadn't made love in weeks.

Without looking up from the *Wall Street Journal,* David said, "Hmm? Late? Oh no. I shouldn't think so."

Sarah Jane studied his handsome head, with its thick, shining jet-black hair and skin the same shade of cappuccino as her silk La Perla robe. She watched his fingers trace the words of the newspaper article as he read. Everything about him seemed so vital, so alive. For a moment panic gripped her, but she quickly banished it.

"Good. I thought we could make it an early night. I'll make you some of that horrid chicken noodle soup that you like, with the dumplings."

David looked up. It was disconcerting the way he stared at her, as if he were seeing her face for the first time.

"Matzo balls," he said dully.

"Sorry. Matzo balls." She blushed. "Not much of a Jewish wife, am I?"

A few weeks earlier, on their honeymoon, David would have laughed at that line. Made some joke about Catholic girls being crap in the kitchen but virtuosos in the bedroom. Now he said nothing. He just sat there, staring. *Something's changed.*

Inside, she was worried, but she made sure to betray no trace of her anxiety in her tone.

"So if I have dinner ready at eight, you'll be home?"

"I'll be home."

David Ishag kissed her on the cheek and went to work.

* * *

Ten minutes later, behind the wheel of his Range Rover Evoque, David plugged in his MP3 player and listened again to the recording Danny McGuire had given him yesterday.

Sarah Jane's voice. *"We can't, not yet. I'm not ready."*

A man's voice, electronically distorted. *"Come on, angel. We've been through this. We go through it every time. The gods have demanded their sacrifice. The time is now."*

Sarah Jane again. Angry now. *"That's all very easy for you to say, but it's not the gods that have to do it, is it? It's me. I'm the one who has to suffer. I'm the one who always suffers."*

"I'll be gentle this time."

A strangled sound, half muffled. Was it a laugh? Then Sarah's voice again.

"He's different from the others. I don't know if I can do it."

"Different? How is he different?"

"He's younger." There was a note of desperation in her voice, of pity even.

Hearing her made David Ishag's heart tighten. *"He has so much to live for."*

The distorted voice took on a harder edge. *"Your sister has a lot to live for too, doesn't she?"*

The line went crackly at this point, and the audio was lost. David had heard the recording fifty, a hundred times now, desperately searching for any meaning other than the obvious one: that his wife and some unknown lover were plotting his murder. Each time he reached this point, he willed the next line to be different. Prayed he would hear Sarah Jane's voice saying: *"No, I can't, I won't do it. David's my husband and I love him. Leave me alone."* But each time, the nightmare recurred exactly as it had before.

"Yes, yes. Friday night."

"I love you, angel."

"I love you too."

With David's help, Danny McGuire and his team had finally managed to tap in to Sarah Jane's cell phone, as well as the two pay phones in Dharavi that his men had observed her using. They still hadn't traced the identity of the man. He was obviously a pro, distorting his voice and using sophisticated blocking software to prevent anyone from accurately tracking his number. But the Ishag mansion was under twenty-four-hour surveillance. Any unidentified male coming within five hundred feet of the place was photographed and, if necessary, stopped and searched.

"You're completely safe," Danny McGuire told David. "If she tries anything, we'll be there in an instant."

But David Ishag didn't feel safe. Not just because Interpol being there "in an instant" might not be quick enough. It could take less than "an instant" for a bullet to penetrate his skull or a kitchen knife to puncture his aorta. But because the real tragedy of all this, the thing he feared most, had already happened. He had lost Sarah Jane. Worse than that, he never really had her in the first place. Sarah Jane, *his* Sarah Jane, didn't exist.

Even now, in the face of overwhelming damning evidence of her guilt—even without the audiotapes, David Ishag had seen McGuire's pictures of the other widows, and the resemblances were too striking to ignore—he couldn't fully make himself believe it. Sarah Jane had looked so heartbreakingly sexy in that negligee this morning. She'd sounded so vulnerable when he hadn't been able to bring himself to laugh at her jokes, or even look at her properly when she spoke to him. Part of him, a big part, still wanted to tell Danny Mc-Guire and Interpol and the rest of the world to go fuck themselves. To take Sarah Jane to bed, make love to her the way he used to and afterward simply ask her about the man on the tape and the lies she'd told him. Challenge her face-to-face to explain herself and give him a rational explanation.

And she would explain herself and apologize, and David would forgive her, and someone else would have committed these dreadful murders, not Sarah Jane, and they'd live happily ever after.

His car phone rang, shattering the fantasy.

"So we're still set for an eight o'clock start tonight." Danny McGuire sounded almost excited, as if they were talking about a kick-off at a football game and not an attempt on David's life. "No last-minute changes. That's good."

"You picked all that up, then? At breakfast."

"Clear as a bell."

David thought, *At least the bugging devices are working properly.* The only thing more terrifying than going through with tonight's plan would be going through it with technical hitches.

Danny McGuire said, "Try to relax. I know it doesn't feel that way, but you're perfectly safe in there. We've got your back."

"I'll try to remember that this evening when my wife's boyfriend starts lunging at my jugular with a sharpened machete." David laughed weakly.

"You're doing the right thing. Come tomorrow morning, this will all be over."

David Ishag hung up the phone and swallowed hard. He knew that if he allowed himself to cry once, the tears would never stop.

"This will all be over."

No, it won't.

For David Ishag, the pain of Sarah

Jane's betrayal would never be over. Without her, he might as well be dead.

At six P.M., Danny McGuire sat in the back of the transit van, dividing his attention between the screen in front of him and today's London *Times* crossword puzzle on his iPad. It was Richard Sturi, the statistician, who'd gotten him hooked on British-style crosswords and Danny had quickly become a junkie. They helped relieve the stress and loneliness of running Operation Azrael, helped him forget how much he missed home and Céline, helped him block out the fear about the state his marriage might be in once this operation was finally over.

The London *Times* puzzle was usually the most challenging, far superior to that of the *New York Times* or *Le Figaro,* but today's setter seemed to be having an off day.

One across: *Wet yarn I entangled.*

As anagrams went, it was laughably easy. As Danny typed in the answer— *R-a-i-n-y*—his mind started to wander.

When had he last been in the rain? A month ago? Longer? It rained a lot in Lyon. Here in Mumbai the sun was relentless, beating down punishingly on the sticky, humid city from dawn till dusk.

"Sir." Ajay Jassal, a surveillance operative on loan from the Indians, tapped Danny on the shoulder. "The catering van. That's not the usual driver."

Danny was alert in an instant. "Zoom in."

Jassal was eagle-eyed. Even up close, it was tough to make out the van driver's features on the fuzzy green screen. It didn't help that he was wearing a cap and had one hand covering the lower part of his face as he waited for the service gates to open.

"You're quite sure it's a different driver?"

The young Indian looked at Danny McGuire curiously, as if he were blind. "Yes, sir. Quite sure. Look at his arms, sir. That is a white man."

Danny's pulse quickened. Ajay Jassal was right. The arm dangling out of the driver's-side window was a distinctly

paler shade of green than that of the
rear gatekeeper waving him into the
compound.

Was this him? Was this the killer?

**Was the face beneath that cap the
face of Lyle Renalto, aka Frankie
Mancini?**

Have we got him at last?

The barrier lifted. Lurching forward,
the driver put both hands back on the
wheel, turning slightly to the side as he
did so. For the first time Danny McGuire
got a good look at his face.

"I don't believe it," he whispered.

"Sir?"

"I do *not* fucking believe it."

"You know the man, sir? You've seen
him before?"

"Oh yeah." Danny nodded. "I know
the man."

It wasn't Lyle Renalto.

CHAPTER TWENTY-NINE

David Ishag pulled into his underground garage. The clock on the dashboard said 7:30 P.M.

In five minutes, I'll see Sarah Jane.

In half an hour, we'll have dinner together.

By midnight, she'll have tried to kill me.

None of it felt real, except his nerves. The tight knot in his stomach, the sweat running down his back. Mentally he ran over the plan again. He would go inside and act as natural as possible around Sarah Jane. They would have dinner. By nine o'clock it would be safe for David to go up to bed. At some point Sarah Jane would join him, and soon afterward her mysterious accomplice would presumably burst in. David's job then was to feign a heart attack, momentarily confusing his would-be killers and hopefully buying enough time for McGuire and his men to show up and make their arrests.

Raj, David's valet, greeted him as calmly as ever. "Good evening, sir. How was your day?"

None of the staff knew what was going on, for their own safety. David trusted Raj implicitly, but Danny McGuire had been insistent on total secrecy.

"It was fine, thank you, Raj. Is Mrs. Ishag at home?"

Please say no. She's gone out. She's changed her mind. She couldn't go through with it after all.

"She's in the drawing room, sir. Waiting for you."

When David walked in, Sarah Jane was facing the window, her back to him. She was wearing a long scarlet jersey dress with a scooped back that David had bought for her in Paris, on their honeymoon. Her hair was piled up in loose coils on top of her head. She looked stunning.

"You dressed up."

She turned and smiled at him shyly. "I thought I'd make an effort for once. Do you like it?"

David's throat went dry. "You look incredible."

Walking over to him, Sarah Jane wrapped her arms around his neck. "Thanks." She kissed him tenderly on the lips and David felt his resolve weaken. He tried to think about the photographs of the other Azrael widows, Sarah Jane's alter egos; about her voice on the police tape, plotting his death. But both those things felt like a dream, utterly unconnected with the *real* Sarah Jane, the Sarah Jane whose soft lips now pressed against his own.

Was it possible to love someone you knew was going to try to murder you?

"Shall we eat?"

Back in the surveillance van, Danny McGuire's mind was racing.

The "new" delivery driver was not Lyle Renalto, as he'd half hoped, half expected.

The new driver was Matthew Daley.

Danny's thoughts lurched wildly from past to present, questioning everything. *Could Daley really be involved? Could he be Azrael's accomplice?*

Every instinct in him told him that this wasn't possible. Matt Daley hadn't met the woman now calling herself Sarah Jane Ishag till her most recent previous incarnation as Lisa Baring. And that meeting had happened *after* Miles Baring's murder, a crime Matt couldn't have committed because was in L.A. at the time.

And yet . . .

What did Danny McGuire actually know about Matthew Daley? Only what Matt had chosen to tell him. That he was a writer from Los Angeles, that he had a sister called Claire and an ex-wife called Raquel and that he was Andrew Jakes's biological son. The sister was real enough. Danny had met her. As for the rest of the story, McGuire had taken it all on trust. What if it was all bullshit?

Forcing himself to calm down, Danny tried to analyze things rationally.

Let's say what he told me was true. Let's say he really is Jakes's son.

According to Daley, Jakes had abandoned him and his mother and sister, apparently cutting them off without a penny. Was that enough of a motive for murder? *Sure.* Matt would have been in his midtwenties when Andrew Jakes was killed, more than old enough to plan and carry out a homicide. *What if he didn't meet Azrael as Lisa Baring? What if he already knew her as Angela Jakes, his father's second wife? And later as Tracey Henley and Irina Anjou, and now as Sarah Jane Ishag?*

But if that was the case, where did Lyle/Frankie fit into all this? And why, more importantly, would Matt Daley have flown to Lyon to see Danny Mc-Guire in the first place? To point out to Danny the links between the various Azrael killings and convince him to reopen the case? Surely, if Matt were involved in the murders, that made no sense.

Unless he wants to get caught.

Wasn't that the classic psychopathic mind-set? That there was no point committing the perfect crime if the world never got to know how brilliant you were? Danny pictured Matt Daley, first in L.A. then later in London and the South of France, waiting for the police sirens, for retribution, for the knock on the door that never came. Perhaps the anonymity had gotten to be too much for him?

"Camera three, sir!" Ajay Jassal's voice brought Danny back to reality. "Daley's leaving."

"Leaving?"

Now Danny was even more confused than before. Wasn't the hit on Ishag supposed to be tonight? If so, why the hell would Matt Daley be leaving, and at breakneck speed too? That van must be doing sixty miles an hour.

He looked at his watch. Five to eight. Dinner would take at least an hour. David wasn't scheduled to go up to bed until well after nine.

"Where's Ishag right now?"

"Still in the drawing room, sir. Audio's picking him up clearly. He's fine."

Danny McGuire made a split-second decision.

"Okay. Follow Daley. Follow the van."

Ajay Jassal hesitated. "Are you sure, sir? If something unexpected happens up at the house and we don't get back in time . . ."

"We'll get back in time. I wanna know where that bastard's headed in such a hurry." Danny picked up the walkie-talkie so he could speak to the men sitting in the second surveillance vehicle, parked on the front side of the mansion. "Jassal and I are in pursuit of a possible suspect. You guys stay in contact, let us know if you need to go in earlier, or if anything happens."

"Yes, sir."

Danny turned back to Ajay Jassal. "What are you waiting for, man?" he shouted. "Drive."

Coiled like a rattlesnake in David Ishag's master-bedroom closet, the man pressed the barrel of his pistol against his cheek, closing his eyes as if embracing a lover. At his feet the blade of a six-inch hunting knife glinted in the darkness.

It was uncomfortable, crouched in his hiding place, but the dull ache in his thighs was a small price to pay for vengeance.

In one short hour it would all be over.

"How's the soup?"

"Very good. Thank you."

"I made it myself."

Really? We're making small talk? David scraped the last of his matzo ball from the bottom of the bowl. He'd worried all day that he'd be too nervous to eat tonight. Danny McGuire had stressed the importance of behaving naturally around Sarah Jane, but what if David couldn't? What if he threw up, or passed out, or accidentally blurted out *Why are you trying to kill me?* over dessert? But as it turned out, he found that he was surprisingly hungry for the condemned man's last meal. And the soup *was* good.

"What's so funny?" Sarah Jane asked. David realized belatedly that he'd been grinning like an idiot, lost in his own thoughts.

"Nothing." He tried to reset his features to neutral. "What's for dessert?" *Death by chocolate?*

"Ice cream. Are you sure you're all right, David?"

It was no good. He was visibly laughing now, powerless to stop the tears of mirth from rolling down his face. He hadn't felt like this since his brief stint as a pot head back in his Oxford days. *I must be getting hysterical.*

"Do you want to go upstairs and lie down?"

Upstairs. The word sobered him up instantly, like a glass of ice-cold water in the face.

So she wants to do it now, does she? Get it over and done with? Why not?

The original plan had been to wait until after dinner to make his move upstairs, somewhere around nine fifteen. But if Sarah Jane was ready now, then so was he. He thought about the SWAT team surrounding the property and remembered Danny McGuire's words from this morning. *"You're completely safe. If she tries anything, we'll be there in an instant."*

He turned back to Sarah Jane.

"I think I will, if it's all the same to you. I don't feel too great all of a sudden."

The catering van weaved its way through the grand streets of Marathi, as fast and nimble as a mouse. Ajay Jassal followed, struggling to keep control of his large, squat surveillance vehicle while the usually mild-mannered Danny McGuire screamed at him to "Keep up! Don't lose him!"

Jassal knew the streets well. But surveillance vans were not designed for high-speed chases. They were designed to stay parked for long, wearisome hours and to blend in with their surroundings. It was a tribute to Ajay's skill that he managed to keep the smaller vehicle in sight at all, bouncing over cobblestones and careering precariously around corners, often into unlit streets. God knew what the ride was doing to their expensive audiovisual equipment.

The catering van was taking them on a tour of South Mumbai's most upscale residential neighborhoods: Walkeshwar Road, Peddar Road, Breach Candy, all of them distinctive for their British architectural leanings. The driver avoided the commercial thoroughfares such as Cuffe Parade or Carmichael Road, preferring to duck and dive through the quieter streets. Clearly, he realized he was being followed.

After twenty minutes, much of it spent driving around in circles, the van headed north toward Wankhede cricket stadium. As they got nearer, the streets thronged with crowds of young men. The blazing stadium floodlights could be seen from miles away.

"Must be a match night," said Ajay Jassal. "I doubt if we'll get much farther. Not by car."

Danny McGuire could hardly see the van now through the dark, heaving mass of bodies. Was Matt Daley planning to make a run for it? Danny looked at his watch. *Eight forty-five.* David Ishag's dinner date would soon be over. They had to get back to the house.

Without thinking, McGuire threw open the door of the surveillance vehicle and began pushing his way through the mob, shouting, "Police!" and grabbing shirts and jackets indiscriminately as he literally flung bystanders out of his path.

Within seconds he'd reached Matt's van. It too was empty, abandoned only a few yards from the gates of the cricket ground. Desperately McGuire looked around, scanning the crowd for Matt's distinctive blond mop of hair. *Nothing.*

Then suddenly he saw him, right at the stadium entrance, about twenty yards away. By the time Danny got there, Matt would be inside, subsumed into the crowd. Gone. Instinctively Danny's fingers tightened around his gun, but he knew he couldn't use it. *Fire a shot here and you'd trigger a stampede.* Just as despair began to wash over him, Danny saw Ajay Jassal sprinting past him, parting the crowds like Moses at the Red Sea, his long legs powering over the hard ground like a cheetah. There was a scream and a scuffle.

Danny forced his way forward, waving his Interpol badge as if brandishing garlic at a vampire.

Jassal had pounced, knocking Daley clean off his feet and pinning him to the ground.

"I have apprehended the suspect, sir," he panted.

Danny McGuire wheezed up behind him. "Good job, Jassal. Matthew Daley, I'm arresting you on suspicion of attempted—" He stopped midsentence.

The man on the ground had turned to face him. His cheek was badly bruised and his brown eyes were wide with confusion and panic.

He was as Indian as the Taj Mahal.

David Ishag stared at the bathroom mirror, clutching the marble countertop for support.

This is it. Any moment now, she's going to let him in.

My killer.

He splashed cold water on his face, willing the dizziness to stop. *Remember what McGuire said. He's right outside.*

All I need to do is collapse to the floor with chest pains the second the guy walks in. Easy.

"David? Darling?" Sarah Jane stood swaying in the doorway. "Are you all right? Do you need a doctor?"

Swaying? That's weird. Why's she swaying?

Spots began swimming before David's eyes. "I . . . I don't feel good." Now the whole room was lurching, like a ship in high seas. All of a sudden he felt violently ill. Never mind a faked collapse. At this point he was about to have a real one.

Then suddenly it dawned on him.

"Do you like the soup? I made it myself."

She's poisoned me! The bitch put something in my soup!

He tried to look at Sarah Jane, but there were at least six identical versions of her leaning over him as he slid to the floor, clutching his stomach. "Why . . . ?" he gasped. "Why are you doing this?"

Tears filled her eyes. "It's all right. Don't panic. I'm going to call an ambulance."

The sympathy in her voice sounded so *real*. But he couldn't let himself fall for it, couldn't allow himself to slip. He had to stay awake, stay focused. McGuire's mikes were all in the bedroom. He had to get in there, let the SWAT team outside know what was happening. With every ounce of his remaining strength, he shouted, "Bed!"

He could feel his throat muscles swelling up, his breath getting short. Soon he wouldn't be able to speak at all.

"Have to lie down. Please."

"Of course, darling, of course." Sarah Jane helped him into the bedroom, a look of deep concern and worry on her face. *Why is she still keeping up the charade?* thought David. *It makes no sense.* Falling back on the bed, he clutched at his tie. He had to loosen it! He couldn't breathe! He waved frantically to Sarah to help him, but she had turned her back and was heading toward the phone.

"I'm calling 1298. Hold on, David. Help is on the way."

* * *

Back in the surveillance van, Danny Mc-
Guire checked his seat belt and clutched
the handrail above the door for support.
Jassal was on clear, straight road now,
his siren blaring. They must be doing
ninety at least.

Danny looked at his watch: nine P.M.
He felt like a royal idiot.

Matt Daley, of course, was still in the
Ishag house. He'd known Danny was
there all along and lured him away with
a classic bait and switch.

Had they done it yet? Had he and
Sarah   Jane—Azrael—killed   David
Ishag?

In the seat next to Danny the sound
engineer was struggling with the van's
complex radio equipment. They had to
get in touch with the other members of
the team, get inside the house before it
was too late.

Danny shouted at him, fighting to be
heard above the screeching sirens.

"Anything?"

The man shook his head. "We're in
range, but I can't get a signal."

The lights of Marathi twinkled in the distance. Soon the Ishag mansion itself would be in view.

"Keep trying."

Sarah Jane hung up the telephone. "They're on their way."

David drifted in and out of consciousness. *What was I supposed to do again? Something about chest pains?* It was so hard to tell what was real and what wasn't. Was Sarah really holding his hand? Mopping his brow? Or was that a dream? She seemed so loving . . . but wasn't she planning to kill him?

He closed his eyes again.

When he opened them, a man was standing over the bed. He was masked and dressed from head to toe in black like the grim reaper. In his hand, glinting silver against the dark fabric of his pants, was a knife.

David contemplated screaming, but his larynx seemed to have swollen shut, and in any case he wasn't as afraid as he'd thought he'd be. He was just very,

very tired. *I'm probably dreaming. He'll disappear in a minute.*

He closed his eyes and drifted away.

"I've got them, sir! Voices. In the master bedroom."

Danny McGuire punched the air with relief. "And the others?"

"Yes, sir, we have contact."

"Demartin, Kapiri, do you copy?"

The Indian policeman's furious voice was the first on the line. "McGuire? Where the fuck have you been?"

"Never mind that. Get into the house, now! They're in the master. Get Ishag out of there." Hanging up, Danny turned back to the sound engineer. "Can you hear Ishag? Is he alive?"

The sound engineer clasped his headphones, closing his eyes in concentration. "I'm not sure. I can hear the woman. She—"

Suddenly the man ripped the headphones from his ears. Danny McGuire didn't need to ask why.

Everybody in the van heard Sarah Jane Ishag's scream.

* * *

In David Ishag's bedroom, the man in black pulled his mask off and smiled.

"What's the matter, angel?" he asked. "Were you expecting someone else?"

CHAPTER THIRTY

From his hiding place, he could see them perfectly. The man in black and the woman now calling herself Sarah Jane Ishag.

She could call herself whatever she liked. *He* knew who she was. And *whose* she was. She was his. His love. His woman.

The urge to jump out at that very moment and grab her was overpowering. But he'd waited too long for this, invested too much time and effort. He had to see how the scene played out.

The man in black pointed to David Ishag. "Is he dead?"

David lay on his back on the bed, as still as stone. Sarah Jane leaned over him.

"No. He's still breathing."

"I didn't expect him to go down so fast. You must have put too much in."

"Don't blame me!" She was angry. "I followed your instructions to the letter. I told you we shouldn't have drugged him first. What if he has heart failure? What if the police find the stuff in his system?"

"Be quiet!" The man in black punched her hard in the face.

From his hiding place in the closet, he could hear the sickening crunch of her cheekbone as Sarah Jane slumped to the floor whimpering. He watched as the man in black pulled her up by the hair. "Who are *you* to tell *me* what we should and shouldn't do? You're nobody, that's who. Say it. SAY IT!"

"I'm nobody," Sarah Jane sobbed.

"You have no life."

Her voice was barely a whisper now. "I have no life."

Hearing her recite the words seemed

to pacify the man slightly. He let go of her hair. "We had to drug him or he'd have fought back. The others were all too old to defend themselves." He held his knife up to the light. Nodding contemptuously at David, he said, "We'll do him later. First it's your turn."

Sarah Jane backed away, scrambling across the bedroom floor on her hands and knees like a frightened crab. "No! Please. You don't have to do this!"

"Of course I have to do it. The others were all punished, weren't they? Angela, Tracey, Irina, Lisa. Why should conniving little Sarah Jane get off scot-free?"

"Please," Sarah Jane begged. The terror in her voice was unmistakable. "I did everything you asked . . . You said you wouldn't hurt me."

But the man in black appeared unmoved by entreaties or tears. He wasn't a man at all. He was an animal. With a feral snarl he pounced on Sarah Jane, pinning her to the ground. One hand tore at her skin while the other pressed the knife hard against her throat. Instinctively she struggled, kicking her legs vainly under the weight of him. He was pulling up the skirt of her dress, jamming her thighs open with his knee.

The man in the closet could wait no longer. Bursting into the room, he hurled himself on the man in black, smashing the butt of his gun repeatedly into the back of the man's skull. Blood gushed everywhere, warm and sticky and vital. In seconds the vile animal hand that had been clawing between Sarah Jane's legs fell limp.

Sarah Jane screwed her eyes shut, not daring to breathe. *Was it really over? Was he really dead?* The next thing she was aware of was the deadweight being dragged off her. Someone, her savior, rolled the man in black's body onto the floorboards with a *thud,* like a sack of earth.

Was it David, poor dear David, awakened from the effects of the narcotic, loyal and protective to the last?

Or had the police finally figured it out, finally come to take them into custody and put an end to all the years of madness. To save her and her sister. To make it stop.

She turned around and found herself gazing into familiar, loving eyes.

"It's all right, Lisa," Matt Daley whispered. "It's all right, my darling. You're safe now."

Matt touched her face, tracing his finger lovingly over each feature. Her right cheek had swollen up like an overripe plum where the bastard had hurt her. He would never hurt her again.

"Lisa . . ." Matt Daley started to cry. "My poor Lisa."

She opened her mouth to say something, but the gunshot was so loud it drowned out her reply. For a second Matt Daley's face registered something. It wasn't pain. More like extreme surprise.

Then his world softly faded to black.

CHAPTER THIRTY-ONE

Rajit Kapiri was in the house. Seconds later Claude Demartin and his three-man team joined him, followed by a breathless Danny McGuire.

"Where are the servants?" Danny demanded..

"In the kitchens," said Kapiri. "I have six armed officers with them. They've barricaded the doors."

"Good. You and Demartin take the main staircase. I'll go up by the servants' route."

"How about two of my guys go with you as cover," said Kapiri. It was a statement, not a question, but Danny didn't object. They had no time for power struggles, not now.

A gunshot rang out.

The three men looked at one another, then ran for the stairs.

"How could you?"

"How could *I*?" The man in black clutched at the wound on the back of his head. He still felt dizzy, as if he might black out at any moment. "He left me for dead, Sofia, in case you hadn't noticed."

Sofia Basta's eyes filled with tears.

"He was protecting me! My God, Frankie. You didn't have to kill him."

Frankie Mancini frowned. It was unfortunate that he'd been forced to shoot Daley. The man was, after all, Andrew Jakes's son. Technically that made him one of the children. One of the victims Frankie had devoted his life to avenging. It was even more unfortunate that the silencer on his gun had failed. A member of the household staff could come in at any moment. The police might already be on their way. They didn't have much time.

"Bolt the door," he barked. But Sofia just stood there, watching Matt's blood ooze into the rug. "For God's sake, Sofia," Frankie said defensively. "I tried to get him to leave Mumbai. I did my best. He shouldn't have been here."

"He came here for me. Because he loved me," Sofia sobbed. "He loved me and I loved him!"

"Loved you?" Frankie Mancini scoffed cruelly. "My dear girl. He didn't even know who you were. He loved Lisa Baring. And who was she? Nobody, that's who, a character who *I* invented, a figment of *my* imagination. If Matt Daley loved anyone, it was me, not you. Now bolt the damn door."

Sofia Basta did as she was asked. She saw the madness blazing in Frankie's eyes. *Poor, poor Matt! Why did he come for me? Why didn't he run, break free while he had the chance?*

"He didn't deserve to die, Frankie."

"Be quiet!" Mancini shrieked, waving his pistol menacingly in the air. "*I* decide who lives and who dies! *I* have the power! You are my wife. You will do as I command you, or on my life, Sofia, your sister will be next. Do you understand?"

Sofia nodded. She understood. Fear and obedience were all she understood. All she had ever known. For a few short, blissful months of her life, as Lisa Baring, in Bali with Matt Daley, she had been shown a glimpse of another way, another life. But it was not to be.

"POLICE!" Danny McGuire's voice rang out like a siren. Pounding footsteps could be heard behind him on the stairs. A second salvation.

Mancini's eyes widened in panic. He handed Sofia the knife. "Do it."

"Do what? Oh no. Frankie, no."

Her eyes followed his gaze to the bed. In all the drama with Matt, she'd momentarily forgotten that David Ishag was even in the room, but now she could see him stirring, the effects of the drug she'd fed him earlier beginning to wear off.

"This is the end, angel. Our last kill. The sacrifice that will win your sister's life."

"POLICE!" Fists pounded on the door.

"It's only right that it should be yours. Do it."

"Frankie, I can't."

"Do it!" Mancini was screaming, howling like a mad dog. "Cut his throat or I'll shoot you both. DO IT!"

Images flashed through Sofia's mind one by one.

Reading "The Book" with Frankie back at the orphanage. How beautiful he was then, and how gentle. *"You're a princess, Sofia. The others are just jealous."*

Andrew Jakes, their first kill, with blood spurting from his neck like thick red water from a fountain.

Piers Henley, funny, cerebral Piers, who'd fought back until they shot him in the head, splattering his brilliant brain all over the bedroom walls.

Didier Anjou, pleading for his life as the blade sank into his flesh again and again and again.

Miles Baring, collapsing instantly as the knife pierced his heart.

Matt Daley, the one true innocent of all of them. Matt who had loved her, who had given her hope. Matt who lay dead and cold at her feet.

She thought of the living. Her sister, her flesh and blood, out there somewhere. David Ishag, stirring groggily back to life on the bed.

"SLIT HIS THROAT!" Frankie's voice, excited, aroused as it always was by blood and death and vengeance.

"POLICE!" Sledgehammers pounded against the door, splintering the wood.

"I can't," Sofia said calmly, closing her mind to the clamor and roar as she let the knife drop at her feet. "Shoot if you want to, Frankie. But I can't do it. Not anymore."

At long last the door gave way. Armed men swarmed into the room.

"Police! Put your hands in the air!"

David Ishag opened his eyes just in time to see Danny McGuire, gun drawn, panting in the doorway.

"You sure took your bloody time," he murmured weakly.

Then somebody fired a single shot.

And it was all over.

PART IV

CHAPTER THIRTY-TWO

ONE YEAR LATER . . .

Los Angeles County Superior Court judge Federico Muñoz was no stranger to front-page homicide cases. Two years ago in this very courtroom, room 306 on the third floor of the Beverly Hills Courthouse, a jury had found a much-loved movie actress guilty of killing her violent lover after years of abuse. Judge Muñoz sent the actress to death row, to the outrage of her fans, family and many in the national news media. Not long afterward, the judge received the first of the death threats that would be made against him periodically for the rest of his life.

He was delighted.

Death threats were what enabled Judge Federico Muñoz to demand a permanent security detail to escort him to and from work. Arriving every day at the imposing white-pillared courthouse at 9355 Burton Way, surrounded by a phalanx of armed guards, made Judge Muñoz feel inordinately important, as did the ongoing media interest in his life. Publicly, of course, he denounced this interest as prurient and mean-spirited, taking particular umbrage at the *L.A. Times*'s dubbing of him as "Judge Dread." Privately, however, he loved every minute of it. Judge Federico Muñoz was already famous in Los Angeles. Now, thanks to the Azrael trial, he was becoming famous around the world.

The trial that had been going on now for two weeks—it had taken the prosecution that long to present their case, so huge was the mountain of evidence at their disposal—could not have been more sensational. Four wealthy men brutally murdered in identically staged and plotted circumstances around the globe. The accused, a married couple in their forties, both blessed with movie-star good looks, caught in the act of attempting to murder a fifth. All the elderly victims had been lured into marriage by the female defendant, known to the media as "the Angel of Death." And yet this woman had herself submitted to violent, sexually sadistic assaults during each murder, administered by the male defendant. Willingly, if the prosecution was to be believed.

Neither party denied the murders, but each claimed coercion, identifying the other as the ringleader. Throw in the soap-opera-perfect twist of a "Robin Hood" motive—all the victims' millions had been donated to children's charities—and the tabloids could not have asked for more.

But they got more. They got a female defendant who had successfully assumed a new identity each time she tempted a fresh victim into her marriage bed, and had apparently undergone multiple surgeries to alter her appearance over the course of the past decade or so, but who remained drop-dead gorgeous. Sitting passively through the prosecution's evidence, only occasionally tearing up when photographs of her husbands' tortured bodies or her own injuries were shown to the jury, the woman seated at one end of the table in courtroom 306 looked as pristine and unsullied as a newborn baby, and as radiant as any angel. The press couldn't get enough of her.

On the opposite side of the dock sat her codefendant, Frances Mancini. The pair had met when both were orphaned at a New York City children's home during their teens. Mancini lacked his wife's radiance, the aura of serenity and goodness that seemed to emanate from her person like light, despite the terrible crimes she'd confessed to committing. Nonetheless he was a compellingly attractive man, with his dark hair, strong jaw and regal, smolderingly arrogant features. Mancini had been shot while resisting arrest in India, and still had difficulty standing up and sitting down, wincing with discomfort each time he moved. When he was at rest, however,

Mancini's thin lips were curled into a permanent knowing smile, as if the whole spectacle of the U.S. justice system had been contrived solely for his amusement. Neither he nor his wife had fought their extradition to the United States despite the fact that in France or England, where they could equally well have been tried, there was no death penalty. Here in California, both defendants were on trial for their lives, in front of a hostile jury and the toughest judge in the L.A. County Superior Court system. Yet Frankie Mancini seemed to view today's proceedings as little more than a piece of theater, a melodrama if not a boulevard farce, to which the fates had generously decided to allocate him a front-row seat.

This might have had something to do with the lawyer for the prosecution, William Boyce. A tall, angularly built man in his early fifties with close-cropped gray hair and a fondness for cheap charcoal-gray suits, Boyce, who was known for his even, measured delivery, was the antithesis of the hotshot attorney one expected to find in such a high-profile case. He was the proverbial "safe pair of hands," competent, professional and painfully ordinary to such a degree that it was often said that the only remarkable thing about William Boyce was how very unremarkable he was. Why the state had chosen Boyce to prosecute such a case was almost as much of a mystery as the homicides themselves. Perhaps the powers that be had decided, in the face of such overwhelming evidence, that a monkey could have succeeded in condemning both the Azrael killers to death row . . . and William Boyce was the closest thing they could find to a monkey.

In any event, it was quite an achievement to be able to bore a jury with a case as sensational as this one, but over the past two weeks William Boyce had managed to do just that, reciting the facts pertaining to the four murders in a monotone that had effectively blunted their emotional impact. He'd spent an entire day getting bogged down in the complex international legal agreement whereby the British, French, and Hong Kong Chinese authorities had consented to the evidence being heard jointly in California. His witnesses had livened things up a bit. Andrew Jakes's Spanish housekeeper, in particular, gasped and sobbed her way through hideously graphic testimony that had made the front pages of all the tabloids the next morning. But all in all, Judge Muñoz could see how the prosecution had earned Frankie Mancini's contempt. Like everyone else in courtroom 306, and those following the trial around the world, he was looking forward to hearing the defense's case. Today, at last, that time had come.

Because each defendant claimed to have been coerced by the other, they had chosen separate representation. Frankie's attorney, Alvin Dubray, was a short, fat man with a permanently untucked shirt and mad-scientist hair. Dubray arrived at courtroom 306 dropping papers from the pile under his arm, looking for all the world like a muddled old grandfather who'd gotten lost on his way to the library. In reality, as Judge Muñoz knew well, Dubray's mind was so sharp and his memory so prodigious that he had no need of notes of any kind. But the bumbling-old-buffoon act had been endearing him to juries for over twenty years and he wasn't about to abandon his shtick now. With a client as cold and unsympathetic as Frankie Mancini, Alvin Dubray would need to endear the hell out of today's crowd.

In that regard, the "Angel of Death's" attorney had the easier job. Ellen Watts was young and relatively inexperienced. This was only her second murder trial. But she had already made a name for herself on the Superior Court circuit as an insightful and talented trial lawyer, manipulating evidence with the artistry and ease of a potter molding clay on the wheel. With her bobbed blond hair and elfin features, Ellen Watts was usually considered a beauty. Next to her client, however, she faded away like a camera flash aimed at the sun.

"All rise."

For the last two weeks, Judge Federico Muñoz had banished the media from his courtroom. (It wouldn't do to be seen as too camera-hungry, and William Boyce was so deathly dull he'd be a turnoff for viewers anyway.) Today, however, he had relented, allowing a select group of news organizations some spots in the gallery. Their cameras, like the eyes of the rest of the room, flitted between the defendants and the three men sitting side by side in the front row. By now, they were all household names in America.

Danny McGuire, the LAPD detective turned Interpol hero who'd spent two-thirds of his career pursuing the Azrael killers and who had helped orchestrate the Indian sting that finally caught them.

David Ishag, the swoon-worthy Indian tycoon who'd been slated as Azrael's next victim till McGuire and his men plucked him from the jaws of certain death.

And at the end of the row, in a wheelchair, the tragic figure of Matthew Daley.

Daley was a writer, the son of Azrael's first victim, Andrew Jakes, and at one time a key Interpol informant. He too had been present the night of the defendants' arrest and was lucky to have survived the bullet from Mancini's gun, which had lodged in the base of his spine. Despite this, Matt Daley had refused to testify against the female defendant, a woman he still referred to as "Lisa." The rumor was that the poor man had been driven to the point of madness with love for her. Watching him gazing at her now, a hollow-eyed, sunken version of his former vivacious self, it was easy to believe.

"Ms. Watts." Judge Federico Muñoz paused just long enough to make sure that all eyes—and cameras—were trained on him. "I understand you are to open the case for the defense."

"That's correct, Your Honor."

Ellen Watts and Alvin Dubray had agreed between them that Ellen would go first. The plan was to get the character assassination of each other's client out of the way early so that they could close in on areas of common ground: weaknesses and inconsistencies in the prosecution's case, and the abuse suffered by both the accused as children. If they could sow enough reasonable doubt in the jury's mind as to who had corrupted whom, and paint both defendants as mentally disturbed, they stood a chance of keeping them both from death by lethal injection. Realistically it was the best they could hope for.

Ellen Watts approached the jury, looking each of the group of twelve men and women in the eye.

"Over the past two weeks," she began, "the prosecution has presented you with some pretty horrific evidence. Mr. Boyce has eloquently familiarized you with the facts surrounding four brutal murders. And I use that word advisedly—*facts*—because there *are* facts in this case, terrible facts, facts that neither I nor my client seek to deny. Andrew Jakes, Sir Piers Henley, Didier Anjou and Miles Baring all lost their lives in violent, bloody, terrifying circumstances. Some of those men have family and friends here today, in this courtroom. They too have had to sit through Mr. Boyce's evidence, and I know there isn't one of us whose heart does not go out to them."

Ellen Watts turned for effect and bestowed her best, most sympathetic nod of respect toward the two of Didier's ex-wives who'd flown over for the trial, as well as to the stooped but dignified figure of Sir Piers Henley's eighty-year-old half brother, Maximilian. Behind him, two women in their late fifties, old girlfriends of Miles Baring's who'd kept in touch after his marriage, glared at Ellen Watts with loathing, but the attorney's concerned expression never faltered.

"I am not here to debate the facts, ladies and gentlemen. To do so would be foolish, not to mention an act of grave disrespect to the victims and their families."

"Hear, hear!" shouted one of Miles Baring's girlfriends from the gallery, earning herself a sharp look from Judge Federico Muñoz and a murmured ripple of approval from everyone else.

"My job is to *stick* to the facts. To put an end to the wild speculation and rumor surrounding my client, and to present to you the truth. The truth about what she did and what she did not do. The truth about her relationship with her codefendant, Frankie Mancini. And the truth about who she really is." Ellen Watts approached the defendants' table, inviting the jury to follow her with their eyes, to look at the woman whose life they held in their hands. "She's been called the Angel of Death. A princess. A witch. A monster. None of these epithets is the truth. Her name is Sofia Basta. She's a human being, a flesh-and-blood woman whose life has been one long catalog of abuse and suffering." Ellen Watts inhaled deeply. "I intend to show that Ms. Basta was as much a victim in these crimes as the men who lost their lives."

Most of the jury frowned in disapproval. Cries of "shame" rose up from around the courtroom, prompting Judge Muñoz to call for silence.

Ellen Watts continued. "The truth may not be palatable, ladies and gentlemen. It may not be pleasant and it may not be what we want to hear. But revealing the truth is my business in this courtroom, and in the coming days I will show it to you in all its ugliness." Roused and passionate, she turned and pointed accusingly at Frankie Mancini. "It is *this man,* not my client, who orchestrated, planned and, indeed, carried out these murders. Knowing that Sofia was vulnerable, that she was mentally unstable, that she was lonely, Frankie Mancini cynically manipulated her, turning her into a weapon that he could use to further his own hateful ends. Convicting Sofia Basta of murder makes no more sense than convicting the knife or the gun or the rope.

"That's all I'm asking of you today: to hear the truth. To let the truth in. Nothing will bring back Andrew Jakes, Piers Henley, Didier Anjou and Miles Baring. But the truth may finally allow them to rest in peace."

Ellen Watts sat down to a silence so heavy you could almost hear it. Some of the jury members clearly disapproved of what she'd said. Others looked puzzled by it. But unlike William Boyce, Ellen Watts took her seat knowing that she at least had their full attention.

Judge Federico Muñoz turned to the other defense attorney. "Mr. Dubray. If you'd care to address the court . . ."

Alvin Dubray stood up, wheezing and waddling his way to the same spot in front of the jury that Ellen Watts had just vacated. He looked more than usually disheveled this morning, with his wiry gray hair sticking up wildly on one side of his head and his half-moon reading glasses comically askew. After a mumbled "very good, Your Honor," he turned to the jury.

"Ladies and gentlemen. I'll keep it brief. I admire Ms. Watts's respect for the truth. Indeed, I heartily endorse it. Unfortunately for Ms. Watts, however, the truth does nothing to exonerate her client. It is Sofia Basta who was the cynical manipulator. She, not Mr. Mancini, entrapped four innocent men and led them to their deaths. And let us not forget that these were successful, highly intelligent men of the world. If Ms. Basta was able to bamboozle *these* men, not to mention senior police officers around the globe and even one of her victims' *children*"—he glanced at the broken figure of Matt Daley, slumped in his wheelchair in the front row—"how easy must it have been for her to control my client, a clinically certified schizophrenic with a lifelong history of emotional and psychological problems. The truth, la-

dies and gentlemen, is that Ms. Basta
is the cold-blooded killer here, not Mr.
Mancini. Thank you."

Alvin Dubray shuffled back to his
seat. Danny McGuire watched him go.
Danny noticed that at no time during
his address had Alvin Dubray looked at
his client or invited the jury to do so.
*Probably because the guy looks so
fucking evil, and she still looks like a little lamb, lost in the woods.* Danny remembered both Sofia and Frankie from
their prior incarnations as Angela Jakes
and Lyle Renalto. Today, as he watched
them in court, his impressions of the
two were remarkably similar to what
they had been all those years ago. She
still seemed innocent and gentle. He
still projected arrogance and deceit. Alvin Dubray had been right on the money
in one regard. Sofia Basta *had* "bam-
boozled" him. In fact, the word *bamboozle* barely scratched the surface of
what she had done. As Angela Jakes,
she had bewitched the former detective. And in a way, she was bewitching
him still.

Judge Muñoz called for a twenty-minute recess before the defense teams started summoning witnesses to take the stand. Outside in the corridor, Danny McGuire approached Matt Daley.

"You okay?"

Danny still felt guilty for having suspected Matt of being the Azrael killer that fateful night in Mumbai. As he looked at him now, so weak and broken, not just physically but emotionally, the idea that he might have killed those men seemed ludicrous. Matt Daley couldn't hurt a fly. Danny's one consolation was that Matt himself never knew of his suspicions. Since the Azrael arrests, the two men had become friends again. Danny and Céline had even stayed with Matt's sister, Claire, and her husband, Doug, when they vacationed in L.A., and the McGuire and Daley families had grown close.

"I'm fine. I'm worried about her, though."

"Who?"

"Lisa, of course." Even now, a full year after India, Matt Daley still referred to Sofia Basta as "Lisa" and still spoke about her with love and affection. As far as the trial was concerned, Matt Daley was in Ellen Watts's camp all the way. Mancini was the bad guy, "Lisa" his confused, misguided victim. "Dubray's a cold bastard. He'll do her more damage than that wet fish Boyce for the prosecution. How can he stand up there and say those things?"

"He's doing his job," Danny McGuire said mildly. "None of us knows the truth yet. We won't till we hear the witnesses' testimony."

Matt looked at him uncomprehendingly. "*I* know the truth," he said simply. Then he turned and wheeled himself away.

CHAPTER THIRTY-THREE

David Ishag looked impatiently at his half-million-dollar Richard Mille watch. The trial so far had been torture. Sitting just feet away from the woman he'd once believed was going to be by his side forever, he'd not only had to listen to the crushing weight of evidence against her, but had contributed to that evidence himself, testifying to the court how he too was conned into marriage and to changing his will by this most deadly temptress.

Not once in all that time had Sarah Jane, as David still thought of her, made eye contact with him. Not once had she sought, with a look or a gesture, to explain herself. But now at last, David Ishag would hear her speak. He was ashamed to admit it, but there was a part of him that still longed for her to open her mouth and prove her innocence. To take what he knew to be the truth and disprove it. To make this nightmare go away and to return home at his side. Of course, rationally he was aware that that way madness lay. Only a fine line divided him from poor Matt Daley, and it was a line David Ishag hadn't the slightest intention of crossing. Even so, the prospect of Ellen Watts calling Sofia Basta as her first witness, as she was widely expected to do, had brought him to an almost unbearable pitch of anxiety.

"The defense calls Rose Darcy."

David Ishag's horror was echoed by a general murmur of disappointment in room 306. The spectators had waited weeks to hear the beautiful woman in one of the defendants' chairs speak for herself about her terrible crimes. Instead, a stooped, frail old woman ascended the witness box, helped by a courtroom clerk. Rose Darcy walked with a wooden cane almost as tall as she was, but despite her age and seeming decrepitude, she gave off an air of determination. Her spun-silver hair was tied neatly and firmly in a bun, and her blue eyes still sparkled brightly in her ruined, wrinkled face.

The court was not to be entirely disappointed, however. For the first time since the trial began, Sofia Basta appeared to be overcome with emotion. Letting out a stifled sob, she clutched the edge of the defendants' table.

"Mrs. Darcy, can you confirm your name for the court?"

"Rose Frances Darcy." The old woman's voice was strong and clear. "And it's 'miss.' I never married."

"I'm sorry. *Ms.* Darcy, are you acquainted with either of the defendants in this case?"

"I am. With the young lady."

The old woman looked across the room at the accused, her eyes welling up with tears of affection.

"I see," said Ellen Watts. "And when did you first meet Sofia Basta?"

"I never met Sofia Basta."

The jury members exchanged puzzled frowns. For a moment Ellen Watts looked equally perplexed. It would be just her luck to discover that her first witness had lost her marbles.

"Ms. Darcy, you just told the court that you know the female defendant. But now you're saying that you never met her?"

"No," the old woman said testily. "I never said that. I've known *her*"—she pointed at the defendants' table—"since the day she was born. What I said was, I never met Sofia Basta."

"But, Ms. Darcy . . ."

"That's not Sofia Basta." Rose Darcy finally lost her patience. "Sofia Basta doesn't exist."

It took Judge Muñoz a moment to bring the court to order. Once the gasps had died down, the old woman continued.

"Her real name is Sophie. Sophie Smith. I don't know where this 'Basta' baloney came from, but it wasn't the name she was born with."

Ellen Watts said, "You said you knew Sofia—Sophie—since birth. You knew her mother?"

"No, ma'am. I'm a social worker. Her mother abandoned her at birth at a maternity clinic in Harlem. I happened to be working at the clinic that night, so I saw her soon after she was born. Tiny little thing she was, but a fighter even then. She spent the first three weeks of her life withdrawing from heroin. Mom must have been using throughout the pregnancy. She was lucky to survive. It was the workers at the clinic who named her Sophie." She turned and looked at the stricken figure at the defendants' table. "She'll always be Sophie to me."

"What contact did you have with Sophie after that night?"

Rose Darcy smiled sadly. "Not as much as I would have liked. Although I probably had more contact with her over the course of her childhood than anyone else. She was a sweet little girl, very loving, very sensitive. But she was troubled from the beginning."

"Psychologically troubled?"

William Boyce lumbered to his feet. "Objection. Leading the witness."

"Objection sustained. Be careful, Ms. Watts."

"Yes, Your Honor. Ms. Darcy, in what way would you say the defendant was troubled?"

"Her psychiatrists could give you a clinical opinion. But from my observations, she was withdrawn, poorly socialized among her peer group, prone to fantasy and self-delusion. Child Welfare Services was aware of her as a problem case. She was moved repeatedly between facilities."

"Why was that?"

Ms. Darcy turned toward her former charge and said affectionately, "Because no one could handle her, that's why. No one understood her."

"But you did?"

"I wouldn't say that, no. After she turned thirteen, she told her caseworkers that she didn't want to see me again and we lost touch. I never did know why."

Sofia Basta was crying openly now,

with every TV camera trained on her beautiful, tear-streaked face.

"That must have been hard for you."

"It was," Rose Darcy said simply. "I loved her."

Ellen Watts's next witness, Janet Hooper, had worked at the Beeches, the home where Sophie lived in her late teens. A heavyset woman, with hunched shoulders and heavy bags under her eyes that suggested she might be one of the chronically depressed, Janet Hooper, it soon became clear, felt none of old Ms. Darcy's affection toward the defendant.

"She was difficult. Rude. Withdrawn. Kinda snooty toward me and my colleagues."

"Sounds like a typical teenager."

"No." Janet Hooper shook her head. "It was more than that. She traded on her looks in a real cold, cynical way. The records from her previous home said the same thing. Once she hit puberty, the boys were all over her, as you can imagine. But she didn't discourage it. She reveled in it."

Ellen Watts frowned. "She became promiscuous?"

"Very."

Alvin Dubray blinked his rheumy old eyes in Ellen's direction, as if to say, *Just what on earth do you think you're doing?* Calling witnesses who painted her client as a calculating slut was hardly the most obvious way to win a jury's affections. If anything, vilifying "Sophie" was his job.

But Ellen Watts plowed on, regardless. "I see. And how long did that behavior continue?"

"Until she was around sixteen, I believe. Until she got close to Frankie." Janet Hooper turned toward Frankie Mancini, who met her gaze with his usual withering disdain.

"Frankie Mancini changed Sophie Smith for the better?"

Alvin Dubray couldn't believe his ears. Ellen Watts was making his case for him.

"Frankie Mancini changed Sophie Smith completely. She was a new person once she met him. Completely under his control."

The first warning signals went off in Dubray's mind.

"Under his . . . *control*?"

Janet Hooper nodded. "Yeah. Like Frankenstein's monster."

Oh God.

"She worshipped the ground Frankie walked on. Did everything he told her to."

Ellen Watts smiled smugly at Alvin Dubray. "Can you give us some examples, Mrs. Hooper?"

"Well, changing her name, for a start. It was Frankie who started this whole 'Sofia Basta' thing. Convinced her she was a Moroccan princess or some such nonsense. That she had a twin sister who'd been separated from her at birth. He created this whole past for her, this whole identity. I think he got the story from a novel. Anyway, Sophie started acting like it was real. She was out of her mind."

"Move to strike," droned William Boyce. "The witness is not an expert and not qualified to comment on the accused's mental health."

"Sustained." Judge Muñoz preened

self-importantly for the cameras, push-
ing back his newly dyed black hair.
"Where are you going with this, Ms.
Watts?"

"Your Honor, the relationship between
Mr. Mancini and my client is key to this
case. I intend to show that Mr. Mancini's grooming of my client was cynical,
calculated and started from a young
age. That she was as much a victim of
Mr. Mancini as the men that he killed.
Let's not forget that during each of these
brutal attacks, my client was raped by
Mr. Mancini."

"Objection!" It was practically a howl
from Alvin Dubray. "She was turned on
by the killing! Sex was consensual."

"With those injuries?" Ellen Watts
shot back. "The police reports all said
'rape.'"

"The police didn't know she was in
on it!"

This was television gold, watching the
defense "team" rip each other's throats
out. After two weeks of William Boyce's
monotone speeches for the prosecution, Judge Federico Muñoz finally had
the spectacular trial he felt he deserved,

complete with a balcony full of salivat-
ing television crews and news reporters. Tomorrow his name would be on
everyone's lips.

"I'll allow it," he said graciously, "but
I hope you have some expert psychiatric witnesses for us, Ms. Watts. The jury's not interested in the opinions of
amateurs."

Ellen Watts nodded gravely, dismissing Janet Hooper and calling her next
witness.

"The defense calls Dr. George Petridis."

A handsome man in his early fifties,
wearing a three-piece suit with a vintage silver pocket watch, Dr. Petridis
was chief of psychiatry at Mass General Hospital in Boston. He radiated authority, and both Alvin Dubray and William Boyce noticed with alarm the way
the jury members sat up with attention
when he spoke. Even Frankie Mancini
seemed interested in what the esteemed
doctor had to say. Throughout his testimony, you could have heard a pin drop.

"Dr. Petridis, what is your relationship

with the defendants in this case?" Ellen Watts asked.

"I treated both of them in the late 1980s, when they were teenagers. I was working as a psychologist for New York State Child Welfare Services at the time, dealing almost exclusively with adolescents."

"Prior to these homicides being brought to light, did you remember these patients at all? Twenty years is a long time. You must have counseled hundreds of kids since then."

The doctor smiled. "Thousands. But I remembered these two. I also keep meticulous notes, so I was able to check my memories against what I recorded at the time."

"And what *do* you remember about the defendants?"

"I remember an intensely codependent, symbiotic relationship. She was a sweet kid with a lot of problems. She was clearly psychotic. I prescribed Risperdal from our very first session, but she was resistant to the whole idea of drugs. The boy disapproved."

"What form did her psychosis take?"

"Well, she was a fantasist. At best, she had a very fluid sense of self. At worst, no conscious identity at all, at least none that bore any resemblance to reality. I suspect maternal, prenatal drug use was a major factor. Effectively the kid was like an empty shell, a mold waiting to be filled with somebody else's consciousness. In a very real sense, the boy 'created' her."

In the front row of courtroom 306, Danny McGuire shivered. *"I have no life."*

"Changing her name was probably the clearest external manifestation of her condition. Sofia was the name of her exotic, Moroccan alter ego. It was a psychotic affectation, lifted from a romantic novel one of the nurses had given her as a child. Frankie recognized her attachment to this story and her need for a past, an identity. He pretty much took the two things and meshed them together."

Ellen played devil's advocate. "Is a seventeen-year-old boy really capable of that sort of sophisticated manipulation?"

"Usually, no. But in this boy's case, absolutely. He was highly intelligent, highly manipulative, a uniquely adaptable and capable individual. He was amazing, actually." Dr Petridis looked across at Frankie Mancini rather like a zoologist might look at a particularly fine specimen of some unusual species.

"In your opinion, was Frances Mancini psychotic?"

"No. He was not."

"Did you prescribe any psychiatric medication for Mancini at any time while you were treating him?"

The doctor shook his head. "There's no pill that could have cured Frankie's problems. We tried talking therapies, but he was highly resistant. He knew what he was doing, with Sophie, with everything he did. He had no interest in changing."

"Correct me if I'm wrong, Dr. Petridis. But are you saying Frances Mancini was 'bad' rather than 'mad'? That he did what he did deliberately and consciously, knowing that it was wrong, that it was evil?"

Dr. Petridis frowned. "*Bad* and *evil*

are both moral terms. I'm a psychiatrist, not a judge. I can tell you that Frankie certainly wasn't 'mad' in the sense of insane. Like most of us, like Sophie, he was a product of his childhood."

"Did he talk to you about that?"

"Oh yeah," said Petridis solemnly. "He talked."

For the next fifteen minutes, Dr. George Petridis outlined the horror story that was Frankie Mancini's childhood. As he spoke, at least two female jurors were reduced to tears. In the front row, the trio of Matt Daley, Danny McGuire and David Ishag listened intently, hanging on the doctor's every word. For Danny McGuire in particular, it was like finally being given the answers to a crossword puzzle that had defeated him for years. With each word, the Azrael murders began to make more sick, twisted sense.

"Frances Lyle Mancini was always a beautiful-looking kid," Petridis explained. "Even as a child, he had the same dark hair, blue eyes, olive skin and athletic physique you see in this courtroom now; the same face and body that would make him so fatally attractive as an adult. But Frankie's good looks were his curse."

"How so?"

The doctor paused before answering. He explained how the first eight years of Frankie's life had been happy. Then one day, a few weeks before his ninth birthday, Frankie's father, a selfish, womanizing naval officer—whose good looks and appetite for risk Frankie clearly inherited—abandoned Frankie's mother, Lucia, and their three children, sailing off to and setting up home in the Philippines with a much younger woman. Frankie's adored mother was destroyed by this betrayal and never recovered her sense of self-esteem, never even laughed again. Frankie described what it was like to be forced to witness this disintegration in his sessions with Dr. Petridis.

"Lucia Mancini wound up remarrying a much older man," Petridis went on. "His name was Tony Renalto. According to Frankie, she hoped that Renalto would provide her young family with financial security and stability."

"And did he?"

"Yes, he did, but at a terrible cost," Dr. Petridis said grimly, and told the court how, as well as bullying and belittling Frankie's mother, the boy's elderly stepfather routinely physically and sexually abused Frankie himself. When Frankie complained to his mother, she did not believe him. The sexual abuse only stopped when, at the age of fourteen, Frankie bludgeoned his stepfather to death with a table lamp.

"He told me during our sessions how he fled the scene of the crime, never to be seen by his family again, and lived on the streets for a year until he was picked up by the police and sent to the Beeches. That was where he met Sophie."

Ellen Watts asked, "Did you report this crime, the killing of his stepfather, to the authorities."

"I did, of course."

"And what happened?"

"Nothing. The police did a token interview. Frankie denied it. The case had been closed two years earlier, with the records showing that Renalto had been the victim of a bungled burglary."

Like Andrew Jakes, thought Danny.

"No one wanted the trouble of opening the thing up again. By all accounts, no one much missed Renalto, and other than Frankie's retracted testimony, there was no evidence."

At the defendants' table, Frankie Mancini sat back and smiled, like a man who'd just learned that his investments had doubled during a bear market.

"Presumably Frankie stopped confiding in you as his psychologist at this point?" asked Ellen Watts. "Once he knew you'd ratted on him to the police."

"No, actually. He continued our weekly sessions. He just made sure nothing was ever taped."

A titter of amusement swept the court. It was remarkably easy to be impressed or amused by Mancini, to fall for his looks and charm. Somehow, smiling and posing at the defendants' table, he seemed dissociated from the gruesome crimes that had brought both him and Sofia Basta here.

"Frankie liked to talk," Dr. Petridis

went on. "It was one of the things that connected him to Sophie and to me. We were a captive audience. Of course, by this point, he was seventeen and severely disturbed. He was homosexual, but had little or no sex drive."

The doctor dropped this bombshell as casually as if he'd been describing Frankie's taste in shirts or his favorite baseball team. The jury foreman's mouth literally fell open, like a dumbstruck character in a comic book. Ellen Watts, however, was prepared for the psychiatrist's answer.

"This is very important, Dr. Petridis," she said seriously. "As you know, there is clear forensic evidence showing sexual activity at all four of these crime scenes. Violent sexual activity. The chances of the semen recovered from those homicides *not* belonging to Frankie Mancini are well over two million to one."

Petridis nodded. "That's consistent with what I saw. In the course of ordinary life, Frankie's libido was depressed. What turns him on isn't men or women. It's control, of either sex—

because he grew up with none. Frankie has a deep-rooted hatred of men who abandon their wives and families, like his biological father did . . . and of old, rich men, like his stepfather, whom he sees as abusers. I imagine that those were the motivating factors behind both the violence and the sex in these homicides."

"Thank you." Ellen Watts smiled across at Alvin Dubray. "I have no further questions."

To everyone's surprise, not least Judge Federico Muñoz's, William Boyce got to his feet. So far he'd declined to cross-examine any of the defense witnesses, considering his case so watertight as to need no further emphasis. But Petridis's testimony had been so convincing, he clearly felt a token parry was in order.

"Dr. Petridis, you say that in your sessions Mr. Mancini displayed a 'deep hatred' of older men."

"That's right."

"Yet you would not describe him as pathological? It wasn't a 'pathological hatred'?"

"In the common parlance, you could call it that. But clinically speaking, no."

"I see. And you also described Ms. Basta as being like an 'empty shell,' a vessel into which Mancini could pour his own consciousness and opinions."

"That's right."

"Yet when Ms. Basta acted out these hatreds, when she assumed them as her own, you say that they *were* pathological."

"Yes, but that's different."

"How so, Doctor?"

"Well, in her case there was transference. She was acting *as* someone else, *for* someone else."

"But wasn't he doing the same thing? Wasn't he, according to your testimony, acting out the fantasies of a disturbed, abused little boy? Wasn't he transferring his hatred from Tony Renalto and his own father to the victims he butchered?"

"Yeees," Dr. Petridis agreed uneasily. "He was. But clinically, that wouldn't be enough to exonerate him on mental health grounds. He knew what he was doing."

"I quite agree. He knew that the men he killed were not his father or his stepfather."

"Of course."

"And so did Sofia Basta."

"Well, yes. She would have understood that. But—"

"No further questions."

David Ishag didn't sleep a wink that night, tossing and turning in his suite at the Beverly Wilshire. Nor did Matt Daley, in the ground-floor spare room at his sister's house, which Claire had converted into a bedroom in order to make it easy for him to come and go in his wheelchair. Nor did Danny McGuire, in a lonely motel room a few miles east of the courthouse.

Ellen Watts had done a good job so far of painting her client, at least partially, as a victim. Despite the prosecution's attempts at undermining Dr. Petridis's sympathetic testimony, she still came across as a disturbed little girl, drawn into a web of hatred, fantasy and violence by the corrupt Mancini. But it was tomorrow's evidence that would decide the fate of the woman each man still thought of by a different name and who, despite everything, each man wanted to spare from execution. Deep down they all still wanted to rescue her.

Tomorrow, that woman would finally speak for herself. She would answer what had become, for David Ishag, Matt Daley and Danny McGuire, the most important question of all:

Who are you?

Chapter Thirty-Four

The television crews were lined up along Burton Way en route to the courthouse as if they were covering a royal wedding. Today was the day the Angel of Death was going to testify in the Azrael murder trial and the sense of excitement and anticipation in the air was almost palpable. People were in the mood for a carnival, it seemed, smiling and joking with one another, cheering as Judge Muñoz's bulletproof Cadillac swept by and catcalling as the armored prison vans bearing Basta and Mancini passed the security barrier and descended into the secure underground lot.

"It's all just a game to them, isn't it?" Matt Daley gazed out of the LAPD squad car in despair. He and Danny McGuire arrived at the trial together every morning. The squad car came courtesy of an old friend of Danny's from back in his homicide-division days. "Don't they realize there are lives at stake? Don't they care?"

Danny wanted to respond that perhaps they cared more about the four lives that had already been taken than about the fate of two admitted killers. But he bit his tongue. Today was going to be tough for all of them, but it would be toughest on Matt. If Sofia—Lisa—incriminated herself up on that stand, death row was a certainty. No one, not even Matt Daley, would be able to save her then.

Inside courtroom 306 they took their usual places, oblivious to the gawking stares aimed their way from the spectators in the gallery. David Ishag was already in his seat. It was tough for an Indian to look pale, but David had achieved it this morning. Sitting rigid-backed in his chair, immaculately dressed as always, in an Ozwald Boateng suit and silk Gucci tie, the poor man looked as if he was about to face the firing squad himself.

"You okay?" Danny McGuire asked.

Ishag nodded curtly. There was no time for any further exchanges. Preening like a squat, Hispanic peacock, Judge Federico Muñoz strutted into court, basking in his short-lived moment in the spotlight and the rush he always got when a roomful of people rose to their feet to acknowledge the importance of his arrival. In truth, though, no one much gave a damn about Judge Dread this morning, any more than they did about Ellen Watts's opening statement. There was a brief flurry of interest when Alvin Dubray announced matter-of-factly that his client, Frankie Mancini, had elected not to testify, a clear sign that his lawyer was shooting for a diminished responsibility/ mental incapacity defense. But even the Mancini team's legal maneuverings were of little interest to those assembled today in courtroom 306. Only when the name Sofia Basta was called, and the slight, slender figure at the defendants' table was escorted to the stand to take her oath, did the room come to life.

"Please state your full, legal name for the court."

"Sofia Miriam Basta Mancini."

Her voice was neither strong nor faltering, but deep and mellow, projecting an aura of peace and calm. David Ishag, Danny McGuire and Matt Daley all remembered that voice and each man felt his heart leap when he heard it.

Ellen Watts started off gently. "Ms. Basta, would you begin by telling us in your own words how you met Mr. Mancini and to characterize your relationship with him."

"I was fourteen. I was living in a home for children in New York, in Queens, and Frankie was transferred there from a different home."

"And the two of you became friends?"

"Yes. More than friends. I loved him."

As one, the court turned to see if Mancini had displayed any reaction to this announcement, but his face remained as regally impassive as ever.

Sofia went on: "In the beginning, he was different. I mean, he was so beautiful and smart and charismatic. But he also treated me differently."

"In what way?"

"He talked to me. He listened. And he respected me. He never tried to touch me."

"Sexually, you mean?"

Sofia nodded. "The other boys at the home, and the men there, the staff . . . they all forced themselves on me." Matt Daley bit his lower lip so hard it bled. "But not Frankie. He was different and he kept them away from me."

Ellen Watts paused to allow the impact of Sofia's testimony to sink in, especially among the female jurors. "You're saying that you suffered sexual abuse while at this children's home?"

Sofia nodded, hanging her head. "I didn't know that's what it was at the time. I thought that was just . . . what happened. But Frankie made me see things differently. He told me I was beautiful, that I was special. I had a book, it was about a princess, from Morocco. We used to read it together. He told me that the princess was my grandmother, he'd found it out somehow. He knew things about my past, like what had happened to my mother and my sister. I had a twin, you see. We were separated."

As she went back into the past, something strange began to happen to Sofia's face. Her eyes took on a distant, glazed expression, almost as if she were under hypnosis.

"The others didn't believe I came from an important family. They were jealous. But Frankie understood. He knew. He loved me."

Very gently, Ellen Watts said, "Sofia. You understand now that that isn't true, don't you? That the story about the princess wasn't really your history. That it was just a story. And the letter from the lawyer, about you and your 'twin sister,' Ella, that was just something that you made up, you and Frankie, right?"

For a moment a look of sheer panic passed over Sofia's features. Then, like someone waking from a trance, she said quietly, "Yes. I know that now. It wasn't real."

"But at the time you believed it was. That was when you changed your name legally to Sofia Basta, wasn't it? Basta was the name of the Moroccan family from the story."

"They told me that later. Yes. I think so."

She looked so confused and forlorn, Matt Daley couldn't bear it. Even Danny McGuire found it hard to believe that this degree of mental confusion could be an act.

"So once you became Sofia, how did things develop with you and Frankie? When did the relationship become physical?"

"Not until after we married. And even then it was rare that we . . . he didn't really want to."

"He didn't want to have intercourse?"

"No."

"Did you suspect that he might be homosexual?"

"No, never. He loved me, he was passionate in other ways. You have to understand, I . . . I had no life and Frankie gave me one. He saved me. I didn't question that. I embraced it."

"So the two of you married and moved to California."

"Yes. Frankie was brilliant, he could have gone anywhere, done anything. But he was offered a job at a law firm in L.A., so that's where we went. It was a new life for us, so he gave us new names. He became Lyle. And I was Angela. We were very happy . . . at first."

"It was as Angela that you met Andrew Jakes?"

Sofia twisted her hands together, as if kneading an invisible ball of dough. "Yes. Angela met Andrew. Lyle set it up." She'd slipped into the third person so naturally, at first people barely noticed. But as the depths of her schizophrenia were laid bare, scattered gasps could be heard around the court as, for one spectator after another, the other shoe dropped. "Poor Angela. She didn't want to marry him. She didn't want him anywhere near her . . . he was so *old*." Sofia shivered. "She felt sick every time he touched her."

"She?" Ellen Watts asked the ques-

tion that was on everyone's lips. "Don't
you mean *you,* Sofia?"

"No! It was Angela. I'm telling you
about Angela, remember? Please, don't
confuse me. It's so hard to remember."
She pressed her hands to her temples.
"Angela didn't want to marry Andrew
Jakes. She was a lovely girl, Angela.
But Frankie made her do it. He said Andrew needed to be punished for what
he'd done and Angela had been created to punish him. There was no way
out."

"And what had Andrew Jakes done?"
Ellen Watts asked. "Why did he have to
be punished? Was he a bad man?"

"Andrew . . . bad . . . ? Not to Angela,
no. He was quite sweet actually. Thoughtful . . . She was fond of him in the end.
But he'd done the same thing as all the
others, you see. He'd abandoned his
family. His children . . . That was why he
had to die."

Danny McGuire saw his life flash before his eyes. *Could it really have been
that simple all along, the link between
Azrael's victims? That they'd all walked
out on their children, the way that*

Frankie Mancini's father walked out on him?

"That's why they *all* had to die. Andrew, Piers, Didier, Miles. It was for the children. The children had to be avenged."

You could have heard a pin drop as Ellen Watts asked her next question.

"Who killed Andrew Jakes, Sofia? Was it Angela or Frankie? Or did they both do it together?"

Sofia answered without hesitation. "It was Frankie." She broke down in sobs.

"That's a lie!" Mancini jumped to his feet. "This is bullshit, it's a fucking performance. *She* chose Jakes as the first kill. *She* picked him out, not me!"

Judge Muñoz sternly called for order, and court officers quickly subdued Frankie and wrestled him back into his seat.

Sofia was still talking, in a trance, apparently unable to stop. "He slit Andrew's throat. It was awful! There was blood everywhere . . . I'd never seen so much blood. Then he raped poor Angela . . . She was begging him to stop, but he wouldn't, he went on and on and on, hurting her. Then . . . then he tied them together and he left."

"And where were you while this was happening, Sofia?" Ellen Watts asked. "Do you remember that?"

"Of course." Sofia looked surprised by the question. "I was where I always was . . . Watching."

Ellen Watts questioned her client for another hour before Judge Muñoz ordered a two-hour recess. Officially this was to allow the other attorneys to prepare their cross-examinations. In reality, the extended break would give the slew of media people time to indulge in an orgy of comment and speculation on Sofia Basta's spectacular performance on the stand so far, earning the Azrael trial maximum exposure and guaranteeing it a place as the lead item on the East Coast lunchtime news.

The second hour of Sofia's testimony had continued in the same dramatic vein as the first. She had interludes of perfect lucidity, when she seemed fully aware of who she was, where she was, and why she was answering questions. During these periods she appeared calm, intelligent, articulate and remorseful about her role in the killings. But when asked to go back to the nights in question, she inevitably slipped back into the third person, talking about each of her alter egos—Angela, Tracey, Irina, Lisa and Sarah Jane—as if they were real women she had known and befriended, dissociating their experiences entirely from her own. In her warped mind, Tracey's love for Piers and Lisa's for Miles Baring were not acts. The love, the sorrow, that the wives felt were real emotions. For each murder, the message was the same: Frankie had arranged, orchestrated and carried out the killings, driven by his own desire for "retribution." He had "created" the various wives to help him. And then he had hurt them—while poor Sofia watched.

The question now was: Was her apparent insanity an act, as Frankie Mancini vociferously insisted, a charade designed to send him to death row while she lived out the remainder of her days in some cushy psychiatric ward? Or was it the truth?

Roused from his usual torpor by the mesmerizing effect that Basta's evidence appeared to have had on the jury, particularly the women, William Boyce opened the session that began after the break aggressively, going straight for the jugular.

"Ms. Basta, when you assumed different identities expressly for the purpose of marrying and murdering defenseless elderly men—"

"Objection!" Ellen Watts screeched.

"On what grounds, Your Honor? She's admitted that much under oath."

"I'll allow it. You may finish the question, Mr. Boyce."

"When you assumed these identities, presumably that required a lot of preparation?"

"I don't understand."

"Oh, I think you do. Before each crime you had to change your appearance, and invent and learn an entirely new backstory for your new 'character.' You'd have had to practice accents, find employment, make friends. Establish a base from which you could engineer a meeting with the intended target, then begin the business of seducing him."

Ellen Watts got to her feet again. "Is there a question here?"

"There is. How long did it take? To *become* Angela or Tracey or any of the others?"

Sofia looked uncomfortable. "It varied. Sometimes months. Sometimes years."

"So you would spend months, or even *years* in training, preparing for your next kill?"

"It wasn't like that."

"Oh? What *was* it like?"

"Frankie would take me away for a while, after . . ." Her voice trailed away.

"After the murders?"

She nodded. "We were supposed to go and visit my sister. We were going to find her together. But then we'd end up moving again. The new names were supposed to be a fresh start. They weren't part of any plan."

"Of course they were part of a plan, Ms. Basta! Did you or did you not know, when you met Sir Piers Henley, that you intended to marry him?"

"Tracey married him."

"You *were* Tracey, Ms. Basta. Did 'Tracey' know that her real husband, Frances Mancini, intended to murder Sir Piers?"

"I . . . I don't know." Sofia looked around her in panic, like a fox cub surrounded by a pack of slavering hounds. Matt Daley couldn't stand to watch. *Leave her alone! Stop bullying her.*

"You *do* know, Ms. Basta. You know very well. Tracey helped Mancini get into the house in Chester Square. She disabled the alarm for him, didn't she?"

"Yes." Sofia's voice was barely a whisper. "But you don't understand. She had no choice. She had to. Frankie—"

"Yes, yes, we know. Frankie 'made' her do it. Ms. Basta, isn't the truth really that you willingly and actively participated in all these murders?"

"No."

"That you and Mancini planned them together, months or even years in advance?"

"I told you, it wasn't like that."

"What was more sexually arousing to you, Ms. Basta? The rape fantasy? Or watching the innocent men you entrapped being mercilessly butchered?"

"Objection!"

"Overruled." Judge Muñoz was starting to enjoy himself. He'd waited a long time for the prosecution to make this bitch squirm and he wasn't about to let her off the hook now. "Answer the question, Ms. Basta."

For the first time, and quite unexpectedly, Sofia showed a flash of anger. "I wasn't *aroused,* Mr. Boyce," she shouted. "I was raped and beaten. I was forced. He told me if I didn't do what he asked, he'd do the same to my sister. That he'd rape her and torture her and kill her. If you think I derived *enjoyment* from that, you're the sick one, not me."

Ellen Watts put her head in her hands.

William Boyce allowed himself a small smile.

"I feel obliged to remind you, Ms. Basta, that you don't *have* a sister. But

I do so appreciate your use of the word *I*. No further questions."

Everyone agreed that William Boyce's cross-examination had been devastating to Sofia Basta's defense. The *L.A. Times* put it most succinctly: "Never in the history of criminal justice has not just a single word, but a single *letter*, had such a profound impact on a case." In one enraged outburst, Sofia had turned all the doubt and goodwill so carefully cultivated by her attorney over the previous few days into hardened certainty: the Angel of Death's "identity confusion" was nothing but an act. And if that was fake, how much more of her insanity defense might be put on?

Ellen Watts did her best to limit the damage, calling Sofia's current, state-appointed prison psychiatrist to give an evaluation of her mental state. Dr. Lucy Pennino was a strong witness and her testimony was unequivocal: Basta was "without question" suffering from paranoid schizophrenia. Like most schizophrenics, her condition was cyclical—it would come and go—and her mental state now, during the trial, was almost certainly more lucid than it would have been during the times of the murders, when she was taking none of the mood-stabilizing medication she was taking now.

"A person suffering from her condition would be highly susceptible to influence by others, both for bad and good. Matthew Daley, for example, seems to have had a profoundly positive effect on Sofia, when she met him as Lisa Baring. During my sessions with Ms. Basta, she has described theirs as being a genuine love relationship. Had she met Mr. Daley before the first murder, rather than after the fourth, it is my professional opinion that the Azrael killings would never have taken place."

It was good stuff, made all the more poignant by the sight of Matt Daley openly, and copiously, weeping from his wheelchair in the front row. But one look at the jurors' stony faces told anybody watching that Pennino's evidence was too little, too late.

Inevitably, Judge Muñoz's summing-up was as black and white and compassionless as was legally possible.

"The question before you today," he told the jurors, "is not whether Frances Mancini or Sofia Basta had unhappy childhoods. Neither do you need to ask yourself whether either defendant has, or has had, psychological problems. You do not need to understand their motives, their relationship or anything about the inner workings of their twisted minds other than this: Did they kill those four men deliberately? If you believe that they did, you must convict.

"We already know that together, Frances Mancini and Sofia Basta carried out these horrendous crimes and that they were brought to justice in the process of committing another. Make no mistake. Had they *not* been caught, Mr. Ishag would not be alive today. And despite his impassioned pleas for clemency for Ms. Basta, the truth is that Mr. Daley too was lucky to escape from her clutches with his life. Had they *not* been caught, thanks to Assistant Director

McGuire's dogged determination, their killing spree would have continued, perhaps for another ten years. More innocent men would have lost their lives in the most unimaginably terrifying circumstances, betrayed and slaughtered by a woman they loved, and who they believed loved them. This court has heard no convincing expression of remorse from either defendant.

"Much has been made of the defendants' mental capacity, in particular Ms. Basta's. In light of this, I am obliged to remind you that according to the law it makes no difference whether she believed herself to be somebody else at the time she perpetrated these crimes. All that matters is whether she intended to kill. The same goes for Mr. Mancini. If you believe there was intent, you must convict.

"You may now retire to consider your verdict. All rise."

Once the accused were led away, the spectators began to disperse. Danny McGuire turned to David Ishag and Matt Daley. "Can I take you both to lunch?"

Ishag looked tired, but Matt looked

gravely ill, white as a sheet and shaking.

"We should get out of Beverly Hills before those reporters mob us."

"Thanks, but I can't," said David, gathering up his notes and stuffing them into his briefcase. "I'm catching a plane back to India tonight."

Matt looked amazed. "Before the verdict is announced?"

"I have to. The jury'll be out for days and I have a business to run."

"You really think they'll be out for days?" asked Matt hopefully. "You think they're that uncertain?"

"I think they're totally certain," said David. "They have to go through the motions of weighing up all the evidence, that's all. Boyce's footnotes alone would take a week to read." He shook Danny McGuire's hand, fighting hard to control his emotions. "Thank you. What Muñoz said was true. I'd be dead if it weren't for you."

"You're welcome. You're sure you won't stay, at least for lunch?"

"Quite sure. Good-bye, Matt. Good luck." And with that, David Ishag strode out of the courtroom and into the blacked-out limousine that was waiting for him, swatting aside reporters' shouted questions like a giant dismissing a swarm of gnats.

Matt Daley watched him go, a stupefied look on his face. Danny McGuire knew the look well from all his years on the force dealing with victims of violent crime. Matt was in shock. The trial, always a strain, had finally become too much for him.

Danny pushed Matt's wheelchair toward the private, police-only exit. "Come on, man. Let's get you out of here."

They had lunch at a tiny Jewish deli in Silverlake, only six miles from the courthouse but a world away from the Azrael soap opera. Danny ordered a brisket sandwich and insisted on some chicken noodle soup for Matt as well as a mug of hot, sweet coffee.

"They're gonna execute her, aren't they?"

Danny put down his sandwich. "Probably. Yeah. I'm sorry, Matt."

"It's my fault." Tears began coursing down Matt Daley's cheeks, splashing into his soup. "If I hadn't started with this stupid documentary, if I hadn't gotten you involved, they'd never have found her."

Danny was shocked. "You can't possibly mean that. If you hadn't done what you did, people would have died, Matt. Innocent people. That woman had to be stopped."

"I could have stopped her. You heard the psychiatrist. If Lisa and I had gotten away like we planned to. If we'd made it to Morocco and disappeared. Frankie couldn't have kept killing without her . . . and she'd never have hurt a fly if it hadn't been for him."

"Maybe so," said Danny. "Or maybe not. Remember, you had no idea back then that Lisa was involved in any of the murders. How do you think you'd have reacted if you'd known?"

Matt was unhesitating. "I'd have forgiven her. I'd have understood."

"She killed your father, Matt. That's

why you got involved with this in the
first place. Because Andrew Jakes
didn't deserve to die like that. Remember? Nobody deserves to die like that."

"No," Matt said stubbornly. "Mancini
killed my father. Lisa was confused. She
thought she was protecting her sister.
She never wanted any of this to happen."

There was obviously no point in talking to him. He wasn't going to change
Matt's mind, and the subject made his
friend intensely agitated, which was exactly what Danny had hoped to avoid
by taking him out to lunch. He changed
the subject.

"How's Claire?"

"She's good. Tired of having me living with her, I guess. It's not easy having a crippled brother around with two
kids and a husband to take care of."

"She'd do anything for you," said
Danny. "Even I could see that. You're
lucky."

Yeah, thought Matt. *Lucky. That's me.*

"She thinks I should see a shrink."

"What do you think?"

Matt shrugged. "It won't make any

difference. If Lisa . . . If they . . ." He choked up, unable to go on, but Danny could guess the rest. *If they execute Sofia, he thinks he'll have nothing to live for.* The jury might not know it, but they were deliberating the fate of three lives, not two.

"Maybe you should go back to work, Matt. Make this damn documentary of yours. God knows you have enough material and no one's closer to this case than you are. People can't get enough of this story right now. You could make a fortune."

"I don't want a fortune," said Matt truthfully. "Not if it can't buy Lisa her freedom."

"You want to tell the truth, though, don't you?"

"What do you mean?"

"I mean you want people to know what really happened. Well, what better way to do that than to make a movie? To get the message out there in a way that millions of people will understand? That's the one way you *can* still help her."

For the first time, something resembling hope seemed to cross Matt Daley's face. It was true. He did owe it to Lisa to tell the truth. He owed it to all of them. Whether he intended to or not, Danny McGuire had just thrown him a lifeline.

Just then Danny's cell phone rang. It was Lou Angelastro, an old buddy of his from the LAPD.

"What's up, Lou? I'm just out at lunch with a friend of mine, taking a break. Can I call you back in ten?"

Matt Daley watched as Danny McGuire's face passed from surprise . . . to disbelief . . . to panic.

"We'll never make it in time . . . Silverlake . . . can you send a car? Yeah, I'll give it to you." Reeling off the name and address of the deli where he and Matt were eating, Danny hung up the phone.

"Everything okay?" asked Matt.

"Kind of . . . No . . . Not really." Pulling out two twenties, Danny dropped them on the table, hurriedly scrambling to his feet. "The jury came back already. They've reached a verdict."

* * *

In courtroom 306, pandemonium reigned. As people scrambled for the best seats, camera crews battled one another for access to the reserved media gallery, using their heavy cameras as weapons. A number of key news teams had already left the immediate vicinity of the courthouse. No one expected a verdict so soon. But when word was released that the jury was ready to return and that Judge Federico Muñoz was expected to call the court back in session within minutes, they all raced back to Beverly Hills, leaning on their horns like impatient rally drivers. Pretty soon Burton Way was as clogged up as the 405 during rush hour. Even the sidewalks were packed, with passersby and devoted Azrael watchers huddling around the two giant outdoor screens where they could watch the verdict delivered live.

For a case of such international scope, it was amazing how proprietary the Angelinos had become about the defendants, claiming Sofia Basta and the chillingly handsome Frankie Mancini as their own. Suddenly everybody cared about Andrew Jakes, the rich, elderly art dealer the pair had slain back in the early days of their killing spree. The Azrael murders had started in L.A. As far as Angelinos were concerned, it was only fitting that the drama should end there. Not since the O.J. trial had the world's attention been so closely focused on the city's criminal justice system. It was important to the people of Los Angeles that this time the guilty parties receive their just deserts. Although they stopped short of openly baying for blood, the mood among the crowd was grimly expectant, knowing as they did that Judge Dread enjoyed nothing more than handing down death sentences. Today, for once, the city was right behind him.

Matt Daley gripped the handhold on the police car's passenger door. Above him, the siren was wailing, its lights flashing brilliant blue and white as they hurtled toward the courthouse. Matt was struggling to breathe.

"Not much longer," said Danny as the

traffic grudgingly parted to let them pass. "I think we'll make it."

Judge Muñoz walked regally into the court. All the assembled lawyers, defendants and spectators stood up. Arriving at the judge's chair, Muñoz paused for dramatic effect, a king surveying his kingdom. There were the attorneys:

William Boyce, who'd almost bored them all to death with his lifeless performance for the prosecution over the first two weeks, but whose cross-examinations had gripped the world and changed the course of the trial.

Alvin Dubray, for Mancini, the bumbling old "fool" who'd said the least but probably achieved the most for his client by keeping him silent and allowing Sofia Basta enough rope to hang herself.

Ellen Watts, pretty, clever, but in the end too inexperienced to rein in her own client. Watts had had the hardest hand to play, trying to paint an evil killer as a victim, an intelligent schemer as confused and insane, a sexually rapacious sadomasochist as a little-girl-lost. And she'd almost done it too, if only Sofia Basta's temper hadn't gotten the better of her.

To the judge's left stood the accused. Mancini looked his usual amused, evil and deranged self. Sofia Basta was equally inscrutable. Staring straight ahead, her arms at her side, the expression on her face could only be described as blank. Not nervous, not hopeful, not angry, not impatient, not despairing. Not anything. She was a blank slate, ready to have the next chapter of her appalling life written for her. This time, with a little help from the jury, Judge Federico Muñoz would be writing that chapter.

It would be her last.

To Muñoz's right, at the very front of the courtroom, three seats remained conspicuously empty. David Ishag, Matt Daley and Danny McGuire were all missing.

Damn, thought Muñoz. Had he known, he'd have waited . . . fabricated some excuse to allow the three key players in the drama to be present at its denouement. But it was too late now. Finally, the judge sat down. Everyone in courtroom 306 gratefully followed suit, sinking into their seats but still craning their necks to keep Basta and Mancini in view.

One by one the jury filed in.

At the barrier that had been set up in front of the courthouse, their driver was arguing with a guard.

"What do you mean 'no more vehicles'? This is Assistant Director Danny McGuire of Interpol. He has all-access clearance."

"Doesn't matter," grunted the guard. "I got orders. Once the court's in session, no more vehicles go in or out."

Danny McGuire stepped out of the car. Bringing his face to within centimeters of the guard's, so close that he could smell the man's garlicky breath, he said, "Either you remove this barrier and let us through *right now,* or I will personally see to it that you are not only fired from this job but that you never find work anywhere in this city again. If

you think I'm bullshitting you, go ahead
and make us turn around. But you have
precisely three seconds to make that
call.

"One.

"Two . . ."

The guard registered the steely glint
in Danny McGuire's eye and made his
decision.

"Mr. Foreman. Have you reached your
verdict?"

The heavyset black man in his midfifties nodded gravely.

"We have, Your Honor."

"And is that verdict unanimous?"

"It is."

Outside, the crowd gazed up at the giant plasma screens in rapt silence. One
showed the foreman standing, with the
seated members of the jury behind him.
All looked somber, as befitted the terrible crimes they'd been called upon to
judge.

The other showed the two defendants. Standing only a few feet apart in the prisoners' box, they looked as detached from each other as two people could possibly be. It was impossible to imagine that they had known each other since childhood, still less that they had worked together as a deadly team for a dozen years and been married for decades.

"Have you reached your verdict?"

"We have, Your Honor."

Danny McGuire panted as he ran down the corridor, pushing Matt Daley's heavy wheelchair in front of him. The double doors of room 306 loomed in front of them like heaven's gates.

Or hell's.

"I'm sorry, sir," the LAPD guard began. "Court is in session. Judge Muñoz . . ." He trailed off when he saw Danny's Interpol ID.

"You can go in, sir." The guard opened the doors respectfully. "But I can't allow your friend here."

Ignoring him, Danny pushed Matt's chair into the court. The room was so silent, and the disturbance so unexpected, that for a moment hundreds of heads swiveled in their direction. But only one gaze caught Matt Daley's eye. For the first time since the trial began, she was looking at him. Directly at him.

He mouthed to her: *"Lisa."*

She smiled.

Judge Muñoz was speaking. "On the charge murder in the first degree, relating to Andrew Jakes, how do you find the first defendant, Frances Mancini?"

"Guilty."

The word reverberated round the room like a gunshot.

"And the second defendant, Sofia Basta?"

The foreman's next breath seemed to take an hour.

"Not guilty."

The gasps from inside the courtroom were heard around the world. Outside on Burton Way, the crowds let out a scream so loud it was faintly audible even through the thick walls of the courthouse. Once the cameramen realized what had happened, they zoomed in on Sofia's face. But whatever reaction she may have had in the split second after the foreman spoke had been erased from her face now, replaced by her usual serene blankness. Matt Daley closed his eyes, falling back into his chair as if he'd been punched in the gut. Even Judge Muñoz, the famous Judge Dread himself, required a moment's pause to regain his composure.

The foreman went on. "In the case of Andrew Jakes, however, we find the second defendant, Sofia Basta, guilty of voluntary manslaughter, due to diminished responsibility."

Judge Muñoz cleared his throat. "In the case of Sir Piers Henley . . ."

Again, the verdict came back, like knife wounds to the judge's heart.

Guilty.

Not guilty.

Diminished responsibility.

It was the same for the other two victims. Only on the charge of the attempted homicide of David Ishag were both defendants condemned.

The sense of disbelief was palpable. Even the usually unflappable Mancini looked shocked, his olive complexion visibly draining of blood. Sir Piers Henley's brother was shaking his head, tapping at his hearing aid in wonder. Miles Baring's old girlfriends both burst loudly into tears, and more than one voice from the gallery shouted, "No!"

For his part, Danny McGuire couldn't share the outrage. Truth be told, he felt only a deep sense of peace.

Sofia Basta would remain safely behind bars. No one else would have to die at Azrael's hands, sacrificed to Frankie Mancini's twisted lust for vengeance. But the lovely Angela Jakes, as she had once been, would be spared the executioner's needle.

Not justice perhaps. But closure.

Danny McGuire was free at last.

CHAPTER THIRTY-FIVE

FOUR YEARS LATER . . .

"I'm sorry, sir. Without a pass there is no way I can admit you."

Perhaps surprisingly, the guard at Altacito State Hospital did look sorry. It was a tough, lonely job guarding the inmates of California's only women's psychiatric prison, and not many of ASH's underpaid staff were known for their compassion. In his midsixties, the guard looked even older, his leathery skin as cracked and parched as a dry riverbed thanks to long years spent in the punishing desert sun. But there was a kindness in his eyes when he looked at the skinny, hopeful blond man, leaning on a cane at the hospital gates as he tried to plead his case.

It wasn't the first time the guard had seen the man. Or the second. Or even the third. Every month, come visiting day, the man would show up, politely asking to be allowed to see Altacito State Hospital's most celebrated inmate. But every month the lady declined to receive visitors.

Controversially spared the death penalty at her trial, the Angel of Death, as she was still known in the tabloid press, enjoyed a relatively easy life at ASH, albeit a life conducted behind bars and under a heavy shroud of secrecy. She had her own room, with a window and views out across the manicured gardens of the facility to the Mojave Desert beyond. Her days were structured but not arduous, with hours divided between work, exercise, recreation and psychiatric treatments, which could be anything from hypnosis to group therapy sessions.

Unfortunately, Matt Daley knew none of this. He worried constantly about

Lisa—to him, she would always be Lisa—being singled out for brutality and victimization by other inmates because of her notoriety. Matt had written scores of e-mails to ASH's chief psychiatrist, begging for news on her condition. Was she eating? Was she depressed? Could they at least confirm that she had been given the letters Matt wrote her religiously every Sunday, updating her on his life and the worldwide success of his acclaimed but controversial documentary, *Azrael: Secrets and Lies* . . . letters to which Matt had yet to receive a single reply. Did she even know that he was trying to reach her? That one friend at least had not abandoned her in her most desperate hour?

The e-mail replies were always the same. Polite. Brief. Straightforward: Matt Daley was not family. He was not entitled to any patient information unless the patient had specifically authorized its release. Sofia Basta had not.

"I know if she saw me, she'd change her mind." Matt told the guard for the hundredth time. "If you'd let me through to the visitors' lounge, just for a few seconds . . . I've come a long way."

"I appreciate that, sir. I do. But I'm afraid you need to go back home."

Sofia read the letter again, running her hands lovingly across the paper, thinking of Matt's hands touching it, the way they had once touched her. It began like all the others.

"Dearest Lisa . . ."

Reading the name was her favorite part. The name felt good. It felt right. Whenever she read Matt Daley's letters, whenever she thought of him at all, she *was* Lisa. And Lisa was the best part of herself. She'd thought about changing her name legally after the trial. *Lisa. Lisa Daley.* It had a wonderful ring to it. But as the days and weeks passed, and the reality of her sentence sank in—they could dress it up all they liked, call her prison a "hospital" and her punishment "treatment," but it was still life without parole—she changed her mind. What use was a new name to her now, in here? There were no second chances, no fresh starts. This was the end.

But not for Matt. For Matt, there was a chance. A future. Who was she to destroy it by giving him hope? By making him think, even for a moment, that there could be any going back . . . ? For Matt Daley to live, Lisa had to die. It was as simple as that.

It was so hard to hold on to the truth. To separate what was real from what was fantasy. She'd lived with lies for so long. But she had tried not to lie to Matt. When she'd told him she loved him, she meant it. Had she met him earlier, much earlier, before Frankie and the book, before Sofia Basta, before she lost the thread of who she was, things might have been so different. As it was, she would spend the rest of her days caged like an animal, surrounded by electrified fences and desert wilderness. Matt's letters meant everything to her. But she owed it to him not to reply . . . To let him go.

She read on.

"I don't know if you are even receiving these letters, my darling. At this point I guess I write them as much for myself as for you. But I can't stop. I won't stop, Lisa, not until you know that I love you, that I forgive you, that I will never give up on you, no matter how many times the guards turn me away."

It touched her that he still said "the guards" rather than "you." Darling Matt. He still wanted to absolve her of everything.

"I can't bear to think of you in that awful place. Please, my darling, if you're being mistreated, you've got to let somebody know. If not me, then your lawyers or even the governor. Even Danny McGuire might be able to help."

Danny McGuire. It was funny, every time she thought of Matt, she felt like Lisa, but every time she thought of Danny, she was Angela Jakes. Poor Angela. So beautiful, so young. She was the first one to be violated, the first one to suffer. By the time she became Tracey, and Irina, and even Lisa, she was stronger, hardened by the litany of horrors, numb to the pain. But Danny McGuire had known her at the beginning, when she was still vulnerable, still raw. He had known Angela, and in his own way, Sofia suspected, he had loved her. Reading his name in Matt's distinctive, cursive handwriting, she almost felt nostalgic.

Perhaps she should send Matt some sort of message, anonymously, just to let him know she was okay. Apart from the obvious hardship of losing her freedom, the routine at ASH suited Sofia well. Half her life had been spent in institutions, and the other half on the run, not just from the police but from her own demons. At ASH, her days were pleasantly predictable. She found the hospital routine a comfort.

As for being picked on by the other patients . . . if anything, the opposite was true. In the outside world, women tended to be too envious of great beauties to appreciate them aesthetically. But here at ASH, with no men to compete for other than the smattering of male guards, and little enough beauty in any form, Sofia's beauty was a passport to popularity. Other women wanted to be around her, despite the fact that she was far from social, choosing to eat alone at mealtimes and declining all group activities from movie night to organized athletic events. But she never left her room without admiring glances. Occasionally the tone of the glances shifted from admiration to outright lust, but unlike the state prison, there weren't many bull dykes at ASH and Sofia had never felt threatened.

Nor was her beauty her only advantage. Through no effort or desire of her own, Sofia had become something of a celebrity within the hospital. Many of the other women admired her, viewing the Azrael victims as rich, dirty old men, men who had callously abandoned their children and who'd therefore gotten what was coming to them. Sofia herself was careful never to endorse this view. Flashbacks to the murders still gave her terrible nightmares, and talking about them could bring on acute anxiety attacks. The only part of the past she held on to was Matt Daley.

"He came again today."

The male nurse's voice wrenched Sofia back to the present. Reluctantly she looked up from Matt's letter.

"You still don't want to see him, huh?"

Sofia shook her head. "I'm tired. I need to sleep."

The male nurse left her, watching through the glass door panel as she lay down on her bunk and closed her eyes. *Could it really be possible for a woman to grow more beautiful with each day?*

The nurse's name was Carlos Hernandez, and he was one of only a handful of males on the psychiatric staff at ASH. His buddies in Fresno had teased Carlos about landing his "dream job." "Welcome to Altacito," they mocked, "population two thousand. One thousand nine hundred and ninety-nine crazy bitches . . . and *you!*" But the truth was that Carlos was lonelier in this job than he had ever been in his life. Yes, he was surrounded by women, but there wasn't a single one with whom he could strike up an acquaintance, still less a friendship or relationship. The patients were obviously off-limits, and the average age of his female colleagues on the nursing staff was forty-two, with the average weight probably around 180 pounds. Not exactly rich pickings. For an institution that housed over two thousand women, it was astonishing how few of them were attractive.

Water, water everywhere but not a drop to drink.

Sofia Basta, on the other hand . . . she was the exception that proved the rule. An anomaly. A freak occurrence. She was older too, in her early forties, according to her birth certificate, but she looked at least a decade younger, and infinitely more desirable than any woman Carlos Hernandez had ever met, let alone dated. Her smooth skin, perfect features and lithe, slender body would have been more than enough to fuel the young nurse's fantasies. But Sofia had something beyond that, an inner calm, a sort of *goodness* that shone out of her like a light. Of course, Carlos Hernandez knew about her mental illness. Take her off her meds and she could snap at any moment, change back into a confused and highly dangerous psychopath, capable of murder. But to talk to her, it was so hard to believe. Sofia seemed like the sanest, loveliest, most gentle creature on earth.

Through the glass he saw her shoulders shaking. It was against the rules, but he couldn't help himself. Slipping back into the room, he sat down on her bed.

"Don't cry," he said kindly. "You don't have to see anyone you don't want to see. A lot of patients here find outside contact hard."

Sofia turned over and looked at him with those delicious liquid-chocolate eyes. Carlos's stomach flipped like a pancake.

"Does it get easier? As time goes on?"

It didn't get easier. It got more oppressive and stifling by the day, the hour, the minute. Carlos Hernandez had seen the toll that a life in an institution took on a human being. The hopelessness, the despair, knowing you would never get out, that this was your world till you drew your last breath. It was bleak. But he couldn't bring himself to say as much to Sofia Basta.

"Sure it does."

"I would see him," Sofia blurted out,

"if I were ever going to get out of here. If I had any future, anything to offer him. But since I don't, it seems cruel. He has to forget me."

"Try to get some rest," said Carlos, pulling the blanket up around her and gently stroking her hair before leaving the room. He glanced up and down the corridor, checking if anyone had seen him, but he was safe. D wing was deserted, as it always was on visiting days.

Carlos Hernandez had never met Matt Daley. But he knew one thing about him already: he would never "forget" Sofia.

Sofia was unforgettable.

Matt Daley drove toward the interstate, his new customized Range Rover the only car on the road. Barren desert stretched around him in all directions, an ocean of emptiness and dust. *Like my life. Desolate.*

The world thought that Matt Daley had turned his life around. And on the surface, he had. After years of grueling physical therapy, he'd learned to walk

again, against all the odds, and now
only used a cane for support. Rarely
was his name mentioned in public these
days without the epithet *survivor* thrown
in somewhere. His documentary on the
Azrael case, produced lovingly on a
shoestring budget because Matt had
refused to cede editorial control, had
received wide critical attention, if not
exactly acclaim. Matt made no secret
of the fact that he was an apologist for
Sofia Basta, pinning the blame for the
Azrael killings firmly and exclusively on
Frankie Mancini's shoulders. Despite
the fact that the jurors at the trial had
effectively done the same, this stuck in
many people's craw, including HLN's
Nancy Grace. Grace had wanted Sofia's head on a platter from the day of
her arrest. Ironically, it was the Fox an-
chor's vitriolic condemnation of *Azrael:
Truth and Lies* that *had* ensured it a far
wider audience than Matt could otherwise have hoped for. Distributed
throughout Asia and the Indian subcontinent, as well as in Europe and the
United States, the film was a resound-
ing commercial hit. Matt Daley was

more than a survivor. He was a rich man, a winner, a success.

None of it mattered.

He hadn't expected Lisa to see him today. After four years he was resigned to her rejection. But he'd hoped.

Hope would be the death of him.

He pulled onto the freeway. Now that he was alone, tears coursed freely down his cheeks as he once again gave way to the pain. Sometimes he fought it. Told himself sternly that he had to do something, to take his depression by the horns and wrestle it down and defeat it. But most of the time he knew.

One day it would get to be too much. One day he would drive toward the edge of a cliff and simply keep on driving. Lay down his burden. Be free.

One day . . .

CHAPTER THIRTY-SIX

Claire Michaels sipped her coffee at a corner table of a Le Pain Quotidien in Brentwood feeling totally content. It was a glorious June day, nine months since her brother Matt's last abortive Altacito visit, and at long last things seemed to have turned a corner in all of their lives. Claire had driven up San Vicente in the new Mercedes convertible Matt had bought her for her birthday last month, drinking in the blue skies and sunshine and feasting her eyes on the blossoming acacia trees that lined the wide, sweeping road. Even nature seemed to be celebrating today, erupting in a riot of color and scent and joyfulness in honor of her brother's big news.

It was all such a far cry from that awful day last October. She remembered it like it was yesterday. Matt calling her from a rest stop on the I-5 sobbing uncontrollably, barely able to speak, to tell her where he was. His breakdown had been total and catastrophic. Claire had driven him straight to Wildwood, a rehabilitation center in Toluca Lake, and signed the papers as his next of kin. By the time she drove away, Matt no longer remembered his own name.

But miraculously the breakdown had been the making, or rather the remaking, of Matt Daley. After only ten days at Wildwood, he was well enough to receive visitors. Within eight weeks, the depression that had dogged him for more than five years now—since the day Sofia Basta, posing as Lisa Baring, drugged and left him in a Hong Kong hotel room—at last seemed to have lifted. Claire cried the first time she saw him laugh again, and not just laugh with his mouth but with his eyes, his whole being, like he did in the old days. He gained twenty much-needed pounds, began to work out regularly and started to talk about the future. Most importantly of all, he *stopped* talking about Lisa, or Sofia, or Andrew Jakes, or anything to do with the Azrael murders. It was a miracle.

There were more miracles to come.

Matt met a woman in rehab, a divorcee and recovering alcoholic named Cassie. The two of them bonded instantly, and despite Claire's initial reservations, when she and her husband met Cassie, they found her to be as warm and sweet and funny as Matt had described her. Last week, after a quick but astonishingly happy, drama-free courtship—much too mellow to be called a "whirlwind romance"—Matt and Cassie announced their engagement.

"Hi, sis. Sorry I'm late."

Weaving his way through the tables, smiling broadly in khaki shorts and a blue UCLA T-shirt, Matt looked the picture of health and happiness.

"Hey." Claire beamed back at him. "Cassie not with you?"

"I just dropped her off at her Pilates class. Why, I'm not good enough for you now?"

"You'll do." Grinning, Claire pushed a small, gold-wrapped package across the table.

Matt raised an eyebrow. "For me?"

"Hey, I can give presents too you know. It's an engagement gift. Don't get too excited, though, it's nothing much."

Matt unwrapped the box. Inside was a simple but elegant antique man's watch, with a battered leather strap and a rose-gold face. On the back were engraved the intertwined initials *M* and *C,* and the date of their engagement. "Nothing much? My God, Claire, it's gorgeous. It must have cost a fortune."

"Not really," Claire lied. "I'm just so happy that you're happy. You deserve it, Matt. You really do."

Matt *was* happy. It wasn't the soaring elation, the addictive thrill he'd felt in Bali with Lisa. But in its own way, he told himself, what he had with Cassie was just as precious. Cassie brought him peace and security and content-ment. She didn't give a damn about his money, she was nothing like Raquel—and she never questioned him about the past. Loving Cassie was a choice that Matt had made, something rational and good that he had decided to do. Loving Lisa had been an impulse, the irresistible pull of a powerful and dangerous drug. Matt would never forget the high he'd felt at the time. But he knew that that drug had damn near killed him. He could never go back.

Matt ordered two soft-boiled eggs and an open salmon sandwich for himself and a duck-breast panini for Claire while she fired questions at him about the wedding. Had he set a date yet? Booked a venue? Who was on the guest list? Were Danny and Céline McGuire coming over from France? Had Matt heard from Danny at all?

Matt answered all the questions good-naturedly, referring his sister to Cassie for all bride-, cake- and flower-related details. But the basics were simple. It would be a small wedding, in the garden of Matt's new, Nantucket-style Brentwood Park home. The Mc-Guires had been invited but were not expected to attend. They'd somehow managed to have three children—three!—since the trial, and their newest baby was still too small to travel, but according to Danny's e-mails they were very happy. Angela Jakes's ghost had finally been laid to rest.

David Ishag had sent Matt a case of champagne back when the Azrael documentary came out and wrote him a very kind letter while he was at Wildwood. But other than that, Matt had deliberately severed all ties with anyone connected to the case or to Sofia Basta. His wedding to Cassie would mark the beginning of a new, happier chapter in his life. The old book was closed.

Twenty minutes later, back behind the wheel of his Range Rover, Matt switched on the radio. NPR news from Washington blasted the familiar, singsong voice of Lakshmi Singh into the car. The first two reports washed over Matt. New growth figures from the Fed and something about global warming from the National Science Foundation that he ought to care about but didn't. He was thinking about Cassie and how cute she always looked after Pilates, all sweating and energized, convinced that she was a mess without makeup when actually she looked more natural and sexy than ever. Swinging the car right onto Montana, he suddenly screeched to a halt, narrowly missing slamming into an SUV in front of him.

"In breaking news," Lakshmi Singh was saying, "Frankie Mancini, better known to the public as one of the two Azrael killers, is reported to have taken his own life while on death row at San Quentin Prison in central California. Mancini was awaiting execution for his role in the murders of four men between 1996 and 2006 and after numerous appeals was expected to be executed later this year. It's understood that Mancini was found hanging in his cell in the early hours of this morning."

The woman in the SUV was yelling at Matt, shaking her fist out the window. Behind him, honking vehicles began to drive around him. Matt was completely oblivious.

Mancini was dead.

Matt had held on to his hatred for Frankie Mancini for a long time. He'd needed someone to hate so he could continue loving Lisa. But now that Frankie was actually gone, Matt felt none of the satisfaction, none of the sense of closure and of justice rendered that he'd expected to feel. Instead he felt . . . robbed. He'd interviewed just about everyone connected with the Azrael killings for his documentary, and during the trial he'd heard Lisa's—Sofia's—side of the story. But the one person who knew the most about what had happened on those terrible nights, and *why* it had happened, had never uttered a word about his crimes. Whatever his motives and feelings, Frankie Mancini had taken them to his grave. Even his death had been on his own terms.

When Cassie got into the car, she'd already heard the news. CNN was playing in the locker rooms.

"Are you okay?" she asked Matt.

"Sure." He still looked dazed.

"I wonder how it happened. I mean, aren't they supposed to have all death-

row inmates on twenty-four-hour sui-
cide watch?"

Matt nodded absently. He wasn't
thinking about Frankie Mancini, or how
he'd managed to outwit the authorities
at San Quentin and take his own life.
He was thinking about another prisoner,
behind another set of walls, only a hundred miles or so north of where he and
Cassie were talking. A prisoner he hadn't
thought about for a long, long time. A
prisoner he'd trained himself to forget.

Was she grieving? Was she suffering? The thought of her distressed and
alone tore through Matt's heart like a
drill. He winced.

"Are you sure you're okay?" Cassie's
face clouded with anxiety. "We can do
the wedding planner another day if you
want."

The wedding planner. Shit. He'd totally forgotten. Like a physical weight he
forced thoughts of Lisa out of his mind.
Our wedding. Our future.

"Yeah. I'm sure." He forced a smile.
"Let's go choose that cake."

CHAPTER THIRTY-SEVEN

Matt and Cassie Daley's wedding day was a triumph. The garden in Brentwood exploded with flowers, the sun shone brightly and the bride and groom looked as happy and in love as two people could possibly be. The small group of family and friends who came to toast their union with nonalcoholic fruit punch—Matt had given up drinking in support of Cassie, and half their friends were in AA—all agreed that the intimate, low-key ceremony was a perfect reflection of the relationship of this adorable couple, both of whom had been through so much. It wasn't their happy ending. It was their happy beginning.

The honeymoon in Tahiti was idyllic, with nothing to do but sleep, snorkel and make love beneath the stars. Occasionally thoughts of another, earlier experience of paradise in Indonesia flashed into Matt's mind. But he banished each one firmly, remembering the mantras he'd learned at Wildwood, little sayings he'd come to believe and that had literally saved his life.

My mind is my own.
I can control it.
The past is gone.

Only the present was real. Only the present mattered. And the present belonged to Cassie. At first Matt struggled, being so totally cut off from the outside world. The private atoll they were staying on was the last word in reclusive luxury, but by design, the honeymoon villa had no Internet access, television or phone. Cassie made fun of Matt's twitchiness ("I swear to God you're like an addict. Is it *really* that hard to go two weeks without Anderson Cooper or an in-box full of junk mail?"), and after a few days, Matt started to relax to a degree he hadn't managed in years. Perhaps it was his imagination, but he felt as if even his back and leg pain was receding. He swam every day in the warm, pale blue waters and often walked from the house to the beach and back without his cane. In every possible sense, his marriage to Cassie was healing him. Matt felt profoundly grateful.

It wasn't until they got back to L.A. that the marriage faced its first big test. Claire Michaels came to meet them at the airport. Both Matt and Cassie instantly knew that something was wrong when they saw that Claire and her husband, Doug, were accompanied by two uniformed police officers. At customs, they were pulled aside into a private room.

"What is it?" Cassie asked, panicked. "Is it Brandon? Is he okay?"

"Your son's fine, ma'am," the older cop assured her. "There's nothing to worry about. We're really only here as a courtesy. In case you had any questions."

"Questions about what?" said Matt.

Claire took her brother's hand. "Matt . . . Sofia Basta died while you were away. It happened last Wednesday, but we had no way to reach you."

"Died?" Matt couldn't take it in. "What do you mean? How?"

"It was an accident," said the policeman. "It wasn't public knowledge, but she'd been allowed some limited freedoms at Altacito over the last six months, as it was felt that her mental state was improving and she was no longer a danger to society."

Matt nodded absently.

"She was on a hiking trip somewhere in the mountains," the policeman continued. "She was with two other patients and four members of the staff when it happened."

Claire took over the narration. "Apparently she slipped and fell into a deep ravine. They called 911, and sent down search-and-rescue helicopters, everything, but where she fell was like a crevasse, incredibly narrow and miles deep. They never recovered the body.

But, Matt, she'd have been dead on impact. She wouldn't have suffered."

Matt stared at his sister blankly.

"They're sure she's dead?"

"Quite sure. One of the guards and one other patient were there with her when she fell. There's no way anybody could have survived that fall. The helicopters were only ever there to try and extract a body."

"Matt . . . honey." Cassie wrapped a protective arm around her husband's waist. "Do you want to sit down?"

"I know it's a huge shock," said Claire. "But we wanted you to know before you went through arrivals. As you can imagine, the media have been all over the story. They knew you were coming back today, so there's a whole horde of photographers and reporters out there all wanting a reaction."

Cassie looked horrified. From their perfect honeymoon to this. It wasn't fair.

The cop caught her anxious look. "Don't worry, Mrs. Daley. We'll escort you outside. We have a car waiting."

The words *Mrs. Daley* jolted Matt out

of his stupor. Cassie was his wife now. His first thought must be for her, not for himself.

"I'm okay," he said reassuringly, pulling her into his arms. "It was a shock, that's all. But I'm fine. And maybe . . ." He hesitated to say it, but he made himself go on. "Maybe it's for the best."

Both Cassie and Claire looked at him wide-eyed.

"Not that I would have wanted it to happen. But if she didn't suffer, maybe that's a better way to go than lingering into old age, behind bars, with nothing to do but dwell on the past . . . You know?"

Cassie nodded. She knew.

Matt kissed her, closing his eyes and breathing in the scent of her, searching for reassurance, for safety, for love. "And for us too. It's awful and it's tragic. But it draws a line. The past really is gone now."

Cassie Daley looked up at her husband and burst into tears of relief.

At last, at long, long last, the nightmare was over. Once and for all.

CHAPTER THIRTY-EIGHT

EIGHTEEN MONTHS LATER . . .

The woman walked into the Starbucks unnoticed. There was already a long line. It was nine in the morning, right after school drop-off time, and the place was packed with moms picking up their iced lattes en route to the gym. The woman wore the same mommy uniform as everybody else: Hard Tail yoga pants, Nike sneakers and a Stella McCartney for Adidas running top just tight enough to emphasize her pert breasts and flat stomach without being showy. Her pretty face was hidden behind a pair of Chloé aviators, and her shoulder-length blond hair was pulled back in a pony-tail.

Matt Daley didn't look up from his computer. He was supposed to be working, coming up with a first draft for a piece for *Vanity Fair* on the comedy business in Hollywood. Having left Azrael behind him, Matt had returned to his first loves, comedy and writing, and was enjoying something of a renaissance in his career. This morning, however, he was goofing off, scouring Marie Chantal online for cute baby clothes. They'd found out a few days ago that, quite *un*expectedly, Cassie was expecting. An elated Matt was convinced that the baby was going to be a girl.

"Is this seat taken?"

The woman was hovering next to him, coffee in hand.

"Oh, no. Please . . ." Matt moved politely to one side to make room for her to sit down. She did so, putting her coffee cup down on the table first. Something about her hand and the languid way she moved her arm caught his eye. She reminded him of someone, but at first he couldn't remember who.

"I'm not disturbing you, am I? It's just that the place is so packed . . ."

The voice. Matt felt the hairs on his forearm stand on end.

Aware of him staring at her, the woman took off her sunglasses. "What's the matter?" She smiled. "You look like you've seen a ghost."

The phone was ringing. Cassie Daley dragged herself from the bathroom, where she'd just finished throwing up for the second time that morning, into the kitchen.

"Hello? Hello?"

Typical. The moment she got there, the person hung up. Perching at the kitchen counter, Cassie poured herself a tall glass of filtered water and sipped it slowly, nibbling at a piece of dry toast. She'd forgotten about morning sickness and how rotten it made you feel. It had been so long since she'd given birth to Brandon, and almost three years since her last hangover. Nausea felt like a novelty.

The ringing of telephones, on the

other hand, was grimly familiar, the sound track to Cassie and Matt's marriage ever since they got back from Tahiti. Claire's warnings at the airport that day about the media circus following Sofia Basta's death had been depressingly prophetic. They'd walked into the hallway of their house to a cacophony of ringing telephones, home, office and cell, all competing for Matt's attention. Even the fax line buzzed insistently like an angrily trapped bee.

"Mr. Daley? This is CBS News. Do you have any comment on Sofia Basta's death . . . ?"

"Mr. Daley, do you buy the coroner's verdict of accidental death . . . ?"

"Matt, hi, this is Piers Morgan. I'm sure you must be inundated with offers right now, but I wanted to call personally to see if I could persuade you to talk to us first."

Some callers were pushy, others respectful. The magazines, though, were the worst. The bitch who called from *Star* actually implied that unless he agreed to give them an exclusive interview, they were planning to run a story about Matt and Sofia having met up for "trysts" on the days she'd been allowed out of the hospital. "Your wife would be shocked to read the stuff our sources have told us," the reporter had the gall to say. "This is your chance to set the record straight."

When Matt told her where she could stick her sources, the woman was as good as her word and ran the story anyway, a preposterous hodgepodge of grainy, blatantly Photoshopped pictures and conspiracy-theory nonsense. It was the biggest-selling issue of *Star* that year.

Cassie was furious. "Sue them! Sue them for libel. Force them to print a re-traction."

But Matt had persuaded her that en-gaging with tabloid morons would only add more fuel to the fire. That eventu-ally, if they continued to maintain a dig-nified silence, the story would fizzle and die. And he was right. Two Altacito guards lost their jobs and the hospital's director was forced to resign. With public lust for vengeance at least par-tially satisfied, and no more salacious revelations forthcoming, the calls finally stopped. But not before Cassie Daley had developed a powerful aversion to the sound of ringing phones.

The message light was flashing. Hitting play, Cassie smiled when she heard Matt's voice.

"Hi, honey. It's only me. Listen, something came up with this *Vanity Fair* thing. I . . . I have to go meet someone. Anyway, I might be late tonight, so don't worry and don't cook for me. Okay, see you later."

He's a terrible liar, she thought lovingly. She wondered what surprise he was planning this time, what secret it was that he didn't want her to know. *Probably something for the baby. Or earrings to go with the necklace he got me last week. Or maybe he's finally booked that trip we've been planning, our "babymoon."* Always generous, Matt had gone into gift-giving overdrive since Cassie became pregnant. He'd even started spoiling Brandon with a cell phone (at nine!) and a cool new thousand-dollar diving watch.

I'll talk to him when he gets home.

He has to stop with the spending. The baby is blessing enough.

Matt closed the door behind them, his hand shaking. The hotel was expensive, exclusive and discreet, just the sort of place where rich men brought their mistresses.

Is that what I am? A rich man with a hard-on?

Sofia Basta sat down on the bed. There was so much to say, to explain. She'd run through this scene a thousand times in her mind, but now that she was actually here, she had no idea where to begin.

"I know you're married now," she said hesitantly. "I haven't come to spoil anything for you. To ruin your life again."

"You never ruined my life," said Matt. "I did that all by myself."

"But I had to see you, to explain. You're the only person I can trust and I needed you . . . I needed you to know . . ." She started to cry. "I couldn't stay in that place. I couldn't. They were burying me alive!"

"Shhhhh." Matt sat down beside her, wrapping an arm around her shoulders. "It's okay." She looked so different. The surgery to her face was radical this time. But holding her felt the same. A wave of longing almost drowned him. He tried to think about Cassie, to picture her face, but her image too was swept away in the flood of desire.

"I got a new passport, a new ID," she murmured through her sobs. "I changed my name . . . obviously. Here." Fumbling in her purse by the side of the bed, she handed Matt a California driver's license. There were the same, haunting liquid-brown eyes gazing into his. The name underneath the picture read . . . *Lisa Daley.*

"I hope you're not angry with me. It felt right."

Dropping the license, Matt pushed her back onto the bed, kissing her with so much force she could barely breathe. She felt the weight of him, the power, the passion. Desperately he tore at her clothes and ripped off his own, biting and clawing at her like a man possessed. Finally naked, he plunged inside her with a scream that was half agony, half ecstasy. "Lisa!" This wasn't lovemaking. This was a man fighting for his life. He was consuming her, inhaling her, breathing her in like a half-drowned man finally breaking through to the surface and desperately gasping for air. It wasn't just Lisa who had come back from the dead. It was the old Matt Daley, the man Matt thought he had destroyed at Wildwood and buried on his wedding day.

"Matt!" She wrapped her legs around him, clasping his face in her hands, trying to hold him at bay, to calm him. She was the comforter now, rocking him like a baby, soothing him with the warmth and wetness of her body, drawing him in. "I love you! I'm sorry. I love you so much." Matt reached orgasm, grasping her hips and thrusting so deep inside her that she felt like he might pass right through her body and out the other side, as if she really were a ghost. But the sweat and heat and tears were no shadows. This was real, this joining of the flesh. An agonized celebration of life, like childbirth. Afterward Matt cried like a baby.

"Don't leave me. Don't leave me, Lisa, please! I'll do anything."

And she knew he meant it.

They made love again, for several more hours, then slept until dusk. When they awoke, Matt ordered room service— two deluxe cheeseburgers and fries— and they ate till their bellies hurt. Finally, at around seven, Lisa started talking. She told him about her illness. How after many years she finally seemed to have broken free of its shadow and was off her medication.

"I was scared at first, going off the pills. But taking them made me feel like I was in a fog. Now, for the first time I can remember really, I feel like myself."

She told him how a "sweet man" named Carlos Hernandez, one of the psychiatric nurses, had helped stage her "accident," rigging up a simple animal trap in the mountains to make it look as if she'd slipped into the crevasse, while in fact she was concealed in a cave just a few feet below the mouth of the ravine. Given that the only witness to her fall was an impressionable girl of nineteen who was being treated for, among other things, acute hallucinations, it was easy for Carlos to steer the rest of the group back to camp, buying Lisa enough time to climb out of the cave and make her way down to a remote hunting lodge Carlos had prepared for her.

"Were you lovers?" Matt was ashamed to hear himself asking.

"Nooooo." Lisa frowned. "I think he would have liked to be. But no. He was my friend. He risked his own neck helping me and he lost his job, poor man. But he knew that I was well again, mentally, and that they would never in a million years have let me out. Especially after Frankie . . . you know. They needed one scapegoat to punish for all those poor men who died. I was it."

"But you lived with Carlos?"

She shook her head again. "No. That would have been too dangerous. He paid for me to go to South America for the surgery. It's funny how easy it is to sneak over the border when you're coming *from* the U.S. I was in Brazil for eight months, recuperating and then working. By the time I got back, Carlos had moved on."

"So you came back to California to be with him?"

Lisa laughed. "My God, Matt. What is it with the jealousy? Yes, I came back for him. To pay him back the money I owed him and to say thank you. But I also knew I had to see you. It was a risk, a big risk. But like I say, I needed you to know."

"So now I know."

Matt stood up and walked to the window. The L.A. cityscape, so familiar to him all his life, looked strange and somehow menacing tonight, as if he'd never seen it before.

Just a few miles away, in a safe, happy place, Cassie was waiting for him. Cassie and Brandon and their baby. Waiting. Trusting. Dear, sweet Cassie.

"You're thinking about your wife?"

Matt nodded. "She's pregnant." The

words were out of his mouth before he knew he was going to say them.

"Oh!" Pain flashed across Lisa's face. She hadn't felt guilty about being with Matt today. What happened, she felt sure, had been meant to happen. The love between them, the bond, was too precious not to honor. And she'd been without him for so, so long—didn't she deserve this, this one fleeting moment of true happiness?

But a baby . . . ? That was different. What sort of a woman asked a man to leave his child? And what sort of man abandoned his family? Not Matt Daley, that was for sure. Matt was better than that. It was what Lisa loved about him.

"You have to go back."

Matt turned around, too exhausted to cry anymore, but his face betrayed his desolation. Even he couldn't quite believe what he was saying, what he was doing.

"Yes, Lisa," he whispered. "I have to go back. I'm sorry . . . It's time to say good-bye."

CHAPTER THIRTY-NINE

Everyone agreed that Mr. and Mrs. Daley were an adorable couple.

Her baby bump was so tiny you could barely see it, but he was always patting it lovingly, guiding her with infinite care through the lobby or out into the sunny courtyard for tea. Sometimes he sat and wrote out there. At other times, the two of them would flip through the listings of homes that some local Realtors had given them. Like so many couples who came here on vacation, the Daleys had fallen in love with the city. Who knew, perhaps one day their unborn child would grow up to call this place home.

Matt looked up from his book as his wife came toward him. It had been a difficult decision, saying good-bye and leaving his old life behind. One of the hardest things he'd ever done. But watching the woman he loved cross the mosaic-tile floor in a flowing white caftan, her face alight with joy and the promise of impending motherhood, he knew he'd made the right decision.

"Do you want to come for a walk?" asked Lisa. "We can watch the sun set over the souk."

Matt Daley did want to.

He wanted to very much.

Morocco was a dream, a fairy tale. It was where they were meant to be. Matt had taken very little money with him when he left the States. He wanted Cassie and the children to have everything. That was the least he could do for them after walking out the way he had, with no explanations other than a kiss good-bye. He did feel guilty. Of course he did. The last thing on earth he wanted was to cause dear Cassie any pain. But the truth was that the man she married had died the day that Lisa walked into that coffee shop. The man she married no longer existed. The best Matt could do for her was to leave her financially well taken care of, with a longed-for baby to remember him by and her son to comfort her. That and to disappear without a trace.

It would be harder for Claire and for their mother, of course. Matt did grieve about that, so much so that he was almost tempted to tell Claire the truth before he took off. But he knew that to do so would be to put Lisa at risk. Whatever else he might do in his life, Matt Daley would never, ever put Lisa at risk again. She was his family now. His destiny.

In any case, it didn't cost much to live well in Marrakech. Lisa had some money that she'd saved in Brazil, and they were both working—Matt writing anonymously as a freelance journalist, and Lisa teaching English at a local school and occasionally selling one of her exquisite paintings to the rich American tourists who frequented hotels like this one, the Palais Kasim, where Matt had booked them into a modest double room while they house-hunted.

Walking through the souk, as they did every evening, they drank in the scents of the market. Fruit stalls smelled rich and sweet, the remnants of the day's produce beginning to rot now in the late afternoon heat. Dirt and sweat, the aroma of thousands of moving, tightly pressed bodies, mingled with the floral tang of wild honey and the nutty richness of the baklava stalls, buzzing and alive with bees.

For Lisa, the sights, sounds and smells evoked a memory that wasn't a memory, but that felt as real to her as the air in her lungs or the baby not yet kicking in her womb. This was Miriam's world, the world of the book, the world of the childhood she'd never had but that she'd wanted so badly she could taste it. And now she was here living it for real, fulfilling her destiny at long last. Not Frankie's twisted, murderous version of her destiny, but the good version, the fairy tale, the happy ending where she got to marry the man she loved—Matt. Matt, who had stood by her when nobody else would. Matt, who knew everything about her . . . well, almost everything . . . but who loved her still.

For Matt, the appeal of the souk, and its pleasures, were even simpler. Here was a maze, a buzzing hive of anonymous humanity where one could fade away, disappear, like a speck of ambergris lost in the dust. It was full of life and warmth and joy and human richness, the most convivial exile imaginable. And yet it *was* an exile. He felt safe here, cocooned by the crowds and wrapped in Lisa's love.

"Take my hand. There's something I want to show you." Smiling over her shoulder, Lisa led him up a narrow, cobblestoned alleyway to a set of steep stone stairs. These wound round and round in a dizzying spiral, eventually emerging onto another narrow street. To the left was a row of ancient bakers' yards, the hearty, yeasty smell of which filled the air, then more stalls of silk and carved wood similar to the ones they had just passed below. To the right was a dead end with a single, dilapidated *riad,* a traditional Moroccan house, rising three stories high, loftily surveying the alley below.

"What do you think? I know it sounds ridiculous, crazy even. But it's exactly how I pictured Uncle Sulaiman's house."

Matt frowned indulgently. "Wasn't Uncle Sulaiman rich? This place looks like it'd collapse if you sneezed on it."

Lisa shrugged. "It hasn't collapsed in six hundred years. Appearances can be deceiving, you know."

They both grinned.

"Is it even for sale?"

"I don't know. But wouldn't it be fun to find out?" Lisa enthused. "We could do it up together, make it our own. You have to admit it's a romantic house. Just think how happy we'd be there!"

Matt thought how happy they'd be there . . . and said a silent prayer of thanks.

Perhaps he didn't deserve his happiness. Perhaps neither of them did. But this was *their* book now, their story. Together, Matt Daley knew, they were going to live happily ever after.

EPILOGUE

The LAPD officer walked into the room and gagged. Then he ran out and threw up until there was nothing left in his stomach.

There was blood everywhere. *Everywhere.* But it wasn't fresh blood. It was old and caked and dark and stinking. At its center lay what must once have been a body, now a gray-green, fetid, oozing lump of slime, riddled with maggots. Only the occasional bone protruding from the filth, clean and white and gleaming, gave any indication that this had once been a human being.

Covering his mouth and nose, the cop walked back in.

"How long has he been . . . like this?" he asked the pathologist.

The pathologist shook his head. "Impossible to say. Two or three months? Could be more. We'll do some tests on the larvae. That might give us some idea."

At the word *larvae,* the detective retched again, but he forced himself to stay where he was.

"Male? Female? Age?"

"Male. Thirty-two. Would have turned thirty-three in June."

The detective was impressed. "You can tell all that from . . . *that*?" He eyed the rotten, bloated corpse with disgust.

"Nope. Your lieutenant just told me. He signed a lease three months ago. All the personal details are there."

Right on cue, the lieutenant handed his boss a single sheet of paper. It was xeroxed, and a little smudged, but the name at the top was clear. The detective stared at it, thinking. He couldn't shake the feeling that it was a name he remembered from somewhere. But the thought slipped away, like the flesh sliding off the poor bastard's bones.

The name on the lease was Carlos Hernandez.

ACKNOWLEDGMENTS

With thanks and love to the entire Sheldon family, especially Alexandra and Mary, for all their kindness and support. I am also grateful as ever to my editors, May Chen and Sarah Ritherdon, for everything they do to whip my rough-and-ready manuscripts into shape; and to the entire team at HarperCollins for their professionalism and hard work. To my agents, Luke and Mort Janklow and Tim Glister in London, and to all at team Janklow—you are the best. Finally, thanks to my wonderful family, especially my husband Robin, for coping with my midbook neuroses, and our four amazing children, Sefi, Zac, Theo and little Summer. Also to my darling sister Alice, to whom this book is dedicated. I'd be lost without you, Al.